Everyone Loves a Jenny Colgan Novel!

SUNRISE
by the SEA

Also by Jenny Colgan

SUNRISE
by the SEA

A Little Beach Street
Bakery Novel

JENNY COLGAN

wm

WILLIAM MORROW

An Imprint of HarperCollins*Publishers*

Excerpt from *Welcome to the School by the Sea* copyright © 2022 by Jenny Colgan.

SUNRISE BY THE SEA. Copyright © 2021 by Jenny Colgan. All rights reserved. Printed in Lithuania. No part of this book may be used or reproduced in any manner whatsoever without written permission except in the case of brief quotations embodied in critical articles and reviews. For information, address HarperCollins Publishers, 195 Broadway, New York, NY 10007.

Originally published in the United Kingdom in 2021 by Sphere.

First William Morrow mass market printing: March 2022
First William Morrow paperback printing: June 2021
First William Morrow hardcover printing: June 2021

Print Edition ISBN: 978-0-06-311166-0
Digital Edition ISBN: 978-0-06-291133-9

Cover design by Yeon Kim
Cover photograph © Keith Morris/Alamy Stock Photo

William Morrow and HarperCollins are registered trademarks of HarperCollins Publishers in the United States of America and other countries.

22 23 24 25 26   SB   10 9 8 7 6 5 4 3 2 1

To teachers,
especially for this past year. Thank you.

Part One

Chapter One

The sun had been out earlier that day, and the family had all gone out to play.

If you were to glance at the family, you probably wouldn't notice anything strange at first.

It would probably make you smile to realize that the children were twins, and that they each took after a parent so convincingly—the boy his father's double, with a shock of unruly blond hair and a wide smiling face; the little girl more cautious-looking, with freckles and her mother's strawberry-blond hair and pale skin.

Look closer and you would also see something flapping around them, and assume there was something wrong with your vision, because what on *earth* was a puffin doing there?

Avery and Daisy had come tumbling down the lighthouse stairs in their usual noisy way.

For the first year or two of their lives, the stair gate had never been opened and had basically confined the children to the barracks of the sunny ground-floor kitchen, because Polly Miller, née Waterford, was terrified of them tumbling down the lighthouse's circular staircases and cracking their heads open. It was an even stupider idea to live in a lighthouse than it had been before the children, love it as they may.

But her hopes of keeping them safe were completely thwarted when, around eighteenth months or so, she looked away for two seconds then turned back to see Avery holding up the bolt while Daisy turned it, and Neil (the puffin) standing on the gate, almost as if it was his idea. He certainly fluttered up the stairs guiltily as soon as Polly caught them. The days of the stair gate were numbered. She remembered it as if it were yesterday.

"Now," she had said patiently, as she had a million times before, pulling them onto her lap on the squishy threadbare sofa, the blond head so like Huckle's; Daisy so like her, "we don't go upstairs."

"Ustairs," repeated Avery. Daisy nodded. "Ustairs . . . NO?"

Huckle had come in for lunch then, and grinned, as the twins scrambled down and hurtled across the flagstone floor shouting "DADA!"

"Are you teaching them that going upstairs is the most exciting thing in the world again?"

"They opened the stair gate. Working as a team."

Huckle hoisted the two little people up, one arm each.

"Oh, you are brilliant," he said, as they giggled, and he nuzzled them both.

"It is *not* brilliant," said Polly. "They start scrambling up there and someone is going to fall and kill themselves."

"I thought that's why we had two," said Huckle, heading toward the stove.

Now, four years on, they had indeed both tumbled down several times, seemingly without injury, and retained the same basic gang setup—boy, girl, puffin—that took getting into mischief to new levels all the time.

"I always thought Neil would have been jealous of the babies," Polly was saying now, as they watched the three of them trying to play swingball—Neil hovering, then flying up when the ball came round—while she and Huckle sat out in preciously warm spring sunshine.

The lawn streamed down toward the rocks, and normally it was too windy to sit out there, but there was a spot, just behind a low wall, where the wind was blocked and you could lie down and feel the sun on your face and just for a moment everything would be warm and lovely. Unfortunately it also blocked Polly's views of the twins, so it necessitated bobbing up and down every couple of minutes like a meerkat, and steeling yourself against the wind.

"Neil was unbelievably jealous of the babies!" said Huckle, astonished she'd forgotten. "You were in a milk coma. A nuclear bomb could have gone off and you wouldn't have noticed unless a piece of dust had gotten on the babies. What do you think all those marks are on the cradles?"

"I thought they were just features."

"Peck marks!"

"Oh goodness. Bad bird."

"He's a terrible bird," said Huckle with equanimity. "Almost like you shouldn't keep wild seabirds in captivity in the first place."

"You shouldn't," agreed Polly. "He keeps me."

When Polly had first moved to Mount Polbearne, alone and nervous years ago, following the collapse of her business and engagement, in short order, a baby puffling had crashed into the bakery one night. After nursing his broken wing back to health, she had tried to release him back into the wild, but he hadn't taken. Neil had decided that living with a baker was infinitely preferable to diving into the cold sea every day to find fish, and Huckle was inclined to agree with him.

They both watched Neil sweep around the children.

"I mean, he *could*—" Huckle started.

"Neil can't babysit!" said Polly sternly.

"I know, I know," said Huckle. "I just thought it might be a nice night to sit out at Andy's"—Andy ran the local pub and a superb chippy—"or even go up to the posh place and have a glass of wine. Without some small monsters wriggling all over it."

"We could call Kerensa," suggested Polly, meaning Reuben's wife, their rich friends who lived on the mainland.

"I'm not in a Reuben-handling mood," said Huckle. "Plus . . . Lowin."

Even though the twins were miles off, they bounced over.

"ARE WE GOING TO LOWIN'S?"

Lowin, Reuben and Kerensa's son, who was now almost eight years old, was the hero of the twins' lives, living as he did in a huge Tony Stark mansion with every computer game and every piece of Playmobil ever made. Lowin, for his part, tolerated the children more or less, as long as they did everything he said in every game and obeyed his every whim, just like the paid staff did. Daisy and Avery were his very willing slaves and were quite happy to go along with whatever Lowin's newest phase was. Normally it was fine when it was an Avengers obsession phase, or a racing cars obsession phase. But

Lowin's latest obsessive phase was snakes, and despite Kerensa's promises, Polly was never 100 per cent certain Reuben wasn't about to buy him a huge boa constrictor and just let him wear it everywhere like a scarf until it ate Neil.

"Not today."

The twins' faces looked downcast.

"But he's getting a huge slide shaped like a snake! The biggest ever!"

"That sounds dangerous," said Polly, getting up. "Okay. It's just leftover chicken."

"That's all right," said Huckle, who was about to hit the road again, repping his honey business. Times had been tough—there had been floods all over the West Country and a lot of businesses were finding it difficult to keep going but he was doing his best. "It's good to have home-cooked food. It's going to be nothing but restaurants and hotel food for a fortnight."

"Say that like you're sad about it," pleaded Polly.

"I am!" said Huckle. And then, more seriously, grabbing her hand. "You know I am."

"I wish I was going off to stay in hotels."

"It's not the Ritz! It's a Travelodge off the A40!"

"I know. But anywhere is the Ritz with you."

They shared a kiss. He hated going away. But he had to. They had enough trouble keeping their heads above water as it was.

"Think of the windows," he said.

"I know, I know."

If they could replace the lighthouse's ancient rattly single-paned glass with English Heritage–approved double glazing, the difference it would make in the quality of both of their lives would be immeasurable. No more icy plunges down the circular staircase; no more painful hauling themselves out of bed.

Although, who knew? The house might never be warm to other people's standards—Polly's mother's, for example, or Kerensa's, or, well, anyone's, really. But to the four of them—the children had never known anything else—it was just perfect. Huckle had put an old TV in the master bedroom, and through the cozy nights of winter all four of them curled up with the electric blanket on, Neil hopping on the nightstand, watching *Moana*, and it was, windows or not, as happy a place as Polly could possibly imagine.

And now spring was coming! And if Huckle made enough this year they were going to get windows *and* a new boiler, so there was very little to complain about, thought Polly, as she headed back into the kitchen, listening to the merry voices of the twins demanding that their father became a tiger MEEJETLY which he obligingly did, growling so fiercely that Polly wondered if Avery would get upset. Daisy would dry his tears if he did.

She added barley and vegetables to the chicken stock she had boiled up from the roast, happily looking forward to when Huckle would be home for the summer, and the tourists would start to arrive for the season and they would be cheerfully flat out. She couldn't wait to feel the sun warm on her face again, not the endless winter storms that had seemed to arrive every single weekend. For months the rain had thrown itself against the windows and the house was full of wet wellingtons and the children got cranky when she couldn't get them out enough, the pleasure of building dens indoors and helping Mama bake having grown stale. The storms had been getting worse—climate change, she knew—and the winters were getting harder.

"What's up when I'm away?" Huckle asked now, following her in while simultaneously half-listening to Avery talk about how Lowin was getting the biggest snake in the world for his birthday.

"Usual," said Polly. "Oh no, I forgot! Reuben's waifs and strays are arriving!"

Chapter Two

At that moment, over in Exeter on the mainland, one of Reuben's waifs and strays had no idea that was what she was about to become.

Caius—"pronounced 'keys,'" as he liked to tell people snottily when they attempted it for the first time, unless they by some chance got it right, in which case he would say, "It's 'ky-us,' actually?"—was banging heavily on his flatmate's bedroom door, but to no avail.

"Marisa!"

It was, fair enough, hard to hear over the racket.

Caius theoretically liked having lots of friends who were DJs, or said they were, but then he made the mistake of asking them to come and play at his parties and it was horrendous and they all squabbled with each other over how expensive their headphones were, and mixed up their stupid boxes and vied to play very obscure stuff, and frankly, it was a racket.

If he'd cared about his neighbors he would have factored that in too, but, being rich and good-looking, Caius so rarely met people that didn't like him that he often found it hard to imagine what that might be like.

The flat was absolutely heaving, mostly with people he knew, kind of, some he didn't, but they were good-looking and appeared well-off, so that was fine too.

But he needed the little room his parents had insisted he let out—something to do with "learning how to take responsibility" or "managing efficiently"; it had been hard to tell, he had been on the worst comedown while they'd been talking to him and he still had his earpods in so it could have been anything.

"Marisa," he yelled again, as loud as he could. He winced. Caius didn't really like shouting; he liked drawling or, even better, not saying anything at all and merely waving a hand at waiters bringing him things.

"Marisa! Come on, it's a party! Can't you make us some canapés?"

Still no reply. He pouted. She must have heard him by now.

Marisa used to be fun. Well, not *fun*, exactly, she had a real job and went to bed at a reasonable hour. But she cooked and smiled and was funny and he quite liked someone kind of looking after him.

Then she'd gone all quiet and sort of vanished and he knew she'd told him why, some family shiz, but he kept forgetting, and it was really terribly tiresome.

"Marisa! People want to use this room! For coats!"

"And also sex and taking drugs," said one of a trio of people in black eyeliner appearing behind him, the other two vigorously agreeing.

"No! Totally none of those things, just probably coats!" said Caius. He frowned. "You know there's tequila out here, right? There's tequila out here and none in where you are, which means I don't understand you *at all*."

Well, they agreed about one thing, thought Marisa. Because she didn't understand herself either.

Chapter Three

Inside her little box room—like many of these expensive new builds in Exeter, the main room was flashy and showy with a big glass wall and a balcony, but the smaller bedrooms were done on the cheap—Marisa Rossi sat on the end of her bed, knees up to her chin, headphones on, the clatter beyond the door more or less white noise.

Another party. Another night when the rest of the world was out and about, having fun.

Everyone else seemed fine. Everyone else always seemed fine.

And, in the scheme of things, losing a grandparent was hardly heartbreaking loss. A lot of people lose grandparents. Everyone, when you think about it.

And they all still seemed able to go to parties. Everyone but her.

But somehow, she could only think of her *nonno*, Carlo: her kind, funny grandfather in Imperia, Italy, descended from generations of shipbuilders—a tradition that had only stopped with her mother, Lucia, who had left for the UK to find a better life, and married a man from Livorno, just down the road. Marisa's father couldn't bear the cold and the rain and left England—

and Lucia alone, with Marisa and her brother, Gino. Marisa tried not to take it personally.

But her grandfather had stepped into the breach, and then some. Her fondest memories were golden: holidays spent in Italy; long days on the hot windy shores of Imperia, as the great big industrial ships rolled past; late dreamy evenings at restaurants as she ate spaghetti vongole and fell asleep under the table as the adults talked and laughed long into the night; cool hands rubbing in cream to sunburned shoulders; ice creams as big as a beach ball; stones underfoot as you ran into the water; the pungent scent of the exhausts of the Vespas of the young men gunning around the town, a contrast with the smartly uniformed *navale* stationed there; the long rolling rhythms of Italian summers.

Abandoned in her teens for holidays with her British friends on cheap packages in the Balearics, drinking shots and laughing uproariously, they sometimes, in her memory, felt like a dream; snatches of an older language tugging somewhere at the fraying edges of her brain, another person, happy and free, in big fussy-bowed dresses her grandmother—who was as stiff as her grandfather was loving—liked to buy her, and which she adored and her mother thought were absolutely awful.

Then life interfered, took her to college and on to Exeter and a job she used to love—being a registrar for the council. Births, marriages and deaths, it required a combination of a love for and interest in people, with a fairly meticulous approach to record-keeping, and nice handwriting. Marisa was not a show-offy type of person at all, but she was incredibly proud of her handwriting.

Then Carlo had died.

"There's no rhyme nor reason," her nice but very

harassed GP had told her, when she explained the insomnia, the constant crying and, increasingly difficult
for work, her encroaching fear of leaving the house and
speaking to people, that seemed to get worse every day.
"Grief affects everyone differently. It seems to me you
have an anxiety disorder, shading into agoraphobia. I
would suggest the best course is antidepressants."

"My grandfather died!" Marisa had said. "I'm sad!
I'm not 'depressed'! This is normal."

"I'm just saying that they would almost certainly
help."

"But then . . ."

Marisa fell silent.

"What if I don't even miss him anymore? What if I
don't feel anything?"

The GP, too, fell silent, wanting to be reassuring;
unable to mislead.

"The wait for counseling is very long," she said,
finally.

"Put me on it," said Marisa. "Please. Please."

"Okay," said the GP.

"Why?" said Marisa. "Why am I the only person who
can't get on with their life?"

The nice GP shook her head sadly.

"It only looks that way," she said. "Don't be fooled
for a moment."

She hadn't been able to make it in time. He'd been out
pruning in the garden, in the big black hat he wore all
the time, probably, and had collapsed. No time to call,
no time to say goodbye to the most important man in
her life.

People saying he wouldn't have known a thing about it, that it was better that way, did not, in Marisa's opinion, know what the hell they were talking about. Did they seriously think he wouldn't have wanted to say goodbye to the family he loved so much: her mother, Lucia; her sister, Ann Angela (actually Anna Angelica but quite the mouthful by anyone's standards); the boys; and . . . well, her?

Somehow, she found the funeral, which she had to dash to, even more difficult. Her *nonna*, or grandmother, garbed in black, was cross and busy in the kitchen, insisting on cooking for thousands and refusing, in Marisa's eyes, to face up to what was happening at all. And there were so many people—cousins, family, friends, bloody butcher and baker and candlestick maker—talking about how much they'd loved him (and, by inference, how much he had loved them in return), that the entire noisy family felt overwhelming on that wet October Italian day, and there was so much shouting and noise and Marisa, who had always been quiet, had retreated further into her shell, worrying that, after all, the love she had felt from her grandfather had meant little, amid the clamor. He had been quiet too. She yearned for his big hand in her smaller one; couldn't believe that she would never feel it again. But everyone else's grief had felt louder, more pressing. And so she had taken hers home, let it sit, forming inside her, more and more layers building up, cementing it in place, holding her down like a ball and chain, and as the months had passed she'd found it increasingly difficult to leave the house at all.

"Do you think you need your aura cleansed?" Caius had said, and she had given him a look, but Caius was one of those people who could never notice when he was being annoying, and probably wouldn't believe you if you'd told him. He'd been sent from the US to do a very expensive course in something or other near some uncle, but Marisa hadn't seen him go once.

"You just need to come out and get pissed up, duh, obviously," said her best friend Olive, but she somehow couldn't face doing that either.

She pretended she had evenings out planned with work colleagues, which was a complete lie, but the other lie would be to pretend she had a date, which she didn't, or she could be honest and say she was occasionally seeing Mahmoud again, but they all hated his guts for being a lazy cadging loser (albeit a very, *very* handsome, fit, lazy cadging loser) so she didn't want to say that either. Aged twenty-nine, Marisa's romantic history was . . . not patchy exactly. But being an introvert meant that often she hadn't quite managed to pluck up the courage to tell people she didn't like them that much, and things could bumble along, or she would lack the courage to make it clear to people she did like that she liked them, and they'd pass her by. When Olive had fancied Keegan, for example, she'd stuck on her false eyelashes and her push-up bra and simply turned up everywhere he was. And now they had bought a flat together and were planning on a baby and Marisa was delighted for them, of course she was, but the world was easier, she felt, on the confident Olives than on the shyer girls. Also, Olive pointed out that Mahmoud treated her like a doormat and the fact that that was completely true didn't make her feel any better.

Anyway, because she didn't like going over to his anymore to watch him play computer games—Mahmoud was generally too lazy or a bit stoned to come over—that didn't matter, and gradually, she'd found, as she sat and read over old letters from her grandfather or dug up old photographs of an evening, that it was just easier not to go out, much easier.

She told herself she'd do it tomorrow, or maybe the weekend.

And she volunteered for more and more of the admin work that didn't mean having to go into the office. Nazreen, her boss, was puzzled—Marisa had always been so good at facing customers—not an extrovert, but calm and reassuring in her dealings with everyone. Now, though, she had become so terribly timid. Facing the public was so much the fun of their job, always had been. But although she couldn't understand it, Nazreen was too busy to question what was going on. Marisa was still as efficient as ever and she let it go.

Oddly, Caius was the one who didn't give up.

"Have you done your ten thousand steps? You know you could probably do with a mantra."

"No thanks."

"MDMA?"

"No!"

"Okay! Hey, what should we have for dinner?"

He looked at her imploringly. When Marisa had moved in he had been pleased: she was nice, tidy, pretty but not his type (which was unusual, as the people who were Caius's type was just about everybody), and best of all, she cooked. Caius didn't eat very much—you didn't stay model thin and cool if you did—but when he did, he liked it to be the very best.

And now, all of that had gone. She looked tired and sad and miserable and there was never any food. This wasn't fun in the slightest.

Inside, Marisa was gripped with fear. What was happening to her? She wasn't crazy, was she?

She just . . . didn't like going out anymore. The world

seemed scarier. Nobody would mind if she just stayed in, would they? She wasn't bothering anyone. Just keeping nice and quiet in the back . . .

And then sometimes at night she would wake up breathless, and panicking, and think to herself, *My life is going by*, and find it hard to breathe, and think that she must, she must do something, and would go and pour a bath so hot she could barely sit in it, the water fierce against her skin, driving away her thoughts in a cloud of steam, staring out at the dark, thinking, *Is this it now?*

Christmas had made everything notably worse. Lucia had wanted a big family get-together to remember her grandfather, and the thought of it had made Marisa a bit panicky. In the end, she hadn't been able to go; to face everyone again, cheery and loud and getting on with their lives.

She'd tried looking for other things to do, and making excuses, but Lucia was having none of it, and in the end there had been a horrible bust-up on the family WhatsApp. Her brother Gino had phoned, then Lucia had, in dramatic tears calling her selfish, and gradually they had ended up in one of those heated family rows. Usually when this happened someone would eventually have to get up and make a cup of tea and, at the end of an excruciating amount of time would have to shout, "Anyone else want one?", and after that everything would be mended. But this time, not being in physical proximity to each other, that hadn't happened. And so nothing got mended. It had shocked both Marisa and her mother, Marisa thought. Lucia was used to Marisa being a quiet, acquiescent little mouse and now she'd made a stand.

Even though, Marisa knew deep down, the stand was no good for her. She should have been with her family.

But guilt added a new layer of calcification to the

stone inside her that was dragging her down and keeping her in; layer upon layer of sadness and grief and worry that was growing too large for her to do anything at all.

She had spent Christmas inside, on her own, fielding increasingly nasty texts from her mother, not so subtly implying she was doing it for attention. She'd gone to working full time from home. Her appointment with the NHS therapist still hadn't come up. And, three months on, things were looking worse, not better.

The morning after the party, Caius came to a decision that was going to make things worse still.

Chapter Four

"So." Caius looked regretful. "Okay, you have to know, first of all, this isn't me, okay? I've spoken to all of my therapists about it and they all agree with me."

Marisa blinked at him. It was four p.m. on a Tuesday, and she was still in her dressing gown. She'd been clicking through a huge pile of pics on Instagram: her friends had gone to a party on a boat last night. The boat hadn't gone anywhere but they'd obviously had an absolute blast, drinking bright cocktails, and for some reason everyone was wearing a ridiculous hat. Or perhaps it was the same hat, passed around. Anyway. They all looked like they were having a ball. They hadn't even invited her. There was a limit to how many times she could say no to everything. They had been concerned and sympathetic to begin with but when nothing changed, and she was doing nothing and had nothing to say and frantically insisted all the time that she was all right . . . well. There wasn't much they could do, even though they loved her, which they did. The wall she had built around herself was as sturdy as that of the flat and nobody had the power tools to knock it through.

Although Caius was giving it a very good try.

"The thing is. You're giving out what is mostly a Very Bad Vibe?"

Marisa noticed she had some tinned spaghetti sauce on her dressing gown and frowned.

"It's quite hard to live with you?"

This was from Caius who had parties every five minutes, left empty bottles everywhere, and had random people showing up all the time of whom Marisa was mostly terrified and hid in the bathroom.

She frowned at him.

"Really? I'm quiet and tidy and pay the rent on time."

Caius took a deep breath.

"Actually, you're spooky and sad and weird? It's a bit like sharing a flat with that toilet ghost in Harry Potter?" He nodded. "You know I'm only being honest like this for your own good?"

Marisa felt herself go numb.

She couldn't get kicked out. She couldn't. She'd have to leave . . . to go where? The idea of finding somewhere new was . . . it was too frightening. Too scary.

Her mum would be happy to have her home, but they still weren't really talking, not after Christmas. She just didn't understand, and she asked Marisa to explain it to her and Marisa didn't understand either.

Plus her mum ran an open house anyway, she had thousands of friends popping in all hours of the day and night, as well as people from the charities she worked for, her choir, her church group . . . it was endless. She didn't really need Marisa.

Marisa and her grandfather, both more reserved, had been peas in a pod, her mother had always said. It always made Marisa happy to hear that.

"I'm not a toilet ghost," she said quietly.

"I know," said Caius, in a reasonable tone. "But say you *were* a toilet ghost, yeah, how different would your behavior be?"

Marisa caught sight of herself in the mirror across the room. Her face was incredibly pale; normally her olive skin lit up at the slightest hint of sun, but she'd spent the entire year indoors so far. Her black hair looked faded and dull; her eyebrows straggly. Her mum would have a fit. She looked much older than she was.

"You're kicking me out?" she said, confused and frightened.

Caius sighed. "I'm not *evil*," he said. "Do I seem evil to you? Is evil what I'm putting out there? It's not really the look I'm going for. I have something for you I think you'll like?"

"Sure," said Marisa, feeling her breath harder to come by; she was suddenly aware of her own body; her heart racing, her chest getting tighter.

"Anyway. It's not like I'm kicking you out . . . I'm just moving in Binky and Phillip."

"Both of them?"

Caius had been carrying on an affair with each of the members of a couple.

"Sure," he said. "Worth a shot."

"I didn't know they knew about each other."

"Yeah, well, I didn't originally plan it like that but . . ."

If the situation hadn't been so awful, Marisa might have appreciated it: typical Caius to be cheating on two people and for them to immediately forgive him and want to move in with him.

He lifted his hand in a "what can you do when you're so attractive?" gesture.

"So," he said, pulling round his laptop and showing her something, "come look at this."

She flinched. Even with Caius, she didn't like getting too close to other people. He rolled his eyes.

"Look! Look at the picture."

She squinted down to see what he was showing her. It was a little chalet perched on top of what looked like a hill, surrounded by water.

"What is that?"

He shrugged. "My uncle Reuben. Lives down in Cornwall?"

Marisa had heard of this legendary uncle, who owned a huge estate, had his own beach, his own tech company, was rich even compared to Caius's incredibly rich family and was also apparently the biggest dickhead anyone had ever met.

"Well, he built these chalets for tourists staycationing this year and then everyone looked at the tearing rain and went to Spain instead so they're just sitting there. And I figured, seeing as you're not really going to work these days it doesn't matter where you are . . . and you want peace and quiet and I . . . don't want that . . ."

It was true. Armed with a letter from her GP, Marisa had finally made an official request to work from home for the foreseeable future. It was a headache for Nazreen and made Marisa miserable and guilty, but it had just got too difficult for her.

"Where is it?" said Marisa suspiciously.

"I mean, it's very picturesque . . ."

"Where?"

"I can't . . . one of those limey words. I want to say Potbeans?"

She looked at him.

"Mount Polbearne?"

Everyone knew Mount Polbearne. It was a remote tidal island off the southern coast of Cornwall; a tourist attraction, but a tiny place.

"You know it?"

"Of course I know it—it gets completely cut off for

half of every day and you can't own a car there and in the winters it gets cut off for months and you're miles from anywhere."

"I thought," said Caius, "that would be *perfect* for you."

The bell rang. Marisa looked up, worriedly.

"Uh, yeah, the guys are just coming over to . . . hang?" said Caius hopefully, as Marisa dived back into her room.

Chapter Five

The party noise that night was . . . prolonged. Marisa tucked her head under her pillow and found she was too exhausted even to cry. Sleeping had been hard for so long—possibly because she was taking so little physical exercise she simply wasn't tiring herself out enough. But this was pushing her beyond her limits.

She looked at the link Caius had sent over. Well. It was there, it was available and it was a lot less than she was paying at the moment to live in a lovely two bed right in the middle of a vibrant city, even though she couldn't take a single step into that vibrant city; she barely looked out of the window.

And what choice did she have? Nobody wanted her, not really. She couldn't face crashing her mother's full life with her sadness and gloom; her mother had loved her own father, of course, but she had taken a more pragmatic view. Life was for living and celebrating: he had been old, very old, and had had a long and happy life with a family he adored and a job which, while it didn't make him a rich man, had made him a satisfied one. So the blubbing and the dressing gowns at teatime seemed to her mother self-indulgent at best; at worst, an active insult to a man who lived and loved and worked his whole life. Marisa didn't know how to bridge the chasm between her mother and herself. She didn't know how to bridge the chasm between herself and the rest of the world.

And the idea of going out and meeting other people, finding somewhere else was . . . it made her freeze. It wasn't possible. Not at all. No.

She looked at the location again.

Her friends all promised to charge down to visit. They also wanted to organize a big leaving Exeter bash for her, but she said she was just too busy at work. Also, she had a feeling Olive was about to get engaged. Which was brilliant, amazing, she should be thrilled for her. And yet she felt nothing at all. It was terrifying. She texted Mahmoud, who just said, *yeah babe, c u round*, which didn't make her terrified, it made her sad—again, with herself, for settling, always, for so little, for always being afraid to ask for what she wanted.

Nazreen was disappointed, of course; she'd wanted Marisa back in the office, and sharply asked how long this was for. There was a limit to how much admin work there was to do. Marisa added this to the long list of other things she had to worry about. Somewhere quiet and out of everybody's way must, she thought, be the right move.

Chapter Six

Reuben had built the new holiday homes when he'd renovated the school—Lowin went there and of course he had to have the absolute best of everything, so Reuben had to do up the school and figured he might as well do a little bit of business while he was about it.

The renovation, however, had turned into a massive nightmare as anyone within touching distance of Mount Polbearne had suddenly decided that their children absolutely had to go to the place with the cool new gym and the music instruction and the small classes and the adorable commute. There were even plans for a music and art department, currently held up in the planning committee as Reuben could only hold off on being rude to people for so long.

Archie, one of the more enterprising fishermen, set up a mainland commuting boat so they weren't dependent on the tides and the children *loved* it. Even Lowin got fed up with being taken privately on the Riva boat and insisted on joining the little outboard motor and wearing his own life jacket with his name written on it. Everyone else's was written on in Sharpie, but his was embroidered. They all had a great time.

The school was a huge hit. But the holiday cottages had hit a snag—the years of terrible weather and flooding had meant they couldn't produce a stable road to them: some of the houses existed, but you couldn't easily drive to them, park at them, get a buggy along the street and so on.

Reuben's new plan was to offer them as longer-term lets to people that wouldn't be packing and unpacking every five minutes, then keep haranguing officials till they either built him a new road or invented hover bikes.

He had tenants turning up; the school music teacher, who was having trouble with the commute; and some irritating flatmate of his nephew (who had been sent to the UK and who Reuben was meant to be keeping an eye on, which meant he just sent him extra money from time to time). Anyway, keeping Caius quiet kept Reuben's annoying sister off his back while she went through her third divorce, so that was always something.

He'd given the keys to Polly the previous week and asked her to let everyone in despite her clear and obvious objections that she was running her own business and couldn't take time off in the middle of the day to do that for him, didn't he have anyone from his multimillion-dollar corporation, or perhaps his wife, you know, the one who didn't have a job?

Good-natured Kerensa had laughed and said of course she did, she was getting her nails done so that Reuben didn't leave her for a twenty-year-old and Reuben had said damn straight. Polly had said, well, it used to be that only Reuben was a putz but it appeared that marriage had infected Kerensa as well and now they were both putzes. To which Kerensa pointed out that they were putzes who were also pouring Polly another glass of Champagne while Lowin's nanny looked after her children. (Polly had her own thoughts about this as Lowin's nanny tended to run after him, while backing him up every time he tried to terrorise Avery, which was often. Daisy versus the nanny, on the other hand, was a surprisingly fair fight.)

So Polly had a new thing to add to her already long to-do list that Monday morning, including reassuring Huckle that his business trip would be worthwhile— sales needed confidence too, and his handsome face had looked so worried that morning. She thought he was brilliant and his honey was awesome and she'd done her best to perk him up. Then there was Avery who had taken to wearing a pair of Daisy's stripy tights round his neck and calling it his pet snake Jiminy, which had caused quite the kerfuffle that morning, as well as the fact that he'd caught the tights on the doorknob on his way out to school and nearly garrotted himself. And now she had Mrs. Bradley standing in front of her sighing and saying, "Pasties again."

"Well, yes," said Polly, trying not to sound stiff. "We are a bakery in Cornwall."

"I'm just saying, you could mix it up a bit."

"I did mix it up! I did chilli bread and nobody would talk to me for a week."

And Neil had got the worst diarrhea of any bird she'd ever known, she didn't add.

"It would be nice to get a little bit of variety."

Polly thought about it. God knows they needed the money.

"Thanks for the input, Mrs. Bradley. Anything else?"

"I'll take four pasties."

Polly smiled as the bell dinged her out, then looked up rather tiredly as it dinged again.

". . . Uh, excuse me?"

The voice was so very quiet she didn't even hear it until the second time. Standing in front of her was a short, round, sweet-faced dark-haired girl, her skin pale as if it hadn't seen the sun for a long time, her eyes wide and oddly frightened.

Chapter Seven

Getting to Cornwall had been difficult. Very difficult.

"Don't worry," Caius had said blithely. "It's much nicer than here, it's cheaper than here and there'll be *no parties*."

Marisa let her GP surgery know she was moving. Still no sign of a therapist.

"Do you want some help with your stuff?" said Caius, cheerily, and Marisa, feeling helpless and swept along in the tide of things, shrugged numbly.

The day before Marisa was due to move out, a massive muscle-bound chap called Phillip and an incredibly buxom woman called Binky showed up and started, politely but firmly, packing her belongings into boxes.

Phillip did nothing but complain about how bending and lifting things would spoil his regimen for muscles and stopped every twenty minutes to eat four raw eggs, which Marisa thought indicated he wouldn't necessarily be a better flatmate than she was, but Binky, round and cheery in large dungarees, seemed all right. Marisa couldn't for the life of her relate to someone voluntarily deciding to take on two men, but Binky seemed happy enough, chattering away merrily, which helpfully meant Marisa didn't have to say anything at all, but learned an eye-popping amount about polyamorous relationships. Mostly, she was impressed by their time management.

"So who do you go in for—boys or girls?" said Binky cheerily, like she was asking about the weather.

"Uh, boys mostly," said Marisa, feeling very colorless and staring at her shoes.

"So, what do you like?"

She shrugged. It had really depended on who came along.

"The world's your oyster!" said Binky, cheerily. "I don't think I've ever had a Cornishman."

"Statistically, you have," said Phillip, unconcerned.

"Well, yes, *statistically*," mused Binky as Marisa put her head down and scuttled out with another box.

Caius presented her with a large bottle of Champagne.

"Here!" he said. "Good luck! I'll be down for Uncle Reuben's parties—he throws the *best* parties—so I'll definitely see you there! Hope you loosen up! And please, please, if you ever start cooking again, look me up, yeah?"

He gave her his most winning smile, the one where his hair fell just so over his eyes, and Marisa almost let him give her a hug, except she didn't really hug anymore, so instead she leaned a little bit, then ducked into her tiny car, where she felt safe, even though she'd barely driven it in a year.

Driving wasn't so bad: you didn't need to confront people when you drove as timidly as Marisa did, and she felt protected inside. That was the easy bit.

By the time she reached the famous craggy outline of Mount Polbearne, the tide was low, so the old road, just wide enough to take a van, was completely uncovered.

It was a gray morning, but a tiny shaft of light from behind the clouds just illuminated the very top of the hill; the old church, half-ruined, that had sat at the very top for hundreds and hundreds of years, set above a winding, motley collection of slightly drunkenly leaning cottages, made of the gray slate native to the area, home for a long time to monks and fishermen.

The monks were long gone; the fishermen remained, but were outnumbered now by second homes, tourist spots, hotels and B&Bs. Even this early in the season, children were crabbing off the dock with their little nets; people strolled up and down the promenade eating ice cream and taking photographs. There were a lot of people, Marisa noted, with slight nervousness. Oh God, she'd have to pass them all to get up. She'd been told to pick up the key from the bakery, and what if she couldn't find it? And she'd have to talk to someone. And oh God, her life was going too far ahead of her and she really didn't like it. Deep breaths, she thought. Deep breaths. I made it, Nonno, she said in her head. I made it this far. I don't like it but I made it.

Polly bit back her first instinct, which was to ask the girl if she was all right—it was beyond rude—and managed to say instead, "Hello, what would you like?"

This was the third new person Marisa had had to speak to today. You'd think she'd be getting better at it. Instead she found she was pressing her back against the wall. Even though this woman, with her strawberry-blond hair, freckles and open friendly face, looked as unthreatening as a person could.

Suddenly the enormity of the situation broke over her. She was in a brand-new place where she knew nobody, she'd been evicted from her flat and dumped somewhere else, she was definitely possibly going to lose her job and she was just never going to get better. She hadn't even told her mother she was moving, that was how bad things had got between them; she knew her mother would only beg her to come home, or snap out of it, or ask her yet again if she was sure she didn't need some antidepressants, or *something*.

And now she was being asked a very simple question, in what should be a perfectly straightforward transaction, and, for the first time, Marisa realized just how bad she'd let things get. Because she was about to have a panic attack.

There was no help for it. She was going to burst, she was going to stop breathing if she didn't get out of the warm scented bakery right now. She couldn't help it; she couldn't breathe. She wasn't going to catch her breath and she was going to suffocate and die and her heart was beating so fast it was going to explode and she couldn't breathe, she couldn't breathe!—she dived toward the door, and fumbled for the handle, her eyes wide. Polly looked at her, concerned.

"Are you okay?"

As Marisa pulled at the door, bright red in her embarrassment, completely incapable of explaining what was actually the matter with her, there was a sudden commotion and what looked like an incredibly unaerodynamic football came swooping in.

Marisa was so startled she forgot for a second she

was having a panic attack, and found herself yelping and then her body gulping, instinctively taking a deep breath as the fresh breeze from the sea outside streamed in through the open door, and then another.

"Goodness," said the woman, running to her. "Sit down here."

She indicated a ledge in the window.

"Breathe slowly. I'm so sorry! God, I'm not surprised you got a fright."

She turned round.

"What have I told you?" Suddenly the red-haired woman was telling off . . . What the hell was that? A bird, yes. It was a puffin, Marisa realized, light-headed. She'd never seen one in real life before. She had no idea they came onto land, she'd thought they all lived up in Scotland or something. To her utter amazement the bird fluttered round the shop then gently came to rest on Polly's shoulder. She realized her mouth was open, and she drew in more breaths of the fresh salty air until she could almost feel herself calming down.

"Sorry," said Polly again. "He knows he's not meant to be in here. Health and Safety doesn't *specifically* mention puffins, but we reckon it's probably implicit. You are a Bad Bird."

But she was rubbing the bird's claw as she said it. The bird made a gentle eeping noise.

"Come on. Away with you. Sorry, what were you after . . ."

Finally Marisa found her voice.

"Um, I'm here for the—"

The door banged and in hurtled two small children who, as was evident by the girl's red hair and the way they ran to her, were clearly the woman's children.

"You let Neil go ahead!" said Polly.

"We spoke to him about it and he promised not to come in here," said Daisy solemnly. "He lied."

"NEIL!" shouted Avery. "COME HERE!"

Neil did absolutely nothing of the kind and eyed them with beady disdain.

Behind them, an extremely large man entered the shop. He took up most of the remaining space in the small bakery, and stared straight ahead, smiling.

"You are pirate?" he asked. He had a thick accent, a mop of dark hair and a full beard.

Polly looked up at him, then realized he was referring to the bird on her shoulder.

"No, I'm just the baker," she said pleasantly. "Neil. Shoo."

She opened the door and the small bird flew out. A thought occurred to her.

"Are you Environmental Health?" she asked the man, nervously.

Daisy and Avery, meanwhile, were regarding the very large, shaggy stranger cheerfully.

"This is Mr. Bat-BAY-ar!" said Daisy, pronouncing carefully. "He's our music teacher!"

"Also, I think perhaps he is a bear," whispered Avery. It was not a very quiet whisper.

"Hello, Miss Miller, hello, Master Miller," said the man gravely, shaking each of their hands. "I am here for key?"

"Of course, you're Reuben's new tenant!" said Polly. "He told me you were coming. You teach at the school?"

"I like having a bear as a teacher," said Avery, again in a loud whisper.

"He's NOT A BEAR," whispered back Daisy, equally loudly. "That's RACIST."

Avery frowned. "But we likes bears."

Mr. Batbayar was examining the baking with some attention. There were pasties, of course, scones, pies, beautiful sourdough loaves and gorgeously tempting cakes in rows, including strawberry tarts. He had narrow brown eyes, and they gleamed.

"I'm so sorry," said Polly.

She felt in her apron pocket and found a jangling set of keys.

"Is Avery being racist, Mummy?" Daisy wanted to know.

Polly grimaced and hissed, "No. Just a bit rude."

"BUT! WE! LIKES! BEARS!"

Polly handed over the key, and a file full of instructions. "Okay, it's all the way up to the top of the hill, past the school."

"Excuse me, Mr. Bat-BAY-er, do you KNOW any bears?" asked Avery.

The man looked at the boy, seemingly puzzled. He clearly hadn't been listening before.

"I . . . you think I am bear like GRRRRR?"

He made a growling noise and lifted his huge hands and made them into a claw shape, and both the children squealed, half-delighted, half-terrified.

"Children!" said Polly, anguished. "Stop it!"

"Oh! Yes. I know many dangerous bears. They are playing piano very bad, but they pay honey so I am not sad."

"Our dad makes honey!"

"Is *he* bear?" said Mr. Batbayar.

This hadn't occurred to either of them and their eyes grew even wider. Polly felt this was getting slightly out of hand.

"So if you follow Sandy Lane all the way up to the end, where the road runs out—they haven't finished the road, I'm afraid, one of the reasons Reuben is letting them go cheap."

The man nodded.

"You're the second on the right."

"Thank you."

He turned his furry face on the children once more.

"And do your practice or I will be EATINK YOU UP!"

The children squealed in horror and ran behind the counter to hide in their mother's skirts.

"Mr. Batbayar is only joking," said Polly.

"I am not Only Jokink," said the man. "*Nyam nyam.* I am hungry bear. Please may I have four of thinks with . . . red, if there are no children to eat at this time."

Polly lifted up four strawberry tarts and took his money.

"Good day."

And he left the shop, the door dinging behind him.

Chapter Eight

"Gosh," said Polly. "Avery, I hope you're not crying. He was only joking."

"NO!" said Avery bravely, although Polly slightly feared for bedtime.

"He's not really a bear."

"But he said he was very hungry and was going to munch me up!"

Polly thought she would have to have a word with Reuben about his hiring practices, not for the first time.

"Um . . . I'm sorry about that," she said to Marisa.

"It's okay," said Marisa, who had managed to calm herself down, and was wondering if people had always been so strange and she just hadn't noticed, or if the world really had changed that much while she'd been sitting alone in her bedroom in Caius's flat.

She quietly steeled herself to open her mouth.

"Actually, I'm here for keys too?"

Polly slapped her head.

"Of course, sorry, what an idiot. I'm Polly, by the way. You must be . . ." She read the piece of paper. "Marisa Rossi? Oh, what a pretty name."

"Um, thanks."

Polly handed over the keys and the file, as the children

eyed her carefully in case she turned out to be a leopard or something.

"Well, welcome to Mount Polbearne. Do you know how long you're staying?"

Marisa shrugged, and Polly gave her an intense look. She remembered turning up here by herself, a long time ago. It had been a strange experience, to be sure.

"Well, I hope you like it," she said, smiling.

Marisa hadn't even thought about whether she'd like it or not. She just wanted to get in somewhere and shut the door and hide away from everything else, and if this place was right at the end of the world, well. That would do.

"I'll take . . . can I take a loaf of bread? And some rolls . . ."

"Oh, of course! Goodness, why didn't I tell that peculiar man to buy some bread too. I can't have been thinking straight."

"Also, we don't want him to be HUNGRY," came a voice from down by her knees.

"Could you take one up to him?" asked Polly. "He can pop in and pay for it any time, I know where he lives."

Marisa was stricken. The idea of going to someone else's house, of having to . . . No. Today had already been bad enough. She couldn't. Why couldn't anyone see that? That life was easy for them and hard for her? Sometimes she wished she could carry a stick around so that people could see there was something wrong with her. Or wear a badge? No, not a badge. Just something people would know to avoid her and not to bump into her or ask her to do things she simply couldn't do.

Frozen, she didn't answer, but Polly didn't notice.

"Oh, he might have brought his own stuff from the

mainland. I wonder if he's going to eat all those straw-berry tarts by himself?"

She chattered on, even as Marisa was mentally breath-ing a sigh of relief. She took the bread and keys, muttered thanks and escaped outside before Polly had a chance to give her directions.

But outside there were people around, walking dogs, boats coming in, people hailing each other and saying hello and she realized she couldn't stay like that either, and glanced at the map in the file of papers, and turned, and putting one foot in front of another, started pulling her suitcase up the hill.

Chapter Nine

The village loomed above her although Marisa barely noticed; the huge church at the top, the houses tumbling higgledy-piggledy down around the mound of it.

In the spring sunshine it looked attractive and inviting, the early morning mist still burning off around the foot of the hill, making it look as if it had just shimmered into view, as if it were purely magical. The lighthouse was on her left, out on its own promontory; the beach scooped beneath the harbor walls and, on the other side, were many clattering fishing boats. Along the harbor front the pub, the fish and chip shop, gift shops, ice creams . . . and the bakery, of course, just there on the corner, in its charming dove-gray.

But Marisa didn't look at any of it. She kept her head down and ploughed on alone, stepping miles away from anyone who approached her on the narrow pavement.

She felt so abandoned, so far away from everything, as if every day sailed her farther away from the life she had once known, once had.

She followed the road as it wove around the hill, each house higher up than the last, sometimes the older stone cottages looking as if they were leaning tipsily on one another, their small doorways opening directly out onto the road. Eleven Polbearne Heights . . . where was it?

She was getting out of breath as the sun beamed down and her suitcase seemed to get heavier and heavier, like dragging a cow up a hill.

The church was just above her now, and the school was to her right-hand side. She couldn't see a lot of houses. Was this right? Her phone signal was blinking in and out. Oh good, that wasn't going to be a lot of help. She was panting now, red in the face.

Just to the right, the cobbles ran out completely and there was a dusty unlaid road turning sharply uphill. There was no road sign on it at all. This couldn't be it, could it? She remembered what the woman in the bakery had said to that man, about the road running out. Could it be?

She turned a steep corner up the cliff, with a sheer rockface just to her left—and there they were.

A little row of four beach houses: two unfinished, but two ready. They looked like overgrown beach huts, with clapboard frames, four of them in a row, painted pastel colors: lemon yellow, sky blue, pink and mint.

Number 11, hers, was the lemon yellow. There was a set of steps up to the high front door, through a tiny patch of ungrassed yard. Underneath was a kind of garage space that didn't look quite finished.

She took out the key Polly had given her. The four glass panes in the entrance showed all the way through; she tried the key, which turned right away, and she couldn't help herself—she felt, for the first time in months, a tiny flicker of excitement.

The house smelled brand-new. Obviously, given the digger parked nearby, nobody had ever lived there.

At the other side of the large room in front of her was a glass door that led out onto a balcony that looked straight down over the other side of Mount Polbearne, away from the town and over the lighthouse and out to the open sea, far below. It was breathtaking.

The ground floor was one large kitchen diner, a windowless bathroom with a real bath, and a small bedroom; upstairs was a mezzanine with a pointed roof, another little terrace and a bathroom too.

The furniture was plain but lovely; a pale stripped wooden floor covered in an oatmeal hessian rug; a plain but incredibly comfortable neutral L-shaped sofa, with pale yellow cushions and . . . Oh my goodness. Marisa practically ran to it. A real fire! But, even better, a fire that looked real but ran off gas so she didn't actually have to chop logs or do anything like that.

It was beautiful. It was the loveliest, neatest, coziest little place she could possibly imagine. It was by far the nicest thing that had happened to Marisa in a very long time. She thought for a moment she was going to cry.

She texted thanks to Caius, who was only twenty-four hours into Marisa not being there and was already wondering why the kitchen surfaces had stuff on them, then started to unpack her bag. There was something about the place that appealed immediately; the quietness, the remoteness. Nobody knew she was here. Which was a little frightening, but also rather comforting. She could be safe here.

She could lock herself away, work, and never come out again. She had everything she needed. She could go out on the balcony, order supermarket deliveries, work from home . . . This was absolutely perfect in every way. Here, she would definitely get better.

Closing the door was the sweetest sound she'd ever heard, closely followed by the silence that enveloped her, although when she opened the balcony doors, the sound of the sea was suddenly very apparent, swooshing gently at the foot of the cliffs far below. Yes. She would stay here, she would finally get her therapist, breathe in the sea air, luxuriate in the peace and quiet away from the stress of other people's parties and the noisy city. She would finally heal. This was perfect.

In the event, she felt this way for slightly less than an hour.

Chapter Ten

Actually, it was more like forty-five minutes.

She opened all the fresh empty drawers, to put away her things—very few, all comfies, most of her stuff was still in the car, with a plan to drop it off for storage—but did that matter?

The downstairs bedroom was carpeted and cozy and had wardrobes covering one wall, and the bath next door, so she chose that over the mezzanine.

She made up the brand-new bed with the brand-new sheets—what a luxury this was, truly, kitted out for holidaymakers—and sat on it, her knees drawn up to her stomach, holding herself close, looking out on a bobbing sea, feeling far away from everything; feeling safe, the gentle lapping of the water in her ears.

At some point she dozed off—properly out of it, in a way she hadn't been for so long, besieged as she was by both insomnia and terrible dreams that would not let her rest. But now she fell properly asleep, and didn't know how long it was when she suddenly jarred awake. At first, she couldn't remember at all where on earth she was.

Then it came back to her. She'd had to move, to Cornwall, and was in a brand-new house that was incredibly quiet except . . .

CRUMP!

The noise that had awakened her came again. As well as some shouting and a fair bit of cursing. Well, it might have been cursing, she couldn't quite tell: the language didn't sound like English.

Carefully, her heart beating fast, she moved out of the bedroom and toward the main door of the little house, where she could see through the kitchen window.

Outside was a group of large, quarreling men fighting beside a van. Terrified they'd spot her through the glass, she half-crouched behind it. They were all shouting at each other in a language she didn't understand, and there was a lot of banging. She couldn't tell if they actually were angry, or whether it was just because she didn't understand their tongue. Then one of them made an unmistakable gesture at another. Oh. Properly annoyed then.

The object of their ire became clear: the lovely wooden steps up to the front door, necessitated by the steep gradient of the hill this far up. Marisa wondered what it was they were supposed to be unloading from the van and manoeuvring up the steps. Perhaps it was a washing machine. She already had one of those, brand spanking new too. Marisa hadn't expected to get so excited about a new washer-dryer, but there you go. It had been a quiet few months

As she watched, though, it became clear this wasn't a washing machine at all. In fact, she watched with mounting horror as it slowly emerged from the van onto a trolley—it was a huge black piano. Not a grand but even so, the idea of them getting it up the delicate wooden steps was somewhat concerning.

There was a lot more shouting and she retreated to

the other side of the sitting room. Oh God. Were they all moving in? With a piano? She thought back. Of course. Her new neighbor. He was the children's piano teacher. But . . . at the school, surely. He was the school music teacher, right? It hadn't occurred to her at all that he would have a piano *here*. Surely he did it all up at the school? This was a rental, who put a piano in a rental?

CRUMP. There was another loud bang on the side of the house How thick were these walls anyway? she wondered. She had assumed that nothing could possibly be worse than Caius's party-threesome house.

Perhaps she had been incorrect in this assumption.

She looked around the pristine sitting room, with its gorgeous views and pale beachy colors. Well, it had been a dream home for . . . almost an hour.

No, no, maybe it would be lovely. It would be lovely. A little bit of tinkling piano. It would be lovely maybe.

SNAP!

Oh my God, was that a step?

Chapter Eleven

Polly hated Huckle being on the road. It had got harder and harder, everything had. Well, no. The bakery was as bustling as ever, but there was a limit to how much you could make selling pasties and gingerbread even if—as she was very proud—they would be the best pasties and gingerbread you could get your hands on for miles around. Of course, part of the reason for that was that she used high quality local ingredients in everything she made, which meant that her profit margins weren't what they might be there either.

Huckle, who had retired from the rat race to raise bees, had gone back into the rat race when he realized just how much it cost to run an absurdly inconvenient home, two children and one puffin, selling his honey for local natural beauty products to spas and hotels.

Which had been fine but his honey business was now looking wobblier and wobblier. Bigger chains had come in, and honey seemed to get cheaper in the supermarket week after week. People didn't really care how organic things were if they were feeling pennies pinching and after a couple of bad seasons and bad weather, they certainly were.

Huckle was the sweetest-natured and most laid-back

of men but he was starting to get a furrow in between his eyebrows.

Life had rushed by the last few years, speeded up as quickly as the lighthouse lamp turned round, lighting the sailors on their long journeys past. From their first meeting at his cottage, wearing his beekeeper costume . . . through their bumpy romance, to her engagement ring, carefully preserved now in a little glass box, made of dried seaweed . . . to the wedding Kerensa had organized for them when Polly was simply too busy to do it herself—nothing they had done had been conventional. But all of it had been fun.

And since the babies had come, they had spent a lot of it in a hurly-burly, even if it had been fun too—nappies and Peppa Pig and talcum powder and rushing out the door and having food on you and first steps and exhaustion and laughter and bewilderment—but they had never stopped moving; everything had always been crazy. But good crazy.

Was that about to stop? wondered Polly. It felt rather like her worst fears were being confirmed, as he rang her—his sweet southern accent without all of its normal jocularity—just to tell her he was coming home early, which pleased her and worried her all at once; he told her which tide he would catch, and she said fine, and he hung up, and in the silence was a stop, immediately filled by the children appearing at her side.

"Where's Daddy? What Daddy saying? Avery and me would like to know, please?"

Daisy was being polite, which meant, Polly knew, that she was worried about something.

Polly pasted a large smile on her face.

"I think," she said, "I think Daddy is going to come home early."

"Hooray!" said Daisy.

"Boo!" whined Avery.

"Stop that," said Polly. She didn't have time for this now. Avery had announced that he was going to be Polly's twin and he hated everyone else in this stupid family and Polly was trying to ignore it—she knew it was a natural phase but she wished he would get over it.

"Maybe Daddy stay away working," continued Avery, taking Polly's hand and giving her a sincere blue-eyed look which he had found very effective on his darling mama even at this tender age. "Then we can get married."

"No, he's coming home and we're going to be a family," said Polly. Possibly a poor one, she didn't add.

It was in the tilt of his shoulders as he walked through the door, the cast of exhaustion on his handsome face even as he collapsed onto the old sofa and let Daisy swarm all over him.

Avery sat and started singing a little song to himself about everyone he didn't hate, mostly Mummy and Neil.

Huckle cuddled his daughter while staring straight over her head, and Polly brought him a glass of wine and he smiled at it, but didn't move to pick it up.

Coldness gripped Polly's heart. She'd been through the agony of losing a business once, many years ago after the banking crash. It's what had brought her to Mount Polbearne in the first place.

But she'd been young then; more than able to pick herself up and start over. She didn't have responsibilities, employees; Christ, she didn't have children.

"Tough week?" she said, tentatively. Huckle turned his tired eyes to Polly.

"I don't want to talk about it," he said, his hands still gently stroking Daisy's hair. He'd lost weight, thought Polly. Whenever he'd been on the road for a few days, she always found herself assessing him for the first time again; even with his suit crumpled and his blond hair in need of a trim, and his blue eyes tired—in fact, perhaps because of those things too—he was still the most attractive man she'd ever seen in her life, still the golden boy she'd come across once, taking off his ridiculous beekeeper hat, insects buzzing on a spring zephyr, hollyhocks growing wild over his head.

She would have taken him straight to bed if the children were not there and if he wasn't patently, completely and utterly exhausted, beyond reason.

"Okay," she said softly, and laid the table for a pork pie, carefully made from a hot water crust which he loved, the insides scented and delicious, a fresh early summer salad on the side, with tomatoes from Reuben's terrible forcing greenhouses; that Polly secretly thought were cruel to plants—the tomatoes, nonetheless, were bright, sweet, red love-hearts of things.

"Don't come to the table, it's okay," said Polly, making him up a plate.

"I should have a shower," said Huckle, his mouth watering nonetheless. The horrible tasteless muck you could buy when you were on the road, on offer in service stations and convenience stores, made him not want to eat at all. Something as simple and as beautiful as one of Polly's special pies made him want to bury his face in it.

"Yes. You smell bad," said Daisy, who was burrowed under his arm. He frowned.

"But the pie smell good," said Avery, as Polly shooed him away.

"Off you go, gannets. You've had supper. Let Daddy enjoy his dinner and you can watch *Moana*."

"*MOANA! MOANA!*"

They looked at the books together. Another hotel chain had moved to a bulk supplier, Huckle explained. They just couldn't make it work.

It didn't matter how many times they went over it. They weren't going to make it. Unless this summer was an unlikely hit. Unless there were a million billion weddings, even though weddings had taken a turn for the quieter, after the last floods. And even then. Unless there was an influx—but after last year, when there had been so much rain and it had been so stormy and damp . . . well.

She sighed and closed her eyes. The heating could come off. They'd done without it before.

She could always ask her mother for help—a problem shared was a problem halved and all that—but Polly knew that if she told her mother, she would fret to the hills and back, which would simply give her another problem.

And if she told her best friend Kerensa, she'd try to give her money, Kerensa being incredibly rich, and that would just be absolutely awful. If anything, Polly spent more on Kerensa than she did on her other friends, just in case she ever looked like she was taking advantage. She took Champagne, not Prosecco; insisted on splitting dinner. She wasn't entirely sure Kerensa even noticed.

And her other friends, dotted around the country, weren't necessarily finding life any easier than she was at the moment and thought that she and Huckle, living in a groovy lighthouse on a gorgeous island in Cornwall, were the luckiest people they knew anyway, even if their children did fall down the stairs about once every three days.

"I could . . . well, I don't think I could . . . I could look for a corporate job," said Huckle, as she moved over and lay down on the sofa, her head comfortably in his lap. It was a terrible position to have a serious discussion from, which, she knew, was why she had chosen it.

"On the plus side, you don't actually smell bad," she said. "Or at least, I like it."

Huckle smiled, seeing she was trying to distract him, and coiled a length of her pale red hair around his finger.

"You're not listening," he said. "I could go back to the office."

He had tried working back at his corporate job once before, back in America. It had not gone well.

She grimaced. "You can't," she said. "It's too far. Even if they'd have you back, which they probably wouldn't. And you're getting too old. They'll be running on cheap interns now."

Huckle shrugged. "Maybe Reuben could find me something?"

Polly winced. "He'd make *you* pay."

"He would."

They held each other. Neil was sleeping in his box but opened a beady eye just to check on them.

"Just you and me, kid," said Polly, hoisting herself up to sit on his lap.

"Just you and me," he said, burying his head in her lovely hair.

"We'll figure something out," said Polly. "But in the meantime I'm going to switch the heating off."

Huckle groaned. The nights were still chilly and the lighthouse got the full brunt of every gust of wind that came along.

"It's a shame you're so tired," said Polly, "given this is the last night you'll see me not swathed in nine layers of old fishermen's jumpers."

Huckle's voice was muffled as he nuzzled in closer to her neck.

"I'm not that tired."

She wriggled on his lap. "Well, that's good."

She moved closer to him, pressing herself against his flat stomach.

"MUM! Come see the song you like! The man is dancing."

Huckle frowned. "This isn't the bit where you fancy the god Maui again, is it?"

"He's a very attractive cartoon god, what's not to like?" said Polly without moving. "Goodness, and I thought I was in the mood before."

Chapter Twelve

Marisa sat, back against the wall, waiting.

Perhaps, she told herself. Perhaps it would be nice—some lovely music, nothing too difficult, a few tunes every night? That would be pleasant, no? Yes. It would be all right. It would be nice, in fact. A little music. Presumably if he was a teacher he'd be good, right? It would be okay. She tried some of the breathing exercises she'd read about. In through the nose, out through the mouth. In through the nose, hold for four: one, two, three—

CRASH!

At first, Marisa thought someone had dropped the piano again. But then there was another powerful crumping noise and two things immediately became obvious: one, that despite the luxury fixtures and fittings and the gorgeous layout, the walls of these buildings were paper thin (this was entirely correct; Reuben only meant them as holiday homes so hadn't bothered with soundproofing. In his own house, which had a totally circular bedroom, you could land a helicopter outside without noticing, and in fact this had happened); and two, this was not going to be "a little pretty music coming from next door."

This was incredibly discordant and loud, banging away as if he were trying to hurt the piano rather than play it. Was he even a musician? she found herself wondering. He certainly wasn't playing like one. It was a horrible sound.

She moved into the bedroom on the other side of the sitting room, but it didn't change matters at all. The only place that was slightly quieter was the bathroom, which didn't have any windows. She ran a bath. Then she put her own speakers on, very loudly in the bathroom. Unfortunately, the blend of the last Taylor Swift album and the (albeit fainter) racket from next door was even worse.

Close to tears, she sat in the bath. This couldn't last forever.

It lasted for three hours.

Any idiot, she knew, would just go and speak to him. Say excuse me, hello, introduce herself, and discuss what was sensible to do. You could even get keyboards that didn't make any noise, she knew, so maybe something like that. Well. There were all sorts of things she could have done.

Unfortunately, over the next few weeks, she found herself completely incapable of any of them. She ordered a very expensive pair of noise-canceling headphones that cut out absolutely every other piece of noise in the house in a slightly off-putting way, but still let the banging and crashing noise through so she felt like now she was in a world where only the horrible piano existed.

Perhaps it would stop when he went to work, she thought.

She thought wrongly. In fact, one of the reasons Reuben had been so keen to put the music teacher into one of his houses was that his plans for a huge glass arts and music structure effectively hanging off the cliff side of

Mount Polbearne, turning it into an "international arts destination" (his words) or "A James Bond dystopian carbuncle" (the views of the planning committee), were still on hold.

So there wasn't just the piano teacher playing. There were his pupils too, and it was something of a toss-up as to who was worse, in Marisa's opinion. Because she heard EVERYTHING.

So every morning the students tripped up the steps, clutching their little music cases, and over and over again Marisa would listen to a reluctant, catastrophic set of scales; followed by "Row, Row, Row Your Boat" and "Camptown Races," fingers haltingly tripping over every new note.

She could make out, when she was in the main room—or, even clearer, the mezzanine, which she'd set up as her own office, a deep growling voice too, presumably his; never angry, but patient, slow and encouraging. How could he stand it? How could he do that over and over again?

It felt like torture. And the worst of it was, everything else was as good as it could be, under the circumstances. She liked the little doll's house. She could get food delivered; she had her work and an internet connection—although she felt guilt at leaving Nazreen to do all the front office work, working with the public while she did all the admin. She was lonely, but she was safe.

Nazreen liked Marisa very much and, even after the GP's recommended working from home period elapsed, was happy to let things carry on as they were and to pass on the boring stuff. Meeting the public, admiring the new babies, taking part in the celebratory weddings; that was the stuff of the job that she loved, that Marisa had used to love too, long ago. Even carefully and sensitively handling loss was a part of the job that could give great satisfaction, if you could do it right.

Nazreen more than anyone could see what was happening with Marisa; had advised against the move and pushed her on the therapist. Now she was biding her time, hoping to inch her back little by little, sooner or later.

Marisa was nowhere near even thinking about going out. But she was thinking about going mad. Or, she reflected gloomily, even more mad.

After a full day of little children—and some older ones—hammering their way dementedly through the same three or four pieces and the endless relentless scales, the teacher himself would then sit down—she could, with her headphones off, hear every creak and noise across the floorboards—and unstring himself, sometimes with great long scales himself, pounding away, but more often with loud, noisy clanging music that he would play over and over again, long into the night, with absolutely no discernible tune, as far as she could tell.

Chapter Thirteen

She tried. She did. In the most un-Italian way—
something her mother always insisted she'd learned in
Britain—with passive-aggression.

She coughed loudly when the music started. Turned
up the television very loudly when the music was particularly discordant and tuneless. Once or twice she even
knocked gently on the wall. Nothing. Nothing made
any difference. How, she raged, curled up in bed, how
could he ignore her, not think about the effect this was
having on his neighbor? How could he be so hateful and
thoughtless?

What could she do? She could phone the landlord—
but that would mean picking up the phone and talking to
someone she'd never met. That was absolutely out of the
question, and if Reuben was anything like his nephew,
he probably wouldn't care anyway.

She could go next door and talk to him. She almost
laughed aloud. No, she couldn't.

She could crank up the music in her headphones to
deafening levels and just go about like that all the time.
It did almost block out the noise from next door but it
didn't allow her to concentrate on work or, in fact, on
anything. This wasn't a permanent solution either, as it
would almost certainly damage her hearing. Although

at this point the prospect of long-term deafness seemed like quite a nice one.

She tried to think of someone to talk to who wouldn't think she was completely ridiculous not to just confront the situation, and couldn't come up with anyone. What if he became angry with her? What if he shouted? What if he played even more loudly? What if she had to leave here? Where would she go?

In the end, the GP's referral came through just in time.

Anita Mehta was a good therapist, and doing her best under trying circumstances (today's being that her six-year-old had discovered the mute button and was constantly pressing it so she would pay attention to him rather than the screen). But today her head was not perhaps as switched on as it might be. She glanced up at the screen, her eyes tired. They were doing Zoom therapy because Anita was based in the South-East; it was a way of getting the waiting lists down. Plus, leaving the house would add so much to Marisa's anxiety it was better practice to start this way regardless.

"Marisa?"

"Hello," said Marisa, shyly. She had taken the laptop as far into the bedroom as she could to avoid the many renditions of "What Will We Do with the Drunken Sailor" being laboriously banged out on the other side of the wall.

Anita introduced herself and explained the basic components of CBT—cognitive behavior therapy—that they were going to use.

"It's baby steps," she said. "Every week I'm going to set you a task—do you have a workbook?"

Of course Marisa had a workbook, neatly filled in in her beautiful handwriting, a freshly sharpened pencil at the ready. Anita was both pleased and concerned at the same time. People who were normally very organized and in control could fight extremely hard to preserve that control, including reducing their world to a tiny space which could not harm them.

"You'll need more people than me," she said. "Are you speaking to your friends? Your family?"

Marisa shrugged, blushing. It felt such an admission of failure to admit that she wasn't really speaking to her mother at all.

"My mum thinks I'm just . . . putting it on."

"Why would you do that?"

"I know," said Marisa.

"No, I'm asking," said Anita, seriously. "What is in it for you?"

Marisa thought about it for a long time.

"Nothing . . ." she started indignantly. Then she paused. "Well," she said. "I suppose . . . I mean, I feel safe here. And outside . . . it doesn't feel safe to me."

"Outside is never safe," said Anita. "That's a part of life we normally accept. But in your brain, right now, there's a little feedback loop that's overemphasizing that."

Marisa shifted uncomfortably.

"I know," she said.

"It's nothing to be ashamed of," said Anita. "And there is no rush to fix it."

"MUMMY!"

A soft toy hurtled behind Anita's head. She placidly ignored it.

". . . well, beyond the NHS rush, of course. But we're not going to rush."

"I have another problem that's making me very anxious," said Marisa, explaining about her noisy neighbor. Thankfully, Anita didn't suggest she immediately run off and confront him or anything else as impossible to her as flying to the moon.

"Good," said Anita. "See it as an opportunity."

"What do you mean?"

"Well, you need to learn how to leave the house. And he is making your house unbearable. See him as a useful motivating factor."

Marisa stared into the Zoom.

"Are you serious?"

"Totally," said Anita. "And this week. All I want you to do is go out and stand on your steps. That's it. That's your homework. Do your breathing exercises—they're in the book. Do a visualization—have you got one?"

"Yes!" said Marisa, feeling ridiculously teacher-pleasing. A visualization was something she was meant to think of when she felt a panic attack coming on: a happy place, somewhere she felt calm and at peace. She was meant to imagine as much of the scene as she could, put herself there until the panic attack had passed. "Do you want to know where I chose?"

"I don't have to," said Anita. "As long as it is special to you."

"Oh," said Marisa, slightly disappointed.

She had chosen the beach at Imperia, in the old town, just as the sun was setting. The sand still held the warmth of the day but wasn't scorching; the old ladies had come out after their afternoon siestas and were standing in the water in large old-fashioned bikinis, gossiping. Other large families were taking their *passeggiata*, their early evening stroll, done up in their finery, looking forward to an *aperitivo* shortly, followed by a good long meal. It was one of the happiest places she knew.

"It's in Italy," she added.

"Very good," said Anita. "Do you still have family there you could talk to?"

Marisa had a lot of family there, absolutely loads. But could she talk to them?

"Is your grandmother still alive?"

Marisa thought of her scary grandmother, always shooing them out of her kitchen and telling them off for dragging sand through the house. Such a contrast to her kind, loving grandfather who was infinitely patient and pleased to see them.

Of course, as an adult she could see that was because he didn't have to do anything in the house; her nonna was fully in charge. But as a child it hadn't seemed that way. Her grandfather was for fun and cuddles. Her nonna was to be avoided at all costs.

"It will be so hard to do this alone," warned Anita. "After all, how's it working out so far?"

Marisa looked around her lovely bedroom and thought to herself, actually, not that bad.

Then she heard a new noise from next door; the sound of someone having a loud, extremely sad telephone call. Every word, she thought. Didn't he realize she could hear every single word, even if it was in Russian? It was completely and utterly infuriating.

"Okay, I have to—" Anita started, and a small hand crept in and slammed shut her laptop for her.

Chapter Fourteen

Lucia, Marisa's mother, had set up her nonna's Skype when they'd been over for the funeral, with great fanfare, even though it was very obvious that her grandmother felt that she'd got through eighty years without using anything so ridiculous, so why did she have to change now?

Nonetheless, looking at it, Marisa felt ashamed, suddenly. She *should* have contacted her grandmother. The fact that she wasn't speaking to anyone was absolutely no excuse. That was the thing about grief and anxiety: it made you so selfish, so stooped in, only thinking about yourself. Marisa was heartsick of herself.

And she didn't have to go outside. Well. Not yet. If she did this one thing first, that would be a tick in her workbook, and that would be her hard thing for the week. Yes. No rush.

She pulled up the computer screen before she got the chance to change her mind, and pressed dial. Listening to it ring, she felt nervous but tried her best to hang on. It was only Skype. She owed her nonna a call. She could do this. She could. She could.

The first thing she saw when the button was clicked on the other side made her catch her breath.

A wall as familiar to herself as her own hands.

Painted a rough blue, with a huge sunburst clock in the middle of it, over a sideboard—far too big for the little room in the small house, part of it blocked a window—but it had been handed down through the family and therefore had to stay.

Inside it, she knew, were screeds of china—far more than could ever possibly be used—gathered from wedding gifts from long ago, great-aunts and -uncles whose dusty pictures hung on the wall, but whose names Marisa had long forgotten, if she'd ever known them.

Her grandfather had four brothers and two sisters, her grandmother two of each, so a relatively small family. Marisa, who was fond of her brother Gino—although she rarely saw him, and he lived in Switzerland now so she hadn't seen him for months—could only imagine the world she remembered from visits as a child; a world where everyone you knew was related to you, where everyone you knew was a cousin, and of course you got on because . . . you were cousins and that's just what you did. She looked at the scene for a long moment, wondering who had answered the computer.

Then she heard the voice.

"*PRONTO!*" came a tiny querulous voice. "*PRONTO.*"

Marisa realized that, without the neighbors around who had helped at the funeral, her nonna probably didn't know how to use a computer. She didn't realize where the camera was, and was looking at the wrong side of the laptop.

Nonna was always in the kitchen, cooking, and came from the generation that seemed perfectly content to do that—she and her grandfather had got married at nineteen, although children hadn't come along until much later.

She ran a tight ship, was always chasing children out

of the kitchen, spoke no English and made rigid demands about everything the children, particularly the girls, ought to be doing and how they should be dressed.

Her grandfather—who would take Marisa down to the pebbly beaches of Imperia and let her pick up pieces of blue glass and put them in his pocket; who would buy her soft ice creams, two flavors swirled together, an indulgence her own mother found rather shocking—had been so easy to love. Nonna was slightly terrifying.

And she had never had any truck with anything more modern than a television so she could watch *Un posto al sole*, which she did, religiously. She also did religion religiously. There was no skipping mass at Nonna's. Marisa still remembered the enormous excitement of the grandparents visiting England—which they did not pretend to understand—for her first communion.

It had been a lovely spring day. All the other girls were wearing light white shifts and simple dresses. She had had the full works: hooped skirt, embroidered cape, white muff, full veil that covered her face, coronet, lace gloves, shoes, a white handbag that contained a Bible blessed in the Vatican, new rosary. Her entire family had cooed and taken photographs of her as she left for the church, waving like a queen. Inside the church the other girls had giggled and made side-eyes at her extraordinary garb, a way of behaving slightly at odds with what the priest kept insisting was their Innocent State of Grace.

"They're jealous," her mother had whispered. And perhaps they were. Marisa couldn't bear to look at the photographs now, though, which Nonna and Nonno displayed so prominently of all their grandchildren. She looked like she should be sitting on top of a loo roll.

"PRONTO!"

"Nonna?" she called out softly in Italian. "It's Marisa! Go round the other side of your laptop. Of your computer. Your computer. Turn it round."

There was a short pause, then the picture jumped and went blank.

Marisa waited. And waited again. Nothing. Had she dreamed it?

She called back on the Skype. Even the picture on the tiny icon made her wistful; one of her and her grandfather, hand in hand on the sand.

The phone rang for a long time. Marisa realized she had almost forgotten her terrifying neighbor for a second, then quickly turned the volume down on the laptop.

"*PRONTO!*"

Now, there was her grandmother's face, looming terrifyingly over the full screen. Marisa flinched backwards in alarm. She also sounded incredibly loud. She nervously glanced to the side. At least the bedrooms didn't share a dividing wall. That really would have been difficult. Mind you, why should she care? If anyone deserved to be disrupted by noise, it was him.

"Nonna?"

Her grandmother's voice boomed. "Marisa! There you are!"

"Sit down, Nonna, you don't need to be so close."

Reluctantly the old woman moved back and was finally sitting in front of the sideboard, at the large wooden table, which was also far too large for the house, on which Marisa had eaten so many meals she could remember the blush of the tomatoes; the clink of ice cubes in pastel-colored plastic glasses; the shape of the netting skirts that covered the fruit bowl, that folded with a snap and that she had been fascinated with as a child, until Nonna had smacked her hand away and told her not to touch them. Lucia, her own mother, wouldn't have hit her in a million years; the child had gone wide-eyed and pale. But she had never touched them again.

"Can you hear me? I can't hear you."

"I can hear you fine. Turn up your volume."

"What is that?"

Painstakingly, Marisa described the right key to press, and was rewarded with her grandmother's look of satisfaction. She could only imagine the volume she was booming out now. Mind you, they didn't have neighbor problems. Their walls were about six foot thick. They barely exchanged a word with their neighbors anyway due to some contretemps, decades before, between their Little Carlo—then a child, now a grown man with a family of his own—and one of the smaller children in the playground over marbles which had ended up in a vowed blood feud. Marisa thought about that. She hoped it didn't run in the family, this type of thing.

"Well," said her grandmother eventually sitting back. "Look at me, on the computer."

Marisa smiled shyly. She'd written to her grandmother, of course, and guessed Lucia spoke to her plenty, but she didn't . . . they'd never quite had the relationship she'd had with her grandfather, and didn't really know where to start.

"How are you doing?" she asked carefully. "Since Nonno . . ."

Her nonna sniffed. She was dressed all in black, her hair lightly pulled back with a great gray streak through it. She looked rather fine, in fact, Marisa noticed.

"Well," said Nonna. "He is with God now."

"You miss him?"

"I speak to him every day."

She crossed herself briefly. Marisa felt herself sadden;

she was hoping for a conversation with her grandmother, not platitudes.

"Well, that's good."

Her grandmother's lips twitched. "And sometimes, now, he listens!"

Marisa smiled at this.

"And I did a computer class!"

"I see that."

"Everyone else said, ah, you are old and behind the times, but Father Giacomo ran a class at the church and now PING! I am on the internet."

"You are on the internet."

"Everyone is very impressed with me," she said smugly. "Especially Father Giacomo. And I have more time now. Now that it is just me."

Marisa thought about it. She had a lot of time in her day—but what had she used it for, but sitting inside and worrying about things? Even her grandmother, it appeared, had got it together enough to take a computer class, for goodness' sake. That was amazing enough in itself. She looked at her grandmother carefully. It was almost like . . . well. She didn't seem in the depths of despair quite as much as she, Marisa, felt herself to be.

"You aren't too sad?" she tried, tentatively. It had been, she realized, so long since she'd spoken Italian—to her mother's alternate annoyance and sadness, she and Gino had started speaking rapid, West Country–inflected English the day they started school and used it as code, and there hadn't been a lot of Italian spoken at home after that. And it had indeed been a while.

But it sounded so good in her mouth, soft and quick and musical on her tongue. She wondered, briefly, if the man next door found it difficult to speak English all day.

His English wasn't good at all. Maybe Russian to English was harder than Italian. Maybe it didn't feel so good in the mouth. Italian had a rhythm all its own; the way every sentence rhymed, the way it had been designed, like so many Italian things, simply to be beautiful, because beauty was important in itself.

"You look bad," countered her grandmother. "Stand up. What is wrong with you?"

"I'm not going to stand up!"

"Stand up!"

She did so, reluctantly.

"Why are you not looking after yourself?" her nonna demanded. "You look tired and bad, not beautiful as you are and should be. You are a young woman, or not a young woman in fact, you are not young, I suppose, but . . ."

"Nonna, people here don't get married at nineteen."

"And women don't get married over thirty," shot back her grandmother. "Well, they do. But to absolute rubbish."

Marisa remembered, not for the first time, quite how awkward talking to her grandmother could be. Now she could only see the top of her head. Which was good because she wouldn't see Marisa going pink, thinking about Mahmoud who, playing computer games in his tracksuit bottoms, normally with one hand inserted down them for some unknown reason while she made him dinner, would have undoubtedly passed her grandmother's threshold for "absolute rubbish." On the plus side, she didn't have to add "missing my wonderful amazing boyfriend" to everything else going wrong in her life, she thought darkly.

"I can't see your face, Nonna."

"My face doesn't matter. My face has been married. Only your face matters. And your face is looking—"

"Nonna. Please don't."

Suddenly, Marisa found herself speaking the truth from the depths of her being.

"Since Nonno died . . . I have been so very, very, very sad."

Chapter Fifteen

Her nonna still didn't get her hairline into the camera, so it was like talking to the top of a hill, but the words that came from her mouth were kind.

"Of course you miss him. Of course you do. We all do. Of course you are sad. Your mother, she cries every day."

It was with a stab of guilt Marisa heard this.

She had thought Lucia was more or less fine about it; she certainly hadn't stopped her normal life of seeing her friends, going to bridge club, going swimming, hanging out in the open air. Her mother's frantic social life had barely slowed down in the last few years, regardless of what was going on in the world. It had always irritated her introvert daughter, that constant rush to be surrounded by people, to be everywhere.

"She needs to be busy. She thinks it makes it better," said her nonna. "Maybe it does."

"Maybe," said Marisa.

"Do not be so sad. He was old and he had a very happy life because he was married TO ME. So there."

Marisa smiled.

"And he loved you and all his children and grandchildren and he sat in the sun and talked to his friends and drank good wine, so there is nothing to be so sad about. You know, some lives are very sad when they finish. You know I had a sister. I was small and I don't remember. But she got measles. She died. I don't even remember it, but it made my mother unhappy for the rest of her life. *That* was sad."

Marisa had known a little about that; her mother often said, if Marisa was looking particularly gloomy, that she reminded her of her own grandmother, who had died long before. Marisa had known even at a young age that this wasn't a compliment; that her mother might rather have preferred an outgoing, charming child she could have taken to her bridge group and shown off, who would have been a popular member of the church community, not a terrified little mouse who hid behind her mother's skirts and didn't say a word unless directly addressed. Even as she'd opened up as she'd got older— you could hardly perform wedding ceremonies and be a total introvert—and found nice friends, her mother still saw her as that mouse, she felt, which had the tendency to make her clam up in her presence, and that of her mother's noisy, carefree friends, who were legion.

"So!" Her nonna's face brightened. "Your hair is terrible, but let me know what has been happening in your life."

"Not very much," confessed Marisa. "But I do have a noisy neighbor."

"I have a solution," said her grandmother when she'd finished. "You take your broom handle. And just— BOOM! Hit the side of the wall. Every time he does it."

"I don't think I can do that," said Marisa. "It's his job."

"Then, at night! Put on very loud music at four a.m. and leave a note saying "This is what you will get, *signore*. Hahaha to you." Also, get a very large dog that barks, *bau bau* all day and all night. And if all else fails, I will send Little Carlo to cause some trouble."

"Um, thanks," said Marisa.

"So, to begin with. Go round to his house. Take the broom. Bang on the door and say, 'This must stop now. Or . . .' "

"Or what?" said Marisa, whose options, she felt, were very few.

"Or you hit him with the broomstick! This isn't difficult Marisa."

"I'll end up in prison! Is prison your answer to this?"

Is prison quiet? Marisa found herself thinking. Probably not.

"Don't actually hit him with your broomstick! But you really must convince him that you could!"

"Is that why you don't talk to your neighbors?"

"No, that is because our neighbors are . . ."

And Nonna used a word in Italian Marisa would have sworn she didn't know.

Chapter Sixteen

However bad Nonna's advice had been, Marisa was still glad that she'd spoken to her and was sorry to hang up. It had been a while, she realized. She seemed to have more or less stopped speaking altogether. And her phone had stopped ringing too.

Enough, she thought. She was going to get through this. She was feeling better already. She had a therapist, and she'd managed to get in touch with her nonna. Two things had gone well already and she'd only been here a few weeks. She'd be down playing on the beach in no time.

She went to bed oddly pleased with herself for the first time in months. She'd achieved something.

Just as she was turning out the light, it started up. A low crumping of chords, all deep low keys, loud enough to make the light shades shake.

She sat up, incredulous.

"Shut up shut up shut up!" she said, teeth clenched. She was dying to shout it, loudly, bang on the walls—but oh my God. What if he answered? What if he was angry; what if he came round . . . She didn't know him at all. What if he was dangerous? He was so big those kids had thought he was a bear.

She felt her heart race, fell back on the bed, cursed

herself for her weakness. She knew she could say goodbye to sleeping tonight.

This couldn't go on. It couldn't.

Marisa agonized over writing the note—it felt so
passive-aggressive, probably because it was.

On the other hand, she didn't know what else she
could do.

But what to say? Could you set your piano on fire and
never play again? Could you give up what was patently
your job and livelihood just because I don't want to go
into the office?

So much of this, she knew, was about her own issues.

No. During the day she'd have to deal with it. It was
the night-time music—the awful modern stuff that
wasn't really music. That was the stuff that really had
to go. He must see that was reasonable, surely. Just the
night stuff.

Then next door they started a halting, punishingly
slow version of "My Heart Will Go On"—this must be
one of his new collection of older lady pianists, who had
suddenly started turning up out of nowhere—and this
stiffened her resolve.

She took out her pen and pad. It felt nice to be writing
by hand again; she'd missed it. She had always taken a lot
of pride in her handwriting, looping it carefully.

Dear Neighbor

she started. Tentative, but friendly. The last thing
she wanted was him coming over to make friends.
And she couldn't remember his name. It was Russian

so it seemed she was unlikely to guess it correctly. But then his English wasn't very good. Maybe he wouldn't know what that meant? She frowned to herself. She was overthinking this. Maybe she should leave it for another time.

The terrible key change in the song was coming up and Marisa found all her nerves tightening in anticipation. There was an agonizingly long pause . . . and then a crash of harshly dissonant notes. She could make out the bass rumble of the man's voice: it was soothing and encouraging. Perhaps he was deaf, she thought. That would make sense of the noise.

The student went at it again, and Marisa found herself completely wound up, like an overstrung instrument.

Dear Sir,
*   As your neighbor . . .*

Okay, so that didn't get round the neighbor problem.

Dear Sir,
*   As I am living next door to you and have to work*
from home I wonder if I could ask you to keep the
music down? It is very loud at all hours of the day
and particularly at night and it appears the walls
are very thin. Thank you.

She was going to write her name and then at the last minute decided against it. He wouldn't . . . I mean, he hadn't seemed an aggressive person, but who knew? She was up here all alone, nobody had a clue where she was.

She chided herself. The piano teacher living next door was very unlikely to kill her. Surely.

Although from what she remembered, he was a very

large person. And, as she'd already seen, absolutely thoughtless.

No, that was madness.

And wasn't Russia quite a violent place?

She was being ridiculous.

She heard his voice again, murmuring. The walls in here were terrible, she thought. If she got close enough she could almost . . .

I mean, she wouldn't.

She shifted herself over toward the wall. After all, what if he was saying, "If you don't play this properly I will kill you"?

As she got close to the wall, his low rumbling voice came through incredibly clearly.

". . . is just notes," he was saying. "You can learn to play notes. Notes can be wrong. Does not matter. But you must learn to trust heart. Celine, she say, heart go on. Do not hesitate. Go on."

"But I keep getting it wrong," came the querulous tones of the student. It was Mrs. Baines, as it happened, one of Polly's best clients, who had fallen in love with Mr. Batbayar because she liked his dark flowing hair and was hoping that he would understand that when she played "My Heart Will Go On" she was actually playing it to him.

Mr. Batbayar did not understand this and thought that someone had sent this woman playing a terrible version of the worst song ever written in order to torture him for a sin he had committed in a past life and was wondering what it might be, and was regretting accidentally killing a spider the day before, which he had meant to pick up and free. His huge fingers on a keyboard were elegant and full of precision. When it came to being around the rest of the world, they were oversized and he had been unusually clumsy. This was spider karma, he had decided, and he was simply dealing with it as well as he could.

I love you, thought Mrs. Baines next to him, who had mistaken his narrow brown eyes remembering a spider for fascination.

"So?" he said, returning to Mrs. Baines, who was pink with effort. "Gettink wrong is our road to gettink right. Do not stop. But do be slower, yes? Fingers cannot run before head is ready. Try it slow slow slow, and put your heart in every note. It will find you."

"All right," said Mrs. Baines timidly. "Could you show me again how to shape my hands?"

"No! You know now! You can do it."

Marisa frowned crossly. He didn't sound remotely dangerous. And as Mrs. Baines started, very slowly and not quite so falteringly, she irritatingly thought he was probably quite a good teacher. She googled "piano teacher murderer" but it appeared to be a vanishingly rare set of circumstances.

She sighed and returned to the note. Still. She couldn't live like this, she really couldn't.

Chapter Seventeen

She cautiously opened her door after Mrs. Baines had left, with much cooing and chit-chat and cluttering of bags and purses as far as Marisa could hear, and information being imparted about upcoming village events, of which there seemed to be an awful lot for a tiny village at the ends of the earth.

Next door, the man had gone back to playing something loud and threatening, occasionally interrupted by huge long runs at the top of the piano which were so unexpected and jarring she felt it get under her fingernails. She was so scared her teeth were nearly chattering.

She looked at the innocuous pale blue door next to her pale lemon one. Well, almost innocuous, apart from a missing step where, she was right, the piano had indeed broken it. She frowned. He should fix that. It pained her tidy heart.

She picked up the note, put it down again. This was ridiculous. She knew what she had to do. Knock at the door. Introduce herself. Politely state her request and why it was necessary for her well-being and mental health that she wasn't being auditorily assaulted all the time . . .

Yes. She would. She would do that. Like a normal

person. She was a normal person. She was fine. She was absolutely fine. She lifted her hand to raise it—

"HELLO, NEW LADY!" came two small voices. Up the unfinished road swung Daisy and Avery, the little twins from the bakery. A tall blond man in shorts, presumably their father—Avery was his spit—was following them up the hill, talking intensely into his mobile telephone, his face worried.

"My daddy is on the telephone and we are going to our piano lesson," said Daisy, as if Marisa was a policewoman asking for a precise account of her movements.

"We don't need Daddy, AS YOU SEE," said Avery, swinging his arms. "BYE!"

Huckle lifted his tired face for a moment then went back to his call.

"We share a piano lesson now," said Daisy in a confiding voice. "We used to have one each but now we have one together and Avery is very naughty."

"Because is SPENSIVE."

Unused to contact with other people for a long time—and completely unused to children of any sort—Marisa smiled in a slightly distant fashion and backed away, even as Huckle hung up his phone and smiled at her apologetically.

"Sorry."

"We don't need you, Daddy," said Avery.

"But! What if!" hissed Daisy, obviously referring to an earlier conversation.

Avery looked scared and piped down.

"What if what?" said Huckle, in an amused voice.

Daisy shook her head, shushing him, with a very distinct "not in front of the children" expression on her tiny face.

"What if what?" persisted her father.

"What if Mr. Batbayar brings his BEAR FRIENDS," hissed Daisy in a stage whisper as Avery took on a hunted expression very similar to his father's only a moment or so before.

At that moment the blue door swung open. The music teacher stepped out, without looking to where Marisa was. She shrank back in the door frame, inside the safety of her own four walls once more, hidden from view.

"Aha! My favorite pupils who are . . ."

It was clear he didn't know the word for twins.

". . . being born on one day that is the same day," he finished triumphantly.

"You mean 'twins.'" said Daisy seriously. "We're twins."

"Tweens."

"Twins."

"I say that."

Avery was trying to see round Mr. Batbayar, which wasn't easy as he took up the entire doorway. Mr. Batbayar looked behind him.

"Just me," he said. "No——"

"Don't say it!" said Daisy.

Mr. Batbayar raised his huge hands and beamed at Huckle.

"You stay?"

"You don't need to stay, Daddy," said Avery.

"I will," said Huckle. "But I'll just take a call outside, okay, you guys? I'm right here."

The two little ones scampered into the house and Mr. Batbayar left the door ajar and disappeared with them into the house.

Huckle smiled apologetically at Marisa.

"Hello," he said. "You're one of Reuben's newbies. How's it going?"

Marisa froze. All she could think of was "Oh, you're American," which was a fairly ridiculous thing to say to someone who presumably already knew they were American. A bright flush stole over her.

But he seemed very nice and gentle. She could . . . she was standing in her own doorway. She was safe. She was fine. She forced herself to stay put.

"Uh . . . it's good," she said. "Bit noisy."

Huckle frowned and looked around. It wasn't like Mount Polbearne to have noise issues; they weren't on any flight paths, and there were very few cars. The masts clattered in the harbor from time to time, that was about it.

Marisa nodded toward next door.

"Oh, of course! Oh, how nice to live next to all that music . . . oh."

He saw her face.

"Well, you get out to work, don't you?"

"Um . . . I work from home."

"Oh. OH." He smiled. "Well, good luck. You might learn a lot."

From the open door came the noise of very small fingers doing their best to find middle C.

"Uh-huh," said Marisa.

Huckle's phone rang again and with an apologetic grin he moved across the road to take the call.

Marisa felt rather proud of herself for at least managing that much of a conversation. Before she could think better of it, she quickly stuck the note in the little ornate postbox on the porch, then disappeared inside.

Then she immediately changed her mind and wanted to go outside again and retrieve it but she couldn't because Huckle was there and instead she decided that throwing herself into work was probably a good way not to have to think about what she'd just done. She then went and redid the entirety of the next year's budget, saving the department about 5 percent, as it happened, and got so thoroughly engrossed, and was listening to Biffy Clyro so loudly through her headphones that she completely missed the knocking on her door the first time. She heard it the second.

Chapter Eighteen

Oh God. She was going to get murdered. The children must have left their lesson, everyone else must have gone. She was completely alone. She glanced out to sea. The sky had clouded over; everything looked heavy and gray.

Perhaps she could pretend she wasn't in.

Bang! Bang! Bang! Bang!

Oh God, how would that even work? She couldn't do that.

She sighed. She knew the note had been a bad idea. He was going to be furious. This was awful. Everything was awful. Her heart was racing. Maybe she could go and hide in the bathroom again.

But she couldn't hide forever.

Maybe she could.

No. No she couldn't.

"Hello!? Hello!?"

Oh, CRAP. Crap crap crap. The worst had happened. There was a pause.

She took off her headphones and stepped forward, swallowing loudly, terrified.

The door swung open. Marisa braced herself, ready for someone yelling at her.

He loomed, the size of the doorframe, his face be-

neath the beard—he had a strong aquiline nose and
Asiatic brown eyes framed with very dark eyebrows,
which wasn't she thought of Russian people looking
at all: she thought they were blond and blue-eyed. Oh
goodness. How cross was he going to be?

But instead, he looked delighted.

"AHA! HELLO!" he roared. She felt trembly.

"I HAVE PERSON NEXT DOOR!"

Well, that cleared up whether or not he knew the word
neighbor.

"I didn't not know I was havink person next door! You
arrive today?"

"Actually, I've been here for three weeks."

His face looked confused.

"Three weeks? But I too have been here three weeks."

He obviously didn't remember her from the bakery.

"But I do not see you come out or come in."

She half-smiled and didn't answer, not wanting to
admit that she hadn't been out once.

"You leave me note!"

He held it out to her, smiling, and indicated that she
take it.

"Thank you for note!"

"Um . . ."

He stood back.

"Can you read note to me, please?"

There was a long pause. Marisa felt her insides turn
cold.

"I can . . . you don't read English?"

"I do! Very much! But. Only when it is in typink. Yes."

Marisa glanced down at her loopy calligraphic handwriting. She saw the problem.

"Ah."

The temptation was huge: to tell him it was a note just

to say hello. As if reading her thoughts he said, with a broad grin, "You send me note sayink hello!"

She blinked. It was now or never. He didn't seem threatening, despite his size.

"Um . . ."

His face looked concerned suddenly. His thick eyebrows furrowed. Despite the beard, it was a very expressive face. She doubted he was much use in a game of poker.

Marisa took a deep breath and found her courage.

"Actually, I was asking . . . do you need to play music so much all the time . . . all day and at night?"

Marisa burbled the last words and mumbled them almost under her breath, half-hoping he wouldn't understand her, but he did.

"I play music at night?" he said wonderingly, almost as if this came as news to him.

"Uh, and the walls are very thin?"

He frowned even more, but didn't say anything for a long time. It looked like he was going over the problem in his head.

Finally he looked at her in confusion.

"You don't like music?"

Marisa bit her tongue so she didn't mention that what she was hearing at night wasn't music.

"But it's all the time," she offered, finally.

"But it is mine job. My job," he corrected himself.

"In the daytime," she said.

"You not have job?"

"I do. I do it here."

"But I do mine there."

They seemed to be at something of an impasse.

"And at night . . . it's just horrible."

Something contorted slightly in his face then and she realized suddenly she'd hurt him deeply.

"I mean, it's just so loud. And I can hear everything."

"But I cannot hear you at all! I do not know you are here."

"Because I am a quiet person."

"Well, the world has quiet people and noisy people maybe."

"Maybe it does."

He peered past her into the pristine little house.

"You have same house. Just you?"

"Um . . ."

Marisa was tempted to lie just in case.

"You have whole house. For you. Overlooking sea. Is beautiful, no?"

"Yes."

"Beautiful house just for you. In beautiful place. Filled with good thinks. With good people. Safe. Is happy place, no?"

Marisa didn't feel in the least happy but she shrugged.

"And you find you haff piano to make you sad. I see. I suppose you haff find something make you sad."

"I'm just . . . trying to work . . ."

He frowned as if completely confused. It was hard to tell whether he was angry or whether it was just the natural timbre of his voice that made him sound very angry indeed.

"I do not like notes. You send notes complaining about music. Where I come from people used to send notes. They send secret notes. To the police about the people who is livink next door."

She stared at him, completely horrified that he would think this about her. He turned, slowly, and descended the staircase. Halfway down he turned back and held out his hand.

"I do not want this note," he said stiffly. "In the daytime there will be music. Is job. At nighttime you must haff what you want. I see."

He looked at it dismissively.

"Although your handwriting is very beautiful."

It was. It was part of her job. He was holding it out.

He didn't apologize for shouting. She didn't put her hand out for the note; couldn't reach out of her own front door. He proffered it again, his eyebrows twitching in confusion, but she did nothing.

Finally, as if this was beyond endurance, he ripped the note in half, once, twice, three times, and threw the pieces up like confetti in the air, so they gently floated down and coated her steps.

Then he returned to his own house, closed the door quietly and silence fell.

Chapter Nineteen

It was the easiest place, she figured, hiding out in the little windowless bathroom. It was tiled in a very bland, hotel style that she liked, as if she was on holiday somewhere—which she guessed was the point—and the towel rail heated up the entire room. Having no windows made it feel cozy and cocoon-like and cut off from the rest of the world. It felt safe. She lit a candle even as the hot water filled the tub and she put far too much bubble bath in it. She took her book, but didn't read it. Instead she got into the water, even though it was far too hot, the pain felt cleansing somehow, sat with her hands around her knees and let big salty tears run down her face.

She was trembling. He had been so angry with her! It had been a reasonable request. Okay, maybe she should have done it in person but . . . well. She couldn't. A polite note was perfectly reasonable. Well. Reasonable-ish.

She thought of his face, so animated and cheerful when he thought she was welcoming him to the neighborhood. She put her head in her hands. She should have done that. She should have found a way to say hello. Baked a cake perhaps. But it had been so long since she'd done anything in the kitchen.

Cooking for friends used to be one of her greatest pleasures. Now she could barely keep herself fed wholesomely. Why must everything be so hard? Everything was hard—she found herself slapping the bubbles with her hand—and nobody understood. And what kind of an idiot thought it was okay to play crunching music all night when you had neighbors anyway?

She remembered belatedly that he hadn't even realized she'd been there. She'd been so successful at hiding herself away that he hadn't even realized she was there.

She turned on the tap so he couldn't hear her sobbing through the paper-thin walls.

All that night, as she tried to follow something on Netflix, she was also keeping an ear out for next door. Part of her desperately wanted him to keep playing—to play louder, if anything. Then he could be the bad guy in this scenario and she could cheerfully reclaim the moral high ground and know she was right in what she did and he was a pig. It wouldn't solve her next problem but it would make her feel better right now.

Instead, there was no piano playing at all. What there was, all clearly audible, was:

1. stomping up and down the woodenfloors
2. occasional sighs
3. the squeaking open of the balcony door
4. more sighing
5. the lighting of something—a cigarillo? Not a cigarette, but a faint scent of licorice and cloves drifted over from the balcony—which was puffed· noisily for a couple of moments, then extinguished crossly.
6. more muttering

This pattern then repeated. Marisa grew more and more alarmed. What if he was actually insane and was plotting to murder her in her bed? Just because she was in the middle of nowhere, at an address that didn't appear on Google maps, on an island that didn't connect to the mainland, with very few people knowing she was there, next door to a very grumpy giant whom she had angered . . .

Marisa took her laptop and retired to bed.

She looked at Skype sadly. There was only one person she was interested in hearing from. And he wasn't around anymore. And her grandmother would almost certainly tell her she was an idiot.

On the other hand, she would almost certainly be home.

"Well, I did tell you."

Being told off by her grandmother wasn't much of an improvement on being alone—but it was a bit.

"I know. But I just . . . I just couldn't in the end."

Her grandmother sniffed.

"Next you'll be telling me you didn't go to mass on Sunday."

Marisa slid past that one as quickly as she could.

"So now I live next to an angry giant who hates me," she said.

"Is he married?"

"Nonna! Seriously, aren't you listening?"

"I'm just saying. Who else are you meeting?"

"Okay, thanks, Nonna."

"Your mother agrees with me. Says you're having a big sulk at the world."

"You've been discussing me?"

"Of course," said her nonna serenely. "What else do you think happens to me that I have to talk about? Also, we are both worried about whether you're eating."

"Of course I'm eating."

"Well, I can see you're *eating*. Are you eating *well*?"

Marisa had hoped it didn't show, but obviously it did. Everything seemed so much effort, and cooking had fallen by the wayside.

"I'm fine, Nonna."

"Good. Go talk to your neighbor. He is musician! Oh, I love music. I think you are very lucky."

"This isn't . . . it's not the kind of stuff you like."

Nonna had started singing to herself.

"Not like that."

"Ask him if he knows 'Voglio Te.'"

"He doesn't," said Marisa shortly. "He knows "Bang Smash Piss Off Marisa.'"

But despite the fractious conversation, Marisa still felt a little better when she finally fell asleep.

Also, something rather odd happened. Her nonna forgot to hang up the Skype. She just wandered off. When Marisa woke up the next morning, she found they were still connected; she could see the kitchen, with the hot morning sunlight pouring in from the back door, and her nonna listening to the radio as she put coffee on the stove.

"Nonna?"

But the old woman didn't hear her, just carried on. Marisa found she didn't mind at all; having the computer connected to Italy was somehow rather nice, like she could just glance through a window and find her there. Even when she finally got Nonna's attention, she simply shrugged and smiled and said, well, that was nice but she had to get on with her day and took her little checkered shopping trolley and headed out to the market, as Marisa threw some bread in the toaster.

And over the days, they both pretended that it was nothing, really, that the Skype was left on, and that they could swap the odd word here and there when Marisa wasn't working, about what Father Giacomo had been saying or what the fishmonger had tried to pass off at the market and how she had told him a thing or two, and Marisa would tell her some old stories from the registrar's, and they would talk about her grandfather and gradually, as the days went by, they fell into an odd sort of pattern—at least, after the microwave lasagne fight, that neither of them referred to again.

Marisa started to lean in to the rhythms of her grandmother's life. She rose early, even with the one-hour time difference, and was always dressed and busy before Marisa hit her first coffee of the day. She took her old much battered shopping trolley out into the blinding sunshine of the Imperia morning, headed down to the market at the old port to discuss fish and fruit with the sellers, and came back and started preparing herself a little lunch—fresh sardines, perhaps, and salad, while Marisa toasted herself yet another sandwich. Then Nonna would take her siesta and wake at five, ready for a chat, just as Marisa was winding down her day, and Marisa would go to bed long before her grandmother, who would play her old opera records; a more comforting kind of music, and so quiet as to be practically imperceptible.

It was surprisingly companionable. Not, of course, that either of them would admit, in a million years, over a thousand miles, and two generations, that they were . . . lonely.

Eventually, in the evening, her nonna started squinting at Marisa's television and demanding that Marisa put on the Italian subtitles to whatever she was watching, and even when Marisa suggested that she could get Netflix herself and watch alongside, she shook her head at that completely outlandish suggestion and preferred to squint through the bad camera on Marisa's laptop and watch that way, so Marisa would stick the laptop next to her on the sofa, feeling slightly ridiculous, as if she had a robot friend, and they would watch together.

The noisy music had stopped at night. Now she never heard him play at all, only his students throughout the day, and some growled phone calls. Apart from that, nothing.

Marisa felt terrible about this. It wasn't fair. They should have found a time when he could play and she would just put up with it.

"Well, you discuss it, you build a compromise," Nonna pointed out, but of course saying things was easier than doing them, and Marisa couldn't bear to make the first move.

"No more notes," said Anita, at their next session. "But you got out?"

"I stood on the steps! For a bit."

"Okay. Bottom of the steps next week. And, ideally, a sensible conversation with your next-door neighbor, but I realize that's a lot to ask."

"Uh-huh."

"How did it feel, when you went out?"

Marisa thought about it.

"You know that film *Beetlejuice*? The really old one."

"Where Winona Ryder has really cool hair?"

"*Really* cool hair."

Both Anita and Marisa were pleased that, for once, they appeared to have landed on something they both agreed upon.

"Well. That's what it's like," said Marisa, more quietly.

"Stripy ghosts?"

"No . . . you know. When she tries to leave the house. The mother."

"Geena Davis! God, she was gorgeous. What happened to her?"

"That's not really the—"

"Do you remember Brad Pitt in *Thelma and Louise*?"

They both went quiet for a moment.

"Cor," said Marisa at the memory.

"I mean, I don't care how old he is."

"Why isn't *he* living next door?"

They both smiled rather soppily at each other.

"Sorry," said Anita, snapping out of it and becoming professional again.

"No, don't worry. I think thinking about Brad Pitt might be the best therapy I've ever had."

"I'm going to write that down."

A ball soared over Anita's head and her face furrowed.

"I bet Brad Pitt's nine hundred kids don't do that."

"I bet they do."

"I bet they do too."

Marisa grinned, feeling a little better.

"Okay, so, tell me," said Anita, returning to business, her dark gaze penetrating even through the screen.

"Well, when she tries to leave the house, it turns out to be perched on a desert, surrounded by vast sandworms."

"I remember," said Anita.

"That's what it feels like to me. Like everything out there is a different world. That everything out there is not safe."

"But you know rationally that the world outside isn't really sandworms?"

"But so does Geena Davis. It doesn't make any difference to whether or not she can get out of the house."

"So leaving the house for you . . ."

"Is like braving sandworms."

"I get it," said Anita. "I do."

There was a long pause.

"Oh God, it's just so stupid."

"Don't. Don't be ashamed. Don't feel ashamed. You have nothing to be ashamed of."

Marisa thought back to what she'd done to her neighbor.

"I think I do."

"Can you make it better?"

"He got so angry and upset."

"Well. Okay. Well. Start small. Sit on your step when the weather is nice. Wave at the worms."

Marisa half-smiled at that. "I can try."

"You can."

Marisa glanced at the time. It was almost up. A paper airplane soared above Anita's head.

"Creative," she said.

"I think it's made out of my passport application," said Anita. She smiled ruefully. "Okay, until next time. And Marisa . . ."

"Uh-huh?"

"Remember, please—I know I keep telling you this. But remember this is an illness. And illnesses—many of them—they pass. Even without treatment. Bodies don't stay sick forever. Ask any doctor to tell you the truth, and they will; a lot of the time, they're just waiting for bodies to heal themselves. And all it takes is time."

Chapter Twenty

Polly was opening up cheerfully, with Jayden her assistant making plaits in the back. There was still a chill in the air, and meatball plaits to go with a steaming cup of coffee were proving very popular. "Tastes like pizza," said Avery, giving them a hard look. The children's greatest dream was of takeaway pizza, something they had seen on American TV shows and occasionally experienced at Lowin's. There wasn't a takeaway pizza place within range of Lowin's house either but somehow Reuben made it happen.

The postie, who hated having Mount Polbearne on his beat—constantly lashed by the weather, nothing but hills, having to time his visits with the tides—came in, looking lugubrious as usual.

"Hello, Janka!" said Polly, who always tried to cheer him up. It had never worked one single time, not even on the golden days, when children paddled through rock pools with shrimping nets; when the sounds of happy laughter could be heard around the ice cream stand, and the whole town bustled with happy holidaymakers, and people thrilled by the beauty and strangeness of the place; little ones, faces sticky, scurrying up the streets and pointing at the lighthouse; the days when it felt like there could be nowhere more delightful to be on earth than Cornwall.

Janka grunted.

"What's up?" she said, fetching him his regulation triple espresso, which she firmly believed did nothing to improve his temper.

"Someone got their magazine subscription mixed up and complained about me to head office," he said, crossly. "Apparently there is a python magazine that is about computers, and a python magazine that's about really big snakes and if you get one you don't really want the other."

He downed his coffee. "Who even subscribes to magazines about really big snakes?"

Polly had a fair idea, but decided now was not the time to drop Lowin in it.

"And," he said, even more crossly. He bent into his red wheelie bag and pulled out a huge box. Both of them recoiled. A very pungent scent was coming from it.

"What even is this? How can it be legal to send this through the Royal Mail? This is toxic waste! This is probably poison! I will probably end up poisoned and all I will have to show for it is a life trekking across that bloody causeway."

"In the loveliest corner of the world?" suggested Polly, gingerly reaching out. "That . . . is it for me?"

He shook his head.

"Marisa Rossi," he read.

"Oh," said Polly. "We haven't seen her."

She thought about that crossly. Given that she'd given her keys and everything, a courtesy visit would have been nice, seeing as they were, you know, the community's bakery. Maybe she was one of those people who thought all carbs were evil. Although she hadn't looked like one of those people.

"She lives all the way up the top of the town," said Janka heavily. "On an *unpaved road*."

He looked at the large box.

"It's actually against health and safety for me to deliver to unfinished roads," he said.

"*Is* it?" said Polly, skeptically. She knew Janka knew that she saw almost everyone in the village from time to time and if he could use her as a kind of free intermediary drop-off point, as she was right on Beach Street, he would. She was fighting this at all costs and made no move to touch the large parcel.

As the stand-off continued, fortunately the bell rang. It was Mr. Batbayar, the very large piano teacher, who came in most days and was, Polly remembered, the girl's next-door neighbor.

"WHAT you bakink today?" he said, recoiling instantly at the smell.

"Janka, you're poisoning my shop," said Polly. "You're going to have to take that out."

"I can get coffee anywhere, you know," said Janka, threateningly.

"No you can't!"

Mr. Batbayar examined the box.

"That is my street."

"It's your neighbor," said Janka quickly. "Can you take it to her?"

"Of course."

"You don't have to!" said Polly, but Janka was already out the door. "Argh. That confounded postie!"

The piano teacher blinked in surprise.

"This is bad?"

"Oh . . . no," said Polly. "I'm just not sure I can take on being local postmistress as well as . . . anyway. Never mind. How are the twins getting on?"

"They are very five," said the piano teacher, making it clear that that was about as much information as he was willing to give right then. "Six red things, please."

"Mr. Batbayar . . ."

"Alexei, please."

"Oh, okay," said Polly. "I'm Polly. Anyway, one thing is, they're called strawberry tarts."

Alexei made a game attempt at shaping his mouth into four syllables that meant literally nothing to him, and smiled cheerfully in the way that often meant people stopped fussing him about his English.

"And secondly, are you eating all of these yourself?"

Alexei gave her a look.

"Um. No?"

"Really no, or is that what you think is the right answer no?"

"The other one," said Alexei. "You try not to sell too many thinks?"

"No, but you could mix it up a bit. Look, I have some beautiful asparagus tarts."

"I loff . . ." He pointed at the little spears. "Yes! Six, please!"

Polly put the strawberry tarts down. He gave her a bear-like look and she picked them up again, and he paid quickly, then shouldered the large heavy box like it was nothing and dinged out of the shop whereupon Polly spent a faintly irritating day explaining what the smell was.

Later that day it was still chilly, but Marisa didn't really notice the weather. Had she been able to step outside she would have seen celandine blooming through the rocks that made up the end of the unfinished road; she would have seen swifts returning to lay their eggs in hedgerows and singing a cheerful song, the white flashes of cow parsley and the daffodils that thickened every hedgerow, as well as the woods full of bluebells back on the mainland.

But she didn't notice any of that. She left the balcony door open for fresh air, but apart from that the seasons were passing her by.

There was a knock at the door. She glanced up from the laptop—Nazreen was out, and she was tidying up the archiving files.

It was becoming increasingly clear to her that, useful as she was, there was less and less homeworking she could actually do. One day they weren't going to need her anymore.

The knock came again, and with it her instant physiological response; her mouth went dry, her hands started to tremble.

"HELLO!" came a loud voice.

Marisa's heart sank. It was him. She knew it was him from next door. Of course it was. She wanted to pretend she wasn't there, that nobody was in, but that was ridiculous.

"HELLO! LADY NEXT DOOR!"

He sounded gruff and impatient.

Okay, she wasn't going to be able to get away from this. Timidly she opened the door.

"I HAFF PARCEL FOR YOU!"

In the morning light he looked larger than ever, his beetle brows jammed together, the parcel, square and wrapped in brown paper, looking small in his hands, even though it wasn't.

"Um . . ."

She started to stutter and he looked at her as if she was completely beneath his worth attentions.

"I put here," he said. Then he did something odd. He picked it up and sniffed it. Marisa blinked at the oddness of his gesture. Who was this guy?

There was a parcel, square and wrapped in brown paper with her grandmother's familiar handwriting, sitting on the top step. They both looked at it for a moment, the man's beard obscuring half his face.

"Um, thank you," she managed. He stood there watching for an instant, as if he were waiting for her to open the parcel, then nodded shortly and made to go back around.

"Mr. Batbayar!"

A tiny little girl was rushing up the unfinished road, splashing in little puddles. She had vibrantly curly hair which shot out behind her and seemed bigger than her head.

"Mr. Batbayar! I have learned ALMOST almost most of it VERY LOUD AND FAST."

His face changed completely, and he beamed at the little girl.

"Vivienne!" he said, as if there was nobody he was more pleased to see. "Well. Now. What we say? Fast is last."

"Fast is FUN."

He grinned wider.

"It is fun. Hello, Mrs. Cordwain."

The similarly frizzy-haired woman smiled happily and followed the little girl up the steps.

"You stay?"

"It's been giving me a headache all week," she said easily. "Another few dozen repetitions can't make any difference now."

"I hear your mother say you do lots of practice," said Mr. Batbayar to the little girl, who smiled with delight and nodded.

"Also . . ." went on the woman, smiling hopefully.

"You want coffee?" said Mr. Batbayar, sounding much jollier than Marisa had heard so far.

"I would *love* one. You make very good coffee."

"No. England coffee is very bad coffee. That is not a hard thing."

Presently the small party disappeared into the house and moments later a very loud and fast and not entirely accurate version of the Skye Boat Song came banging out from the little blue house next door.

Marisa stood there with the parcel she had been so delighted to receive only moments before, feeling suddenly very sad. How easily they had found the conversation, how relaxed the curly-haired woman had been, going out and about and into someone's house. And they had both looked right through her.

Well. At least she had a parcel. Clutching it like a miser, she went back into the house and sat down. She recognised the wobbling antique handwriting and the sunny stamps; they had arrived on every birthday card of her childhood. It occurred to her, for the first time, that of course it must have been her grandmother who chose and wrote those cards, took them to the little *ufficio postale* and sent them safely on their way, in good time. Huh.

She realized very quickly why he had sniffed it.

Inside, carefully wrapped, she found treasure.

There was Barilla pasta and Mutti tinned tomatoes,

straight from the store. Carefully wrapped in straw was a tiny pot of home-made tapenade scented with everything good. There was a jar of tomatoes her grandmother had dried herself on a corner of the little sunny terrace where it was too hot in the afternoon but glorious at any other time of day. A big hunk of parmesan, and, instantly recognizable from the second she'd picked up the box— the smell of it pervading everything, overpowering and absolutely enchanting and something that had probably perfumed the entire Mount Polbearne postbag (Janka did indeed complain about being expected to deliver it: head office had regrettably replied that unless it was a fungus that was likely to explode they were unable to intervene in this instance)—a large brown truffle.

She buried her nose in it; it was extraordinary. Deep and rich and heavy with scent; to be used sparingly and stored carefully, otherwise it would contaminate the entire rest of the house and, quite possibly, the street. She immediately fetched a Tupperware container, and sealed away her treasure carefully.

There was more. Local sea salt, and even some potted basil so she could grow her own, although what could possibly thrive in the harsh rocky salted sand of her new home and survive the brisk westerlies she couldn't imagine. A jar of plump shiny black olives, a twisted vine of garlic which would have smelled amazing if they hadn't been pushed sideways by the truffle, and a bottle of exquisitely good first-press olive oil.

She pulled them out carefully. It was amazing. The one thing her grandmother could have done for her right now that was as close as could be to putting her arms around her and giving her a hug. She glanced over at the Skype, but her nonna wasn't in view.

She smiled ruefully at her nonna's bossiness. It genuinely did hurt her that she wasn't eating properly.

She thought of her dinner for that night—a stodgy and not very appetizing ready meal, with microwave noodles and almost certainly not enough vegetables—and sighed. It had been so long. The joy she had always found in making food.

"SO!"

The voice from the laptop startled her. She sat up. It was Nonna, of course, returned from her siesta.

"I got your parcel!"

"I see!" The woman was grinning broadly.

Glancing behind her, Marisa saw all the tins laid out on the countertop.

"It must have cost a fortune to send."

"Yes, it ate in very heavily to the money I had to spend on designer clothes for the Christmas ball at the Duke of Lombardy's."

"Aren't you a little old to be sarcastic?"

"Oh yes, you go to so many balls."

Marisa grinned. It was strange. Her grandmother was as snappy as ever, but somehow, she'd gotten used to it. She wasn't so freaked out anymore. She thought about Anita and what it said in the book. Repeat the thing you're scared of . . . until you're not so scared. But talking to Nonna was easy. It was everything else in the world that was difficult.

"Well. Go on then!"

"Go on then what?"

"Tell me at least you have an onion."

"If you think for one second I'm going to cook with you standing there shouting at me, you are very wrong about things."

Her grandmother folded her arms.

"I will watch and not say anything."

"That is not possible for you."

"It is completely—"

"See, you're at it."

Nonna made a zipping noise with her mouth and sat back with her arms folded, pulling a cardigan around herself, even though Marisa had looked at the weather forecast and it was a balmy seventy-nine degrees in Imperia that morning.

She moved self-consciously toward the countertop and dug out one of the rather ageing onions she had ordered online when she'd first moved, thinking optimistically it would get her cooking again. It had not, when it came down to it, and they had sat there in the dark cupboard beside the sink, like a reproach.

She selected one of the knives from the holder. They had never been used. Everything here was so new.

"What kind of knife is that?" came from behind her.

"I don't know. Ssh!"

"Well, you can't cut anything with that knife."

Marisa sliced through the onion, far away from the tips, just as her grandfather had shown her, long ago, to avoid crying.

"That's too far down to cut an onion! You are wasting half an onion."

"I am going to hang up now," said Marisa.

"But you can't do this alone!"

"Well, I'm going to give it a try."

"Just put me on mute."

"But then you look like one of the Muppets."

"Do not be rude to your nonna."

"I think *Un posto al sole* is just starting."

However much fun shouting at her granddaughter was, it wasn't worth missing *Un posto al sole* for, and Nonna, sniffing, backed down.

"I won't be far away."

"I'll call you if I forget what pasta is."

"So young and such a smart mouth."

Chapter Twenty-one

Marisa felt briefly guilty that her nonna had gone to all the trouble of sending so much food and was now being denied the pleasure of shouting at her as she cooked it.

But somehow, even just setting the butter sizzling in the brand-new pan was helping to make her feel better. It was soothing. She added some pretty music, kept quiet so she couldn't be accused of double standards.

While you were chopping, it almost didn't matter that you were far away from home, stuck somewhere you were too scared to leave, held prisoner by grief. When the knife was so sharp it nearly took your fingers off, when the oil was gently heating in the pan, sizzling quietly, and gradually, without rushing, the onions starting to softly melt, no rush. When all of that was going on, nothing was too bad.

Next she grabbed the garlic, that was a gentle purple around the base; cracking the papery shell with the flat of her knife, breathing the scent in deeply. She chopped rather than mashed the garlic; it was in wafer-thin slices which would gently color in the good oil.

She felt her breathing slow as the delicious scent hit the air, and opened the bottle of Valpolicella, the last thing, carefully tied up in bubble wrap, that her nonna had put in the box, and set it to warm next to the pan.

Next she pulled out a large pot, boiled the water for the pasta, adding plenty of salt, then gently stirred the tomatoes and fresh basil and even more salt into the pan with the onions, giving everything time to gently blend together. So simple, but with good tomatoes—and these were very, very good tomatoes indeed—there was nothing better. She dug up a little grater from one of the cupboards for the rough hunk of parmesan.

Everything was perfect. She put a note up on Skype to say so, and to say thanks, and to her extreme surprise got back an emoji of a person with their mouth zipped shut.

Then turned the heat down, grinding a few sharp turns of pepper in the top.

Next door, the women with the curly hair was leaving.

"Oh, that smells amazing," Marisa could hear her say, close as anything. "Is that your dinner?"

There came a long sigh.

"No," said the deep voice, sadly, as if he was starving to death which was clearly very far from the case (although he had already eaten all the asparagus tarts, but he had underestimated the ability of small children to sniff out a strawberry tart, then make beseeching eyes at their piano teacher). There was a pause on the other side of the wall.

"Oh, dear. Hey, you must come down and eat with us sometimes. We like to be neighborly round here."

Marisa felt a sting at that. Neighborliness.

The woman lowered her voice. "Be nice to have some company, actually. It's tough being a single mother sometimes."

Marisa frowned. Now he was being *hit* on?

"Thank you," said Alexei, and she heard the heavy tread as he moved toward the door.

"It's such a friendly village!"

"Good, good. Thank you, Vanessa, I see you next week."

The door closed behind them and once more, Marisa heard that heavy sigh.

Oh, for goodness' sake. She went back to stirring the sauce that was reducing so beautifully on the stove. She was a perfectly neighborly person, thank you very much.

It hadn't occurred to her that she might not be the only lonely person in Mount Polbearne.

The wind outside was growing chill, and she went to close the balcony window. As she did so she realized that he was standing out on his own balcony, separated from her by a wooden fence, with a gap in between, and a precipitous drop down the cliff side.

It was a tremendously lovely view when you looked straight ahead out to sea; a slightly concerning one when you looked down.

He was smoking one of those strong-smelling cigarillos. He hid it immediately when he saw her.

"This is bad too?" he said, unsmiling.

"No. It's fine," said Marisa, timidly. He nodded stiffly. She glanced back at the oven.

"That is smellink very good," he said, just as she moved to the door.

She blinked rapidly, trying to play down the panic response.

"It's just dinner."

"Ah, dinner."

She blushed, shyly, just at having the conversation.

"You don't have any dinner?"

"I have dinner. It doesn't smell good like your dinner."

Something in her softened—perhaps it was not having to go outside, and the fact that he didn't seem quite so scary when he was a far drop away.

"Well," she said, wondering if she dared be so brave. But he didn't seem angry anymore. Just hungry.

She thought about what Anita had said, and what Nonna would say.

"Would you like a plate?"

He thought about this for a moment. His narrow dark eyes looked serious, as though this was a very complex suggestion. Finally, he came to a conclusion.

"I could not take your food."

"I have enough. Bring me a plate."

"How you get food on my plate from there."

They both eyed the gap.

"You throw spaghetti? Is high risk."

"How did you know it was spaghetti?"

"I can hear it roll over. It roll over."

Maria glanced around. It was indeed rolling over—boiling over, of course, was what he meant—and with a quick gasp she leapt to save it. She couldn't find a colander anywhere, and shouted, "Colander!"

"What is this?"

"Thing . . . holes . . . sieve . . . water . . . pasta . . ." she shouted, breathless, until eventually a colander came flying onto her balcony and she dashed over and grabbed it. His colander was sky blue. These houses were ridiculously color-coordinated. Well, she had to give him some now.

She drained the pasta and tossed it with the light garlicky *pastasciutta* sauce in the pot, then quickly unbagged a small arugula salad. She filled a plate, added a glass of wine, and carefully took it over to the balcony.

"Aha!" said Alexei excitedly, reaching out his big bear arms to grab it over the barrier. Amazingly, he could reach.

"Don't drop it!"

"If I drop it I go after it," he said. "Thank you very million times."

"Um . . ." Marisa blushed again. "It's nothing."

Then there was a pause and she retreated into her house to eat her own meal, odd as this felt.

She had forgotten, she realized. She had forgotten the taste of real food, made properly. There was nothing complicated about it, it was just superb ingredients, handled properly. The garlic was soft and sticky and aromatic and delicious. She practically licked the plate. She called her grandmother back over to the computer halfway through. Her grandmother ignored her the first four times. Then she limped over, making a fuss of her back and her arthritis as if it had been agony to come the four steps from the parlor.

"You are calling to tell me I was right."

"Yes," said Marisa. "You are always right."

"I AM," said her grandmother in satisfaction, straightening up.

"Thank you," said Marisa. "It was the kindest thing to do."

"Your *nonno*, he loved my cooking."

"We all did."

"Yes. I should have been worse, then I wouldn't have had to do so much of it."

They both smiled. Then suddenly, as if from nowhere, came a quiet little noise.

"What's that?"

"I don't know," said Marisa.

The tinkling noise continued and Marisa realized it was a very soft, sweet rendition of a tune that even she knew on the piano.

The tiny noise played in little ripples, tinkling like a waterfall. It was absolutely like nothing else she'd ever heard emanate from next door before. She and her nonna both fell silent to listen.

" 'Clair de Lune'!" said her nonna, happily. "I love it! I thought you said he was terrible!"

"He normally is," said Marisa. "Huh."

The sweet, soft piece played—and then finished. And there was no more noise, even as Marisa worried suddenly that this truce in maneuvers might result in the hammering starting up again.

But no. He played it, as a little benediction—perhaps he thought it was a tiny thank-you, Marisa wondered, and then left it in peace.

"You have dinner and now you have music," said Nonna. "I do not think maybe that everything is as bad as you think."

She paused momentarily.

"Perhaps next you will even cut your hair."

Chapter Twenty-two

The walls really were incredibly thin. So it was two days later, when she could hear the twins plonking at either end of the piano, that she heard another noise, from the other side of the house. Confused, she moved toward it.

It was—definitely, unmistakably—a sob. Marisa crept closer to the wall, where there was a little window above the cupboard that held the washer dryer and the mop.

There it came again. It wasn't a wail; it wasn't shock or pain. It was very clearly the sound of someone crying, but desperately trying to keep it quiet. It was a sound Marisa knew better than anything.

She began bargaining with herself. She could open the door, just a bit. Just to see. She had promised Anita to go to the bottom of the steps, that was all. That wasn't far. Someone needed help. It was a basic human feeling she was having, nothing to worry about or even think about. Old Marisa would have done it without a second thought. Her mother would be making them soup right now.

That decided it. She couldn't bear what would happen if Nonna found out that she'd ignored someone crying outside her door. She'd probably end up having to do nine decades of the rosary.

She opened the door a tiny crack. Polly jumped back about a foot.

"Oh my God! I didn't think there was anyone here!"
Marisa half-smiled.

"But you gave me the keys."

"I know, but nobody's seen you at all since Huckle did a couple of weeks ago and Alexei brought your parcel . . ."

"Who's Alexei?"

"Your next-door neighbor."

"Oh," said Marisa, slightly abashed.

"He's nice," said Polly.

"Okay," said Marisa. "But I've been here all along!"

Polly wiped her eyes, trying to pretend she hadn't been crying at all.

"What have you been living on?"

"I get deliveries," said Marisa, fidgeting and uncomfortable with the conversation.

"Oh," said Polly, whose lip looked like it was about to start wobbling again. "Well, if you ever want to, you know, support local businesses . . ."

Marisa felt ashamed.

"Uh," she said. "it's all very new. It's been a big move, it's been . . . quite difficult."

Polly nodded.

"Are you okay?" said Marisa.

"I'm . . ."

Polly was still cross at this person not buying her bread from her, but her face was so concerned and it was so exhausting, so very, very tiring having to keep up a cheery façade, day after day, not frighten her customers, maintain a cheery line of banter and happiness so as not to worry the twins, and this was the only person in the village she didn't know, asking kindly and sincerely, and the temptation to unburden herself was almost overwhelming.

"I'm sorry," said Marisa when it became clear Polly couldn't go on. "I didn't come to the bakery. I have a . . ."

It hurt, it really stung to say it out loud.

"I have an anxiety disorder."

There. It was done. The world did not, a part of her noticed, implode at her saying it.

"And . . . sometimes it's very hard for me to get out and about."

"Oh," said Polly again, instantly changing from resentment to empathy. She could only imagine. "Oh goodness, I am so sorry. That sounds tough."

Marisa shrugged. "I can . . . I can still . . . do you want coffee?"

Polly found herself agreeing and following her in—partly out of nosiness. She was desperate to see Reuben's chalet.

"They're really beautiful!" she said. "Wow. Reuben can be a putz, but this is just lovely."

"I can't believe he had trouble renting them," said Marisa.

"Oh no, he didn't, it's just the stupid road."

Polly's eyes moved to the wall, where the plonking noise from the twins continued.

"Do you get that *all day*?"

"It's not so bad," said Marisa, almost without thinking as she went to the coffee machine.

Then she paused. It was true. Kind of. She had really stopped noticing the piano lessons during the day. They blended into each other like background noise on the radio. She played her own music through headphones and just generally got on with things. In fact, she'd almost applauded the other day, when Mrs. Finnegan had successfully made it all the way to the end of "I Know Him So Well" without collapsing halfway through, which had elicited a joyous shout of encouragement from Alexei.

"It was at night that was driving me crazy. When it was just him."

"Is it not nicer when he plays?"

"No! Oh my God. No. Weird, weird music."

Polly smiled.

"Well, you won't have to put up with the twins for much longer."

"Why not?"

Marisa brought over two little espressos. Then she colored, realizing it had been so very long since she'd had company she had completely forgotten to ask people what they wanted to drink.

"I'm so sorry . . . what would you like?"

"I'll never sleep," said Polly, smiling at the tiny cup. "But hey ho. I never sleep anyway. It can't do me much more harm. Thank you."

Marisa remembered suddenly a little packet of biscotti had turned up in her care box and jumped up to get them.

"Oh, look at these!" said Polly, who couldn't resist anything sweet. "Oh, they're wonderful. We should sell them in the . . ."

Her voice trailed off.

"Why aren't you coming up here any more?"

"Oh. We . . . I need to cancel piano lessons. They're just a bit pricey. Don't tell anyone."

"I can't," said Marisa. "I don't know anyone."

"Okay, well, don't mention it to your landlord."

"I've never met him."

In fact Polly knew that the second Reuben found out they couldn't afford the lessons, he would insist that he paid for them. And that was too awful. When she and Kerensa had first been friends, of course she admired

Kerensa's drive, her iron discipline with her diet—but then she knew Kerensa loved her too, appreciated her sense of humor, liked having her around. They were equals. The idea of their longstanding friendship being reduced to a begging bowl of inequality: oh God. They had lost their money, she couldn't bear to lose real friends too.

"Are . . . things not doing well down at the bakery?"

Polly sighed. "We've lost a lot of the holiday trade—it's tough all over for everyone, and my husband's business and . . . Oh, I don't want to wang on about my problems."

"We all have problems."

"We do."

"Everything will get better."

"Do you really think that?" said Polly, skeptical.

"Well," said Marisa. "I know I seem totally rubbish but . . . I never thought I'd make it here. And I did. I never thought I could move. I couldn't even . . . well. You probably didn't notice but I just made it all the way to the bottom of the steps to see you. Which I couldn't have done before."

"Seriously?" said Polly. "Wow! Well done then!"

Marisa couldn't help smiling.

Polly raised her cup.

"I can see why you order stuff in. This coffee and biscuits are absolutely awesome."

"From Italy," said Marisa.

"Oh, great."

"But as soon as I can make it to the bakery, I'll get my bread from you."

"Is that a promise?"

"Yes," Marisa said, firmly. "Yes it is."

Next door a terribly clunking duet was making its way

to an end. There was a lengthy pause and then BANG! all four tiny paws finished simultaneously and on the right chord.

Marisa and Polly grinned at each other.

"Did you hear that?"

"YOU ARE NINJAS!" came the voice from next door, loud enough to be heard in the kitchen. "YOU ARE MY TWIN NUNCHUKS DUET NINJAS!!!"

"How come he knows the word for ninjas and he doesn't know the word for strawberry?" grumbled Polly.

Chapter Twenty-three

Predictably, Avery had a lot of questions about nun-chucks as Polly thanked Marisa for the coffee and headed on down the road. Mr. Batbayar watched them go. Marisa, buoyed, stood out on the steps too.

Marisa gave him a half-smile, which he tentatively returned, then vanished into his house and returned her freshly washed lemon-yellow plate and fork.

"I am sorry," he said, staring at the ground. "When I did yellink at you."

"It's okay," she said. And then, surprised at her own daring. "How much is a piano lesson?"

"You want piano lesson?"

He looked totally bemused. Obviously he had her down as a total music-hater in every conceivable way.

"Oh God, not for me."

He half-smiled. "Noooo, not for you."

". . . if I was to pay for the children? But, not with money."

"Actually, I would say money is good."

In fact, Marisa had a plan. She had been a little taken aback by Polly pointing out—correctly—how she didn't contribute to the community, as well as the curly-haired woman talking about neighborliness. And she wasn't exactly spending her own wages.

She could see how proud Polly was. Of course she wouldn't take charity.

On the other hand.

"If I said, you can play at night that's fine and also maybe if I cooked for you when I was cooking . . . could you maybe keep teaching the twins?"

This all came out in a rush and he frowned as his serious careful face worked through what she meant.

"Ah," he said sadly. "You mean, to hear me play that would be a great sacrifice for you but you would do it to help another person."

"No!" said Marisa. "Well. Is that what I said?"

He nodded sadly, his big bear face looking glum.

"I'm sorry," said Marisa.

He put his hands out in a "well, what can you do" gesture and turned back around and went back in without giving a clue as to whether that was a yes or a no. She sighed, and went and turned the Skype on for Nonna.

"What's the matter? You look even sadder than normal. It's really bad for the face, looking sad all the time. What happened?"

Marisa sighed.

"I tried to do something good. I don't think it worked very well."

Her nonna listened to the whole story, sniffing occasionally.

"Well," she said finally. "I think this is easily solved."

"I'm glad to hear it," said Marisa, surprised.

"Do you have any lambs' liver in the freezer?"

Marisa gave her nonna as sharp a look as she could manage through the laptop camera eye.

"NO!"

"Oh. Okay. Not quite so simple. Let me think. What do you have?"

"Is this about food?"

"Everything is about food," said Nonna.

In fact, inspired, Marisa had done a slightly more adventurous online shop. Okay. There were a few microwave meals in there. But there was a lot of fresh stuff too. Possibly more than she needed. Possibly.

"Um, chicken . . . potatoes . . ."

"Okay! Stop right now. That will do. You have mushrooms?"

Her grandmother immediately instructed her to slice some of the truffle incredibly thinly and put it on a layer of butter under the skin of the chicken leg, then whisk up a mushroom sauce before making truffle mash, which included more butter than Marisa privately thought any human should eat in a year or two, but on the other hand her grandmother was eighty-four and still swam in the sea with her friends every weekend, so who was she to judge?

"You will need Madeira for the mushrooms. Or brandy."

"Why would I have either of those things?" said Marisa.

"You're an adult," retorted Nonna.

"Well, I don't."

"Well, you'll have to find some."

Chapter Twenty-four

It was a glorious evening, and Marisa took the potatoes—which she was mashing with plenty of salt and cream—to the little balcony terrace.

To her right, the sun was setting in a light medley of gold and pink. It was wonderful. She glanced around at the houses meandering up and over the hill, down the other side to the northern edge of Mount Polbearne, and the thin land bridge that came and went and joined her little end-of-the-world yellow house to the mainland and the rush and dash and fuss of the rest of the world. She glanced back into the lemon house. She was happier where she was.

The chicken roasting started to smell heavenly; so good it felt unfair, like leaving a trap for a hungry dog. Sure enough, eventually, the shaggy head appeared on the balcony.

"I am thinkink we should be better . . ."

He had looked up the word but it had gone from him. ". . . nybor?"

"*Were* you," said Marisa, continuing to mash. His eye strayed irresistibly to the potatoes. There was clearly lots. "You don't have any cooking sherry, do you?"

His head tilted.

"Sherry? It's . . . Spanish wine."

He vanished and came back with a Rioja, proffering it willingly.

"Um, no. Like. Sweet wine. Is it? Yes."

"Oh!"

He vanished again and returned with port.

"What . . . do you have an entire bar in there?"

"Yes." Alexei nodded gravely.

"What? How? Why?"

"My friends . . ."

He looked slightly caught out then, as if he hadn't meant to mention them.

"When I move . . . they said, you must take alcohol, you move to England. They buy me presents. Was funny."

He said the last words quietly, as if it didn't seem funny anymore.

"But you're *Russian*," said Marisa. He looked as if he didn't know what she was talking about.

"So?" he said.

"Why did you . . ."

She was about to ask why he had moved there but he had disappeared once more.

"What you want?" came from inside his blue house.

"Okay," said Marisa. "Well. If you really have everything. S-H-E-R-R-Y."

He disappeared then eventually came back with a very expensive-looking bottle of Amontillado.

Marisa couldn't help cracking a smile.

"No way! Well."

"You want?"

"It's too good for cooking."

"You drink it?"

"No. Do you?"

"No! Was for new English . . . friends."

They both looked awkward then and Marisa didn't say anything.

Therein followed a small problem of how to get it over the balcony. It didn't occur to either of them just to open their front doors. Instead Marisa grabbed one of her big yellow striped towels and held it in the gap between the two balconies, and he gently lowered it in.

"Thanks for this," she said. "Would you . . . like to eat?"

She could tell he was still annoyed with her and desperately wanted to swallow his pride and say yes.

"Well, what are you having for dinner?" she asked him.

He frowned. "Is fine."

"What?"

"Cabbage that is stuffed."

"That sounds . . ."

"Is very good."

"Okay," she said. "Supper will be about fifteen minutes. I'll leave it up to you what you do with the cabbage."

"Is very good," said Alexei, with feeling.

"Well, bring it. I'll see you on the balcony."

Marisa returned to where the chicken was browning beautifully and put the potatoes back on the heat. She added garlic to melting butter and threw in some chopped onions, sprinkling them with a huge splash of the expensive sherry. The smell was absolutely divine.

Quickly she made up a salad, slicing her precious sun-dried tomatoes into little sharp-tasting shreds with the kitchen scissors, but letting long luxuriant thin slices of parmesan settle onto the arugula leaves. Then she threw the mushrooms into the hot butter with the onions caramelizing gently, and ground a large amount of white pepper into the mix. This she poured over the chicken with its crunchy aromatic skin, added the completely luscious mashed potatoes and the sharp little salad, then carried two hefty platefuls out to the balcony.

Alexei arrived at about the same time with some pale-looking cabbage on his plate. He looked at her plate and he looked at his plate. Then he took his plate and hurled the cabbage off it over the side of the rocks, till it splashed into the water below.

It was so unexpected Marisa let out a bark of laughter, and after that it felt very odd not to sit out with one another and chat, or so Marisa thought. Alexei, however, gulped down his food like a bowl had just been set in front of a dog, in complete silence. Then he looked up, noticing she had barely started.

"Is very good," he said, still chewing.

"Okay," said Marisa. "So. Um. Do you like being a piano teacher?"

There was a pause.

"Um," said Marisa eventually, when it became clear he wasn't going to fill it.

His beetle-like eyebrows came together.

"You play the piano?"

"No."

"Any instrument?"

"No."

"You sing?"

"No."

"When you are happy? Or in the shower? You do not sing? You have no music?" His face looked sad. "It is sad to have no music."

Don't start, thought Marisa. Don't tell me about sad. She used to love music, used to go to gigs all the time. Here she just used it to block out the rest of the world, to block out other people's music and noise.

Out over the sea a gull called out. The waves pounded onto the rocks below. It was as quiet as it had been since Marisa had moved in.

"Well," she said carefully. "Silence is nice too. Listen?"

The push and pull of the water came back and forth. Another gull answered the cry. The lighthouse flooded their windows, briefly, and off again. There was the distant clatter of the masts of the fishing boats, clicking in the wind.

He did listen, tilting his large head to the side.

"Well," he said finally. "Perhaps that is just a different type of music."

"Perhaps it is," said Marisa, quietly.

Chapter Twenty-five

"This is very odd," said Polly, looking suspicious as she fussed around the kitchen first thing in the morning. Huckle was staying at home. He was trying to do mail-out internet orders. It was not going so well. People got cross with him and ordered the wrong amounts or ordered different things or sent things back they hadn't used or, worse, sent things back they patently had used, including honey they had eaten half of then decided they didn't like, or cream they'd broken the seal of, or ancient gifts they'd received a year ago they'd suddenly decided they didn't want, and the site collapsed all the time because their broadband was so awful. It was horrible, especially for Huckle, who liked people on the whole but he had to admit that if you were running a mail-order internet business, people were not very good at showing you their best side.

"What?" he said, looking up wearily. The sun was just coming up and Daisy and Avery were supposed to be getting ready for school but instead had decided to throw raisins in the air to see if Neil could catch them. He couldn't, but he was having a very good time trying.

"That puffin is getting so fat he's unaerodynamic," said Huckle. "You should call the *New Scientist*. 'Impossible Creature Can Fly.'"

Neil came to an undignified screeching halt above a raisin that had fallen on the floor.

" 'And Make Holes in the Floor,' " said Huckle. "Stop feeding Neil."

"It's EXERCISE," yelled Avery, scurrying around the kitchen with his arms outstretched. "Why can Neil fly and me not fly?"

"That's a very good point," said Huckle. "Probably because you're not fat enough."

Avery immediately started gulping handfuls of raisins from the packet. Polly rolled her eyes and started clearing up.

"I *was* saying . . ."

"Oh sorry," said Huckle. It was very difficult with small children, they had both found, to ever get to the end of a conversation.

Polly tried to catch Daisy to brush out her strawberry-blond hair. Nicely done it was a heavenly cloud. Left the way Daisy liked to leave things, it looked like a witch's mane and would take nine times as long to be attacked by a comb the next time, with Daisy in floods the entire time, deeply remorseful for not having combed it more often, but somehow even more determined to never let a comb near it subsequently. It was a battle Polly could already see stretching far into the distance, possibly forever.

"What?" said Huckle, as Polly wrestled with the Tangle Teezer. It was the single most expensive item for hair Polly had ever bought. It was worth every penny.

"I've forgotten," she said.

"YAY, NEIL, TWO RAISINS!"

"OW!"

"Okay then . . ."

"No, hang on . . ."

She looked up. "I got an email from Mr. Batbayar."

Huckle looked no more enlightened.

"The piano teacher."

"The BEAR!" screamed Avery. "Neil, we will teach you to peck out the eyes of a BEAR."

"Don't do that, smalls," said Huckle. "What did he say? Is he upset at the cancellation?"

"Actually," said Polly. "I hadn't mentioned it, I was about to, then I had coffee with that new shy girl up there and we overran and I forgot. But, he said that the twins are doing so well he entered them for a scholarship and apparently they got it! For twins. Apparently loads of twins play the piano together."

Huckle screwed up his face.

"*Really?*"

He fired up YouTube and searched "twins piano duets."

"Huh," he said.

There were indeed vast numbers of twins, often identical, playing duets on huge pianos.

"Well," said Polly.

Hearing the name of Mr. Batbayar, Daisy and Avery had marched over to the ancient upright they'd rescued from the old schoolhouse before Reuben started developing it—literally nobody else had wanted it—and started banging away loudly. It sounded appalling.

"Perhaps," said Huckle, "there weren't many entrants to the scholarship."

"They do need to get them young," said Polly. "I suppose it will mean a lot of extra practice."

"And he didn't know they were about to give up? This isn't him being sneaky?"

"No! And why would he, anyway, he doesn't know

us, and I can't believe rural piano teachers make enough money they can hurl it all over the place."

"Cor. Well then." Huckle beamed proudly. He thought absolutely nothing was beyond the scope of his twins.

"What's that girl next door like? Why has she never been seen in the village? She's incredibly mysterious."

"Ooh, no, she's not! She's got agoraphobia."

"Is that the stay-in one or the go-out one?"

"Well, why don't you think about it for five seconds?"

"I'm very tired."

Polly smiled at him.

"Goodness," said soft-hearted Huckle. "I hate to think of anyone shut in."

He looked out to the frothy bright waves gleaming, a distant rain shower heading their way under a cloud, but sun showing promisingly either side of it.

"I know," said Polly.

"That's terrible," said Huckle. "Is there something we should be doing?"

"Leaving her a trail of cakes, that kind of thing? Not sure," said Polly thoughtfully. "She seems nice though. I get the impression she's had a bit of a rough time. I think she's come here to get over it. Not everyone copes."

Huckle put his hand over his eyes.

"We will though," she said, going over to him and putting her arms around him. "We will."

"How?"

"We could Airbnb the lighthouse. People love that kind of thing."

"But where would we live?"

"We could move above the bakery."

"It's ONE ROOM!"

"It's a nice room."

"For two adults, two children and a bird. I'm not sure that's going to work out."

"We could find somewhere cheap on the mainland. Away from the beaches and the nice bits."

"Yeah," Huckle sighed.

"You know when I first arrived here it was all cheap," said Polly. "I paid nothing for that flat above the bakery."

It was now occupied by a posh Pilates teacher whom Polly scuttled past most days before she got a lecture on her terrible posture.

"Yes," said Huckle. "And then you only bloody gentrified the bakery, didn't you? And sent it all upmarket and lovely and then people started moving in and then a posh restaurant came along and then bloody Reuben set up his stupid posh school and then everyone wanted a second home there and now nobody can afford to live there anymore, especially not us."

"I know," said Polly. She lowered her voice. "We could maybe sell the lighthouse?"

Huckle rolled his eyes.

"Yeah, no, clever people want to move here," he said. "Not idiots that want to live in a lighthouse."

She smiled and they intertwined their fingers.

He looked over at the beef wellington she was whipping up for supper, her fingers easily entwining the pastry.

"Can't you do something like that for the posh second-homers?" he said.

"I don't know," said Polly. "The locals want bread and cakes and pasties and I don't think the posh folk eat bread at all. Plus they're never here."

"There must be something," said Huckle. "Because we can't sell our home. Maybe our best option is to let the twins grow up to become musical geniuses and make their fortune in the world of piano duets. Is that a thing?"

"Let's hope," said Polly. "I'll just say thank you to Mr. Batbayar."

"Also tell him to shave off his beard so the children will stop training their pet bird to peck out his eyes if he turns into a bear."

"I'm not sure if that will translate into Russian."

Chapter Twenty-six

Anita had warned her that the process was—or could be—one step forward, two steps back, but Marisa was too buoyed by the success of her scheme to listen.

And she so enjoyed cooking with Nonna, and sharing it with her neighbor. Well, apart from the night where Alexei suggested a plum wine which came from his unfathomably deep liquor cabinet.

For the plum, Nonna suggested duck, and Marisa, to her absolute astonishment, was able to order it from a nearby farm and when it appeared, tragically covered in feathers and with the head still attached, Nonna talked her down off the ceiling and patiently, after going out and finding her own from somewhere—Marisa was scared to ask in case she'd just headed down to the nearest lake and lassoed one—walked her through butchering it, a faintly unpleasant affair but still, oddly, in its own way quite affirming; she felt in touch with her hands and the food she was preparing, that something really was happening. She played a podcast and almost—almost felt like a normal person, doing a normal thing.

Unfortunately, what Alexei had taken to be plum brandy, due to a fancy swirly label he couldn't read properly, was plum sake, and so unbelievably strong that they were both completely trolleyed by the second glass, poured with Alexei's rather generous hand, and the duck breasts burned on the hob but they didn't care as they were laughing too much, so it wasn't exactly the evening they'd planned, especially when Marisa made the mistake of saying, "Okay play something now," and he had said, "Oh, music is only when drunk, I *see*," and then tried to play something and got completely bamboozled and ended up ploughing the tune into a wall.

But it was still fun, and the following evening Marisa salvaged what she could of the duck and sliced it very thinly and reduced the sake down to its essence and made a cold plum and sesame seed duck salad with bean sprouts that was formidably delicious because she couldn't bear the idea of the duck dying in vain, so it all worked out as well as it possibly could.

"But I still have to pay you for the lessons," she protested, picking up a groceries delivery on the front step after enduring the twins' faltering attempt at "Three Blind Mice" for a solid forty-five minutes. (Huckle sat outside, pondering what the talent was, exactly, that Mr. Batbayar had spotted that he couldn't quite hear.)

"We're drinking through your friend's bar, and lessons are expensive."

Alexei frowned. The evening light was cresting the hill, about to disappear behind their houses.

"Yes. There is a thing."

"Name it."

"My hair. It is like a crazy wild man in the woods."

It was true, his dark hair went everywhere; there was absolutely loads of it, straight and in his eyes.

"Isn't there a hairdresser in the village?"

"There is. It is a lady . . . She is pupil."

Marisa wondered if it was one of the ones who brought love songs but didn't like to mention it.

"And she has a lot of questions always for me." He looked pained.

"I do not want to be rude but . . ."

"So what . . ."

She looked at him. "You don't want me to do it."

"Just makink it straight at back. I cannot see it."

"I can't cut hair!"

"Will be fine."

"It won't be!"

"Marisa," he said. "You have no faith in yourself."

"I know that!" she said, despairingly. "That's why I'm here."

He looked at the sun, moving toward the sparkling sea, and his eyes took on an inquiring look.

"Can't I just give you cash?"

His face took on a stubborn look.

"No. Hair. Stay here."

He went in and returned with a bowl of water, his own hair dampened down, and a pair of scissors.

"These are kitchen scissors," she exclaimed.

Of course they had a pale blue handle.

"They are not . . . used scissor. So. They are anythink scissor."

He sat at the edge of his steps with his back to her so she could reach through the divider. Then he brandished the scissors and a comb behind him.

Marisa sighed. "If this is a disaster . . ."

"Everythink can be disaster," said Alexei. "Still. We try."

He leaned back his head on her side of the steps, and she felt the weight of it in her hands.

"Don't lean too far."

"Thank you. Don't die for haircut. Is good advice."

Marisa began to comb out the bushy head. He had his eyes closed, and she understood why: it was oddly personal this, to be so close to someone, especially when you had access to scissors. It had, she realized, been a long time since she had been in such close proximity to another human being, particularly a stranger. Mahmoud didn't really count.

That seemed so awful; to lose something as fundamental as touch.

She combed everything in a straight line, then did what she'd seen hairdressers do and held a line of it between her fingers, then snipped it off.

"Hmm," said Alexei.

"What's the matter?" said Marisa, panicked.

"Well, now I think, perhaps my power is in hair."

"Like Samson?"

"Yes. Perhaps if you cut hair, I not play anymore."

"Great!"

He laughed ruefully, but there was no rancor between them now.

His hair was thick and long. Marisa made another straight line of her fingers, and snipped.

After the first shining dark locks fell to the ground—which did feel in fact, rather like a shame—it was much easier. She cut and shaped round the bottom of his head. There was a scent to him, feeling so intimately up close; like woodsmoke. It was pleasant, like whisky, a hint of the cigarillos; pencil sharpenings for some reason, and tobacco, and something a little sharper, like oranges. It was an old-fashioned smell.

He sat perfectly still under the bright blue sky, the only sound the *snip snip snip* as she tried to tidy everything up, and, if she was entirely honest with herself, not really wanting it to end. His face with his eyes shut was much more expressive and pleasing than when hunched in a permanent grimace.

She felt she should speak, but she was concentrating. Plus, if everyone in the village asked him too many questions, she didn't want to add to it. And she didn't want him to ask any questions back.

It was not unpleasant, feeling her hands on his head, in the sweet spring air.

"You should cut your beard too," she said.

"Now you are professional, I see."

"Ssh, don't move."

He obediently closed his mouth. High above, a pair of gulls circled lazily in the soft air, cooing to each other.

"You do not ask questions."

"You said you don't like it."

"Well, now is too quiet."

She snipped gently.

"I ask you. Why you never go out?"

"I have . . ."

She had told Polly. She could talk about it.

"It's an illness. Called agoraphobia. I'm getting better though. I'm on the steps! I am talking to you!"

"So you hide at end of world?" he said, musing. "Well, I'm glad you do better."

"Why are you here?" said Marisa in answer.

"Oh." He sighed. "Is long story."

"You have a lot of hair."

He smiled.

"Don't move."

"Well. Is not long story. Is old story. Beautiful woman. She not want me anymore. 'Go away, Alexei.' So. I go away. Very far."

He sighed.

"Very far."

"You're done," she said, having finished the rest of the job in silence, wondering what on earth the woman was like, what had happened that had made his friends send him a bar to hide himself at the foot of a country he wasn't even from. No wonder he didn't want to get his hair cut in the village.

When he finally sprang up, shaking off the hair down below into the dirt of the unpaved road, he realized he didn't have a mirror.

"Well?"

Marisa smiled. She was quite proud of her handiwork. Now, his hair softly and lightly covered his head, one stray here or there but mostly just a gentle covering, with a longer quiff on front. He pulled his hand through it distractedly.

"It's lovely," she said, then bit her lip. "Well. I hope you like it."

"Perhaps I will not be frightenink all the children," he said.

"I don't think they're frightened really," said Marisa. "You're not that frightening a person. When you get to know you."

There was an odd moment there as his face looked sad suddenly; his eyes far away.

"Well. I am glad you are thinkink that."

Chapter Twenty-seven

Anita was pleased, of course she was. But she had seen this before; the teacher-pleasers who rushed ahead with their books, who thought they were doing perfectly, and then hit a wall at the first setback. She hoped Marisa wouldn't be like this but she couldn't be sure.

After all, Marisa couldn't live like this forever, with a next-door neighbor with a bottomless drinks cabinet and a computer grandmother, Anita said, rather sternly.

Then she had paused and said, as World War Three appeared to be breaking out above her head, briefly, that it did in fact actually sound rather nice and then she remembered herself and ordered Marisa to go for a walk up and down the street.

And Marisa was going to—when she could hear Alexei was safely ensconced with a student; when it was a lovely day, which it was, and she could go out and turn right, up toward the cliff edge, not back down toward the village, on the unmade road, so she wasn't going to run into anyone and she could stay close to the center of the road so it would be perfectly safe and she was not going to panic and if she did, she would only be two steps away from the house. So. She was not going to panic. If she thought she was going to have a panic attack she could head back to the house. She was going to do it. She was.

And then the phone rang.

It was just the office but somehow—the way you just know sometimes—she just knew. As if the timbre of the ring was somehow different; ominous, like a tolling bell. She didn't believe people could be psychic but there was something about that ring, like the ring she'd got when her grandfather had died, when things were about to go badly wrong.

Nazreen's voice was so kind.

"Marisa, I have to give you the heads-up."

Marisa didn't say anything. Her insides froze.

"I'm having to make changes to the office—savings. And, we love you, you know that. But for an administrator, you're really expensive."

Marisa nodded, unable to speak.

Of course she knew it was true. A registrar who couldn't go out and perform weddings and deal face-to-face with the public was absolutely no use at all to anyone. She had always known this. It was just now it was coming home to roost.

Marisa had a huge lump in her throat suddenly and couldn't swallow or speak.

As if hearing what she was thinking, Nazreen continued, "Obviously we can speak to HR if you feel you want to make it official?"

"No," Marisa managed to choke out finally. "No, it's fine . . ."

"I have to drop you down two grades and put you part time," said Nazreen. "Unless . . ."

"I know."

For a second, Nazreen couldn't hold the professional façade together.

"Oh, Reesie. You used to *love* this job."

Marisa couldn't speak again.

"Remember the babies? How good you were with all those old ladies?"

Marisa nodded.

"Remember we had *two Pocahontases* on the *same day*?"

Marisa smiled. "Oh that was a great day."

"It was a great day. I still think you should have told the second one about the first one."

"Absolutely not," said Marisa, whose ability to sincerely intone, "Wow, that's a beautiful name" had become second nature over the years.

"Don't you miss it?"

Did she miss it? What was Nazreen thinking? Did she think she didn't miss the nervous young couples giggling and poking at each other and coming in to register their banns—or, sometimes, the stiff awkward pairs who were possibly just like that or possibly getting married for other reasons or both. Marisa could not bring herself to get dismayed at people getting married to stay in a country where they did well for themselves. Nazreen, who was older, told her about the old days when gay people would marry someone of the opposite sex just to get their parents off their backs, or for their visa or for a baby or for their cultures or a multitude of different reasons, and how the weddings could be hysterical—if their friends showed up—but so sad at the same time. Marisa had been an assistant on Equal Marriage Day, and for three weeks she had witnessed the opening of the floodgates—never been so busy; never known such an overspilling of joy and happiness from couples, some of decades standing, finally legally married in front of their families and friends. It remained an absolute high point of all their professional lives.

And the joy of being the registrar of the baby for

people you'd married, a year or two years—or, in one heartbreaking and joyous day, ten years—later, or of every nervous father, stumbling over middle names, awkwardly spelling things out, occasionally followed two days later by a leaking furious mother demanding that that was not in fact what the baby was to be called *at all* and having it gently explained to them that it was a historical record and they would need to go and speak to a priest about getting the baby baptized something else and then they could fix it, which often saw the luckless chap end up in a very bad way.

She missed it all. She missed the momentary relief she could give to the solitary widows, whose harassed-looking children would bring them in, with all the dull miserable work of bureaucratic paperwork on their hands, each member of the family shipwrecked on their own island of solitary grief—or, often, something more complicated than that—trying to help each other, and how grateful they were when she took them into the comfortably furnished room, made tea, listened sympathetically to the story of Frank's or Albert's last days, let them take their time; filled in the big book with her careful calligraphy, honed in additional classes she'd taken. There was something reassuring about the scratch of the pen, she'd found. She didn't know what it was. As if by writing something beautifully it gave it more heft, gave it more reality, these huge milestones in people's lives: birth, marriage, death. Recorded and made real. Whenever she handed over the completed and printed certificates, with the red seal, people would stroke them, stare at them, as if they hadn't believed what had just happened to their lives until she had written it in the book, like some recording angel.

That had been the person she was. And look at her now.

"I miss it so much," she whispered, her voice cracking.

"You have to find a way back to us," said Nazreen. "You have to."

And her voice rang out, clear and loud; almost as loud as the little gremlin in her brain who kept telling her she had failed, her job was gone; she was a failure, she was wasting her life, she was ruining everything; she was a disaster and everything was terrible and nothing would ever come good again, and the world around went black and closed in on her, even as she put down the phone and all thoughts of a walk were completely forgotten.

Chapter Twenty-eight

Being right, reflected Anita, was in no way satisfactory.
She had so hoped Marisa might prove the exception. The
forty-five minutes of sobbing that was currently taking
place indicated that this was not the case.

She didn't want to be directive, but maybe—just
maybe—this setback could be a breakthrough. Remind
her of what she wanted back in her life; what she truly
loved: being with people, out, and part of the world.

"This is making you so sad," she pointed out, unnec-
essarily, as Marisa wrung out yet another lemon-yellow
cloth napkin.

"Yes."

"But it's not about your grandfather, is it?"

Anita's tone was gentle, but deadly serious.

"But I miss him."

"Yes, but he didn't raise you . . . he lived far away. He
loved you and you loved him. I realize you miss him.
But I don't think he's the reason you've found things so
difficult, do you?"

Soberly, Marisa shook her head.

"This is you, Marisa. It's you who has made yourself
so scared, who has tied yourself in knots. It's been—and
I don't mean you didn't love your grandfather; of course
you did—but I think your grief has become more than

this, don't you? You've let it engulf you. It's nothing to be ashamed of, lots of people find life gets on top of them at points."

"But everyone else seems fine."

"Pff," said Anita. "Yeah, whatevs. You would think you were totally fine, if you could see yourself in your beautiful house, cooking away."

Marisa shook her head. "I feel sometimes like I'm the only one left grieving."

"And I have to show you that that is not true and that there are ways to live and grieve at the same time."

"What do I do?"

"Well," said Anita slowly, "you carry on. You stay the course. You walk farther away from home. You don't think about your job or your granddad or your future or anything else. You put one foot in front of the other."

Chapter Twenty-nine

It's hard to say, really, when happenstance comes along.

Marisa, if asked to be brutally honest, would say that it was flotsam, something floating past when she felt she was in a shipwreck and she had grabbed at it, desperately trying to keep her head above the waves.

Polly, being of a more optimistic disposition, would put it down to serendipity. Regardless, when she lightly knocked on the door of the little yellow house when the twins were at their lessons, she wasn't at all prepared for Marisa in the kitchen.

"Oh," she said. "What are you making?"

Marisa had just added a thin stream of milk to the bowl.

"Just *crespelle*," she said. She had laid out nutmeg for the bechamel and was trying to dry the spinach, not entirely successfully.

"Spinach is the wettest thing in the world," she complained.

"I know," said Polly. "They should feed it to camels. Did Reuben not leave you a salad spinner?"

"I think I'm pretty committed to paper towels."

Polly smiled. "So, what even is it?"

"Well, I make . . . they're like little pancakes really. Then you stir the spinach into the sauce . . . my grandfather used to let me do it. The colors blend just so beautifully, it's like magic. Then you add lots and lots and lots of pecorino. And then some more. And too much pepper also. And probably some prosciutto if you've got some kicking about. And you fold it over and pour more sauce on top and stick it in the oven until it's all bubbling and delicious.

"Oh my God," said Polly. "That sounds amazing. You're making me hungry."

She thought for a moment.

"Does it make children eat spinach?"

Marisa shrugged. "Italian children already eat spinach."

"Yeah yeah yeah," said Polly, watching her, a thought growing in her head.

"I don't suppose they'd scale up?" she said, watching Marisa whisk her bechamel neatly.

"What do you mean?"

Polly frowned. "Just a thought I had. Can you show me?"

Marisa shrugged again—she still wasn't very used to having people around—and heated up the pan to cook the first one.

The spinach swirled into the bechamel sauce was like marbling, the bright green against the creaminess, and hypnotic to watch.

"Wow," said Polly, then she smiled apologetically. "I don't get out much."

"Neither do I," said Marisa and Polly jumped back in horror. "Oh God, sorry, I didn't mean . . ."

"It's all right," said Marisa, smiling to show she wasn't really hurt, although it stung a little bit. But that was hardly Polly's fault.

The butter sizzled in the pan as she started to turn the *crespelle*.

"You seem to be making a lot," observed Polly. "Are they all for you?"

Marisa flushed bright red. "Um, sometimes I feed my neighbor," she said.

"No wonder takings are down," grumbled Polly. "You get all your provisions sent in from Italy and now you're taking my clients."

Deftly Marisa lined up the *crespelle*, lined them with a thin layer of the lightest most beautiful Emilia-Romagna prosciutto that made Polly's mouth water just to smell it, filled them with a layer of the bechamel, then flipped them and poured more in the top, popping them into the oven to bake. Next door there was some dramatic banging of something which may or may not have been related to *William Tell*. Polly glanced at her watch.

"Um . . ."

"About fifteen minutes?" said Marisa. "Tea?"

Polly smiled gratefully.

I wonder, she thought, as she left finally, collecting the cheerful children. I wonder if I could get that girl to help me cook for the poshos? She wasn't usually quite so mercenary, but this was something else. She told the children about it. They looked immediately dubious.

"So it is green," said Avery.

"So it's not pizza," said Daisy.

"Well, thanks, my market research council," said Polly, taking a hand each and letting them swing and bounce off her all the way down the road, blown by the wind behind them and their loud singing, all the way back to the lighthouse.

Chapter Thirty

Marisa had felt so happy to feed Polly: she had forgotten the satisfaction of it. With Alexei she occasionally felt you could boil a shoe for him and he'd wolf it down at speed, but Polly was a baker, a professional, and she'd really, really liked her food. She couldn't help but feel proud, even when Polly said she could come work for her anytime and Marisa had laughed at the impossibility of it.

But she had meant to move forward in her book; she really did.

The next day, however, the weather was utterly filthy. A great wet rain cloud had moved in fast over the Atlantic, and doors were banging and the fishermen's masts were rattling and everything was blustery and wet.

Marisa could tell the lesson next door was coming to an end; there was a pattern to it, as he induced the pupil to round up, just one last time, make the final cadence, play the final notes with a flourish, play loudly, or fast, or however they wanted, so he could send them off with a "well done!" or a "YOU ARE BRILLIANT!" which is what everyone got when they managed to make it to the end of a piece.

Well. No time like the present then. She stood out on her balcony again, breathed deeply the way the book said. In through the nose, hold, out through the mouth. In through the nose, hold, out through the mouth.

It had rained solidly all night, leaving puddles up and down the muddy unpaved road.

Now it came down in a steady stream, choppy on the sea, even as a slightly milder breeze came as a reminder that although it was late spring and flowers and gangling unfurling leaves that opened everywhere insisted that the whole joy of summer was coming—to her, to everyone—the British weather was not always done with you. Birds sheared across the tides, impossibly beautiful, even the hated gulls.

Okay. She was going to do it. She was going to dive in. Run through the raindrops, just for a second. She could do it. She *could*. She ran—literally, ran—across the floor toward the front door. She was going to pull it open and then run down the steps and she was going to be free, to run just like she used to, like there was nothing in her way, like she was free, and happy and everything in her life was as simple as it was when her grandfather would take her down to the beach and she could run for miles along the sand, splashing in and out of the watery puddles there, knowing the only thing waiting for her out in the whole wide world was a cuddle and a gelato . . .

The door opened with a bang. She had, it quickly dawned on her, massively underestimated a wet Cornish day on an island.

Alexei was waving farewell to his young pupil who was disappearing around the bend in the unpaved road, standing on the steps busying himself with a pile of sheet music. This, however, she only noticed after the shock she got when opening her front door with the balcony door also open. A massive gust blew through the wind tunnel they created, something she had never done before. As Alexei turned to politely say hello and, less politely, wonder what they were having for dinner, seeing as there had been nothing the previous evening, the gust took the pile of papers from out of his hand and sent them dancing all the way up and down the wet street: as high as the roofs above them and straight into puddles; some out to sea.

"*Chy'ort vozmi!*" shouted Alexei suddenly, dashing after them. "Get them!! GET THEM!"

But the shock had taken the wind out of Marisa's sails; she stared, open-mouthed, at the scene of dancing manuscript paper and found herself frozen at the top of the steps, just as she had always been. The sandworms had returned. The world was cold, noisy, hostile. Her feet were retreating of their own accord.

Alexei moved nimbly for a big man, and was snatching papers out of the sky, but Marisa could do nothing at all; she was completely paralyzed by fear, even as one soared straight through between roofs where their houses met and carried on to sea. Several came to rest in the deep puddle next to where the drain ran down the hill, caught up in the filthy brown water. The ink on the pages—she could see even from where she stood that it was not printed, but instead was just handwriting ink— was running off the page even as she looked, and she saw dissolving black blobs that were musical notes, and she saw writing on it, half-dissolved; but it was Cyrillic and she couldn't read it.

"HELP ME!"

She wanted to. With all her might. But she couldn't.

When he finally picked up all he could of the ruined manuscript he turned back to her, his expressive face like thunder.

"Why you not helpink me?"

His face was completely uncomprehending.

"Look," he said, holding up a sheet, the ink running and completely illegible. The water dripped off his nose and down his hair, making him look crosser and sadder than ever.

"But! Your hair is important? You not get wet?"

"No . . . I . . . I didn't . . . can I buy you another music book?"

He snorted, too distraught to speak. The piece beside Marisa, the messy ink blots running, was completely washed away now, ground into the mud.

He stormed up the steps.

"I'm sorry . . . I'm sorry. I thought I explained—"

"How can you not go outside? Is not real! YOUR HEAD IS LYING TO YOU! IT IS TELLING YOU LIES! DO NOT BE LISTENINK TO IT!"

He was properly yelling now, shaking the sodden ruined paper.

"DO NOT BE LISTENINK TO WHAT IT IS TELL-INK YOU!"

Abruptly he turned and stormed inside, banging the door hard. The motion made the little peaked room above her front door judder slightly, sending water straight down the back of her neck.

That night the discordant music started again; loud, furious, over and over again, never the same, never right, as he tried to retrieve what had gone forever.

Marisa sat in the bath, feeling back where she started. He had *known* she wasn't well. He was completely unsympathetic and horrible about it. Didn't give two shits as long as he was shoveling her food down his gob every bloody night. And now he was punishing her for messing with a few stupid pieces of stupid paper. When obviously he was the one with anger management issues. Well, sod him. Sod him.

What happened next was almost certainly caused by a combination of things: the kind words of friends like Polly and bosses like Nazreen, and Anita's hard work, and her nonna bringing fresh ingredients and good food and family back into her life just exactly at the point where she truly needed it.

But Marisa didn't see all that. She just heard, sitting in the bath, the heavy loud angry music and it stirred something in her. She wouldn't say it was a good thing it stirred in her, it made her feel angry, because the music itself was so angry. But somehow it fitted; she found it fitted with the storm outside which, even as it had grown darker, had intensified; was now howling through the house, making the lights flicker, pounding rain against the windows and the roof, making the wooden chalet that she loved so much, that felt so sweet and secure, suddenly feel flimsy and lightweight.

The music rose to a great discordant crescendo, just as the wind howled outside and suddenly Marisa stood up. She felt wild, and furious, and pent up, and full at the same time and as if she didn't quite know what to do with herself, even through the fury, and she realized that, of all the odd things to feel, this was important; because it was life she was feeling. Not being removed from life, or dull to it, or simply removed. She felt real, passionate, irritating, infuriating life, pulsing through her veins, her blood rushing to every part of her, and almost without warning, because her stupid brain could take over and second-guess or talk her out of it or panic, she moved toward the door. She remembered the furious man in the rain, screaming "YOUR HEAD IS LYING TO YOU!"

Your head is lying to you. Everything, she felt. Everything in the world was lying to her. That things would be all right. That adulthood would come naturally; that she would grow up, and own her own home and be great at her job and have loads of friends and a buzzing social life and know where she was going in life. And instead she was trapped indoors by her own mind, terrified of her own shadow and desperately, horribly sad.

The music grew even louder, it seemed, following or focusing on the movements of the storm.

And suddenly, she was there. She flung the door open, hard, let it bang against the side, and, before she could think about it, dived into the rain.

She charged up to the end of the street—she'd never even been there before—in her light striped pajamas, nothing on her feet. She didn't notice anything; not the water beneath her feet or the mud squelching. Her brain was bursting, her blood pumping and these things overcame her mind, overcame her worried side, her anxiety, and once she felt fully out of range, she came to the top of the road, overlooking the wild sea, the sweeping clouds, the distant lightning, and she found herself screaming at the top of her voice.

Alexei thought he heard something outside in the storm, and stopped playing abruptly. He had been trying to reconstitute the music he had lost in the rain. Of course he knew he should have made copies, he was always being told to take copies and how important it was, but he had got caught up in the moment, been too impetuous. It wasn't fair, he knew, to blame the poor girl next door. It wasn't her fault. He realized that. He had been cruel and angry about something else, and taken it out on her, and he absolutely hated himself for it.

He remembered that he had shouted at her and felt worse than ever. Shouting at women wasn't something he would ever have thought of as part of his makeup and he was heartily ashamed of it now, especially as he knew she was unwell.

He put down the lid of the piano, feeling guilty, and got up and went out, into the filthy night.

It was still wild outside and he knocked sharply on the door.

"Marisa? Marisa? Is me. I am sorry."

There was no answer from the little lemon house, and he left it a moment or so and tried again. Still nothing. He tried harder, but then realized he had to give up.

He'd absolutely messed it up and she wouldn't forgive him and frankly he didn't blame her for not opening the door in the dark to a strange and possibly deranged man. It wasn't news to Alexei how physically imposing he was; people had been remarking on it since he grew six inches in a year when he was fourteen years old. Normally he tried to preempt the situation by being gentle. Because he knew, when he wasn't, he was a more frightening proposition than most pissed-off people would be.

Deeply disappointed in himself, and vowing never to bother her again—and regretful too, both about his missing music, which she hated so very much, but also that he would now lose access to her frankly astonishing cooking—he trudged through the rain back into the little blue house, just in time to miss Marisa, drenched to the bone, black hair plastered down her back, taking big gulps of the electric air, slowly walking down the middle of the road, that was now more like a stream, soaking, freezing, but somehow feeling better than she had in months and months.

Marisa's bath was still warm as she got back in it, finding herself shaking. But she wasn't shaking from panic or fear: she was just cold. That was all. A normal physiological reaction to the weather outside. Somehow, screaming into the air had tired her out—but a good tired, a proper full-blown tiredness, rather than the aimless, scrolling confusion of other times, when she was enervated but not exhausted.

The water had felt so good on her face; the wind far sharper and brisker than she remembered; the air bristling but sweet, the vistas so far and so dramatic; nothing to be seen ahead except the occasional brisk sweep of the lighthouse, warning sailors on a night like this to stay well away.

And inside herself, deep down, was a tiny fist of triumph. She had done it! She had gone out! She had broken the seal of the doorway; she had made her way through the desert of sandworms, through the abyss that lay beyond the lemon-painted steps, and she had survived. She had triumphed.

She hugged her knees close to herself in the cooling bath, marveling that she had managed it, listening, but hearing no more music from next door. However, it had helped.

And then she got herself to bed, and she slept better than she had in months.

Part Two

Chapter Thirty-one

It wasn't like the dam inside Marisa had broken. It didn't change immediately. It didn't even change noticeably, but it was as if the storm had weakened the structures; had washed away some of the roots of the anxiety and fear that had got inside her so deeply—just as, even though she didn't know it then, a lot of water had buried itself deep inside the structures of the island, with results that would be worse than she could possibly have imagined.

But she managed. To walk a little every day.

Alexei had stopped talking to her completely. The night music stopped too. But she still heard that big bear growl as he cajoled his students and played along with them and then at night she would have to cope with her nonna saying what had happened to the boy who lived next door who she used to feed, what was his family like, why couldn't he play them music anymore, she loved music, and Marisa would hush her and turn on the television.

But she was happy to be able to tell Anita she was moving forward. She hadn't left her own road, to be sure, and she only went when she knew nobody would see her, i.e. when Alexei had a lesson. But it was definitely something. And she even got to enjoy the seasons changing; spring roaring in with extraordinary speed, flowers appearing between cracks in the rocks, and an eruption of green which raised the heart beyond all sense. She would see a solitary dog walker from time to time, and she never ranged farther than within sight of her front door—but it was something. It was out, as long as there were no people and no situations she might get herself into that would bring in that dreaded panic response.

The open air didn't make her panic.

"Slowly, slowly," said Anita, delighted. "Just keep breathing. Just keep moving on."

"But what about my job and my life and my friends and the world and—"

"You can't do anything about that until you get well," said Anita. "Listen to me. And your grandmother."

"All she does is shout at me for not slicing zucchini thinly enough," grumbled Marisa, who had indeed been on the end of a rather cranky Skype call the evening before as they had both tried to grill lemon zucchini with blackened garlic in olive oil and Nonna's had been light and crisp and delicious-looking and Marisa's had been soggy and fibrous.

"Good," said Anita. "Do you know what you're not thinking about when you're slicing zucchini?"

"Everything else?"

"Correct. You're not overthinking everything else."

Chapter Thirty-two

One of Anita's children had upended a chocolate milk-shake on her computer screen, she was informed by text one May morning, and therefore there was no therapy that day. Marisa decided to take a book out onto the balcony instead, which probably was therapy even if it wasn't the type she'd been deliberately encouraged to take that week, which was leaving the house, going to a shop and buying something.

But she'd received another wonderful care package from her nonna—she decided to send back, by return, the best she could do, which was to copy out, painstakingly, her grandmother's favorite Bible verses in her most beautiful writing. Her nonna had always loved her penmanship, and it was no hardship on a sunny afternoon to inscribe the words, even more beautiful in Italian than they were in English.

> *Perciocchè io son persuaso, che nè morte, nè vita, nè angeli, nè principati, nè podestà, nè cose presenti, nè cose future; nè altezza, nè profondità, nè alcuna altra creatura, non potrà separarci dall'amor di Dio, ch'è in Cristo Gesù, nostro Signore.*

I am persuaded that neither death, nor life, nor
angels, nor lords, nor leaders, nor the present, nor
the future, nor the heights, the depths and no other
creature can separate you from the love of God,
from Jesus Christ our Lord.

They were pretty verses, whatever you believed; and comforting too, the concept of a huge blanket of love that could never let you down.

She sat in the May sunshine, copying the lettering upside down—her work was always tidier and straighter when she thought in lines rather than the actual meaning of the words, and as the warmth shone on her shoulders, felt oddly content.

Alexei's four o'clock came in: she was as used now to the timings as she was to the ticking of a clock. It was a young skinny nervous lad—she'd glimpsed him—with acne and a constant look of worry on his face which belied what a terrific player he was. You couldn't tell by looking at people, was the one thing Marisa had learned. Very confident people would stride up with expensive-looking "special" sheet-music bags, but then stumble and falter their way through everything. This young lad had . . . well. She didn't know enough about music to know what it was. But when he played, she liked to listen.

He was working on something she wouldn't have known, but it was a tuneful piece of music that seemed to work like a clock; one bit would start in one hand, then the next would click in somewhere else on the piano, then it would go back to the other side, but slightly changed, like the time had ticked over into somewhere else. She didn't know the first thing about classical music but . . . she liked it. It was energizing and fun.

Alexei, however, was much sterner with him than she

heard him with other pupils, and he was certainly never remotely impatient with the children.

Here, though, even though it sounded fine to her—lovely, in fact, a pleasant accompaniment as she carefully scrolled, *"nè cose presenti, nè cose future"*—nor the present, nor the future—in her black ink pen onto a piece of good paper she'd ordered. Her nonna framed them and put them up around her house, interspersed with the many, many photographs going back to the mists of time. Alexei stopped the music every few seconds, it seemed, to rap out a short command or a correction.

She supposed (correctly) that it was because the young lad was good, seriously good, and this was how he had to improve, but she wished he'd just let him play. She heard the bear growl insist "faster," and the piece sped up, but badly, something went terribly wrong somewhere, the fingers fumbled and the whole thing came to a crashing halt.

There was a silence from next door. Marisa found herself tilting her head to hear what was going to happen now.

"Now, what was that?" said Alexei finally. "We are in a competition here?"

"No," came a humbled voice.

"No. Am I scary person?"

There was a slight pause at this as if it were possible the answer might be yes.

"I am big person. But am I scary person?"

Yes, thought Marisa.

"Uh, no?"

"NO!" roared Alexei cheerfully. "SO! You are not scary! And I am not scary! And there is nobody else here! So! Why are you scared?"

There was silence. Marisa felt slightly guilty but

didn't lean back or dare even start lettering again, in case she alerted them to her presence.

"You must play like no one listens, like no one cares! If you play fast it must sound like you play slow, that you do not care."

"But I do care."

"Aha! And that is why my only job as teacher is for gettink you out of your own way!"

It was such a complicated syntax from the Russian it took Marisa—and, clearly, the boy next door—a moment or so to work out what he meant.

Getting you out of your own way. It struck Marisa forcibly. What would that be like? If she could get out of her own way?

"Now," went on Alexei, "I want you to play. But this time you do not think nor of the notes nor of the music nor of me . . ."

Marisa half-smiled, looking at her work. Nor of the heights, nor of the depths, nor of the present, nor of the future . . .

"Think of . . . what you had for lunch three days ago!"

"What?"

"Play and at the end I want to know. What you haff for lunch three days ago."

"But . . ."

"Do it!"

Tentatively, the boy started to play.

And, almost delighting in her own ability to tell the difference, Marisa nearly clapped her hands. Stripped of thinking about what he was playing, the boy's fingers obeyed the part of his brain automatically while, presumably, the front bit responsible for harboring nerves and anxiety and the world around vanished; kept busy wondering whether it had eaten a ham and cheese toasted sandwich or a pasta salad on Tuesday and whether Tuesday had been wet so it would have been a hot sandwich, or sunny in which case if would have been something lighter . . .

The difference was astonishing: the halting sense was gone and instead of it being one hand of the clock and now another, the entire piece danced together as if there was no gap between the low notes and the high notes, that they were all part of the same shimmering continuum, imbued, now, with joy and optimism.

She very nearly clapped again at the end, transfixed by the final rippling sound of the closing notes, but next door there was only silence.

"You see," growled Alexei finally.

"That's . . ." The young man sounded quite jolted. "Hang on, does this mean I have to think about lunch whenever I play?"

"It means," said Mr. Alexei, "you have to be gettink out of your own way."

"Thank you," said the boy.

There was another pause.

"Uh. It was tomato soup."

"I don't care."

"Okay, thank you."

Chapter Thirty-three

About two weeks after the first storm, came the second. It even had a name this one, Storm Brian, scheduled to cross the Atlantic at terrifying speed, hit the north coast first, then come straight across to Mount Polbearne before travelling on to the coast of Northern France.

Spring storms were common, but seemed to be more severe this year. Polly was worried; the lighthouse could take anything the weather could throw at it, and had indeed been built for that very purpose, but the bakery was on very low ground right along the harbor, with only the old crumbling walls protecting it from the wrath of the seas. The beautiful gray paint job done by her ex, Chris, seven years before, was very faded now and desperately needed redoing but they just didn't have the cash. Huckle kept offering to take the black and white lighthouse paint and just stripe the bakery too but Polly kept refusing for the plain and simple reason that it would look absolutely ridiculous and she couldn't bear having to explain it to everyone.

But the water had risen high with the last storm and she kept looking at the weather forecast satellite picture as the ominous circle of tight lines moved closer and closer.

"Stop looking at that thing," said Huckle. "You'll scare everyone."

"I *am* scared!" said Polly. "It's dangerous! For everyone along the seafront!"

"Well, everyone just needs to go visit people farther up the hill," said Huckle. "Come on. This is an island in Britain. How on earth could it not be very used to having storms?"

Being from humid Savannah, Georgia, which had vast electrical storms and excruciatingly damp heat in the summertime, Huckle had always found the British attitude to any kind of faintly extreme weather highly amusing (unless he was attempting to catch a train that had been cancelled because there were a few leaves on the line).

"ARE WE HAVING A STORM?" said Avery. He had been very, very impressed by the lightning they'd had the previous month. Daisy and Neil had been less impressed and had both been found in the cupboard under the winding staircase, trembling.

Huckle gave a "*see?*" look at Polly and went and picked up Daisy who was gazing up with huge eyes.

"Storms," he said, "are just the people upstairs moving their furniture."

"WHAT PEOPLE UPSTAIRS?" said Daisy, suddenly even more petrified.

"What on earth are you talking about?" hissed Polly. "Is that meant to make her feel better?"

"Oh," said Huckle. "My mom always told me it was just God moving furniture and I thought it might help. It helped me."

"OH, IT'S GOD," said Avery flippantly. "YOU KNOW? GOD? IN THE SKY?"

"Is he upstairs?" asked Daisy in terror.

"Yes," said Avery.

"No!" said Polly.

"He's everywhere," said Avery confidently.

Polly didn't want to get into this right now.

"Listen," she said, coming to sit on the old squashy sofa in front of the woodburner next to Daisy in her father's arms. She beckoned to Avery, who joined her, and Neil sat between them on Polly's shoulder.

"*We* are in the safest place we can be. They built the lighthouses so safe that we can make other people safe and look after sailors."

"In case they crash. BANG!" said Avery cheerfully. He slid off her lap and started acting out a dramatic shipwreck scene. "OH NO! BANG BANG! ARGH! I HAS FALLEN IN WATER ARGH I DIE!"

He performed a dramatic death scene then looked suspiciously at Daisy.

"Come on! You can be a dying sailor! Argh!"

Daisy shook her head mutinously and clung to her father.

"It's going to be okay," said Polly for what felt like the billionth time that year. "It's going to be fine."

"It might not even hit us," said Huckle. "It might go straight past."

Polly glanced at her weather app. That wasn't what the bright warning sign was saying. That wasn't what it was saying at all.

You could feel it; you could taste it on the tip of your tongue. A tingling, something crackling in the air. A smell of ozone—not the normal ozone smells of waves and droplets and the usual bright salty air, but something different, slightly electric.

Down in the village, Polly noticed the quick furtive

moves of the customers, who were buying extra bread, commenting on the sandbags that had been placed along the harbor front. Andy from the pub next door wandered in, conferring anxiously on the phone with someone. He confessed he was considering getting off the island tonight but realized he couldn't—but he'd moved all his valuables upstairs.

"Seriously?" said Polly, glancing around. The only truly valuable thing in the shop, apart from the cash register, were the very expensive ovens Reuben had bought her when she started the business, but they were bolted to the floor. Goodness knows what she could possibly do with those.

"Some of the old folk are going up to the school. They're setting up camp beds."

"You're kidding."

But as more and more people came into the shop it became clear the rumor was true: they had put up camp beds in the classroom—school had been canceled that day in case the boat couldn't get back, much to the delight of the children—and were inviting any of the older people in the lower reaches of the village to evacuate there just in case.

"Of course I shan't be," Mrs. Baines was loudly proclaiming to anyone who would listen. "This is just government interference as usual! They're going to put chips in us! Same as that mast! Ever since they put up that mast there's been nothing but trouble, haven't you noticed? Do they think we're stupid?"

Polly gave the traditional tight smile.

"My house has been standing for two hundred and fifty years," went on Mrs. Baines. "I'm not scared of one little storm."

But by two p.m. it was clear that this was not one little

storm. The sky darkened, little by little, and then faster and faster, as if more and more clouds were arriving and crushing down on top of the previous ones in an effort to find room to fit. They shaded dark gray to almost purple; the effect, along with a change in air pressure that made people's ears pop, was very unsettling.

"I'm closing up," said Polly on the phone.

"Good," said Huckle. "Come home."

"How is everyone?"

"It's a three *Moana* day," said Huckle. "Only for Daisy. Avery is cool with it."

"Okay," said Polly. She glanced around. "Well, we sold everything."

The harbor walkway, though, was completely deserted.

Just as she said that there was a sudden crack of thunder.

"Come home, please," said Huckle. "Oh hang on, do you need help moving the sandbags?"

The rain started to pitter-patter.

"This would have been a terrible time to mention it if I did," said Polly. "It's okay. Andy's doing them for me."

"Well, come then," said Huckle, as another flash of lightning zinged. This storm, Polly ascertained, was absolutely in no way messing about.

So she went to lock the door, and looked around her clean pretty little shop, with its shining glass and silver display cases; the shelves of loaves—empty now—above her head; the basket for the baguettes. Impulsively, given it weighed an absolute ton, she grabbed the huge expensive coffee machine they had bought years ago at that trade fair when they were—to be absolutely fair—completely hysterical and jittery from drinking too much coffee—and placed it upstairs outside the Pilates teacher's door—she'd gone back to the mainland, wisely, Polly felt.

Then she went back downstairs, and found herself patting the lintel of the Beach Street Bakery, leaving her hand for just a second, thinking of how much that little shop contained; as much as her heart.

Then she locked the door tight and ran like the wind in the direction of the strong, solid lighthouse and the little circle of people and animals that were everything she treasured and everything she called home.

Chapter Thirty-four

The first storm, the storm that had taken Alexei's music, had been sneaky. It had threaded its watery fingers beneath the roads, through the cracks in the rocks. It had weakened the roots that held the earth together; even as the rain had dried away and everything looked like it had gone back to normal and the sky had shown up blue, even as all those things had happened, beneath the earth water gathered and did what water always does, even slowly: destroyed everything that got in its way, invisible and unnoticed.

When the first storm had hit mostly dry land it had run off. When the second storm arrived, it had nowhere left to go.

The darkness was oppressive and heavy as the first heavy raindrops started to fall. Marisa sat out looking at the balcony to get a good view. She was aiming to feel as she had before; to be at one with the elements, to practice her breathing.

It took her about five minutes to start playing Candy Crush instead, and she told herself off and reminded herself what Anita kept saying to her: don't push your feelings away. Let them engulf you. Feel them and acknowledge them, know that they will pass, that they're just feelings and feelings aren't everything.

It was easier said than done when there was a good Facebook argument going on she wanted to look at, but she did her best.

And in fact, Storm Brian was starting to put on a pretty good show. The thunder was constant, and she could see lightning glance, as if someone was flicking a light on and off outside, even if she didn't always catch the forks. The rain crashed against her windows; so hard it sounded like hail. She went forward to watch it more closely. The sea was foaming hard, a maelstrom of white, foaming like a washing machine. She shivered, thinking of boats out there on the sea. But they wouldn't be out, would they? Everyone knew this storm was coming. They would have found safe harbor, wouldn't they?

Even as she thought this, she caught the very distant outline of a huge container ship on the horizon. Goodness, she thought, concerned. Those things never fell over, did they? But even so she thought how frightening it must be, facing the great walls of crashing waves. Or perhaps they were used to it.

The thunder grew louder, if anything. But having been through the last storm she found she didn't mind quite so much; was feeling rather cozy, if anything. She even started thinking about what she would make for supper—was considering a little eggplant parmigiana and had got those precise ingredients in, even if, sadly, just for one. She turned on the oven, then glanced out the back window. Already the little road was turning into a stream once more, with nowhere for the water to drain properly. Well. She could batten down the hatches and wait it out. And all the while knowing that if she had to get out, she could. She couldn't believe how much better she felt than the last time.

She noticed that the oven had turned on, but the extractor hadn't, just as she heard another, more distant, crack. She frowned, turned on the kitchen light. Nothing. Oh goodness. There was a power cut. She checked her phone, which was charged, because it was always charged. Even when she used to go out, Marisa was the kind of person who always kept her phone charged.

Okay, she thought. Okay. Don't panic. She had 4G on her phone. She had charge. She had . . . She frowned. Did she have candles? Of course she did! In her bathroom!

Lighting all her scented candles at once gave a very distinctive odor to the room but it gave the place a rosy glow. Marisa added an extra sweater, and set about eating what was in her freezer. Thank goodness the oven was gas.

She should probably go and see Alexei, she thought. He almost certainly didn't have a candle—what man had candles just lying around the place, unless they were trying to seduce someone, which as far as she could tell he absolutely never tried to do.

She wondered about his love life. Another musician maybe? A cellist, with hair to her knees. A great amazon of a person, who could look him in the eye. A girl or a boy? An amazon girl, she decided, with big long lily-white arms that were absolutely hypnotizing as they swayed to and fro: beautiful Valkyrie legs either side of the cello. He would have been completely hypnotized, playing along with the orchestra—did they have a piano in orchestras? Marisa wasn't a hundred percent sure— and then he'd had to come to Britain to get this job and he'd had to leave her behind and he was full of powerful jealousy and that's what made him so angry and making such crashing music all the time . . . Ooh, perhaps she was married to the chief of the orchestra, and he had a passionate Russian desire for her that could never be assuaged and therefore he'd had to flee his mother country to try and forget her, even though he never ever could. Marisa would have liked to have been the kind of terrifying girl no man could ever forget but she wasn't quite sure how that would work.

So he'd gone to the farthest spot in the world to get away from a doomed love affair and now he was being regularly propositioned by the women in the village but his heart was true only to the cellist and—

Her reverie was interrupted by a steady banging on the door.

"Marisa! Marisa!"

It was him.

Chapter Thirty-five

Startled, she jumped up, leaving the spoon in the ice cream, which wouldn't balance, so she just took it with her.

She opened the door, the rain pouring down the lintels, the wind blowing round her ankles.

"Um . . . ice cream?" she said as she saw his large startled face.

"This is not ice cream time," he said brusquely. Ah. Obviously their fight was not forgotten. No wonder the imaginary cellist had left him, she thought, crossly.

"This is obviously a time for ice cream," she said. "The power's off, didn't you know?"

"Of course I know," growled Alexei. "I know what power cut is. But—we must go!" he said. "Everyone must go. Is the . . ."

He waved his enormous hands crossly, searching for the word. Marisa looked at him.

"The thing! That is between us!"

"The door? The steps?"

"The big thing!"

"You?"

He flapped his hands, even more het up.

"Is not funny! Come! The road. The road on the sea. The road that is on the sea."

"The causeway?" gasped Marisa.

"Yes! That! It is washink away! We must go!"

Marisa peered out fearfully into the flashes of lightning, the sheeting rain.

"Yes!"

"I don't think—"

"Yes! Everyone is needed."

"But I don't know what I could do."

He regarded her with that long unblinking dark gaze.

"You have tools?" he growled, not willing to continue the conversation. He dropped eye contact entirely.

"What kind of tools?"

"Tell me you have tools, we discuss that later."

"Uh . . . no," she said.

"Lantern? Flashlight?"

She shook her head. "I have . . ."

She ran into the kitchen, panicking, and returned with a soup ladle.

He nodded.

"I have no time," he said.

And his vast, yellow-clad form—he had somehow acquired a fisherman's sou'wester, presumably from whoever had woken him up—disappeared into the crashing rain and the storm and as she watched him go, she saw, in the distance, other doors opening, and the shouts of men and women as the village joined together to try and save their own community, to try and save their world from the vagaries of the storm and the weather—and she was the only person sitting there and doing absolutely nothing, as worthless as she was.

Chapter Thirty-six

"Peow peow peow peow!"

"I am not sure," said Polly carefully, "that shooting at the storm will make it go away."

She had tried to make things cozy—they had lit the hurricane lanterns with which the lighthouse was always well supplied, and the fire was banked high, which just about made up for the fact that of course the television was off and the very loud streaming of *Ratatouille*, a film Polly loved as much as the children did, was no longer placating Daisy. The child was no longer small enough to be comfortably hoiked around in the crook of Polly's arm, but Polly was doing her best.

Huckle glanced at his phone.

"Holy crap," he whispered, as Daisy stiffened.

"Is Daddy *swearing*?"

"Nooo," said Polly and was almost relieved when Daisy slipped down and announced to Avery that apparently holy crap wasn't swearing and they could say it now whereupon they started galloping around the room chanting "ho-lee crap! ho-lee crap!" as Polly sidled up to look at what Huckle was showing her on the phone. She closed her eyes. It was a text from Andy. The harbor wall was crumbling and the causeway was losing its cobbles. Oh my God.

"Do you remember when they wanted to build a permanent bridge?" she asked Huckle wearily, who nodded. They had turned it down: happy to live half on an island, half-connected to the land, as the causeway rose and fell through the tides, giving them the best of both worlds, just as it had been for hundreds of years.

Polly frowned.

"Do you think it's possible we should have just let them?"

Huckle was already shrugging on a huge outdoor coat and checking his boots were dry.

"Right now I do."

"We can't lose the causeway! It's been there for eight hundred years."

"Well, that might be part of the problem. And the rest of the problem . . . probably human beings."

"HO-LEE CRAP! HO-LEE CRAP!"

Polly screwed up her face and ran to make him up a flask of coffee.

"Be careful out there."

"I don't even know if we can save it," said Huckle, grabbing a flashlight and one of the hurricane lamps. "If you see me back in five minutes . . . I'm not sure that's good news."

"Be careful," said Polly, going up toward him and nuzzling his neck briefly, breathing in his lovely warm scent. He held her closely.

"Of course," he said. "Although you know I have good life insurance. You could replace the windows."

"Do not even *joke* about things like that."

He kissed her on the forehead as she tipped the hot coffee into the flask and, instinctively, added a couple of spare buns to his pockets. She could tell he was doing his absolute best to be brave, and loved him to distraction.

"See you later, kiddoes."

And he walked out of the lighthouse and into the maelstrom. Neil eeped and vanished up Polly's sweater, as freaked out as she was. Polly watched Huckle go, then steeled herself, set her face, turned, with difficulty, back toward the room.

"Okay, kids!" said Polly. "Who wants a story in front of the fire and some hot chocolate?"

"Yay!" said Avery, and even Daisy brightened up at the thought of hot chocolate.

"Marshmallows?" she asked innocently.

"Maybe."

"YAY!"

"I love storms," said Avery happily.

Chapter Thirty-seven

Marisa stormed around the house, feeling alternately tearful and furious; cross with Alexei for asking something she could not give, and cross with herself.

She felt her breathing rise, then, as she stared out the balcony window, did her best to let it pass. The futility of her fury was no use to anyone right now. It felt like a self-indulgence for nobody but herself. And it was a waste of everyone's energy, right then.

It was not her. It was not all she was. It was her brain, lying to her once more. And she wasn't going to let it.

She looked around the room. And moved purposefully forward.

Down by the water's edge, it was becoming Sisyphean. It was meant to be low tide, meaning the causeway was uncovered, but the water was running high anyway, loosening the cobbles as it surged upward; great waves cracking against the sea wall.

The people of the village had formed a human chain, dumping sandbags and rocks to try and bulwark the wall against the incoming tide, to keep it standing and keep it safe.

But Beach Street already was a river, a morass of water, mud, hideous bits and pieces floating in it, the current growing stronger every moment, and Huckle reckoned they were fighting a losing battle; puny humans against the terrifying power of wind and water was no fight at all.

The water poured down the back of his neck and his waterproofs, freezing him through; even as he shouted and yelled at other men. Someone had found a supply of timber, and they were passing it hand over hand to try and brace the wall. That huge Russian piano teacher was tossing them along as if they were twigs. The boats were bouncing up and down and smashing off one another; anything not properly battened down, or anchored too close to another boat, was not going to survive the swell.

One or two people—second-homers, Huckle knew straight-away; their Land Rovers were too clean and shiny—had parked up close on the harbor wall and he told Archie, the fishing captain who was in de facto charge of the mission, to get the message out to move your damn car before you lost it—but everyone's internet was down; phones were draining of charge, there was no power anywhere.

The women not on the line of getting materials along to the sea defenses were rapping on doors and moving up the people who had felt they didn't have to move earlier on; helping to carry valuables to upstairs rooms; comforting distressed older folk.

Huckle took a quick glance at the Little Beach Street Bakery. Despite the sandbags, the water had already reached the level of the low letterbox. The old wooden doors, warped and ageing, could not possibly last for long. He couldn't believe it. All that work, all those

years of love and care, the life they were building together, brick by brick, day by day, the business for him
and the bakery for Polly, the lighthouse, the children.
Nothing else was remotely important to him, other than
their family and the life they had created against all the
odds; against most people's expectations, particularly
his family's.

Not an angry man by temperament, he simply carried
on trying to build the barricades higher and higher, bol-
ster everything they could. Old ladies were being ferried
back and forth up to higher ground with a collection
of what they obviously considered essential—Huckle
thought he saw a sewing machine, but it couldn't be,
could it? Plenty of small dogs, though, already unset-
tled by the storm, who thought their owners were being
kidnapped and decided to protect them by sharing out
the odd nip or two, which felt particularly unfair to the
brave and sodden volunteers.

Polly had a million things she wanted to do to help—she
should be making up flasks of hot coffee and brandy at
the very least—but, she realized, the world didn't care
and what was going on didn't really matter when you
were faced with the sadness of a very small five-year-old.
She felt the pull of the village, which needed all hands on
deck, even as the storm roared on outside, like a clutch
of furies, screaming their rage out across the sky; tearing
the world apart.

But instead she sat on Daisy's bed. There was space
for each of the children to have a room; they were little
round things, cut in to the second floor, but they had

never been parted since they were babies and still shared a room, with a baby monitor going up to Polly and Huckle's room on the third floor.

They didn't need it now, the twins were perfectly capable and galloped up and down the stairs like mountain goats—were surer in their footing than Polly and Huckle, having never known anything else, and also being rather less likely to split a bottle of wine on a Friday night—but Polly liked overhearing their little dreamy conversations, their arguments about whether it would be good to fly and how it was good to have Neil but also they really wanted a dog and would it be a big dog or a little dog and what would they call the dog, which usually ended in a fight of some kind as Avery wanted to call it Iron Man and Daisy wanted to call it Buttercup.

She marveled, as she always did, at their astonishing ability to be endlessly curious about the real world while also cheerfully inhabiting the childhood world of their own, where superheroes and names for dogs and marshmallows in your hot chocolate were every bit as important as the storm outside. Because they were lucky, she knew. They all were.

She was surprised it had been Avery at the window ardently pointing out bolts of lightning and shouting "peow peow." It was odd, since the normally redoubtable Daisy wasn't usually the timid one. Avery was generally far more sensitive. But tonight it was Daisy's turn, and she huddled in her Totoro duvet cover, with her Totoro toy under her arm. Normally the large fluffy thing was incredibly calming, but tonight he wasn't doing the trick at all.

She clung tightly to her mother, her head in Polly's chest, and Polly found herself wishing she could still nurse her, which used to remedy all ills.

"Sssh," she said. "You know it's going to be okay. And everything will be fine and we will go and see Lowin."

"Lowin is getting five hundred snakes for his birthday," came the muffled voice. "I don't think I want to go."

"No, he isn't," said Polly, hoping she was telling the truth. "And even if he is, they won't be real ones."

"He says they're going to be the biggest snakes in the world."

"Well. We'll go and play in the non-snake sections."

But Daisy was tearing up in a way that could only get worse and soon she was simply crying for her daddy.

"He's helping to fix things," said Polly, holding her tight.

"But Daddy's terrible at fixing things!"

Polly wished she hadn't made so many jokes about Huckle's DIY prowess.

"He's in the storm!"

"Yes. Because he is a very good and brave daddy."

"I. WANT. HIM. TO. COME. HOME."

"I will shoot the storm!" said Avery. "Peow! Peow! Peow!"

He took aim into the room with his Nerf gun. This was always a disaster; Neil loved the Nerf gun and would swoop acrobatically to try and catch the bullets and everything would end quite badly.

"Put that down," said Polly automatically even though Avery could see his advantage in that she couldn't get up and leave his sister.

"Shan't," he said craftily, and Polly shut her eyes as another burst of thunder cracked overhead and Daisy let out a tiny scream.

Chapter Thirty-eight

Just do something, Marisa told herself. Just get to it. You don't have to go anywhere, you don't have to do anything. Just do it.

And by the light of the candles—and the lightning strikes, which turned the sky into a fireworks display—she pulled and kneaded the dough, turned up the oven, used up the very good olive oil and the bright crystals of sea salt.

She baked cakes, little yoghurt cakes, and she made focaccia, as well as she could in the hottest part of the oven, sprinkled with rosemary and salt and smelling like heaven; and she wrapped everything up in tea towels and wished she had a flask, but took a full teapot and some cups anyway. Then she stood at the front door. And she knew she couldn't open it, and at the same time she knew that she could.

What did she have for lunch two days ago? she asked herself, desperately. Could she get herself out of her own way?

She held her basket closer and put on her raincoat, all the while saying to herself, "Lunch two days ago. Lunch two days ago."

It had been halloumi, she thought. Grilled with sun-dried tomatoes and rocket leaves. It had been delicious;

she had added a tiny amount of balsamic vinegar, not too much, because it had a tendency to drown everything out. Nonna had sniffed as she disapproved of "foreign" cheese no matter how much Marisa inveigled on her to try it. Halloumi. Yes. Get out of your own way.

She pulled open the door. There was a maelstrom beyond; a vision, in fact, as close to the idea of hell, of the sandworm vista that her brain could have conjured up for her.

And the day before that, what had she had? Leftovers, probably; she'd roasted a chicken and normally she would have saved it for Alexei. That was probably what she was planning when she had bought it but of course now he wasn't talking to her because of his stupid pages, so she had ended up . . .

She had one foot on the top step. This wasn't like charging out in a fit of fury, or going to the top of the road. She was going somewhere. She was going somewhere to talk to people.

Chicken. Roasted chicken, with the waxed lemons from her care box rubbed over the skin; with far more cloves of garlic roasting than she could possibly need, just for greediness and the fact that, for all its hardships, it wasn't a bad thing you weren't going to run into people at close quarters when you'd eaten half a bulb of garlic.

Two steps. She was shaking all over.

And the night before. What had she had with the chicken, on a Sunday night when Nonna wouldn't let her watch television because it was unholy on the Lord's day and they'd had to listen to hymns and chat instead but somehow it hadn't mattered so much because although in English she felt so awkward, such a failure, a mental health problem, someone off work, in Italian she felt simple and secure and basic. She could talk about food, and weather and listen to Nonna slag off the neighbors, which seemed a bit worse on a holy day but woe betide mentioning that.

And she was on step three.

Food. Food was helping. She thought hard. Back to a big plate—one of her earliest memories, truly a big plate of steaming seafood, in shells, that had seemed wondrous and a little frightening to her and Gino, and her grandfather had shown her how to scoop out the mussels with a little shell, hot and scented with garlic and lemon; and they had both discovered the delicious chewy strings of the deep-fried calamari, which they liked immediately, making squid faces at each other; too hot to eat, greasy, slippery and salty, but chewy too, exploding like sunshine in their mouths as their mother fussed around putting on sun cream and hats and forcing them under umbrellas and everyone went quiet and lay down for their *pisolini,* and a drowsy peace would descend over the beach and everyone there, and full of seafood and with the promise of an ice cream later if she lay quietly, curled up next to her beloved grandfather, Marisa would drift off . . .

She was in the road. The rain was pelting her, hard, the thunder still roaring overhead. She concentrated on the sound of the sea, the salt, even rough and ferocious as it was, provided her with the thinnest silvery line. Get out of your own way, she whispered to herself. Get out of your own way.

She kept that thinnest line between her memories, pulling her down the hill toward the water. Memories of happy meals with lots of people. Wonderful dinners when they'd all crammed around tiny student tables, everyone bringing a dish. Although as soon as they re-alized how much better Marisa was at cooking than the rest of them put together, they had eventually left her to it. A fragrant fish stew with the best part of a bottle of white wine in it. A perfect, plain cooked salt cod eaten in Ischia with her last boyfriend but one. The rest of the holiday had been a disaster and they'd broken up but it was almost worth it for that fish, in her opinion. In fact it absolutely was. Just remember the happy things. Just think back. Get out . . . get out of your own way.

Her foot plunged ankle-deep into the running stream of the road, but she didn't stop.

She clung tightly to the boxes she was carrying; inhaled their scent. Bread. Fresh bread on a camping trip with her family when they'd been washed out and had to spend the night in the car, turning up to the bakery as soon as it opened and the warm fragrance of the warm focaccia after a sleepless night. The slices of wedding cake that turned up weekly in the office, as grateful newlyweds remembered their ministrations—Nazreen hated fruitcake so the rest of the office normally got all of it, and Marisa loved marzipan, all year round.

The croissant *marmalata* that made them know that they were on holiday, the first things they always got, sometimes even at the airport as soon as they disembarked at Genoa, filled with sweet orange jam that you could never find at home; the announcement that you were here, where her mother would relax and feel at home, even though to her and Gino it was a foreign country.

Lucia had left Italy to make money and do well and raise her children and she had done all of those things.

But she had done them in the rain; in winters when the dark seemed to settle for months; where everyone worked all day and scurried home to lock themselves in sealed houses and watch television. When her mother first learned she got forty minutes at school for lunch, she thought it wouldn't be physically possible. When one of Marisa's friends came around for dinner and announced that she normally ate in front of the television, Lucia's eyes nearly bugged out of her head; Marisa had heard her telling Nonna that night on the phone, who was convinced that doing that kind of thing would lead you straight to hell. Her father had said, before he left, that the British knew how to make money, but they didn't know how to live.

But she, Marisa, loved her home country.

She loved Mars bars and *Dick and Dom* and going to Nando's and eating fish fingers at six p.m. at her friends' houses and talking about going to college and nobody remotely concerned about marrying a nice Catholic boy the family knew and settling down next door to everyone you'd ever known. She loved the amazing music and TV and the grand history and the jokes and all sorts of different people living hugger-mugger together; the beauty of the countryside, the down-to-earth people; her mother's amazement that the government bureaucracy actually worked.

She loved to visit Italy—but she was British. And while this saddened her mother, it delighted her grandfather, who was overjoyed at his proud independent grandchild, and would always squeeze her hand and tell her he was proud of her.

Marisa could see the villagers now down at the docks, hauling at rocks and sandbags, digging, and doing their best against the rising tide of water.

She had done it.

Chapter Thirty-nine

She moved on, desperately looking for Alexei's face; or at least a face she knew. She saw the blond man who was the father of Polly's twins. His face was drawn and exhausted-looking.

She waved tentatively and he didn't look pleased to see her.

"Everyone should be indoors," he said in his American accent. "You shouldn't be out unless you can help."

Too timid to talk, Marisa held up her boxes.

"Food."

She opened the boxes and took out the roll of paper towels and passed around the warm bread and as much tea as she could pour out.

The helpers fell on it with signs of enormous gratitude. Marisa found herself looking around for Alexei—he was normally easy to see—but he was over on the other side of the port trying to help move cars out of the way with several of the seamen, and didn't seem to spot her.

"This was brilliant," said Huckle, his mouth full. "Thank you. I'll keep some for the others. You should get out of the weather."

"Can I help?"

"You did."

He looked at her.

"Could you . . . could you possibly make some more? Maybe take it up for the old people? They'll need breakfast."

He looked at the bakery, sadly. The water was already all over the floor, the rain still showing no signs of shopping. He dreaded telling Polly.

"I don't think we're going to be open tomorrow."

"Um, I can try," said Marisa, "but I think that's everything I had in the house."

Huckle blinked, the water running down his nose.

"You could go to the lighthouse," he said. "We put everything there."

"It's two o'clock in the morning."

"Nobody's asleep," said Huckle grimly.

Marisa thought about having to go up to someone else's house. On the other hand, it was Polly.

"The old folk are really going to need something in the morning."

"You all are," said Marisa. That decided her. "Okay. I'll go. I'll do it."

Chapter Forty

Marisa had to knock on the back door several times to make herself heard over the wind and the rain. Would this storm ever blow itself out?

Finally, she heard a tired voice say, "I'm coming, I'm coming."

Polly opened the door to a drowned rat; she barely recognized her at first.

"Come in, come in," she said, as Marisa slightly pitched forward into the incredibly lovely warmth of the kitchen, where an Aga was radiating heat. The kitchen had always been the warmest room in the lighthouse, due almost entirely to it not being in the lighthouse; it was in an ugly late sixties flat-roofed pebble-dashed extension which, for all its failings, at least benefited from double glazing.

"Oh my God! Are you all right? It's wild out there. I've just got the children off to sleep."

"Aren't you going to sleep?"

Polly didn't want to say what she'd been doing in the ten minutes since Daisy finally gave up the unequal struggle against dozing off, Avery having exhausted himself shooting at the lightning.

Staring out of the window she could see the hurricane lamps of the people working down below, desperately trying to shore things up. But she could see in the dim light that the water was still running; that Beach Street did not look normal, with cobbles, but instead shining and reflective and liquid; that the bakery could not hold.

She had been crying.

It was gone and they were going to be ruined, even as she watched the men and women of Mount Polbearne work for all they were worth, with every last breath.

"Um," said Marisa. "I made them some food, but it's all gone and your husband thought maybe we should make something for the morning and maybe I could do it as it's not so far? And I don't have any flour left. Your husband suggested I come here . . ."

All of this came out in a rush as it was one thing having Polly in her house, where she was safe, but being in someone else's felt like a different kettle of fish altogether, but Polly knew what she meant and couldn't believe she hadn't thought of it. And thank God, Huckle was okay.

"Of course," she said. "We moved all the flour here as a precaution."

She turned to Marisa and pasted a smile on her face.

"First, let's get you out of those wet clothes," she said. "That was amazing of you to do to that."

"It was the least I could do," murmured Marisa. But she was still incredibly pleased to hear praise—genuine, well-meant praise. Nobody had found her much of anything but a weird disappointment for so long, no matter how patient with her they'd tried to be.

"It's going to be jogging bottoms and they're going to be too big for you," warned Polly, heading toward the door and returning with a big, old and worn but still cozy clean towel. "I'd like to tell you that I was an immaculate dresser before I had the children but I'm afraid I would be lying to you."

Marisa found herself smiling.

"Dry is absolutely a hundred percent of everything, thanks."

Polly came back—and oh, the bliss of changing out of wet clothes and into big fluffy dry socks, a clean T-shirt, a red hoody and, in fact, a pair of dungarees which were the first thing Polly could find to hand that was clean.

"Oh, you look rather cute, that's annoying," said Polly when Marisa had changed. "You should keep that red hoody, it suits black hair. It looks mad with red hair, I don't know why I bought it."

She also looked a bit mischievous.

"Okay," she said. "I dug this out as well. If we're going to be up all night baking . . ."

Marisa nodded.

"Well. I think we need some help."

And she pulled from behind her back a very old dusty bottle of Prosecco that had been brought for a party and forgotten all about.

The kitchen being so far from the children's bedrooms, they could happily whack on the radio, which they did, avoiding anything that gave frightening weather updates and sticking to a nineties station that offered up a comforting menu of Britney and the Backstreet Boys, much to their delight, even though Marisa was really too young for them, and Polly had to stop while the dough was proving and put the videos on so she could choose a favorite.

They danced as they molded pies and muffins, flour liberally sprinkled all over the kitchen, including on Polly's nose, and Polly started laughing at Marisa's horrified reaction to noticing bird prints in the flour.

"We're going to kill the entire village," Marisa had gasped.

"Well, bit too late now if that's what's going to happen."

Neil himself had vanished up onto the curtain pole, almost as if he was well aware that goodies took time to bake, and taking a small snooze accordingly. Marisa looked at him, looked at the prints, shook her head and burst out laughing again. Polly didn't think it was quite *that* funny.

That was because she had absolutely no idea how long it had been since Marisa had laughed aloud in somebody else's kitchen; had no idea how much Marisa had feared she would never do so again.

The Aga divided up neatly and they did pies, vegetable and cheese muffins, and kneaded up loaves for the day ahead.

"Do you think you'll be able to use the bakery?" said Marisa. Polly shook her head very quickly.

"I'll worry about that tomorrow." She frowned. "Let's just keep busy."

And they drank Prosecco and kneaded bread and made muffins and scones—which got a little wonkier as time went on—and Marisa stayed in the kitchen while Polly ran out with tea as often as she could, and at four a.m. the tide, having hit its heights and done its worst, finally turned and started back down again. And as the storm finally began to die away there was nothing to do after that but to wait for the sun to rise as it always did, and survey what they had left.

On Polly's instructions, all the helpers trooped back, utterly exhausted and muddy but delighted that their unstinting efforts had saved the causeway from being destroyed completely. She would need repairs—but she still stood.

They kicked off their boots—steam rose all around the kitchen till it looked like a laundry—and dried out in front of the fire, being stuffed full of coffee and fresh bread until they felt like bursting.

There was much jolly bravado—after all, nobody had been lost, although one Mini was currently floating off in the direction of France, and nobody had had to be rescued by a coast guard that already had enough on its hands last night to cope with a village that hadn't helped itself. As well as that, half the Royal National Lifeboat Institution volunteers were from the village anyway, and were already pretty busy, but they had managed to protect their population.

"Did you really save the causeway?" said Marisa, so amazed she found her voice to ask the friendly, tired-looking Archie.

"Well, most of it," he said, eating a scone so fast Marisa wasn't sure it had touched his throat. "We've got the stones. They'll need to be put back."

"Did you not want to wait for the fire brigade? To make it safe?"

"But this is us," said Archie, his lined face kind. "We are Mount Polbearne. We can't lose a single brick. If a brick in the causeway is lost, it's a piece of the chain.

Every brick matters. Every brick is connected to every other brick. It's a part of us. We all have to join up. That's what community means."

His voice was kind, but there was a reproof in it too, and Marisa realized that however much she felt she was hidden away, here in a tiny community like Polbearne, she had been noticed—as, presumably, had her bussed-in groceries and distant deliveries. She had not played her part, even though these men and women had risked everything to save the causeway: for her and for everyone else here.

She nodded, then proffered up the plate again.

"Thanks," he said. "Did Polly make these?"

"I did, actually."

His pale blue eyes met hers then for the first time.

"Well done," he said. "They're very good."

The furniture and floors of the population who lived nearest the water's edge . . . well, that was a different matter. Those going up the hill vowed to take the fresh baking up to the schoolhouse, where the evacuated residents were gathered, Mrs. Baillie telling once again the story about how she was a real-life evacuee (which indeed she was; she had been sent to Cornwall from London as a four-year-old. By the time the war had ended she was a strapping, dairy-fed nine-year-old with an accent thick as clotted cream who worked the fields with her kind adopted family—who still spoke a few Cornish words—and returned only rarely throughout her life to the East End slum, and the hardscrabble family of thirteen children she'd been born into).

Then those lucky enough to have been untouched

would grab as much sleep as they could before the great clean-up would start in the morning and a reckoning could be made. Huckle and Polly didn't mention the bakery, didn't even look at each other. Andy was looking somber, but his beer barrels were watertight so he'd probably be all right. Polly was hyped up on a combination of Prosecco and coffee and couldn't stop baking, which Huckle noticed; it's what she did when she was nervous.

Marisa had waved tentatively to Alexei as he came in, filling the door frame, but he hadn't seen her at first. Then he'd given her a quick glance as if to say, well, of course, here you are, in front of the fire surrounded by food, nice and cozy, I see you can get out when you want to go somewhere nice and, too tired and anxious to explain, she had simply offered him a plate of food, which he had not so much eaten as inhaled. He had sat on the window seat at the far side of the kitchen, while the chatter and gossip continued around them, and in the middle of the tumult had at some point fallen asleep. But it was not for long, because Daisy and Avery, up at dawn despite their disrupted night, had been only too delighted to wake up and find a party going on—with cakes too!—and, charging downstairs, had immediately clambered onto their favorite teacher and had awoken him by pulling hard on his beard.

"Ach," he had said, abruptly jerked out of his dreaming state, but, Marisa couldn't help noticing, his confusion turned instantaneously to sweetness.

"Get away, you *solnyshko*," he said. "What is rule?"

"No climbing on the piano teacher," said Daisy sensibly.

"No climbing on piano teachers, thank you very much." He stretched and yawned, covering his mouth with his sleeve.

"BUT!" said Avery. "We is brought HONEY!"

He presented the tub. "Oh, I love honey," said Alexei, reaching for it. Daisy and Avery swapped a look that said, there we are, proven right yet again.

He is so lovely, Marisa found herself thinking. To everyone who isn't me.

Chapter Forty-one

Polly left it as long as possible to go to the bakery. Huckle tried to get her to have a sleep but she wouldn't, instead moving around the kitchen cleaning up and putting away tins and ingredients. Everyone had stumbled home to snatch some rest, but she'd need to alert Jayden, her colleague, and, frankly, she had to have a look herself first.

"I'll go and get out the insurance papers," said Huckle, even as he was falling asleep himself, the twins safely in front of the TV now the power was back on. "But, you know . . ."

Polly did know. It was simply impossible to properly insure a tidal island that got cut off at every high tide, and they had all seen the problems people had had over in the West Country with the 2018 floods. Even if they were up for any money, it would be a long time coming.

Polly sighed and pulled on her wellies.

"I'll come," said Huckle, but his eyes were already closing and his voice was trailing off.

"I'll call you if I need you," said Polly. "Don't let the twins eat the leftovers."

"LEFTOVERS?" said Avery who appeared to have the ears of a bat.

"I'll be back at lunchtime," said Polly. "We'll have them then."

"Leftovers now!"

"Come on, Neil," said Polly, grabbing her raincoat and pulling on her wellies. "Let's go."

It was impossible to believe when you stepped outside that there had been a storm at all. The sky was a fresh-washed blue, a few innocent-looking clouds drifting by. The sun bounced off the wet cobbles like a billion glistening diamonds, rendering the whole of Mount Pol-bearne almost too bright to look at.

Polly hadn't brought her sunglasses, and wished she had, but was too bone weary to go back and get into a whole "leftovers" conversation again.

Instead she trudged onward. After a few moments she was joined by someone—Marisa—whom she thought had left ages ago.

In fact, Marisa had been standing near the lighthouse, trying to give herself the courage she'd found last night to get back up the hill again, past everyone. Willpower, she'd found, was something that came and went. Or perhaps, when she thought about it, it was something you had a finite supply of and once you'd used yours up for the day you had to plug yourself back in to whatever your battery was—in her case, a chat with her nonna, in her house, cooking and watching TV.

But seeing Polly made her feel safe, somehow. Even the little bird that seemed to follow her wherever she went cheered her up.

A thought leapt up in Marisa that she was being creepy and a bit of a stalker, but Polly's face brightened to see her, and she tried to tell her brain to quieten down.

"Hello," said Polly. "I thought you'd headed home."

"I'm . . . I'm going," said Marisa. "Do you mind if I walk with you for a bit?"

"Not at all," said Polly, remembering Marisa's condition. "I'll walk you all the way if you like. But I can't promise to be good company. I'm going to inspect the damage."

"Does this happen often?"

"It's getting worse and worse," said Polly glumly.

They crossed over onto Beach Street. There was still water running down into the drainways but most of it was gone.

What was left, however, was grisly. A thick black layer of silt and rubbish; mud and bits and pieces of flotsam; a foamy scum covering everything. It looked solid and unshiftable. Big wads of paper were bunging up the drains. Men from the council were already out cleaning up. There was a big truck along the road, sucking up as much of the rubbish as it could manage. Polly briefly thought how much the twins would adore watching a big muck-sucking truck, but continued on her way.

The front door of the Little Beach Street Bakery, all glass, the bottom pane repaired so many years ago when Puffling Neil had been thrown against it during another storm—was completely impassable, the door warped, and a thick sticky layer of mud gummed up the entrance completely.

Marisa followed Polly round to the back door to the kitchen, which thankfully was a little higher up off the main road, and was untouched by the water.

Going into the dark kitchen—Polly didn't dare turn a light on in case the water and the electrics had become horribly tangled up somewhere—was a dispiriting experience. The thick mud and water had got into everything and the smell was horrible; damp and rubbish and worse, infiltrating every corner of the once immaculate kitchen.

Tears pricked Polly's eyelids. Everything they had worked so very hard for. Everything lost. Everything ruined.

"Oh wow," said Marisa suddenly, out of the blue. "Oh my goodness! Look at these ovens!"

The ovens were state of the art; Reuben had bought them as a gift when Polly had considered opening the shop, he wanted a baker so much.

"Are they ruined?" said Polly, her lip wobbling. "God. They were expensive too."

"I know!" said Marisa. "That's what I mean! They're amazing! Polly, I don't think they're ruined at all. They'd withstand a nuclear attack, these things."

Polly was looking around, blinking and not really listening.

"I suppose I'd better start with the hose," she said. "Andy's got a power hose I can borrow once he's finished with it. If I hose it for . . . God knows. Two months?"

"I can help," said Marisa, but she was still distracted. "But you know, these are the ovens they have in the very best places."

"Well, nice of you to say . . . Let's hope the electrics aren't completely shonked."

"They make . . . I mean, they go up to about five hundred degrees!"

"Six fifty, actually."

"You know they make the best pizza in the world?" said Marisa.

Polly looked up at her suddenly, her senses pricking.

"I thought that was wood-fired ovens?"

"No, if you get it hot enough you'll still get a blister on

the bottom. Then the sides caramelize slightly if you're quick, then it'll come out dark and sticky and crunchy all at the same time."

"God, that sounds good," said Polly.

Marisa frowned. "Do you serve pizza?"

"We're a baker's. Most people would consider that fancy foreign muck. We do bread, cakes, pasties and biscuits . . . but I was looking to diversify . . ."

Both of them felt an odd excitement bubble up and Marisa tried to rein herself in, to stop herself sounding too excited.

"I mean . . . you could do it at night."

"Yes, that's what I need," said Polly, wryly, who was truly very tired. "A longer working day."

But she was interested, and Marisa was genuinely enthused.

"They are lovely," she said. "They remind me of Italy."

"Is that home?"

"Oh no," said Marisa. "Britain's home. But my family is Italian."

"You look Italian. Oh God, sorry, is that all right to say?"

"It's fine. Good, in fact," said Marisa. "I am. And I like looking like my family. I spent a lot of time there when I was little. Then last year . . . my grandfather died."

"I'm sorry," said Polly, and she sounded genuinely sad, which was more than a lot of people had managed to muster. She knew for most people the loss of a grandparent was a sadness, not a tragedy.

But Polly had lost her own father too recently to not feel profoundly affected by anyone losing a loved one, and was too soft-hearted not to mean it.

"It's been tough," said Marisa, and then had to catch herself. "Sorry."

They were, after all, standing ankle-deep in the ruins of all of Polly's hopes and dreams.

"It's been rough for everyone," said Polly. "It's been rough all over. We can't keep bursting into tears. Well. Maybe we can. But we'll be all right."

And that was when Marisa made up her mind.

"Let me help," she said. "Let me help get the bakery back on its feet."

Polly looked concerned and excited all at once.

"Do you mean it?"

"I've lost half my job," said Marisa.

"I mean, it would have to be a kind of . . . I mean, I could only pay you depending on how it went," said Polly.

Marisa smiled and, for the first time in a very long time, showed a flash of what looked suspiciously like confidence.

"With these ovens?" she said, dark eyes flashing. "I think we'll be all right."

And Polly found that, somehow, she wasn't crying anymore.

Chapter Forty-two

Andy's power hose was in massive demand, so they first went at it, exhausted as they were, with big wire brushes, starting with the most important job: wrenching the main door back open. Once Huckle woke up, he brought up the twins in their wellingtons, warning them to stay outside in the backyard and play in the puddles rather than, as they were perfectly capable of doing, somehow falling on a concealed rusty nail and ending up airlifted to hospital for tetanus.

The door was ruined, that much was true. Completely done for. Huckle patiently set to work unscrewing its hinges to lift it out altogether. The forecast for the next few days—stretching into the next week, in fact—was irritatingly fine, which meant that they should be able to carry on cleaning up, which was good, but also that they would miss all the tourists, who were being told to walk over at their own risk until the cobbles were properly reset in the causeway, a frustratingly slow and delicate task, and nothing could drive over either.

Archie's mob were making up for the damage done to their fishing fleet by running the boat taxi service twice as often as usual, and bringing in large boxes of supplies, thankfully.

The bakery door unhooked, the water started to rush

out, down back toward the sea, leaving behind a slow-moving pile of silt and dirt and crap.

"At least there's no carpet," said Huckle. "You should see Mrs. Baillie's place. All floral carpets, all done for, and it will stink for one hundred and forty-five years."

It was true, the heavy flagstones were practical—no peeling laminate or floating tiles. But it was still dispiriting to see her beautiful glass units all scratched and cracked by the thrown-about water; the chiller cabinet for cakes completely destroyed. The cash register was safe, thankfully; she had unplugged it and put it up above with the knives and many of the dishes, so that although the units were a mess, her expensive equipment was safe.

They opened every window that could open, checked the electrics were okay, and set the extractor going and Andy, bless him, once he'd finished in his chippy, kept the power-hose unit on his back and came straight over to theirs.

"Ghostbusters!" said Huckle drily as Andy lowered his visor and gave them a salute, but they were all incredibly pleased regardless.

They sluiced on and on until there was just a grim black patina on the floor, which would need hands and knees scrubbing. The girls looked at it in dismay. Huckle looked at the both of them and ordered them home for a nap. It would keep.

There was piano music coming from next door as Marisa finally let herself in, filthy and utterly exhausted. A melancholy, sad song. He must think she was still at Polly's. For some reason she didn't mind it so much.

She fell into the shower, and the water ran black

off her. She left the hot water on for a very, very long time, leaning her head against the shower wall feeling a mixture of emotions—pride, sadness, excitement—all coursing through her at the same time.

The music was still going as she came out, finally clean, put Polly's clothes into the washing machine, pulled out some fresh cotton pajamas and crawled between the fresh sheets on her bed even though the sun was high in the sky. The soft bed and stiff cotton felt like heaven to her bone-weary body; she remembered, smiling, the little bird marching through the flour; the children crawling up Mr. Batbayar and startling him awake; the excitement of the ovens. What could she do? she wondered. If she could get out of her own way, what might she do?

Next door, the little song tinkled on. But it did not keep her awake.

Chapter Forty-three

By the next day, the town was mobbed. Everyone was
wandering up and down Beach Street. Many were helping; cousins and friends had shown up, waded in over the
broken cobbles or commandeered rowing boats to sweep
out and try to dry out the old cottages and fix things up.
People had come from miles around, particularly after
a news helicopter had done a broadcast on television,
showing the devastation to the ancient causeway. It was
truly amazing, Polly had thought: people had come from
miles away, with blankets (not really necessary) and
mops (very, very necessary).

The weather stayed glorious so the streets were full
of people, whom Andy promptly managed to oblige with
beer and fish and chips, and the grocer's, set back from
the main drag, got rid of as much ice cream as they had
in stock and had to order more.

But Polly was still faced with the endless scraping
task of trying to clean up the ovens and was still without
a working door. She was baking at home but that had to
go to the workers, so selflessly giving up their time to
put the town back together, so she was missing all the
trade, even when all the fishermen trooped up the hills
and presented themselves as her personal cleaning army,
announcing as their slogan, "RECLAIM THE PASTY!"

In the early afternoon, an unexpected quiet fell on the harbor side, and Polly looked up. Everyone was staring at a ridiculous vehicle that had appeared on the causeway. It looked like a convertible on the top and—no, surely not—a boat underneath, and had a big sign on it saying AQUANDA.

A crowd gathered. As it neared the submerged end of the causeway, the car took a sharp right turn and, as the crowd literally gasped, launched itself, taking a cut through the waves and sending a jet of water behind it.

The audience gasped again and some of the children started clapping as the car/boat spun a wide circle in the sparking water and came to a halt in a skid on the beach.

"Stop smirking," said Polly to Huckle, as they both stood watching, the twins, who had been given little mops of their own, dashing out breathlessly.

"LOOOOK! AT! THE CAR!"

Avery was hopping up and down with excitement.

"IT'S A BOAT!"

"Do you need to pee, Avery?"

"NO! YES! BUT! AFTER THE BOAT CAR!"

Well, if the worst came to the worst, he was outside and already filthy, thought Polly to herself, failing to win Mother of the Year for the fifth year in a row.

"Oh, come on, it's cool," said Huckle, nudging her elbow.

"It's ridiculous!" said Polly. "I bet it cost more than the entire contents of this shop."

"It's his money," said Huckle.

"I know, I know," said Polly. "I'm being bitter. Ignore me."

"IT'S! A! CAR! BOAT!"

"It is," said Polly laughing. "A! CAR! BOAT!"

The doors of the water car came up sideways like a

DeLorean, and Reuben and Kerensa stepped out, both grinning broadly. Between them was Lowin, wearing a T-shirt embroidered with a huge cobra, and looking like someone who knew exactly how jealous of him every other kid there would be, and enjoying every second of it.

"WHOA" said Avery. "Lowin is *my* friend. I'm go say hello."

And he dashed across to the harbor's edge where Lowin was mounting the steps.

"HI, LOWIN! HI! HI, LOWIN!"

Lowin gave him a slightly disdainful look as he took his parents' hands and carried on, as if he were a young prince inspecting his town.

"HI, LOWIN! HI! HI, LOWIN! HI!!!"

Polly hit her head on Huckle's shoulders.

"Just think about his therapy bills," said Huckle, soothingly.

Thankfully, kind Kerensa gave Avery a cuddle. Daisy would almost certainly have been coy and careful about what she wanted but Avery could not be.

"CAN I COME IN YOUR CAR BOAT!"

"'Fraid not, kid," said Reuben. "I'd have to insure you for four million. Hey, hi!"

He waved at Huckle and Polly, who came down to greet them.

"Wow, it's been pretty rough here, huh."

His face, however, was beaming.

"How long have you had that thing?" said Huckle.

"Don't ask," said Kerensa. "He's been so desperate for a chance to show it off."

"They only ever made four hundred," said Reuben.

"And the rest are at the bottom of the sea," added Kerensa. "Have you got anything to eat? The boys are starving."

"Sure am," said Reuben.

In response, Polly showed her the wreck of the Little Beach Street Bakery.

"Oh, man," said Reuben. "Oh, man, that's bad. Are my ovens all right?"

"They will be."

"Good, good."

He turned to address the crowd that had gathered round.

"I got something for you all," he said, in a way that made Polly a little anxious. Being in Reuben's debt could be an uncomfortable place to be.

"I'm going to buy everyone . . . new doors! Water-tight, waterproof, whatever the water thing is. You can have 'em! New doors, new weather-proof windows! All on me."

Polly speculated, correctly, whether Reuben had just made any large investments in glassware firms as the locals cheered.

"Yeah yeah yeah," said Reuben. He looked back at Polly.

"Are you absolutely sure you didn't bake anything at home this morning and were keeping it for emergencies?"

Of course Polly had.

"Great," said Reuben, digging into the wicker basket with jam tarts, lemon curd, and cheese twists she had made up for the helpers. He had got steadily chubbier over the years, even as Kerensa had got thinner and thinner, in the manner of the very rich, and he stuck both paws in.

"Thanks for the door," he said finally. "Seriously. I'm buying you an awesome door, girl dude."

"Oh yes," said Polly, distracted. Of course it was a

kind offer, of course it was, she was so grateful. And of course she didn't want his money; they were friends, after all. But a new door . . . it didn't begin to touch the sides of what they were facing, not really. Nowhere near.

She swallowed down that thought. New doors would be great.

"Thank you," she said. "I'm so grateful."

"I just need one thing in return."

Of course he did.

"I need you to cater Lowin's birthday party."

"Oh." Polly blinked. This wouldn't be a small affair. "What is it? Some friends from school?"

It wouldn't be sausage rolls and a caterpillar cake, she could tell.

Reuben barked with laughter.

"No! Ha. No way. No, it's going to be an EVENT! I'll get the party planner to contact you."

"You have a party planner? For an eight-year-old?"

"Well, he's going to be eight, aren't you, Lowin?" said Kerensa, hugging the boy's round head affectionately.

"Whatever," said Lowin, grabbing two of the jam tarts, sniffing one, and throwing the lemon curd away whereupon Neil, followed by about sixteen huge sea gulls, immediately pounced on it, setting up a hell of a racket.

"Well, of course," said Polly. "I'd . . . I mean, of course."

"There's going to be a DJ," said Kerensa. "And loads of Champagne. Seven-year vintage, clever, huh? You're going to *love* it. And you can invoice us a lot more than the cost of the door," she added in a low voice.

Polly thought about Reuben's parties she'd catered over the years, and smiled as politely as she could.

"'Scuse me," said Daisy, from down somewhere by

Polly's knees. "Is there going to be a LOT of snakes at this party?"

"Does he *still* like snakes?" said Kerensa distractedly. "It might be car boats now. Or football or something."

Little Daisy's face brightened. This had obviously been on her mind for a long time. Polly squeezed her hand tightly.

"Good," Daisy said in a breathy whisper.

Chapter Forty-four

Sometimes, there is just one step. One tiny last step; a little nudge, just to push you over the edge. And luckily for Marisa, hers came soon.

It was Nazreen on the phone, sounding anxious. And on a Saturday too.

"Hey, how are you doing?" she said. "We still miss you at the office."

"Thanks," said Marisa. Her first new admin part-time pay check had been a shock, she had to admit. But she was getting by. In a funny way, the office and Exeter were fading from her mind. Mount Polbearne was feeling more and more like home.

"The thing is . . ." said Nazreen. "I haven't replaced you. And there's nobody else around. And. Could you? Just cover this one? It's urgent and there's nobody about and I know, I know you're not well but . . ."

And she explained.

Marisa took a deep breath.

"Have they got a Registrar General's letter?"

"Yes. You know it's just over the causeway . . ."

"We're cut off!" said Marisa. "No, I can walk it. Or there's boats . . ."

"You sound a lot better," said Nazreen, a smile in her

voice. "Great. Can you get yourself over there? He's a Mount Polbearne boy, his mum says."

"What's the name?" said Marisa. Nazreen was delighted. She'd obviously decided to do it.

Marisa didn't recognize it.

"No local gossip?" said Nazreen.

"I don't . . . I haven't. Well. Not much gossip," said Marisa, although in fact she'd got quite a grip on several of the villagers just through helping Polly. Everyone knew Polly.

"Be careful," said Nazreen. "I know these places can be triggering."

"It's okay," said Marisa. "I can do it."

Marisa had only done one other Registrar General's letter in her career. They were rare, heart-rending occasions. There was only one reason people were allowed to get married without due notice.

The small cottage hospital was indeed just on the other side of the causeway. Marisa had got Archie the fisherman to take her and sat hugging herself in the galley of the boat, her eyes half-shut, telling herself to get out of her own way; if ever a day wasn't about her, it was today. Fortunately, Archie was happy to chatter on about how busy they were, and hadn't it been amazing saving the causeway and what a great place they lived in.

The perspective on Mount Polbearne from the sea was really quite something; the ancient rock rising from the water, in the days where if you wanted to get somewhere fast, doing it by water was the express way. The imposing old cathedral at the top, the houses wound around it, its strange, proud solitary shape, with the beautiful golden sand at the bottom of it. Looking at it, and hearing Archie's excited chatter, made Marisa feel oddly proud of her adopted home, even if it wasn't what she would have chosen. It shone brilliantly outlined against the bright blue sky as the boat bobbed up and down and she found herself taking deep breaths, not because she'd remembered, or because it had been something to tick off in her book, but because the fresh, salty air felt so very good.

She had a little wobble as she got to the hospital. The person she was dealing with had been having every dose of radiotherapy and chemo the hospital could throw at them, just to keep them alive for long enough to see this day. It was a huge responsibility.

The doctor, Indira, came and met her, smiling, but grimly.

"His immune system is severely compromised," she said. "Can you mask up? Anything could carry him off."

She held out a mask and a plastic apron.

"Of course," said Marisa.

"We had to limit guests," she said. "He's . . . not in a good way."

In that case, Marisa wondered why it mattered, but didn't say so, just snapped on the gloves.

"And it can only be ten minutes, can you do that?"

Marisa nodded. She glanced at the names.

"Can I have a word with Linnet beforehand?"

Indira shook her head. "No. Sorry. I can't tell you . . . time is of the essence. Let's go."

Marisa followed her, Indira's Crocs clopping on the highly polished surface of the linoleum, feeling nervous, even though she'd done the ceremony a hundred times.

The High-Dependency Unit was hushed, with figures looking like spacemen slowly pacing to and fro.

Undeniably, the hospital had done its absolute best. The bed had been moved to a private room at the very end of the ward, where there was a set of French doors out into a garden. Normally shielded with blinds, these had been pulled up, and the door opened, just a tad, to let the sunlight and fresh air stream in.

Flowers had been hung around the outside of the windows, their scent blowing in on the breeze.

Lying on the bed was a diminished young man who kept taking long draws from the oxygen mask next to him. He was wearing a pale blue suit that was far too large for him, and a flower in his buttonhole. His long hair had been combed to one side.

"Hello," she said, conscious to speak loudly. "Are you Denys?"

The man nodded. Another man stepped forward. His hair was dreadlocked and in neat rows, his eyes full of pain.

"Linnet?"

He nodded.

Indira stayed, along with another nurse, to act as witnesses, but Marisa became aware of a group of health-care staff lining up behind her, heads bent solemnly, to observe. One, she was pleased to notice, was filming. Linnet and Denys each had their mothers there, who were themselves holding hands, and trying not to cry too loudly. That was the limit of people it was safe to have in the space.

"Shall we start?" she said, making her voice as warm as she could. She had a few notes on a piece of paper.

"I know this place and time are not ideal for the wedding you would wish, to pledge your lives to each other. But my job is to assure you that love is here, and that this wedding and this marriage are as legal and as real as any other, as the love you bear for one another on this day and on every day."

The mood was solemn when suddenly, to Marisa's horror, she saw a hand creeping round the bottom of the French doors. Everyone stopped and all you could hear was the sound of machines beeping.

The hand had a plug and was trying to fit it in a socket that was just to the right of it.

"What the hell?" said Indira, starting forward.

The owner of the hand slowly straightened up outside the French windows, also wearing a mask, standing well back and putting his hands in the air as if someone was pointing a gun at him. It was, to Marisa's total astonishment, Alexei.

"Sorry. Sorry. I late. Sorry!"

"What the hell are you doing?"

Carefully, Alexei pushed the French doors open a little and revealed a large electronic keyboard.

"Sorry. Everyone in village know there is wedding, I think, wedding sad without music."

"Well, I'm afraid—"

"No way," interjected Linnet. "Are you going to play for us?"

He squeezed Denys's hand who squeezed back, and they looked at one another.

"What you like?"

"You can play anything?"

"I try."

"Hang on," said Indira, watching in astonishment as, over the garden, figures started appearing, bright in the sunshine, and clearly dressed for a wedding; more and more. It looked to Marisa's eyes like the entire village. Mrs. Baillie and Mrs. Bradley and dozens and dozens of friends wandering over the hospital grounds in their finest wedding clothes, hats and flowers, bottles of Champagne, waving madly. Denys had to take a long draw of oxygen but started waving and grabbing at Linnet, who now had tears in his eyes.

"I can't allow this," said Indira. "You're all going to have to go—"

"Ah, Indira, come on. As long as they stay outside, what harm can it do?" said another female doctor. Everyone backed up a few feet. There were curtains separating them from the rest of the ward and the patients. Everyone stared at the fierce doctor.

Indira rolled her eyes.

"It will agitate my patient."

"Good," said Denys, with some effort from the bed.

"Make it quick," said Indira to Marisa, who opened her book.

"Do you know . . . "As"?" said Linnet. "It was . . . is . . . it's kind of our song."

"ABSOLUTELY NO SINGING," said Indira.

"Mr. Steven Wonder?" said Alexei. "Of course. He genius like Shostakovich."

And, gently, he bent down and plugged the keyboard in, and to Marisa's absolute astonishment, after all the horrible clatter she'd been subjected to, set a gentle grooving rhythm on the keyboard, and started playing, sensationally, the uplifting song, picking out the melodic line with his top fingers, as if he had three hands.

It was, it turned out, almost impossible not to sing along. It was absolutely impossible not to dance to the groove and everyone dotted around the garden started to jiggle just a little, as did the line of nursing staff behind them. Even Mrs. Brodie was tapping a foot.

Linnet and Denys stared into each other's eyes and mouthed how they would love each other always. At the very final chorus, one of Linnet and Denys's friends could not contain themselves anymore, and in a voice of extraordinary power from behind a tree, belted out the last chorus, which meant automatically Alexei kept on playing it, until, gradually there was an entire choir singing, a chorus of people out in the garden, joined by more and more as you could hear the windows open all over the hospital.

The mood of the entire room changed completely. The sadness evaporated: there was clapping, and smiling, and eyes full of happiness. When the song ended, the applause rang from every window and doorway.

"All right," said Marisa, smiling. "Before you are joined in matrimony I have to remind you of the solemn and binding character of the vows you are about to make. Marriage, according to the law of this country, is the union of two people, voluntarily entered into for life, to the exclusion of all others.

"Now I am going to ask each of you in turn to declare that you know of no lawful reason why you should not be married to each other . . ."

She was hustled out as soon as they had both legally signed the register, but she couldn't help smiling all the way out in the corridor, for overcoming something she had been dreading, and as soon as she reached the car park and could pull off her mask, she took in the fresh air in gulps, thankfully, feeling guilty for what she had left behind—but she had done her job.

She glanced around for Alexei, but he was nowhere to be found. Faintly, though, she heard the faintest suggestion of "Don't You Worry 'Bout a Thing" across the dingy car park. She guessed he was busy. There was a party going on back there, whatever the hospital authorities had to say about it. She considered joining them, but decided against it. She felt depleted. But it was done.

Chapter Forty-five

Nonna wanted to know everything, of course.

"Oh, a wedding," she said happily. "What did the bride wear?"

"There . . . uh . . . wasn't a bride," said Marisa, a little tentatively. She wasn't entirely sure how her nonna would deal with this. There was modern and there was something a little too far for Italian grandmothers in Imperia.

"Oh! Two men. Well, good."

Marisa smiled. "You don't mind?"

"Well, now our pope is gay, who should mind?" said Marisa's grandmother, to Marisa's profound surprise.

"Is . . . wait . . ."

"So. There was a cake?"

"I don't know—you know I don't stay at these things."

Her nonna sniffed. "But you don't do weddings anymore. You could have stayed there."

She could have. Nonna was right. Alexei had woken her up stumbling in at goodness knows what time, humming a jolly song to himself and shouting good night to friends out the door. He seemed to have made friends with half the village.

"Well, I did go," she said.

"That is true, yes. Good girl."

She told her about Alexei turning up to play.

"You don't cook for him anymore?"

"No," said Marisa, conscious that the twins were playing next door. "No. We kind of . . . he doesn't really like me."

"Men like anyone who cooks for them," said her nonna. "You should take him a plate. What are you making tonight?"

"I thought . . . saltimbocca?"

"Oh! Good, very good. Take him a plate. He is from a good family?"

Marisa laughed. "I don't know, do I?"

"Although. You know. Piano teachers. They don't make any money. Ever."

"So? Anyway, that doesn't matter. I don't make any money these days either."

"So. You need to find someone who has nothing to do with pianos. He is Catholic?"

"He's Russian, Nonna."

"Oh. Heathens. Never mind."

"This is a ridiculous conversation anyway. We're just neighbors. Who don't like each other."

"Okay. Well. Best not go. You cook for a man, that means something. They are simple creatures."

"Not these days."

"I know men."

"You don't know men! You married Nonno at nine-teen!"

"If I know men, and a beautiful girl who perhaps needs to lose three kilos and cut her hair and put some lipstick on her beautiful mouth from time to time because she is definitely not getting any younger, if a girl like this arrives and says, 'Oh, I have made something delicious for you I live all by myself next door and you live all by yourself next door, I *see*,' what is the poor man to think? Men, they are not clever. And heathen men are even worse!"

"No, I think," said Marisa heavily, "I'm just going to concentrate on the saltimbocca for now."

"You told your mother about the wedding?"

Marisa swallowed. "Not yet."

"Marisa. You should. I love you. I love Lucia. I love Ann Angela."

Ann Angela was Marisa's aunt. She and Lucia fought like cat and dog, and Marisa hadn't seen her in a year either.

"I love my girls, and I am not getting any younger," said Nonna, threateningly. "You must stop fighting."

"You walk for miles and you swim in the sea every day," said Marisa. "You're going to live to be a thousand."

"Even if I do," said Nonna, "call your mother."

Marisa still remembered the awful, recriminatory texts from Christmas. Her mother telling Gino she was doing it for attention, competitively grieving. It still hurt.

"One thing at a time, Nonna."

She heard him next door after the twins' lesson, still humming a very happy Stevie Wonder song. The evening was pinkening, the sunset on its way. It looked to be a doozy. The food was in the oven; it smelled wonderful. She thought of a million reasons why she shouldn't go next door—she didn't really look brazen, like Nonna thought, did she? Anyway, it was ridiculous, he was mostly yeti. And he didn't like her. But he was keeping his side of the bargain and she owed him.

She was nervous, she found. Very nervous. She

hopped in the shower, even though she didn't really need one. Blow-dried her hair, carefully, all the while listening to hear in case he went out again. She added lipstick, half-smiling to herself at how much her nonna would approve and give her a cynical nod. But she stopped short of a dress. She wasn't—wasn't—a wanton hussy. Absolutely not. It was human company she needed, not the ridiculous complication of anything more than that, particularly with someone who you could hear every single time they turned the tap on. It would be like getting off with the person in the next room in student halls. Which she had done, once upon a free life, many many moons ago, and had been incredibly embarrassed at the time but, looking back, she thought it was rather sweet. It had gone terribly wrong and she'd been mortified for the next eight months, but wasn't that what being young was for?

Anyway. He didn't like her. But he should stop hating her. She could call that the aim of the evening.

Chapter Forty-six

Marisa was incredibly nervous grasping the big heavy earthenware pot and going down one set of steps and up another. The road was still muddy, even after two days of sunny weather had dried out most things. But she knew she was so, so lucky to live up high. She'd been texting Polly about possibly getting together to discuss her idea, but the bakery didn't even have a door yet. Still, thought Marisa, Polly would obviously be fine. She was one of the most capable people Marisa had ever met. Polly would have been amazed at how many people who met her came to that conclusion.

Out of the sun the air was still chilly, and Marisa was glad Polly had let her keep the scarlet hoody. The wind blew a little color into her cheeks—already pink with nerves—and she took a deep breath, abruptly instructed herself to get out of her own way—and rapped at the door.

The door was flung open in consternation by Alexei who looked worried, as if he'd forgotten a lesson—then incredibly surprised to see her there. He didn't move, just stared at her, his brown eyes blinking slowly in confusion.

"Um, hi?" said Marisa. She offered up the dish. "I . . . I have . . . I mean. Did you have plans?"

Alexei shook his head.

"I haff no plans," he said. He still looked puzzled. "Balcony is shut?"

"Oh," said Marisa. "No. I thought . . . I thought if you like . . ."

She swallowed painfully. The stupid part of her brain, the stupid blushing part, still wanted her to turn around and run away, just toss the heavy dish in the air and get back to safety.

"I wanted to say thank you for what you did at the hospital. And perhaps you would like to eat . . . together?"

"Oh!" His face still looked puzzled. "Of . . . of course . . . come in . . ."

And he stood back from where he was blocking the doorway.

His house, despite being identical to her own, except blue instead of yellow, could not have been more different.

Whereas she had added very little, keeping everything pristine and exactly more or less as she'd moved in to it, here something very different was happening.

The neat little table and chairs had been moved to accommodate the piano, which she noticed was actually against the far wall; as far away from her house as it could possibly be. The table itself was piled high with sheet music, and with empty sheets of music paper, the five staves drawn. Marisa wanted to look at it; as a stationery nerd it appealed to her, and she could have written beautifully on it.

The sofa was covered in intricate throws, and there were plants everywhere; hanging and jutting out. A music stand stood tall, and next to it a clarinet, which she'd never even heard. Pictures hung on the walls and books were piled up and jammed on every available surface, in Russian, French, different languages. It didn't look like it would leave him a lot of room to get around. Finally, as he had promised, in the kitchen was lined up an entire bar's worth full of the oddest liqueurs and spirits Marisa had ever seen.

"You weren't kidding about the bar," she said eventually.

"Why would I kiddink?" he said, a little defensively.

"No reason," she said. "Is your oven on?"

He looked at her. "I have magic oven?"

"No, obviously not, I just wondered . . . if you turn it on I could heat up supper."

"Okay," he said. Then he stood for a long time in front of the oven.

"*What* have you been eating?" said Marisa crossly, coming up behind him and setting the temperature on the exact mirror image of her own cooker.

"Polly is very good to me. And the fish and chips are good."

"You can't eat fish and chips every day."

"Life is very sad," said Alexei. He turned back to the drinks trolley. "So! What would you like?"

"What are you having?"

"You are surprise guest."

"Okay, what would you normally have?"

Alexei narrowed his eyes. "Well, I would put some vodka in a cup."

"Yes?"

"And . . ."

He shrugged.

"That's what you have?"

"I am Russian."

"Okay," said Marisa. "Okay, I really don't want that. Do you have any red wine?"

He did, and she brought it near the oven to warm it up a little and stirred some into the sauce. It was very quiet in the house. She looked at him and wondered why, and then she suddenly realized.

"Oh my goodness," she exclaimed suddenly, before she could even think. "It's so quiet in your house compared to mine!"

"Why?"

"Because you're not living next door to you!"

He smiled, pushing his thick hair away from his face. He would need another haircut soon, and looked rather wistfully toward his piano.

"How did you become a piano teacher?" she asked. She decided the best thing to do was just to dish up and serve as if she was in her own house; she knew where everything was and Alexei didn't seem helpless so much as completely and utterly disinterested. The bowls hadn't even been moved, had never been used and she had to rinse them. She made up a salad, lifting up the untouched salad servers.

"You don't eat enough salad."

"No," he said, looking gloomy. "You sound like my mother. But I eat many, many bananas.."

Marisa smiled. "I'll let you off then," she said, tossing the light herby salad with a little dressing she had brought over, using some of her precious balsamic vinegar as she did so.

"Sit down," she said. He had to clear a space piled high with pictures and books and music on the table and she wiped it down.

"How did you move in with so much stuff?" she asked, looking around.

"I know," he said sadly. "I had to leave so much behind. No drums. No cello."

"Thank *God*."

"Not for me," he said. "But I have friends . . ."

He sighed and looked sad suddenly.

"I had friends."

She placed the food in front of them and poured large glasses of the wine, that, warmed and decanted, had grown full and sweet.

"So how did you end up here?" she said.

"Is long and boring story," said Alexei dismissively.

"Not to me," said Marisa. "Nobody ever tells me stories any more. Everyone's forgotten about me, here at the end of the world."

She didn't mean to sound self-pitying, but somehow she did. He looked at her, those narrow brown eyes penetrating and clear. It was very odd; for someone who barely spoke the same language as her, she found him incredibly easy to read. She could see in those expressive eyes, with their long lashes, the exact way in which he turned over her question, looking for nuance, deciding within himself whether he was going to speak and how. He did it with everything. At first she had thought he was dopey or simply didn't understand. Now she realized what a rare gift it was: to think before speaking.

"Well," he said.

Chapter Forty-seven

It was so odd, thought Marisa, that they could be the same age—well, he was a few years older; thirty-four to her twenty-nine, and yet his life could be so different. He told her his father was Mongolian—"You know?"—she absolutely did not know—but his mother's family did not approve, and there was trouble from the start.

The marriage broke down, his father returned to Ulan Bator—that part of the story Marisa absolutely could empathize with—and his mother had had to move in with her own mother, in her horrible vast block, one of thousands, on the outskirts of the city, where it was always either boiling or freezing, where there was never enough hot water; where stray dogs roamed the buildings.

He had nothing but the old broken-down piano in his grandmother's house; she had nothing, but sacrificed everything to keep that.

"Oh, the neighbors hated me," he said, quietly, and Marisa winced. She couldn't bear to think of the little boy, confused and sad, only wanting his piano. How awful she must have been to him.

"I'm sorry," she whispered, but he wasn't really listening.

"Oh but then . . . good thing happens! I get scholarship. To Germany!"

"You speak German?"

"*Ja! Können wir Deutsch reden?*"

"No," said Marisa. "*Italiano?*"

He shook his head tightly.

"And that was . . ."

"That was amazing! The food, the supermarkets, the friends, the people . . . Oh, such wonderful country."

He smiled happily.

"This isn't helping me understand where Cornwall comes in."

"So I play in Germany then I get work there as repetiteur. At the Munich Opera."

He visibly swelled with pride.

Marisa shook her head.

"I play piano. For dancers to practice and singers to practice and everyone to practice."

"That sounds like a very important job."

He beamed. "I love it. I know everyone. Everyone knows me. I tour Germany, I go into schools. Oh how I love it."

"And then . . ."

Marisa had drunk quite a lot by this point or she wouldn't have brought it up. His face collapsed instantly.

"I haff girlfriend. She is ballerina."

"Seriously?" She tried not to make her surprise too obvious. "How did that work then?"

"Ballerinas very strong."

"Okay."

He sighed and looked into his glass. "We were in love. So in love."

His face was heavy in the soft light.

"What happened?"

"She was dancer, I was repetiteur, you see?"

"No."

"She was star! She needs another star. I am not star."

"You're very good!"

"Oh yes, very good, very good, many peoples are very good," he mumbled, seemingly to himself. "So. She find star. She dance with star. She want me to play for practice while she dance with star."

His large hands curled involuntarily in the anguish of the memory.

"Everybody knows."

"Oh dear."

"So. I come here. I will show her. To become famous composer. To be brilliant genius for the world and Lara will see that I am not useless."

He hung his head.

"I am useless composer. You cannot even listen to me through a wall."

"Of course you're not useless! Nobody is! That's ridiculous!"

But hadn't it been what she'd been thinking about herself?

"But why *here*?"

Alexei waved a large paw.

"Oh, Reuben, he is good friend to Russians."

Marisa ignored that.

"But I don't know anything about music! You know that! If I don't like it, that means it's probably brilliant!"

He half-smiled at that.

"Ach. And we have eaten well and it is a beautiful night and life says, we must be merry."

She looked at him as he picked up the now-empty wine bottle and frowned.

"Where did that go? I am talkink too much. I am sorry."

Marisa shook her head. "No," she said. "I'm glad you told me."

"Now. Tell me about you. What is wrong with you?"

She sighed. "Well, do you ever get stage fright?"

"I used to."

"When you're shaking and trembling and terrified?"

"When I auditioned in Munich, oh. Well. Yes."

"I feel like that. All the time."

Her hands twisted together and she stared at the floor.

"I see."

"What do you say?" she asked suddenly. "When your pupils have stage fright? What do you tell them?"

He looked grave. "Well. I say Tazlaswit."

She looked up. "What does that mean? Is it a Russian phrase?"

He looked puzzled. "Tazlaswit. Tazlaswit. You know?"

"I do not know!"

"Shek it off! Shek it off!"

His meaning finally dawned on her and she burst into peals of laughter.

"You mean Taylor Swift?"

"Tazlaswit. I said that."

She laughed. "Shake it off?"

"For sure. You need to just do it again and again and again until you are not scared anymore. You shake it off."

"Oh," said Marisa sadly. "That's what my therapist says and what's in my book. You can only get better by doing it a lot. I hoped there was another way."

"Everything is practice," said Alexei.

He stood up and walked over to the freezer, pulling out of it a vodka bottle with the label in inscrutable Cyrillic.

"Now we have been talking of old days," he said. "You will join me?"

Marisa shrugged. She couldn't work out if this was

a good idea or not. On the other hand, when was the last time she had done . . . anything? Spontaneous or otherwise.

"Sure," she said.

He opened the cap, poured the freezing liquid into two small heavy glasses, passed her one then held his up.

"*Za zdarovye!*"

She smiled.

"*Za zdarovye!*"

They clinked glasses.

"No," said Alexei. "You must look me in the eye. Or is bad luck."

She raised her chin and gazed into his brown eyes. She realized as she did so how very long it had been since she'd done just that; the curious intimacy of looking straight at somebody. It didn't seem to bother Alexei in the slightest; he didn't break her gaze. Not in a creepy way. He was simply—and somehow, given his upbringing—comfortable in his own skin, in being with other people. He had got out of his own way.

"Okay," she said, holding his gaze.

"And how would you say it?"

"*Salute*," she said.

"*Salute*."

Chapter Forty-eight

Marisa wasn't sure how much later it was, but she found she was laughing hysterically. Alexei was trying to tell her a story about something that he and his friends had done with some snow, but he had lost all his English and kept switching to German, punctuated by some fairly loud swearing at himself and had ended up trying to act the entire thing out, to Marisa's increasingly hysterical guesses.

"Polar bear!"

"I am not polar bear! I am elegant . . ."

He tried to mime again.

"Hedgehog! Fire engine! Dump truck."

They were both in hysterics by this time.

"I am full of elegance and grace," growled Alexei, stumbling over one of the many lamps glowing around the little room which gave it a cozy air, against the pitch-black of the view outside, flooded every thirty seconds by the lighthouse. He had also lit a small black cigarillo which smelled of cinnamon and cloves and was constantly leaving it teetering dangerously on large piles of paper.

"You're a fire hazard!"

"You are fire hazard oven is off oven is on oven is off. Ssh. I thinkink."

"You must know!"

Marisa stared at him once more. That huge rugby player's physique of his was not graceful in any way, but she didn't hate it. There was something very reassuring about an intensely broad pair of shoulders, after all; a broad trunk, like a tree.

"But! WHAT are you DOING?"

He tried to glide across the room and knocked over a huge pile of old records—they weren't even LPs, Marisa saw looking at them; they were fatter and older. Gramophone records. She picked them up, surprised at how heavy they were.

"Be careful!" she scolded. "I am not sure sport is for you."

"Is for everyone," said Alexei, hurt.

"What is this?" she said, holding it up. She'd seen albums before but this wasn't the same thing at all.

His face softened.

"Eroica," he said softly.

"Pardon?"

He took the plain white paper sheet, looked around and turned a big switch on a cabinet he had against the back wall. It was the oldest record player Marisa had ever seen, older than her nonna's, which had a 78 setting. But before he did so he set it down sadly.

"But I forget," he said. "You do not care for music."

"I . . ."

Then she went for the truth.

"I just don't know much about music. I don't know anything about classical music. I quite like . . ."

Suddenly fessing up to how much she liked Polly's Backstreet Boys albums felt a little pointless to mention now.

"Well, I like pop music. But I don't know anything

about what you play. It just sounds . . . so complicated and noisy and . . . a bit boring."

"Borink," said Alexei looking sad.

"I just . . . I just don't understand. I never learned an instrument. I don't . . . I just don't get it."

He nodded. "I see."

She hated to see him sad again.

"You could . . . you could show me," she said, quietly.

Again that long calculation with the brown eyes and the long eyelashes. Was that him thinking, or was it his circuits translating English? She couldn't decide what he was like at all, it was the oddest thing. But she found she liked looking at him while he thought about things. It was quiet in the softly lit room for a moment.

"Huh. Aha," he said. "Come with me."

She stood up—slightly wobbly—as he refilled their glasses and carried them carefully over to the piano. There were piles of things everywhere but nothing on top of the piano except for two stubby pencils on the sides.

There was one bench, which he sat on, and a chair, on the left-hand side, which he indicated for her to sit on. They were close; closer than Marisa would normally think of as comfortable. Or maybe abnormally. It had been so long. She was once again closer to Alexei, she realized, than she had been to another human being in a very long time.

It felt so strange. There was a heat coming off him; she felt the hairs stir on her arm, right next to him. His side was touching her elbow, but he seemed completely oblivious of the physical contact. She could think of nothing else; as if her elbow seared touching him. He was going through a huge pile of sheet music, humming and hawing to himself, while she felt every tiny pressure of him next to her, every movement, a warm human smell of him—the top of the piano, she noticed, was covered in pencil sharpenings, which explained the woody scent that clung to him, as well as the cloves from his little cigarettes. Even the thick wool of his jumper brushed her like an electric shock and he was completely oblivious; buried in the loose papers with the strange little black markings on them, musical notes and lines and curves and odd squiggly characters that indicated who knew what, but made up a language he could read.

She looked down at the piano keyboard in front of her. She'd never sat in front of one before. She must have banged a few notes at a friend's house. But to actually sit in front of one.

She found she was nervous. It was the proximity, she knew. The two of them so close, the night so quiet. The alcohol had gone straight to her head, she was out of practice with it and felt extremely peculiar. Experimentally, she leaned, just the tiniest way, to the right. Just the tiniest piece of pressure on his body, the tiniest breath of leaning. He didn't notice. His bulk, his warmth though, felt incredibly comforting.

"Aha!" he said, still completely oblivious. He pulled something out, with the same odd scribbles on it as everything else.

"Okay," he said. "We shall try this."

"What is it?"

"You will know it," he said. "If you have ever seen film or watch TV it is everywhere. Some people say aha it is everywhere I hate it now. BUT! Because something is everywhere that does not mean BAD EVERYWHERE."

He placed it with a flourish on the stand. It appeared to be called after a gymnasium.

à Mademoiselle JEANNE de BRET

1ʳᵉ GYMNOPÉDIE

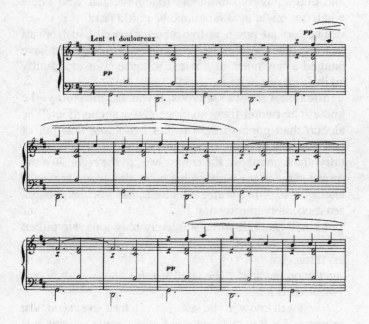

"Am I just going to watch?"

"No! You are going to play with me and feel with me."

"I can't play though! Not at all! Not a note."

"Not a note," said Alexei. "TWO NOTES!"

He looked down at her hand.

"You haff very small paws. That is my bear joke."

"I get that."

"I show you?"

"Uh . . . yeah?"

He lifted her small pale hand in his huge one. It was only when she felt it she got some sense of the sheer size of the man. Her own little fingers completely disappeared in the gap between his thumb and his second finger. The nails were very short and neat and tidy, squared away against the enormous long fingers themselves.

"You're hands are huge," she said nervously.

"Of course," he said. "Tiny hands have hard job on the piano."

Marisa frowned. "I suppose so."

It felt nice, her hand in his large one. But before she had a chance to relax into it—and she didn't feel in the least bit relaxed—he had taken her smallest finger and put it halfway down the bottom half of the piano. Then he opened the music and put it up on the stand.

"Here are two notes," he said. He took her pinky up again and put it down on one. "This is D. It lives between two friends, you see?"

He indicated the two black notes surrounding the white one.

"D feels very safe and comfortable here with his good friends, D Flat and D sharp. They are all happy. It is cozy bed. Stay here."

She depressed the note with her finger and it made a slippery loud plinking noise.

"Good," said Alexei considering. "Although it is late. Perhaps he is quiet and a little sleepy and you do not have to hit him so hard."

She tried again more tentatively and this time produced no sound at all.

"Well, and also we continue and push maybe a little harder," said Alexei, and Marisa was conscious of holding her breath and found her mind wandering, unavoidably—it was the vicinity of another living human being, she told herself firmly, and months and months of deprivation, it had absolutely nothing to do with just him. It could have been anyone, so there, how could she possibly be expected to control her own mind wandering?

But she couldn't help but wonder—couldn't help it— as he showed her how to play hard and soft, alternately pressing then lifting her finger, that if he had that much control over just one finger, what could the rest of him possibly be like?

She finally found a way to play the note, even as she felt her breath running a little faster than normal.

"And now, give me your thumb," he said, and she held it up willingly, happy to be guided.

"This is a G," he said, placing her thumb a little further up. "Poor old G. There are three friends in this group." He indicated the cluster of black notes above the white one. "Sometimes they are friends, sometimes they are mean, sometimes they make a gang and sometimes they are horrible. G is pure but she gets lost sometimes. She is a good note. Not like B," he continued, mysteriously. "B, he is absolutely bastards. Ублюдки. So."

She looked down at her hands.

"Do not move your hand now. They will stay there. G is first, then D. Thumb then finger. When I say now, you play one and then the other, yes? And hold them down, keep them down, keep your hands on them."

His voice was gentle and low, his accent less harsh and his brown eyes were boring into her, trying to make sure she'd understood. Feeling intensely engaged, she did so, one after another.

"Good, good," he said, and she couldn't help it; she felt something inside herself loosen, like a knot falling away.

"Okay," he said. "We begin. I excusink myself in advance as I have to reach down over you when I play. I am sorry."

Marisa swallowed hard. "That's okay."

He smiled at her.

"You start. Slow slow slow. Now."

Marisa pressed down the bottom note, and he reached down his huge left hand and, just above her, played a jumble of chords, soft and low.

"Now. The other one."

Marisa obediently moved to the D, to be rewarded by an answering group of chords just above her hands, as his arm moved right over hers.

"Now! Again."

She did it, as she did so realizing she was getting into the rhythm naturally, and that, in fact, she did recognize the music. She almost jumped in pleasure as, as well as playing along with her low bottom chord, his right hand started to pick out the melody in the right.

"I know this!"

"Ssh! Keep playing . . . now . . . and yes . . . yes . . ."

She did know it, the lovely lazy French melody, familiar from countless films. It sounded beautiful.

"Okay, you do not play now," he whispered in her

ear and stretched over her to play even further down the keyboard, trapping her arm under his. She sat there, trembling, until the music circled around and landed back at the beginning and she played the notes, softly and gently, and realized on some distant level that both of them were breathing in and out in time to the melody. The spell cast around the low-lit quiet room and she felt woozy, dreaming in the music as he took the lead, his heavy presence beside her, and almost entirely on top of her when he took the lower part, a complete contrast to the light airiness of the music flowing from his fingertips. Then, finally, after they had repeated the short piece over and over again, he no longer had to tell her when to play, and she found herself right inside the music, ready and waiting for her turn to come again, even if it was only two little notes, over and over: she felt entirely engulfed by him and the music, even closing her eyes the better to let the melody fill her, and his strong body against her, and the thrill of being a part of it and the thrill of being so close to him and the way they were joined, over the piano keyboard.

When the last note started to die away it felt like a terrible loss, the dying ringing in the air, and she missed it already. Alexei moved; shuffled up the stool as if realizing suddenly how close they had been, and that made her heart jump as if electrified, the realization that he had thought . . . well, who knew what he thought, but her brain was so jumbled and overstimulated she found herself too jumping back as if she had touched something hot; stumbling upward off the seat, her face bright scarlet, and she turned around and just for a second, just for a moment, she thought with a terrible clarity that she was going to kiss him; and worse, he was looking at her too, with those big eyes that missed absolutely nothing and she saw he had noticed it too, and noticed her panicked reaction; that he missed nothing, and that made it infinitely worse.

She jumped up.

"I . . . I . . ."

She was out of breath too. This was ridiculous.

"Is strong music," said Alexei, but Marisa was panicked.

Nonna had been right. Turn up on a stranger's doorstep bearing food, what are they supposed to think? Oh God, that appraising look. She felt like Vanessa showing up with biscuits and . . . oh Lord.

Face aflame she backed away, and he looked startled and worried, as if he'd done something wrong.

"I'm . . . I'd better go."

"You not like the music?" he asked.

"Thank you," she said very quietly. "That was . . . I. Yes. Very much. Thank you."

"You played beautifully."

"I didn't play at all!"

His face frowned, his brown eyes looking thoughtful.

"You were lost in the music, no?"

She reluctantly nodded.

"Is okay. Then. That is playing. That is all there is to playing. The rest, is just exercise. The music you have."

He too had stood up and was backing away rather anxiously, as if they both realized they had got too close; that there was a sudden quiet in the room; mostly embarrassment, some small, tiny, tiny sense, the smallest of—

No, Marisa thought to herself. She was being ridiculous. She had been on her own for so long she was going crazy. The thoughts that were going through her head . . .

She just needed not to look at his hands, not to even be thinking about his hands. His huge, strong, gentle hands, when he had literally spent the entire evening tell her how much he was in love with a ballerina.

"I have to go," she stuttered, realizing as she did so that she was completely betraying herself.

He looked suddenly flustered as if he had done something wrong.

"Yes, is late . . . I walk you home . . ."

"Uh, I live just there," reminded Marisa.

She looked around desperately.

"I am sorry," said Alexei.

"Why? I mean, thank you! I mean . . ."

They both stood, far apart.

"I will get . . ." She was looking for her bowl but he misunderstood and rushed to open the door for her, as if desperate to show he wasn't about to trap her there or that he even wanted her there, which made her feel worse than ever.

"Of course, good night, good night. Thank you for dinner."

Too flustered to bother about her dish, Marisa turned on her heel and fled. Just as she set foot on the steps, to go next door, she turned quickly back to see if he was looking at her, but he wasn't, his dark eyes trained on the piano, and she turned back feeling ridiculous, and half-stumbled down the steps, just as his eyes now turned to her and watched her go.

Chapter Forty-nine

"So. Good family?"

Marisa was suffering from her first hangover in six months, and the weather was dreary and raining and she was in absolutely no mood for an interrogation from her grandmother, bathed in sunshine and shelling peas in her little kitchen. Who? Marisa thought through her foggy head. Who even shelled peas anymore?

"Why are you shelling peas?"

Nonna held them up.

"The brighter, the sweeter," she said. "Lilies of the field who do not weave or spin."

"Yes, yes," said Marisa, who was exhausted. Nonna brought her near-sighted little black button eyes up closer to the screen.

"You look tired. What time did you get home?"

"Um, not too late," lied Marisa through her teeth. She hadn't even noticed what time it was.

"You didn't *drink*?"

Her nonna's face was stern.

"Noooo . . . a little bit. He is Russian."

Nonna sniffed.

"Nonna! Things are different these days."

"You go to a man's house, you take him food, you

drink with him, you come home and you look terrible. Is this what you had hoped for the evening?"

Everything had seemed even worse in the cold light of the morning. Her nonna was right, she had offered herself up on a plate, and he had patiently explained how he much he missed his ex. And oh my God, of course, all the old ladies of the village who came up to practice Celine Dion songs for him. She was absolutely in that category too. She groaned. How could she have made such an idiot of herself?

But the worst thing was, when she put that to one side, she had felt the evening was . . . it was wonderful. She had liked him. Laughing together and drinking vodka, and how touchingly he had taken her into his confidence, talked about his life; it had been a real conversation, not idle chit-chat or the desperate flotsam of Tinder dates, where you talked about other dates you'd been on, or whether you liked dogs or pudding. It had been a real sharing of their lives.

And then when he showed her how to play . . . her fingers still tingled at the memory of it, of feeling engulfed by the music.

And then she'd gone and spoiled it all.

"Do you like this boy?" said her nonna.

Marisa shrugged her shoulders. "It's been such a long time."

"I think that says yes."

Nonna was now adding the peas to some broad beans and making a mint dressing for the freshest, lightest salad Marisa could imagine. She wanted nothing more than to be sitting in her nonna's courtyard, the sun pouring in, drinking sparkling water and waiting for lunch.

"I just don't meet anyone else."

"Well! Get out! Meet other people! Come and visit your nonna!"

"I would love to," said Marisa avidly, even though the idea of getting to a crowded noisy airport and dealing with queues and strangers and boarding a plane was up there with nipping over to NASA and signing up for the Mars mission.

"Now it is lunchtime. Get some sleep. Do not take him any more food until you know his intentions are pure."

"His intentions are nonexistent," said Marisa.

Nonna sniffed. "He is a man, you are a woman. If he likes women, there is nothing wrong with you."

"I think," said Marisa, "that's the biggest compliment you've ever paid me."

Chapter Fifty

The weather cleared up in the afternoon and as well as her hard-won moving outside, Marisa couldn't bear sitting in, listening to the piano lessons next door, each one an agony. His patient growl; the clumping repetition of the students' slow lines. All of it was painful to Marisa and she pulled on her coat and did what she said she'd do; she managed to go down to see Polly.

It was nearly the end of the day for Polly who was waiting on the children returning and hadn't really been expecting Marisa back, considering she wasn't well, and hadn't wanted to get her hopes up.

The new door had arrived, conveyed with great fanfare by Reuben, and of course she had been very grateful; she was very grateful, but she couldn't possibly say now how much they were still in trouble.

Marisa kept close to the walls of the houses again, remembering to do her breathing—although thinking about meals didn't help as it led her back to the previous evening—as she headed down the hill.

People smiled and nodded at her and she did her best to return them. Here and there were houses still open and drying out, and there was a large collection of ruined furniture down on the docks waiting for the refuse boat that was coming to take it away.

Still, Mount Polbearne made a pretty sight in the watery sunshine. The houses were being repainted already, many of which had long needed it, and there was a faint smell of fresh whitewash in the air. Now the day had cleared there were lots of people out on the street, calling to one another, borrowing tools and sharing biscuits. Obviously what had happened had been terrible but there was a definite sense of everyone coming together. Andy had even restrung the fairy lights above his beer garden, in defiance of the storm, lending a promise of lovely light evenings ahead. It was nice to see them. I could sit in a beer garden, thought Marisa, defiantly. She could. Could she?

The bakery was winding down, almost empty. Polly smiled and waved to see her; Jayden had already gone for the day.

"Hey!" she said.

"Hello," said Marisa. "I came to talk about . . . well. Things I was thinking of for the bakery."

She started unpacking the rucksack she'd prepared that afternoon. Polly beamed.

"I wasn't sure you weren't just chewing the fat. Are you serious?"

Marisa held up her apron.

"I am completely serious. You have a hot food license, right?"

"Sure do, class one," said Polly proudly.

"Okay. Well. Want to fire them up?"

They turned the closed sign around on the bakery and cleared a workspace through the back, as well as whacking the ovens up to 500 degrees. It got very hot inside the bakery very quickly.

"Phew," said Marisa. "This will dry you out."

"I know," said Polly. "Also Reuben bought us some

super-duper triple-glazed door which he thinks is brilliant but it doesn't let any draughts in. Also, it's too heavy
for my old ladies. It's going to kill someone. Or, more
likely, their dog."

Marisa winced. "Ah."

She unpacked the huge jar of fresh tomato sauce that
had been simmering on the stove for hours.

"Oh my God," said Polly as she opened it. "That
smells like heaven! What's in it?"

"Not much," said Marisa. "Good tomatoes, lots of garlic, onions, olive oil, salt, a bay leaf and a lot of thyme."
She thought for a second. "And really, the bay leaf is
mostly for luck."

Polly dipped a spoon in and tasted it.

"Oh my God, that's amazing!"

"Thyme is the best bit."

"It's so rich!"

"A good sauce and a good base . . . but that doesn't
mean anything if you don't have a good oven," said
Marisa. "And *boy* do you have good ovens."

The twins came cantering round the back, home from
school.

"What did you learn today?" said Polly.

"Health and Well-being!" recited Daisy.

"Mummy, do you SMOKE?" said Avery, looking
panicky.

"Have you ever seen me smoke?" said Polly, confused.
Daisy came up to her and took her hand gently and with
an air of very mature concern.

"Do you smoke, Mummy?"

"Of course I don't smoke!"

"Because if you smoke you will die."

"TODAY," said Avery, his face looking frightened.

"And it will kill us also!" said Daisy, hers grave.

Polly knelt down.

"I don't smoke," she said. "And even if I did, I wouldn't die today."

"YOU! WILL! DIE!"

"I don't smoke."

"You promise?" said Daisy, her face a mask of despair. "Never ever?"

"I think if I haven't started now I'm probably all right," said Polly. Marisa thought back to Alexei's little cigarillos with a fond smile that quickly turned into a wince.

"PROMISE," said Daisy and Polly took them both in her arms and hugged them and promised faithfully never to smoke and they bounced off with an Empire biscuit each to play with the new door while Polly watched them go.

"I think that's the easiest win I've ever had," she mused. "Good old Health and Well-being."

"Well, it will be until we have our smoking break," said Marisa and Polly stared at her for a couple of seconds, then smiled.

"Well," she said.

"I know," said Marisa. "Oh my God, I made a joke. Not a very funny joke," she added.

"I know, but . . . I mean, that's a good sign, isn't it? I mean, I'm not an expert . . ."

Marisa held up her hands. "I'm here, aren't I?"

Polly smiled. "You are. DON'T GO NEAR THE OVENS!" she shouted in at the children as if this wasn't something that hadn't been drummed into them since they were nine months old.

"DON'T SMOKE!" came the rejoinder.

"Are we going to do that thing where you throw the dough up and down?" asked Polly back in the kitchen when they were aproned up with gloves on, and Marisa was throwing about her good flour with abandon on the shiny worktops.

"Yes," said Marisa. "Gets good air bubbles in."

Together they twisted and threw up the dough and chatted and laughed until the twins came to the door curious as to who was having such a good time; and while it felt incredible to Marisa to laugh again, Marisa didn't realize that Polly felt the same way. She had worried so much for so long and it was really good to get back to what she was used to: throwing dough and getting her hands covered in flour and chatting nonsense. It was just so normal and it felt such an age since she'd been able to be normal. Even when she and Huckle did their best to keep it light, it didn't always feel like it when there were school shoes to buy and electricity bills to pay and lighthouse inspections to arrange. This was more how it used to be, when she was starting out and had nothing to lose.

They dressed up the twins in their little mini aprons and let them toss their own dough, then Marisa showed them how to spread the sauce round and round, not missing the crust, and let them go wild with the toppings—not much; a good chorizo, some very finely sliced peppers that would be only singed in the oven; fine, silvery anchovies—Avery slipped one in his mouth thinking it was chewing gum and was shortly to be found performatively retching over the large industrial sink while Daisy told him off—and perfect juicy olives.

She wouldn't, however, let them loose on the fine silky mozzarella; it was too precious and expensive. She sliced it super fine and spread it over the fine hand-stretched bases.

"Okay," said Marisa, sprinkling on herbs, "now, put an olive on top."

"They look like grapes but Avery they are NOT GRAPES," said Daisy, anxious to avoid a rerun of the anchovy fiasco, but Avery had learned his lesson.

Marisa frowned. "Oh, you should try an olive," she said. "They are good things to like."

Daisy and Avery looked at her suspiciously.

"Or maybe," she said with a smile. "Wait for the pizza?"

"Pizza! Pizza!"

"How long in the oven?" said Polly.

"Three minutes, tops," said Marisa, grabbing the long-handled bread server. "Wear your oven gloves, it should be absolutely blistering."

The children backed toward the shop door as the oven was opened and the high-pitched roaring came out. Polly had never had the ovens so hot before; it was a furnace in there.

"Okay," said Marisa, lining up plates behind her and bringing through the tray of uncooked pizzas. "Are we ready?"

And, lithely, she tossed first one then another into the fiery envelope of the furnace, which immediately roared even higher as slick drops of the olive oil in the dough plopped into the flames.

"Wow," said Daisy.

"This," observed Avery to himself, "is a very dangerous day."

Marisa fed in the bottom two, then deftly turned the top ones again. Dragging one toward her, she turned it, then the other, remembering the thrill of watching the pizza man in Imperia do it just this way, then being allowed to help. Italians didn't pretend to love children in their restaurants; they genuinely did. Although, in retrospect, no way was she going to let the children here help.

"Okay," she said a couple of minutes later. "Stand back!"

And she flipped the first two pizzas onto the plates where they just about landed in the right spot.

"Don't touch," warned Marisa, but Polly already had a friendly hold on the little ones.

The smell in the bakery, though, was a rival to the early mornings, when the warm scent of fresh bread permeated the entire street and made people walk toward the shop like zombies. This was a different smell but equally beguiling and the children began to edge forward, even with Polly clinging to their collars.

Marisa took a cutter and tore apart some slices and handed them round, blowing for the little ones. After much waving and jumping up and down, eventually it was cool enough to take a bite.

"Oh my God," said Polly after a moment's reverent silence. "Oh my God. I'm going to have to throw out all my clothes and just wear a muumuu. For the rest of my life. And I don't even care. Reuben will have to widen all the doors."

Marisa smiled.

The dough was crispy on the bottom, with air bubbles black and twisted, and the inside deliciously chewy. The sauce was a perfect balance of sweet and sharp, fresh and savory and delectable on the tongue. The slightly golden-tinged mozzarella had melted with a brown crust on the top of it.

It was the kind of pizza you dream about finding but never do; or if you're lucky, you'll be in a small Italian village, late at night, down a twisting cobbled side street and you swear you will find it again but you never do, and you never forget it.

Polly couldn't help herself.

"Oh my God," she said. "We're going to be rich."

"Yay!" said Daisy and Avery, their faces smeared with sauce.

Chapter Fifty-one

And to Marisa's astonishment, things moved quickly after that. The most difficult bit, she realized, writing in her workbook, had been getting down the hill.

As half-term approached at the end of May, with the promise of sweet weather, the tourist crowd began gradually to return to Mount Polbearne.

It wasn't like how it had been, of course, not teeming crowds—for starters, they hadn't finished repairing the causeway to make it safe for cars so people were still coming in boats or walking tentatively over a temporary metal gantry. The local news had done a small feature on the children who went to school by boat, which had been picked up all over the world and launched lots of inquiries, so Reuben was happy and, with people travelling less off the island, Alexei, Marisa could hear, was busier than ever.

But from the second the bakery shut at four, till they reopened at six, there was a palpable sense of anticipation in the town, and plenty of daytrippers furious they had to wait about till later, till the ovens stopped producing bread and cakes and moved on to pizza instead.

"We still need repainting," said Polly. "We should do something with a pizza theme."

"I am not sure that's wise," said Marisa. "I think the gray is nice."

They had tentatively agreed to work together for a couple of months and see how things went before formalizing their agreement. Marisa didn't think that with such a tiny population—about 1,500 souls all in—they could possibly sell that much pizza five nights a week to make them sustainable, but Polly pointed out how many visitors they got, and also, they were quite shocked to discover, an astonishing number of people would happily eat pizza at least once a week, or even more often.

"At least it's the very best kind," said Marisa, fulfilling another order for the Gillespies, whose myriad small boys at least burnt it off charging up and down the hilly streets of the town looking for cats to frighten or tourists' children's sandcastles to stomp on.

Plus, of course, the second-homers, who tended to bring large house parties full of people and were more than delighted to find what was essentially a super posh all-natural-ingredients gourmet pizzeria on their doorstep. Huckle pointed out to Polly that this was making things worse instead of better and she had agreed with him without actually knowing what to do about it.

Marisa now worked a couple of hours on admin for the council, paid part-time, made up a new batch of sauce every day, then at five headed down to the bakery to work like a demon until nine p.m., when, to the horror of the drinkers in Andy's bar, they did last orders, causing a massive last-minute scuffle. Andy was relatively good-natured about it, given they were cutting into his fish and chip business, but more tourists was more tourists for everyone, and so in the end he couldn't really complain. It was long hours—but it was, amazingly, working.

Chapter Fifty-two

Marisa's strange new hours meant that even though she was coming and going—quite happily, on that same route—she didn't see Alexei at all, which was probably quite useful after the hideous embarrassment of their dinner.

He hadn't been in for pizza, which was a mystery because she had, quite despite herself, ended up meeting almost every single person on the island as there was no one who could resist at least trying it, and once they'd tried it, they normally came back for more, except for Mrs. Bradley, who thought it was foreign muck and didn't say exactly those words but looked like she might every time she asked Polly in a very enunciated fashion for BATH buns and EMPIRE biscuits, and said, "I'm sorry, but . . . does it smell like garlic in here or is it just me? Goodness. Garlic in a bakery, I can't get my head around the newfangled way of doing things at all," and pretended to laugh.

It did produce another problem, though; once she got home at ten, she found herself still too wound up and unable to sleep and would watch television, drink tea, try to email friends she'd been out of touch with for far too long—and stay up till one in the morning or so, then sleeping in much longer than usual as her workday had turned topsy-turvy.

Except, of course, every morning Alexei would be welcoming students and performing scales by eight a.m. or so, clanging into her early-morning woozy dreams.

Well. Serve her right. But even though she was embarrassed about her drunken night, she thought one thing might work—tell him he could play in the evenings. If she did it right . . .

It still felt insulting: I'm not here in the night any more so play as much as you like. But that seemed all right, didn't it? She couldn't do much about the mornings, but she could at least improve something. A little bit.

Anita was surprisingly insouciant about it.

"I thought you'd have a view," said Marisa suspiciously. Anita beamed.

"Marisa," she said. "Look at you! You're going out to work every day! Three months ago you couldn't leave the house. I asked you to do a tiny thing every day, and you took it and ran with it more amazingly than I could ever have expected. I almost never fix anyone . . ."

She swallowed and realized she'd obviously gone too far.

"I mean, it's very difficult often for people to get over certain stubborn anxiety issues. Some of them really bed in and people find it very difficult to overcome them."

She couldn't stop smiling.

"But you—look at you. You've made friends. Created interpersonal relationships . . ."

"Yes, a really bad one!" said Marisa. "That's what I need to talk to you about."

Anita's eyes danced. "I'm not that kind of therapist, I'm afraid. I'm signing you off."

"What?"

"You have a job, a functional life, a social life, your family . . ."

Marisa frowned. She didn't have her whole family, not at all.

"Look at you, not even panicking at me telling you I'm leaving," said Anita, still exuberant.

Marisa realized she was doing what Alexei did when you told him something: listening to it, letting it sink in before forming a reaction. She swallowed hard.

"I . . . I think. I think maybe I can manage."

"Terrific," said Anita. "I have a bloody parents' night. I think you're my last bit of good news for the day."

"But first," said Marisa, "note or knock on the door? What should I do?"

Privately, Anita thought Marisa should fling open the door and jump on whoever lived next door regardless of what they were like, drawing the line only at actual murderers.

But giving a professional opinion was what she was paid for, and the correct professional opinion in this situation was to smile, and say, "Marisa. You are ready to decide that for yourself."

Chapter Fifty-three

Marisa still preferred being in the kitchen to facing front, and it helped her, not having to face anyone. But it couldn't last forever, and as the weeks went on and spring turned into summer, she couldn't help but start to very shyly smile at a few regulars here and there. Polly didn't push her, was careful and gentle with her, and their friendship deepened day by day.

Polly liked, too, the way the children had taken to her. It seemed a cliché to think of her doing particularly Italian things, but Marisa didn't ever mind the children in the kitchen, as long as they stayed well clear of the ovens, and was happy to make them wash their hands and put on their little aprons, whereupon she'd give them a job to do and supervise them carefully. There is no quicker way to most mothers' hearts than someone taking their children seriously.

And she was tidy, which was useful. And they both liked listening to the same nineties musical radio station which also helped as they could occasionally have a quick vogue around the back kitchen when Polly was on the edge of total and complete collapse.

Gradually, slowly, Marisa got on nodding terms with the Kuelin family, who were delighted with the ability to feed all the children once a week without it taking an hour and people throwing things at the wall; Samantha and Henry, the second-homers, who liked to badger her about what local ingredients she got from Italy and talk about stuff like *terroir* and, while obviously being very annoying, were so genuinely and intensely interested in how she made her food the way she did that she ended up opening up to them completely, and ordering the precise strain of her grandmother's tomato plants for them.

There was Mrs. Baillie who was furiously interested in her next-door neighbor and whether he had any lady visitors (not including herself, Marisa noticed, rather ruefully), and was it true he was a great composer who had left a tragic love affair and Marisa said politely that she didn't know and Mrs. Baillie had sniffed and said, oh well, he was going to love her new rendition of "Eternal Flame" and Marisa had made a mental note to prepare herself for that.

And there was Reuben, of course. Reuben didn't care if you were shy or not, it meant nothing to him. Actually, he quite liked it as it gave him more space to tell you about all the awesome things he'd done and how much money he had. Marisa was actually genuinely quite frightened of him, partly because he *was* frightening and partly because they were attracting so much business she was worried he was going to turf her out of her house and lease it to some rich people, finished road or not.

Inch by inch, little by little, though, Marisa felt the dread lifting, found herself looking forward to work, happy to be there, pleased to see the regular customers and happy to be useful and supporting Polly, who was drooping but still would not and could not stop.

The only person it was really going to kill was Polly; the hours were absolutely punishing. Jayden could open up some days, but not every day, and she found it incredibly difficult to sneak back and nap in the afternoon; she just seemed to have lost the habit since the children were born; always a tiny bit on edge, in her sleep, for one of them falling out of a window. It had switched something in her fundamentally.

And she missed her evenings with Huckle—even as he picked up all the slack; cooking, bath times, stories, everything they used to share he was now handling every night by himself, willingly and without complaining—but she missed them very much. Bedtime stories were her favorite part of the day; the children, finally worn out, sweetly scented, Avery's fair hair combed out neatly into a parody of a little American boy, exactly like Huckle at that age; Daisy in her pretty flowered pajamas, one either side on Avery's little truckle bed. The room wasn't big enough for two full beds set apart and they refused to be separated, so the truckle it was. One day they would get a bunk bed. It was the great aspiration of their childhood and they spent many happy hours bickering over who was going to sleep on the top bunk, and working out a complicated rota system somewhat hindered by Avery's slowness to grasp the days of the week and being constantly frustrated that they were an odd number.

They had drifted through *The Big Red Bath*; Moomins, *Goodnight Moon* even though it terrified them both; *In the Night Kitchen* likewise; *Charlie and the Chocolate Factory* but not the *Great Glass Elevator* as it was Very Very Strange; *The Gruffalo* more times than Polly could count, and she had been gearing them up, as they neared six, to enter Narnia for the first time . . .

It was her favorite part of the day, sleepy and cozy and knowing Huckle was downstairs, with supper on the way, and perhaps a glass of wine poured and the fire roaring and Neil doing little bird snores in his cardboard box.

She knew, every night, as she yawned over the accounts in the bakery, that this was absolutely the best thing for them; that Marisa, completely unexpectedly and out of the blue, had saved them all; that it was an extraordinary stroke of luck.

But oh my God she was so bone weary.

"Can't I toss pizza?" said Huckle. "How hard can it be? I'll wear a nifty hat and everything."

"Well, obviously you *could*," said Polly. "But it doesn't solve the problem of both of us being at home to spend time together and have a cuddle and all the things I want."

"I tried to give you a cuddle last night," observed Huckle. "And you snorted and did a massive snore right in my face."

"Well, exactly. And I can't afford to hire someone yet," said Polly. "But this is . . . it's going to be good for us."

"I can tell that," said Huckle, "because you look so bright and breezy about everything."

"This is a problem," said Polly.

"You know what would probably bring in enough to hire someone a couple of nights a week?"

"Don't say it."

"Catering Lowin's birthday party."

"I TOLD YOU NOT TO SAY IT!"

Polly caught Marisa doing her breathing exercises one night, and instead of being scornful—which Marisa, for some reason, had thought people would be—was incredibly interested and insisted they sat down with a cup of tea and try them together. Poor Polly lasted precisely fifteen seconds before dozing off so quickly she almost toppled off her chair. Marisa thought she had never needed Alexei so much; he needed to come and play something rousing in front of the kitchen. And just as soon as the thought of him stopped making her blush bright red, she was absolutely going to send him that note.

Chapter Fifty-four

Marisa would have told Polly what she was doing, but Polly would have gotten overexcited—being an old married lady meant she loved to hear about other people's love lives. And she wouldn't have told Nonna because Nonna of course would have implied that what she was doing was very sluttish and she shouldn't be chasing a man who hadn't even come to visit her since she'd been over which was, frankly, not a bad point.

And she couldn't have told anyone how much mental energy she was expending on the whole thing because it was embarrassing, kind of how she was at fourteen, mooning over Ishmael Mehta in her chemistry class, who had the most directional haircut in the entire school, with a Nike swoosh shaved into his skull.

So she kept it to herself. And worked on it very slowly, and carefully, upside down, sitting out on the sunny afternoons—and occasionally dozing off, if it was quiet or there was someone good in, like young Edin, the talented boy from next door, who kept getting better and better, and she could happily doze off listening to that, feeling relaxed as he played.

Until finally it was done, and she took a deep breath and put it an envelope and, once more—and, ridiculously, equally nervous this time as last time, although for completely different reasons—picked a time when he was very busy with the twins, hammering away on either side of the keyboard at a deafening pace as ever, and slipped it under his door.

Of course this was a mistake with five-year-olds in the room, on a par with leaving an unattended box of strawberry tarts. Marisa didn't know a lot of five-year-olds. The music next door stuttered to a halt.

"There is POST! There is POST! POST CAME!"

There was a scramble of little footsteps.

"We will get your post!"

Marisa was for once pleased she had somewhere else to go that wasn't home. She set off down the hill at a brisk rate to avoid answering questions. Huckle, who was sitting across the street looking at his online banking on his phone for the first time in months without wanting to cry, glanced up and smiled.

"Hey, can I get my wife back anytime soon?"

She smiled at him.

"Soon as we run out of pizza you can."

He rolled his eyes then came down to join her.

"Listen," he said. "Thanks. We really owe you for what you did."

Marisa blinked. That was exactly how she felt about them.

"Are you kidding? I really needed a job."

It had never occurred to her that she had helped them. She hadn't thought anything was going wrong at all with Polly; had thought, apart from a little bad luck in the storm, Polly had the most enviable life she could imagine. A bakery, a lovely husband, two beautiful children, a bird . . . well, she wasn't particularly desperate for a bird but even so. Polly seemed so sorted. It made her heart lift to hear praise.

"And . . ."

She had been about to go further but didn't. She didn't want to say that Polly had saved her in a deeper way, that she, and her nonna and Anita and, yes, Alexei too . . . that these people had built her a key, piece by piece, to unlock her prison door.

"Well. It's just cool," she managed eventually.

Huckle beamed. He was a sunny soul.

"There we are," he said. "The universe had a plan."

"I don't think the universe ever has a plan," said Marisa.

"Ssh," said Huckle. "The universe will hear you and *totally* mess up the plan." He glanced back. "Okay, let me go get those monsters. They're meant to be extra talented but I have to say, I'm not hearing it."

"Oh, I do," said Marisa quickly, not wanting him to suspect what she had done. "It's really obvious when you live next door."

"Well," said Huckle, beaming, and the pleasure Marisa felt at making another human being happy outweighed the fact that she had patently lied to do it. She found herself wondering briefly what Father Giacomo would say to that but shook it out of her mind and headed down into the village to start another busy evening shift trying to explain to people why she didn't allow pineapple on her pizza although they were welcome to add it at home if they wished. Neither did she do "stuffed crust" or anything with the word "feast" in it.

Because she had found her voice: and she said it with a smile, and by the time people had eaten their first slice, they simply didn't mind.

She and Polly found an easy rhythm working together, even if Polly did it on several cups of very strong
coffee.

"You know," Marisa said, "it's not difficult, not really.
Couldn't Jayden do some nights?"

"Hmmm," said Polly. It was still a question of money,
but she also found it incredibly difficult to leave the
business at such a fledgling stage. She needed to see
which bits of the evening were noisy, which were quiet,
how it ebbed and flowed; what would happen when the
novelty wore off.

The phone rang. It was a house in Looe, the town on
the mainland directly facing them. Could they possibly
deliver their pizza by boat?

"We had one a week ago," explained the woman on
the other end of the line, "and I just can't stop thinking
about it."

Polly and Marisa looked at each other.

"It'll be freezing," said Marisa. "I don't think so."

"The price of the boat . . ." said Polly.

"I know," said the woman. "But it's REALLY good
pizza."

"We need drones," said Marisa as Polly put the phone
down.

"Don't get ahead of yourself," said Polly, smiling.
"Drones, really."

"Not really."

"Okay," said Polly. "Sorry. Sleep deprived."

"You really should . . ."

"I know, I know. I will take a night off when—"

"Three margaritas and two pepperoni please!"

It was Jayden.

"I can't get you working in here," said Polly. "You'll
eat all the stock. Have you got guests in?"

Jayden had the grace to look a bit embarrassed.

"Yes," he said, unconvincingly. "We totally do."

"How's married life?" said Polly.

"Well, I think we're finally getting to the stage where we're comfortable with each other," said Jayden, who had always been in awe of his pretty young bride, Florrie.

"Don't get too comfortable," said Polly. Although it was a losing battle trying to stop Jayden's natural physique becoming completely spherical. It was simply how he was built.

When he had been a fisherman, a long time ago—and hated it to the very depths of his being—he had managed to stay in reasonable shape with the intense physical labor. Working in a bakery was simply not the same as being on a fishing boat in a force five for thirty-six hours into the eye of the storm.

Not having to gut fish made Jayden happy every single day of his life. His sole deepest fear was that Florrie would get on *Bake Off*—she was an excellent patissier—and leave him for Paul Hollywood. Apart from that he led the life of almost total contentment, the kind won by contemplating every day how you have escaped a terrible fate.

"I think being comfortable is very nice," he said, and Polly grinned and gave him a stonking staff discount then thought better of it and waved him away without asking for anything—she paid him what she could afford, but it was little enough.

"No, don't do that," moaned Jayden.

"No, I mean it. Take them. You're opening up tomorrow and I'm having a lie-in."

"Nooo," he said. "Because I love this pizza. And if you don't let me pay I can never come back as often as I

want to have pizza. I can never come back again otherwise I'll be the big elephant who ate all the pizza profits
and that will make me so sad. Pleeeease."

Polly took his money, even though she felt bad doing it.

Chapter Fifty-five

The night flew, Marisa noticed, in the same way her old job had done. When you worked with people you liked, and you were busy, it wasn't really hard, it was kind of . . . well, not fun, you still had to clean the oven. But that endless, slow dragging sense of time that had been sitting on her while she'd been at home; the sense of waste that grief and illness had given her. That had gone.

One night they'd even brought Nonna down on the laptop to see the ovens. She had of course sniffed that they weren't using wood burners even when Marisa attempted to explain that they weren't fitted, it would take hours to get them up to temperature and there weren't any trees for miles around. She had nonetheless seen a smile creasing that old face, along with something that looked like pride.

"So my Lucia goes all the way England, and you work in a takeaway," she said. "That is the way of it."

And Marisa hadn't minded the sting in her words at all.

"I like it," she said. And she wasn't lying.

"Don't tell your mother," said Nonna, and Marisa winced. That was the one piece of her life that was still broken, that still hurt when she probed it, like a cracked tooth.

But she still had a half-smile on her face swinging uphill on a mild warm night, clear overhead, a few stars popping out, thinking of Jayden and his commitment to the pizza place (Polly's Pizza it had become known as, swiftly and inevitably) being so strong he'd insisted on handing over money when it wasn't even called for. She was so busy, she almost forgot to agonize about the note.

Well. It was gone now and there was nothing to be done about it.

It was only when she turned into the little road, happily enjoying the scents of the night air, the calling of the gulls shearing out across the water—although of course when local people complained about their rat-like qualities she absolutely publicly agreed with them—that she saw him; his large form perched on her balcony, outlined in the moonlight.

He stood up when he saw her, spread his arms wide, and Marisa suddenly got a terrible pang. Imagine if he was waiting for her, every night, just waiting to welcome her home. Imagine if that was her life.

She thought of Huckle—he and Polly must have been married for ages—desperate to get his wife back home again. Even of bloody Caius unable to live without his little coterie. Sometimes it felt like she was the only person by herself. She had been focusing so much on just getting herself out of the house that she hadn't stopped to consider what it would be like having nobody waiting for her when she came back to it.

Was he cross? She didn't think so. Not this time. Surely. Surely? Her heart started to beat a little faster in her chest.

Chapter Fifty-six

"Marisa!" He stood up. "There you are." He frowned. "You work every night now?"

"Not Sundays. I can't believe you haven't eaten our pizza."

He patted his stomach sadly.

"I think pizza is not for me."

"You'll like mine."

"That is exactly what I am thinkink is my problem—I will like it too much. BUT! You did not do this."

He was waving the note.

She smiled. "I did."

He shook his head. "But! Is amazink!"

"Oh, it's not . . . could you read it?"

"Of course!"

She had done her best; decorated the paper with leaves and birds.

Плеасе плаы
ин тхе евенингс

And it said, simply, "Please play at night."

"You are never here at night." His face fell as he held the beautiful card. "So you don't have to hear my terrible noise."

"No, just that you can . . ."

He shrugged. "But I have nothing to play."

"What do you mean? You can play anything!"

His head tilted to one side.

"I mean this . . . it is so beautiful."

"No, forget about that," she said. "What do you mean you have nothing to play?"

"My music . . . it was lost in the mud . . ."

"But don't you have copies?"

Gradually she realized, and saw at last why he had been so upset.

"That was *your* music . . . you wrote it?" she said. "Of

course! You are trying to be a composer! Oh my God. I am so sorry."

He shrugged.

"Oh God," she said. "So when I was complaining . . . that was your own compositions?"

"I am very unsuccessful composer."

Marisa closed her eyes. "For that girl?"

He shrugged.

"And you lost your music. Oh God, I am so sorry. I am *so* sorry."

"I think it was way of saying, Alexei, no more composink for you. Is no good. She does not love you, nobody loves your music."

"No," said Marisa. "It was me! I was so sad and I couldn't bear it and . . . maybe I just didn't know how to listen."

"You hated it," he said sadly.

"I know nothing about music!" said Marisa. "I think we've established that."

"No, your first note was right."

"My first note was a mess. This note . . ."

Alexei looked at it and smiled. "Your spellink is many wrong."

"Well, I'm very sorry about that."

He picked it up and turned away. But Marisa was so tired of being misunderstood, and so sorry for what had happened.

"Have you eaten?"

"You are hungry?"

She smiled.

"I don't eat pizza every day."

He frowned.

"But it is my turn to feed you. Come, come."

She wasn't tired, just a little enervated. She wanted

to go in, very much, wanted them to be friends again. "Going into that strange man's house late at night is a very very bad idea," she could hear her nonna sitting on her shoulder.

Okay, she thought. Well, if she was all mucky and sticky from work, she couldn't possibly misbehave herself again. So.

She glanced at her watch.

"I mean, if you don't have anything in . . . it's late."

"It is late. But yes, I have food for you. Come!"

He looked nervous as she lightly climbed his blue wooden steps, her hair swinging in her ponytail, that had got messier and messier as the night had worn on. She was pink-faced from walking up the hill, and any makeup she'd applied earlier had long worn off.

She looked pink-cheeked, and busy and young. Her mother would have suggested about a foot or so of thick black eyeliner, but she looked rather lovely as she was.

Inside the house, with its usual ramshackle collection of books and papers and musical instruments and tasseled coverings on the tables, and lamps everywhere, there was no smell of cooking, Marisa noticed, as she walked over to wash her hands without even thinking, because of course the sink was in exactly the same spot as in her own apartment.

"Oh!" she said.

"No, is fine." He gestured. The soap smelled good, of almonds.

"Do you actually have food?" mused Marisa looking around.

"Yes! Sit!"

As she sat down he went into the fridge.

"No vodka," said Marisa immediately. He popped his huge head back round the side of the fridge.

"*Nyet. Nyet* vodka for you," he said mock severely and then, to Marisa's extreme surprise, brandished a bottle of Champagne with a label shaped like a tri-pointed shield.

She blinked. "Seriously?"

He looked at it. "I think so."

"But that's . . . that's Champagne."

"Yes!" he said. "Very important."

He popped the bottle without asking her, and Marisa felt a little fizzy herself, just at the very idea. Champagne! It reminded her of so many happy times, happy days, excitements, parties, weddings, everything that seemed to have vanished for her recently. Hearing the pop—and the fizz, and the mumbled growling from Alexei as it went all over him and he couldn't stop it—felt like it was unleashing something inside her. She found herself smiling and clapping her hands together. He realized how seldom he had seen her smile. He bit his lip to stop himself grinning too enthusiastically and poured them two glasses, bringing hers over.

She looked at it. "I have done nothing to deserve this," she said.

Alexei shook his head.

"Look at what you have done," he said, quietly, those brown eyes as steady and thoughtful as the rest of him was full of motion and energy.

"The little girl who hides and is silent like tiny mouse. And now she work, she laugh, she moves. She makes most beautiful notes. Of course of COURSE we must have Champagne."

She looked at him, and they swapped a look then, and her heart beat a little faster, as they raised their glasses.

"*Za zdarovye*," she said.

"*Salute*."

And they looked at each other steadily as they drank,

and the Champagne exploded inside Marisa like fire-works, and suddenly she felt herself tingling all over.

The toaster pinged, and he quickly went over to it. His huge hands fumbled with a tea towel, and he pulled out four slices of toast.

Marisa grinned. "We're having toast?"

"What is wrong with toasts?"

"Champagne and toast?"

She thought about it."

"Well, maybe . . ." she said.

"NOT JUST TOASTS!"

He jumped up and opened his fridge and pulled out a little glass pot of white stuff. Then he grabbed some grass-like shoots and a pair of scissors. He put these down on the table.

Then finally, reverently, he pulled out a tin and a tiny mother-of-pearl spoon.

Marisa's eyes went wide.

"No," she said. "Is that what I think it is?"

He held it up to one of the lights. The gold tin shimmered.

"*Da*, of course," he grinned. "My friends they do not forget me."

He shook the large tin of caviar happily.

"SO! We have *smetana*! We have toasts! We have . . ."

He looked at the chives balefully, then waved his hands, as if the concept of even trying to learn the word would be forever uninteresting to him.

"Green thinks!"

And reverently, he opened the tin.

"I think I should tell you," said Marisa, "I haven't tried caviar before."

His eyes were completely startled.

"But you are cook! You care about food!"

"I know, I know," said Marisa. "We don't really eat it in Italy. And . . ."

To say that she had always thought it looked weird and slimy seemed frankly a ridiculous thing to say. What a coward she was.

She heard that little voice inside her head calling herself a coward and clamped down hard on it. She was not being a coward tonight.

"And?"

"I . . ."

She felt herself go pink.

"No reason. I was a bit squeamish about it."

"I do not know this word. You mean squashink of eggs?"

"Something like that," said Marisa.

"Okay. It is okay to squash them. There are no babies inside eggs. Just like chicken egg. But much much much more delicious."

He deftly spread the white stuff—sour cream—on the thinly sliced toast, snipped off a few ends of the fresh chives, then dolloped a large amount of the tiny black marbles in the middle of it. Then he proffered it to her.

"Um," said Marisa.

"Is very very good with Champagne."

Marisa took a swallow of her drink. The Champagne was so delicious. Alexei was watching her and she found herself giggling and unable to steel herself to eat.

He held up his hands.

"Ah, no. I have got it wrong for Marisa. Always I get it wrong for Marisa."

"What do you mean?"

"I play too loud, I shout, I do not say good morning, I get cross with you." He looked at the floor. "I do not always haff words for you, Marisa."

His voice had gone very low.

"And the language I speak you do not hear."

He glanced at his piano.

"And the language you speak we do not share."

With this he looked at the food. Then he looked back at her, sadly.

"I wish I knew how to talk to you, Marisa."

Marisa was suddenly flaming red; embarrassed and confused and completely at a loss. This wasn't in the Cognitive Behavioral Therapy handbook. Nothing like this. Nobody had ever spoken to her like this before, ever.

In utter confusion, she popped the toast straight into her mouth before she could think of another thing.

The saltiness of the fish contrasted with the sharp creaminess of the sour cream, the fresh shock of the chives—and of course the bread was Polly's from the bakery, so even the toast was absolutely perfect. Her eyes shot open.

"Well," she said, looking completely shocked.

Alexei had been staring at the floor after his long speech but now he looked up at her.

She swallowed, covered her hand with her mouth, went to take another bite.

"This is . . . this is amazing," she said.

His face cracked into the broadest grin and he immediately started spreading more sour cream on the toast, and heaving big lumps of caviar with the tiny, delicate mother-of-pearl spoon.

"Yes!" he said, pouring her more Champagne. "It is wonderful!"

"Oh, that was good," she said, after half the caviar tin had been devoured, and Alexei had looked at it regretfully and Marisa had said, yes, but think how happy you will be tomorrow that you left some and he listened to that and nodded at the sense of it, and they refilled their glasses, and she sat back, quietly on the sofa, her shoes off, her feet tucked underneath her.

His eyes were thoughtful, watching her. "You are always so quiet."

"I am so quiet because all the voices in my head were shouting at me at once all the time, anytime I tried to do anything. I didn't have room to make my own noise."

The Champagne had loosened her tongue. But it was also that way of his again; the easy slow way he had of tilting his head, of listening and weighing and measuring every word he heard. Perhaps that was being a musician, she thought; having very strong listening skills, so that you heard not just the words but the spaces between the words.

"I was trying to hide from the voices that were so loud . . . that told me every day about everything I couldn't do and every way in which I was failing and no good and . . ."

She looked into the glass.

"Well, it never worked. And I am so sorry I was so cruel about your music. It felt like something else shouting at me. Even though I know it wasn't."

He looked at her. "It must haff been so hard for you."

"What do you hear in your head?" she asked. "Genuinely curious."

He blinked. "I do not think of it."

"No," said Marisa. "I suppose healthy people never have to."

He was playing with the tiny mother-of-pearl spoon

in his huge hands, turning it over and over as he contemplated the question in his slow way.

Then he grinned suddenly and she noticed he was tapping the spoon on the table top.

"Well," he said. "I suppose I think in my piano. So! If I hear thunder I think, well, crash crash that is Rachmaninoff, and if I hear rain I think, well, Debussy is here, he is playing in the raindrops, and when I hear a police car I think, well, modern music is full of challenges . . ."

Marisa looked at him. "I like you," she said, simply.

"That is good," he said. "Truly or because I live next door?"

"Truly," said Marisa. She laughed. "My grandmother wants to meet you."

He looked from side to side.

"She is livink here? She is even quieter than you? She is in cupboard?"

"No!" said Marisa. "We Skype. Like, a lot, like most days. She's in Italy."

"Oh!" He nodded. "I hear you one night! Talking."

He smiled, rather roguishly.

"Is much noise. You must stop. I write note."

Marisa stuck her tongue out at him. He raised his arms.

"Well," he said. "She can meet me. You want her to meet me? Now?"

"It's late! In Italy it's very late."

Mind you, thought Marisa, her nonna stayed up half the night, she knew that already.

"I want your babushka to approve. Is important. Family."

He dug under a large pile of papers until he found what he was looking for: a large old black laptop that looked a zillion years old.

"You can call her!"

Then he opened it and Marisa stared at the neatly laid out keyboard—all in Cyrillic.

"Ah," she said. Alexei frowned.

"Ah. I see problem."

"I could get mine. This is ridiculous!" said Marisa, giggling.

"Go fetch computer grandmother!"

Marisa slipped back into her own house, gulping the cold air eagerly as she did so. Everything seemed to be moving very quickly. She was slightly drunk, this was probably why it seemed like a good idea but . . . She leaned against the door. Oh my God. Was this the stupidest thing . . .

She looked around. Her spotless house that hadn't changed an iota since she'd moved into it. Compared to Alexei's warm, messy, human, personal space, it felt clinical; empty. Cold.

Tonight, she didn't want to feel cold.

She checked her bra quickly. No. Don't be stupid.

She looked at her face in the mirror though. Her cheeks were rosy pink, her eyes were sparkling from the Champagne. She looked . . .

She looked all right, she told herself firmly. If she was talking to a friend instead of herself she would be so honest and so kind, and say such nice things and tell her she looked lovely.

"You look lovely," she breathed.

She didn't change her bra. She did use a bit of mouth-wash.

Then she grabbed the laptop, her fingers slightly shaky.

Just as she did so, she heard from next door the gentlest, sweetest melody playing. It sounded like a lullaby, soft and simple, but repeating, the tune twisting round and back on itself, changing and becoming deeper and more melancholic, or lighter and frothier, every time it moved up and down the piano. It was completely hypnotic and quite lovely.

She was about to head back, but before she did she leaned, full length, back against the wall, spreading out her arms and her fingers. She could feel the vibrations of the music through the plaster, feel it move through her whole body. She felt, suddenly, filled with it, consumed with it, the voices in her head quelled, simply following the tumbling cascading melodies reaching out to her, in a perfect moment of knowing that all she had to do was to walk two steps down and two steps up and she could fall into the house and the arms of the man who could make that sound on a piano; and if he could make something so pure and so beautiful out of an old piano, what on earth could he make out of her?

Chapter Fifty-seven

She pushed at the open door, softly, trying not to disturb him. He turned round immediately, his hands leaving the keys.

"No," she said quietly. "Don't stop."

He kept staring at her, unable to express how much those were words he wanted to hear. There was no music in front of him.

"You wrote that?" she said quietly.

He shrugged. "I write it now."

"That's amazing."

He smiled wryly. "I make it pretty for you."

"You don't have to do that!"

". . . because you are pretty."

She held up the laptop.

"Are you sure?"

He stopped playing then.

"Babushka? Of course. I want approved."

"Yes."

She opened the computer and they sat on the sofa far apart, then as they realized they couldn't both get in the camera at the same time, they squished up closer. Marisa was suddenly very aware of his leg next to hers; his thigh felt enormous. All of him was so very solid. She resisted a sudden, very strong instinct to touch his leg. But she very gently felt the pressure of his against hers; returned it, gently. Even this, the briefest of touches, of connections between them, sent her heart rate sky high; made her tingle all over; unable to be conscious of anything else happening.

Her hands fumbled opening the laptop; she needed two shots at remembering her password even as he politely averted his eyes, which made her giggle.

Finally, leaning over him—and conscious, at all moments, of every single thing about him—she got onto Skype, and looked up to see if the little green light indicated her grandmother was online.

"It is *very* late," she said.

He looked at her.

"Ah, you are right," he said. "It is such a shame you must go home."

"ALEXEI!"

He grinned. "Family is very important," he said. "If she haff not approve . . ."

Marisa hit him with a cushion.

He looked at her, and gently ran his huge hand down her face. She shivered. Then he took it away.

"I look smart?"

She laughed. "No," she said truthfully. His jumper had holes, his hair was disheveled and needed cutting again. But she liked the way he looked. His solidity; his unmoving strength; the directness in him.

The Skype number rang on.

"She is sleeping, I am hanging up," said Marisa. "It's nearly midnight there."

Normally this was nothing to her nonna, who ate at nine p.m., but Marisa had generally gone to bed long before now, and Marisa didn't want to startle her.

But no: the screen blinked and winked in. Alexei

quickly ran his thick fingers through his tangled hair and rubbed his beard as if suddenly regretting having one but realizing it was too late to change now.

Marisa suddenly panicked. This was ridiculous. It wasn't like she was going to sleep with him. But her grandmother would think that she was! All she wanted to do was . . . well. She wanted to kiss him. And as a joke it had got completely out of hand and now she desperately didn't want to . . . she made a decision.

"I'm going to hang up."

"Why?" said Alexei.

She turned to him in a sudden flash.

"Because," she said, smiling at him, "maybe I want to do something with you I wouldn't want to do in front of my grandmother . . ."

"*Pronto?*"

The voice was crackling and weak coming through the computer and they both jumped apart, even though they had barely been touching. Marisa closed her eyes.

"Nonna?"

Her grandmother wasn't her normal tidy self. Her hair was out of its tight braid and loose around her face and she was unfocused and confused.

"Nonna, did I wake you?"

But her grandmother was in her day clothes, not her nightwear. The lights were on in the kitchen. She just looked bemused and dazed.

"Who is that?"

"Nonna, it's Marisa, it's me."

Alexei frowned. "She is okay?"

"Are you all right?"

Marisa leaned forward to the screen. "I didn't mean to bother you so late, I'm so sorry."

Her grandmother shook her head. "Is it late? I don't know. I think . . ." She looked confused. "I think I fell?"

"Oh my God," said Marisa. "Are you all right?"

"I was on the ground and then . . . then I heard ringing . . ."

She turned around confusedly, as if looking to see where she was in the room, and to her absolute horror Marisa saw a dark patch covering the back of her grandmother's hair, which if you looked closely enough through the small screen was sticky with blood.

Chapter Fifty-eight

It is, Marisa learned, impossible to access a foreign country's 999 system. That was the first thing. The second thing was having to wake up her mother who genuinely was asleep, and whose voice of panic—what is it?—would have irritated Marisa had it not been the correct response. Lucia went immediately to phone Ann Angela.

Marisa and Alexei kept the feed on, with Marisa talking to her nonna through it, getting her to sit down and not move, but to grab a towel for the bleeding.

Nonna was talking rubbish, garbled sentences that went round and round, and mixed Marisa up with Lucia all the time. At one point she squinted at Alexei, who was googling hospitals in the area but coming up with nothing, and, in a moment of sudden clarity said, *"Questo è l'uomo così grande?"*—This is the big man?—and Marisa leaned forward off the phone to the nearest hospital to say, "This is . . ." but her grandmother then suddenly burst into tears and Marisa got back on the phone to the *ospedale*.

They held hands, helpless on the other side of the world, Marisa keeping up a comforting stream of nonsense sounds to her grandmother, saying not to worry, not to fret, everything was going to be okay, and even as she did she felt her grandfather, closer than ever before, picking up her knee, rubbing it where she'd fallen over on a stone, holding her close and telling her everything was going to be okay, soothing her, making her feel like she was in the safest pair of arms in the world and passing the job on to her.

"You are going to be safe, *you are going to be okay,*" she said, over and over again. "*There you are, little one, everything is going to be all right, everything is going to be fine, my little one, my darling, my little mouse.*"

As her grandmother's panic gradually subsided she moved closer and closer to the screen, her eyes fixed on Marisa as if she was the only person there; as if she could reach out and touch her.

"*Help is coming, I promise, we are going to make it okay, it's going to be okay.*"

And Marisa felt the strength of her grandfather go through her; felt for sure and absolutely that she was speaking to herself, not just to her grandmother—that this was something she believed and something that was within her power.

"*Andrà tutto bene, andrà tutto bene.*"

And at last the ambulance men arrived.

They burst into the house, presumably simply knocking through the flimsy lock, if indeed her grandmother bothered to lock the door at all. It was quite frightening and Marisa wished she could see their faces—she could only see their middles—as they asked Nonna her name and what had happened.

"Hello!" she cried through the screen. "*Buona sera!*

Buona sera!" until an ambulance man bent down and listened as she went through a concise description of her grandmother's symptoms and where to find her medication. The man nodded and then gave her a smile.

"Signora, you have done very well," he said, rather flirtatiously. Or perhaps, reflected Marisa later, she had just not been talking to enough people, again. You could say what you liked about Alexei but he wasn't flirtatious. He was simply himself at all times, which was astoundingly attractive in its own way.

"If you hadn't called?" He expressively extended his arms. Marisa couldn't bear to think about it. She nodded and watched as the stretcher came in and her nonna, her great all-powerful nonna, was raised up on it so tiny she looked like a little child lying there, intensely fragile; so close to the screen, so very far away. Marisa found herself reaching out a hand to touch her, even though it was of course impossible.

When the door of the house in Italy had finally slammed shut, everything went very quiet. Alexei went to shut the computer screen, but she wouldn't let him. They had stayed online together so often. She couldn't bear it. She found it comforting to see the kitchen; the pots hanging on the walls, the old painted tiles, the plethora of ladles. The ambulance men hadn't shut off the laptop on her grandmother's side, and, as long as it was plugged in, the connection should hold. She wasn't going to cut hers off either. There was still a connection between them. She wouldn't let it go.

"I need to phone my mum again," she said. Alexei nodded and got up.

"You did very good," he said. "You did not panic, you did not get upset. You were exactly in the moment and exactly right. What I tell my students. You should talk to them! Do not think of self. Just think of what needs to be done."

"Thanks," said Marisa, barely listening. She looked up at him.

"It isn't . . . none of this is what I thought would happen."

"I think it is best good think that it did."

She nodded. "Oh God. I can't . . . if we hadn't . . ."

"Do not think like that."

"No."

She looked around.

"I think . . . I have to plug my laptop in. I think I'd better go home. I'll have to speak to Gino—that's my brother—and there's going to be lots to do."

"Are you sure you not want to stay here? I make tea? Help you?"

She was tempted but shook her head.

"No, it's . . . it's family stuff. I should be next door, get it sorted."

He nodded. "Well. I would say get some sleep but I do not think there is sleepink for you," he said. Then, gently, "I cancel my morning lessons."

"Oh no, don't do that."

"Too late," he said. And he led her to the door. And carefully, and for the very first time, wrapped his huge arms around her and gave her the biggest, gentlest sweetest hug. And she closed her eyes and leaned in to it, realizing it was so long—so long, such an endless, endless winter—since someone had hugged her like that, had had their arms fully and wholeheartedly around her, a deep embrace so close she felt joined to his body. She rested her head against his chest—she only came up so far—thinking how wonderfully comforting it would be to stay there forever.

"I shall keep candle burnink for your grandmother."

"Don't do that," said Marisa dreamily. "A fiery inferno is absolutely the last thing we need right now."

And she held on to the hug for longer than would have been normally seemly or even necessary but it was necessary, and Alexei was steady and gentle and didn't move or pull away, but happily stood with his arms around her, his huge hands stroking her shoulders in a comforting rhythm, his jumper growing wet with her tears.

Chapter Fifty-nine

Nonna had a busy night. She had given herself a nasty bang on the head and they were doing MRIs and looking for brain damage and other difficulties.

Marisa too had not paused. Finally, at two a.m. she had accepted that nobody was going to be able to know any more that night and had tried to get to sleep but anxiety and Champagne were churning around her gut and she didn't have a hope of dropping off. She stared into the starry night, praying to her grandmother's God that he would spare her even though she couldn't help thinking that her grandmother's God would probably want to call her home as much as she did.

At five thirty dawn started creeping in over the sea to the left of her window, and the stars started to fade and disappear. As if somehow tacitly giving her body permission, now that night was over, insomnia loosened its grip and she fell into a deep sleep, not waking till well after ten, less thick in the head than she thought she would have been and extraordinarily grateful to Alexei for postponing his lessons that morning; even more grateful when she went to the balcony to open the window, to see placed on the table and chair outside a croissant and a glass of orange juice.

"Thank you," she shouted out, but got no reply; the

croissant was hard, he must have fetched it from Polly's hours ago.

Nonetheless, she gnawed on it and made herself a coffee, glancing at the empty room, now bathed in sunlight, and calling her mother, who was, understandably, perpetually engaged.

Lucia was packing, and Gino was heading down from Switzerland.

"She won't need you," Lucia was saying, trying to sound positive, but coming over as brisk and making assumptions about Marisa that made her bristle. "She might not even recognize us."

Her mother sounded nervous, of all things.

"Are you . . . I mean. Are you better?"

Marisa was surprised. That her mother would even acknowledge her illness.

"I . . . I am definitely getting better," she said.

"You don't have to come," said Lucia. "If it's too hard. It's not like you're close."

"We are quite close actually," said Marisa. "We've been talking on Skype."

"Your grandmother on Skype?" said Lucia. "Darling, are you absolutely sure? She thinks women priests are sent by the devil. God knows what she'd make of Skype."

"Mum, that's how we found her, remember?"

"I thought she'd just got startled by the ringing noise of her big square telephone."

"Well, no, that's not what happened."

Her mother sighed. "Well, I'm flying out of Bristol today to Genoa," she said. "If you can make that flight? It's in two hours."

"You didn't even ask me," said Marisa.

"Darling, she's a grandmother you haven't seen for ages, never particularly got along with and barely mention, and you, as you keep telling me, have a serious disease which means you can't leave the house or be with your family! You can hardly blame me for this one!"

"No," said Marisa. "You're right, I can't. Have a safe trip. Call me as soon as you're there."

She hung up and looked at the computer thoughtfully.

Even the airport website made her feel terribly anxious. The thought of all those people . . . the queues, the anxiety you could always taste in the air at airports, of panic and mislaid documents and screaming children and worry and . . .

She felt her breathing speed up. What if she got there and Nonna was dead? What if she didn't leave now and was too late? But if she went now, what if she had a panic attack on the plane and they had to land it halfway over or not take off and everyone would be so furious and scream at her and she wouldn't get there anyway, she'd have such a meltdown it would be impossible to continue . . .

She found it hard to breathe and went back out onto the balcony again, trying to take in big gulps of air, trying to think of her happy place. But then her happy place was on the other end of a plane and that was blocking everything else out.

She put her head between her knees like Anita had told her; concentrated on her breaths, in through the nose, hold, out through the mouth, on taking her brain somewhere else, but she couldn't get a grip, could feel her throat tighten and gulp, her leg jerk pointlessly outward, because this wasn't a step, it wasn't a step that had taken her outside, and down the hill, and into the village and into a job. Getting on a plane by herself to go to another country was a crazy idea, a huge enormous leap, an impossible concept.

As she did so, the door next door opened and closed and she could tell by the pacing across the floor that it was young Edin and, suddenly, scales were ringing out, solid and identical, up and down the keyboard, rigid and unchanging, in a tight clear rhythm, and as they went—doh ray me fah so lah te doh, she remembered that much from *The Sound of Music*—and back again, she felt herself starting to breathe in time with the notes, an in-breath on doh ray me fah so, then holding it, then the same as it came down again.

Slowly, gradually, following the music tightly, she found herself bringing it back and calming down. He started to play something light and quiet, as if all of his fingers were dancing of their own accord, with a sweet joy. It sounded so incredibly easy, and yet it could not be: the idea that ten separate fingers were doing ten separate things made her head explode.

She could even hear Alexei humming along almost despite himself, in a gentle rhythm that mirrored the beating of her own heart as it gradually slowed and re-found its natural equilibrium, and if she had been able to think further she would wonder if Alexei had asked Edin to play exactly this piece for exactly this reason, and she would have been right, for Alexei believed in the sacred power of Bach in the way that her grandmother believed in the sacred power of the Virgin Mary.

Chapter Sixty

An excellent solution struck Marisa forcibly. She had money now; everything she was earning from the pizzeria she was just salting away; she had nothing to spend it on but rent and food and nowhere she wanted to go, not really, except for next door. So she could buy the plane ticket.

And it was nearly the summer holidays; he could take time off.

And, assuming everything went well—and she couldn't for a second allow herself to believe otherwise—she could tend to her grandmother but also show him her Imperia, show him the long walkways where the boats came in, and the little playground where the children played, and the funicular railway that had so enchanted them when they were young. They could sit in the beachside cafés, under striped umbrellas, and eat *fritto misto* and drink Prosecco. It would be . . . it would be lovely. It was a bold ask, but there were spare rooms in her grandmother's house, she wouldn't be suggesting anything untoward, of course. Just friends. They could be friends going. She thought again of the feeling of his large body against hers the previous evening.

And he could lead her through the airport, through the

crowds; he could be with her, at her back as she stood in the queues and fussed through the vast wide-open white spaces of the airport, filled with people and panic and fuss and personnel and loading on to the flight and the anxiety of the flight and if she was on the right one and if she was going to the right place . . .

He would be there for all of that, solid, unflappable, kind. And it wouldn't be so bad. And when they got there, and everything was fine—everything would be *fine*, she told herself. *Fine*—then. Then . . . then it would be lovely.

She had to choose her moment. She checked her messages, called her brother who was taking a train from Switzerland. He sounded concerned, but not distraught; he was going to comfort their mother, she discerned, more than being desperately concerned for Nonna herself. There would, Gino assured her, be a million-billion cousins and second cousins descending on the sleepy rural hospital.

"I'll just call everyone Anna-Maria," he said. "It's bound to be one or the other."

"I'm not sure that's helpful," said Marisa.

"You sound much better," said her brother, cheerily. They hadn't seen each other since that awful Christmas, when he'd come to hers for a couple of days on his way up to their mother's and she'd sat in her room watching TV and not paying him much attention and he'd felt bad for her, but couldn't cheer her up in any way and couldn't get her to go to her mum's for Christmas so he'd gone himself. Given it was her mother's first Christmas without her own father, and she was having it without her only daughter as well, Marisa winced now to think how much she had ruined everything. But Gino was an airy, laid-back personality—like her granddad, whereas she was, she realized, more and more, much more, like her nonna—and didn't bear a grudge.

"I . . . I think. Well. I was. Definitely getting better."

"Moving to the middle of nowhere! I can't believe it helped."

"Me neither."

"You making pizza though. I thought the whole point of being second generation was that you joined the professional classes."

He used a mock reproving tone that made her laugh. He always put on a posh voice; from when they had both started school and talked in English all the time to irritate their parents. He had done it as a joke. As he'd grown up and gone to university in England, it had kind of stuck. She had even met groups of his friends who called him "Gene," which was extraordinary.

"I know," she said. "Nonna is horrified, thinks I've gone way downmarket from working in an office."

"Well, I think what you're doing is amazing," said Gino. "The worst mistake I ever made was to live in the German bit of Switzerland and not the Italian one. The food, *che schifo*."

Marisa smiled. To be having an easy conversation with Gino again was wonderful.

"So . . ." His voice was deceptively casual. "You're coming down? Mamma says you and Nonna had got really close."

Marisa took a breath. "I . . . I'm just going to . . . organize a few things. But yes."

"Great," said Gino. "I'm really hoping she'll recover. The second she sees us. And then: the beach!"

"Gino!"

"What? I'm an optimist. She's tough as old boots. Plus, there's still snow up here."

Chapter Sixty-one

It wasn't *entirely* cynical, to rustle up a plate of antipasto, roasting some sweet peppers and onions in the oven with the best oil, slicing the salami thinly, chopping squares of tiny salty white goat's cheese. She toasted yesterday's bread, which still turned up golden, and spread it thick with salty butter, then added an ice-cold Peroni—it was the most beautiful day outside—and went up and stood at her flung-open balcony door. It didn't take long.

"How is she, your nonna? She better, she fine?"

"Here." She went to hand over the tray. He looked at it and frowned.

"Take it! It'll drop down the cliff."

"She is so well you can make me lunch?"

He took it in one big paw, still eyeing her suspiciously with those narrow brown eyes.

"I have a proposition for you," said Marisa, nervously. Then she was cross with herself, she should at least have waited till he'd drunk his beer. Sure enough, those disconcerting eyes looked at her steadily.

"Huh," he said.

"Um," she said, staring at the floor. "I was thinking. Maybe . . . um. I thought. You might like to . . . take a trip with me. To Italy? It's so beautiful there."

Her face flushed.

"I have heard it is very beautiful," he said gravely.

"Have you been?"

"To Milan, yes . . ." His voice sounded faraway and Marisa cursed herself for asking. His girlfriend was probably dancing at La Scala or something.

"But not the Riviera?"

He shook his head.

"You'll love it."

She pointed to a dark cloud on the horizon. "And look. The forecast for the next week is horrible. And there are lots of bedrooms in my grandmother's house and I can buy your ticket and it's . . . I mean, the food is amazing and . . ."

She realized she was gabbling and this had come out completely the wrong way, even more so as he didn't change his calm restful expression. He put down his beer.

"Marisa," he said. "You want me to come with you to visit your grandmother?"

"Um. Yes."

"You should just ask me."

Marisa blinked. "Would you come with me to visit my grandmother?"

There was a long pause.

"No," he said.

She looked at him, stricken, aware that the hurt and sadness would be showing in her face.

"Fine," she said, making to turn away.

"Marisa!" he said. "Wait!"

She half-turned back in case he was going to say he was only kidding but his face was as solemn as ever.

"It is hard," he said, "to go by yourself, yes? To get there?"

She nodded.

"And you think I will make it easier?"

She felt ashamed, that he had seen through her so clearly. He frowned.

"And then what? I go everywhere with you?"

"No!" said Marisa, feeling annoyed and ashamed. "I thought you might like to come with me."

"Very much," he said. "I would like nothing better than to be eating ice cream on a beach with you, Marisa, *kotyonok*."

"But you won't."

He looked pained. "You are doing . . . look at how well you are doing. When I meet you you are terrified. You are mouse. And now, you work with Polly, you go out, you make friend . . ."

Marisa couldn't bear to ask him if he meant himself.

"You are doing well. You can do it. But you have to do it yourself. It is no use having . . ."

He mimed something which she didn't get.

"You are so terrible at miming," she said, swallowing a lump in her throat.

"Things for helpink your legs."

"Crutches."

Her heart fell. Was that really how he saw her? Last night? Truly?

"You need to go be with your family," he said. "You have come so far. You cannot stop now."

"But—"

"I have pupils with exams, I have end of term concerts, I have busy things to be doink also."

She nodded.

"But mostly, I think this is for you. Can you do it?"

His eyes looked at her.

"I . . . I don't know."

"I do."

Chapter Sixty-two

Marisa stormed off the balcony. Her phone was ringing before she'd even closed her bedroom door, before she was ready to collapse in storms of tears.

It was Gino.

"Sweets," he said, "we think . . . we think if you want to come, you should come now."

He said it calmly and Marisa couldn't do anything other than thank him and hang up.

With trembling fingers she checked on flights. There was a late flight to Genoa from Bristol. Without allowing herself to think about it, she booked it.

There were plenty of seats free. He could have come, she thought. He could have. If he'd cared about her.

So all his words last night, all the cozying up to one another. It didn't mean anything. He was still heartbroken for some ridiculous girl she could never match up to and she was literally the girl next door. And vice versa.

And now she would have to do this herself.

She called Polly, who was both dismayed and instantly sympathetic, and explained she'd be away for a couple of days, but she'd forgo the money so she could get Jayden in—he spent enough time there anyway, he could easily handle the dough, and she'd make an extra load of sauce that afternoon they could freeze.

Beyond that, she couldn't think.

Polly was full of sympathy—and concern too, for losing her, plus worry. Remembering that timid mess who had shown up all these months before.

"Are you okay going to an airport and getting on a plane and stuff?" she said, which nearly made Marisa balk again. "Can't you get the GP to prescribe you anything? Like a sedative?"

"I'm too anxious: they don't really work on me," admitted Marisa. "I work myself into such a state worrying they're going to knock me out and I'll go crazy or fall asleep on the wrong plane or have to get removed, that they don't really do what they're supposed to do."

"Oh goodness," said Polly. "What about a gin and tonic then?"

"Same deal," said Marisa. "So scared it'll make me crazy it makes me crazy."

"I am so sorry about your grandmother," said Polly. "You always speak about her so much."

"Just because . . ." Marisa's voice cracked a little. "She's normally so annoying."

Polly smiled. "Do you need a lift? Huckle can take you to Exeter when the tide comes down."

Marisa had been about to say no, but realized that actually every last piece of help she could get would be good in this situation.

"Yes, please," she said. "Are you sure he wouldn't mind? The train fare is more than the flight."

Polly snorted. "It would be. No. He won't mind."

She didn't add, although she could have, that Huckle's gratefulness to Marisa was boundlessly huge.

The twins had to come, of course, and were delighted by this turn of events; they didn't get a lot of trips in the car.

Not only did they get to squabble over one filthy and very badly cracked iPad in the back seat—they had begged Marisa to "borrow" her phone, being canny, before Huckle sternly told them to button it—but there was the promise of that impossibly exotic thing, the McDonald's Happy Meal on the way home. Therefore they both decided to sing the entire way, leaving Huckle and Marisa not much space for talking, which Marisa didn't mind. She looked out of the window, trying not to feel her anxiety grow as Mount Polbearne grew small in the side mirror behind her, touching distance, then gone. She wanted to reach out, run back, but she couldn't.

"You gonna be all right?" said Huckle, in his sunny way.

"I think so," said Marisa. "No. Yes. *Yes.* I can do this."

"If it helps," said Huckle, "nobody likes airports. Everybody hates them. Everyone's feeling the same as you, just on a slightly different level."

Marisa looked at him.

"Is that true?"

"Of course. Hellish places."

Marisa looked at her hands.

"That does kind of help, actually," she said.

"There you go. Also, you get a run-up."

"What do you mean?"

"Well, you walked down to the bakery. Then you got in a car. Then you'll be getting on a train. You're working your way up in steps. Plane is just the next bit."

"You're a very helpful man," said Marisa.

"Good," said Huckle. "Now could you invent a honey pizza, please? Just to help things along."

"There is a cheese and honey pizza! With pine nuts!" said Marisa.

"Is there?" said Huckle. "What's it like?"

"Revolting," said Marisa. "I mean, if you think that's a drawback."

"Okay," said Huckle, as Daisy and Avery sang a loud and extremely rude song off the radio. "Well, I might have to think about it. Do you know how long you'll be away?"

Marisa shook her head shortly. Neither of them wanted to state the truth: until they knew the outcome, either way.

"I wouldn't mind if Polly stopped doing pizza for a couple of weeks," said Huckle. "She needs rest."

Marisa nodded. "She does. Also think of how much pent-up demand there'll be when I get back."

Huckle looked at her and smiled.

"Well, look at you, all optimistic and stuff. I think you're going to be okay."

They pulled up outside the station which the twins mistook for the drive-through and started shouting about chicken nuggets.

"Thank you," said Marisa. Inside the car had felt safe and private and contained. Outside, the world was bustling and busy and nothing like the quiet of Mount Polbearne at all, and full of people shouldering their way through normal life, whatever that was. It was undeniably unnerving.

Huckle hefted her wheelie suitcase out of the boot and watched her wheel off into the crowd, worried about her, and slightly worried about his wife if they never saw her again.

Chapter Sixty-three

She very nearly didn't make it. It was the smell of the airport; that mix of booze and anxiety and diesel and duty-free perfume: all sorts of things bubbling up to fuel her nervousness.

It felt so familiar; the desire to press herself against the wall, to render herself invisible. There was comfort in it, somehow, the old familiar panic; the comfort of the familiar even as she knew it was coming, a storm pulling up around her, a tornado, and she was standing directly in its path, her breath growing shorter, her hands trembling with the inevitability of everything she couldn't do, of all the way she had yet to go, of how very, very difficult it is to change, meaningfully, to change yourself, to get away from what is comfortable to you; all of it is unspeakably difficult, to step out with the sandworms, and she didn't want to. She'd rather take the punishment beating of the panic attack, even as she leaned against the wall, felt her vision clouding over.

No. No. She wouldn't. She wouldn't. She couldn't just wait to be engulfed in this chest-squeezing, appalling thing she thought might kill her at any moment She wasn't having it.

She clenched her fists and remembered what Anita and the book had said: try to control your breathing and think of your happy place. Your calm place. Remember it. Find it.

She shut her eyes tight. She could feel other people passing her, sense them looking at her, a girl in an airport corridor.

She focused hard on the sand between her toes, her grandfather's hand . . . but it wasn't enough. She couldn't feel it, couldn't block out the roaring in her ears, the sound of the PA announcer, the tightness in her chest, the beads of perspiration on her brow . . . It was so hot, why was it so hot, why was she so fricking hot? She felt she was going to pass out . . . everything was going a little wobbly around the edges, as if the world was zooming in and out of focus, and oh God was she going to faint, and she tried to focus on the beach, the beach with her grandfather, but all she could think of was her nonna being taken away in an ambulance, and sometimes people did die and—

"Excuse me, are you all right?"

It was a young, friendly-looking girl in glasses, Afro, backpack, looking concerned.

"Oh, thank you so much," Marisa managed to stutter out to a perfect stranger. "I'm fine . . . thanks for asking. I just hate flying."

The girl smiled. "If you hold on to the armrests really tightly, you know, that's what keeps the plane in the air."

Marisa felt herself trying to catch her breath.

"You're all right," said the girl. "Are you all right?"

Marisa closed her eyes again. And this time she didn't see the beach. Instead she saw a blue room, with a sea view, with lamps, and food, and a piano. She breathed in.

"Through your nose, that's it," said the girl. Marisa half-opened one eye.

"You seem to know a lot about this."

"Anxiety?" snorted the young woman. "Me and half the world, mate. You're hardly the only one."

And Marisa thought about all the people around her who had picked her up and dusted her off—even this complete stranger—and, somehow, came back to herself.

"Thank you," she said. "I'm all right. I'm all right."

"Course you are."

And the girl bobbed on her way up the line, as Marisa remembered a bottle of water in her bag and, gratefully, took a long pull, then sagged against the wall.

The long queue of people had mostly disappeared, everyone had got onto the plane, and she was about the last to go, a few people hanging around. She stood up and looked at the queue, and made a decision.

Chapter Sixty-four

It was after midnight when the plane landed in Italy, but the air was still warm in the airport. Gino was standing in the arrivals hall looking worried. When he saw her his face widened into a huge relieved smile.

"SIS! I didn't think you would . . ."

"I had help," said Marisa, thinking about it. "I had a lot of help. Really. A lot."

"And you did."

Marisa thought back to the person locked inside her room at Caius's like a cell.

"Yes," she said. Then, "How is she?"

"You can't go in till morning," said Gino. "But . . . she had a stroke, Mars. It's not looking good. You know, she's really, really old."

"Yes, but she's . . . she's so . . ."

She had been about to say that Nonna was so young, but of course she wasn't. Marisa found it hard to believe that she had ever been young.

"She's so . . . spirited."

"Is she?" said Gino, who had a very strong memory of being sternly told off when he once put his fingers in a pudding. "I don't know if I buy that whole 'illness is a battle' thing," he said.

"I know," said Marisa. "But sometimes it feels that

way. How's Mum?" she added, as casually as she was able as they walked to the rental car.

Gino snorted. "Are you kidding? Desperate to have her girl home. Desperate."

But she still felt very nervous.

The tiny house was just as she remembered it, with the same squeaky gate and weeds overgrowing the little crazy paving path. But the herbs were growing strong and well; it was all Marisa could do not to stop and check for weeds and take them a little water; the tomatoes, she knew, would be pushing through the green stage in the suntrap back garden. In the warm night, everything was releasing the scents of her nonna's beautiful garden into the world; deep lavender, herbs, arugula. It was a scent that went right to the very base of her brain, took Marisa back to being very small indeed, and she was constantly surprised to find things at shoulder height she had expected to have to reach up for.

Lucia was half-dozing in the little sitting room in front of the television showing, inevitably, *Un posto al sole* as Marisa came in.

Marisa felt once again the shame go through her; how she had rebuffed her mother's concern, brushed off her need for her, ruined family meals and holidays and many other things her mother had had planned for them as a family after the tough times. She deserved to be rebuked, she knew; she had been ill, but illness had made her selfish and made things so hard between them.

One turn from her mother—looking very like her own

mother, suddenly, her face relaxed from sleep—put paid to all of that.

"*Mia bambina*," said her mother, still half-asleep, almost disbelieving, stirring in the chair. Tears sprang into her eyes immediately.

"You came! You came home! You came!"

She stood up and pretended to poke Marisa firmly, even as she engulfed her in an embrace far larger than her petite height.

"For me you don't come. But for my mother?!"

Marisa understood, though, what she meant. It was forgiveness; it was a benediction. She draped herself over her mother's familiar shoulders, let herself soften and be swept up in her embrace.

"My darling girl," said her mother again. "We thought we'd lost you."

"I was lost," said Marisa.

Her mother sat them down and pulled back, looking into her daughter's face.

"Who got to find you?"

"She made it here, Ma," said Gino, who had a slightly keener understanding of what had gone on.

"She made it all this way."

"She *did*."

Her mother hugged her again.

"Although you know you could cut your hair."

And with that, Marisa knew all was well.

Gino opened a bottle of their grandfather's excellent Barolo, and they sat up despite the late hour; caught up. Lucia wanted to hear all over again about the little pizza restaurant in the bakery at the end of the world, was alternately horrified and delighted by her baby setting up on her own, even if she had given up a very decent 9–5 to do it and was now wearing an apron instead of a suit.

Gino, on the other hand, was still doing marvelous things in Switzerland and Marisa was perfectly happy to hear his funny stories about his job and his friends, and even contributed one or two of her own, although she could tell they both were glancing at each other whenever she mentioned her next-door neighbor, so she stopped doing so quite abruptly. Which her mother noticed, and finally, leaned over.

"Tell me all about him," she said.

And oh, the bliss of doing so. Of talking about him. Even with how things were left. She found she wanted to talk and talk about him.

"Well," said Marisa. "I don't know. I mean, it's a bit nuts that he's just next door and the only man I've met in, like, a year."

Her mother nodded.

"I can see that would be a problem."

"And also he's getting over a very painful love affair."

"Ah."

"With a ballerina."

"Oof."

Both Gino and her mother looked very sorry for her.

"And has he shown any interest in you?"

"He made me dinner," said Marisa. "Well, he made toast."

"Had you cooked for him already about nine thousand times?" said Gino.

"Shut up," said Marisa.

"Is he kind?" said her mother.

Marisa thought of how he had refused to come with her.

But then she thought of everything else about him. His patience with his pupils. Playing at Denys's wedding. The way he had taken on teaching the twins for nothing without a second thought.

"Yes," she said. "He is kind."

"Handsome?"

"In his own way."

"Oh my God, a moose," said Gino.

"SHUT YOUR FACE!"

"It's all right," said Gino, cheekily, whose last boyfriend had looked like a young Robert Redford. "Personality is what really matters."

"Shut up! I like the way he looks. He's kind of big."

"Moose big," said Gino wisely, till she giggled.

". . . and half-Mongolian and he has these brown eyes that just look at you and well, I don't really see the rest."

"Which is probably just as well?"

It was so strange. Despite the elephant in the room and the way they kept looking at their phones in case the hospital had been in contact, they had a lovely evening, and Marisa was nearly half-asleep by the time they called it a night and made their way to bed; Lucia in her mother's room, Marisa and Gino sharing twin beds in a spare room.

On her way there, yawning with tiredness, Marisa passed the laptop. It was still plugged in—she realized, suddenly; of course it was still plugged in.

She pressed a button so it jumped into life. Sure enough, there she was, peering into her own home, back in Cornwall.

It felt incredibly odd, as if she had passed into another

realm, was looking to find herself back there, or staring through both sides of a telescope at once.

She noticed how neat and tidy the room was; how devoid of character. It looked cold, even in the moonlight. She glanced around her nonna's kitchen: ancient recipe books stained and lined up; vast old glass jars full of pasta and different types of beans; flour and sugar and polenta; a huge box of tomatoes; a straining bag for making mozzarella, something Polly had suggested in the bakery and Marisa had instantly backed away from. Photos everywhere, of loved ones. The sweet scent of the garden, a tiny window always open for the night air. Her grandmother had made her home exactly as she liked it. There must be a way for her to do the same with her own.

Even with Gino breathing heavily in the bed next to her, she was still asleep as soon as she crawled in under the heavy starched cotton sheets and eiderdown. Her nonna had never quite got to grips with anything as newfangled as a duvet. Outside, she could hear cicadas squawking in the warm air, a noise as comforting as a lullaby. She meant to have a think back over the day, be mindful as Anita would say, think about what she had been through and what she had done; be thankful for what she had managed and hopeful for the trials and days ahead, even find a way to forgive Alexei.

But she couldn't. She was asleep.

Chapter Sixty-five

One of the things that had most tormented her about her grandfather's death had been how sudden it was.

So she didn't even pretend she didn't want to cling on to her mother's and brother's arms, tight, as they marched toward the hospital. She clung to them both, nodding to the staff as they marched up to the old faded yellow façade of the little Ospedale Imperia, sitting above the industrial port, asking the nurses for directions. Marisa felt incredibly nervous as they made their way up in the lift to the fifth floor.

They were directed to an end room, with two beds, one occupied by a large woman snoring loudly, and there in the corner, eyes half-open, staring at nothing, her mouth twisted deeply down on the left-hand side, was the tiny swaddled figure of her nonna.

All three paused before they went to her; she was so fragile and small in the bed. And those beady eyes, so quick to miss nothing at all; to see them focusing on nothing was sinister.

Lucia was straight to her side, grasping her hand, practically kneeling, putting Nonna's hand to her face. Gino stood to one side, looking rather awkward. Marisa slowly stepped forward, and sat at the foot of the bed, staring into her nonna's eyes.

There was something; a little flicker of recognition. "Nonna."

Her grandmother tried to lift her left hand, but it was useless and could do nothing but twitch. Her other hand was in Lucia's. Her voice made an indeterminate, slightly wet noise. Marisa instinctively looked around for a tissue, and gently moved up and wiped the dribble from her face. The old lady leaned her face into Marisa's palm, Marisa's hand, and Marisa stroked her, quite naturally.

She'd expected to be terrified, repulsed. But she wasn't at all. She felt nothing but love, suddenly, for her grandmother and, wider, for her family.

She thought back to Alexei's refusal to accompany her and knew that he had been right; these were not moments that could be shared.

"Mamma?" Lucia said, and once again there was a twitch of the head, some recognition.

Marisa asked if she wanted some water and the old lady nodded so indistinctly you could hardly notice it, unless you were looking very closely, but Marisa's heart leapt to see it; there was still someone in there, who understood what was going on.

She sat on the bed while her mother bustled off to talk to the doctors, gently helping her grandmother sip then wiping the excess off. Gino frowned and looked at his phone, after distractedly patting his grandmother on the arm. That was okay, thought Marisa. He was there. They were there.

The next hour was spent awkwardly, as they sat and stroked her, asking her questions she couldn't answer, making silly conversation about nothing at all; looking at the doctor to read her face. At one point Marisa patted her nonna's arm, only to find, suddenly, that her sleeve was being gripped, hard, by her grandmother's good hand. She looked at the others, then leaned in.

"It's okay," she said. "It's okay. Tell me. Take your time."

There was obviously something she desperately wanted to say; her mouth was moving, incoherently. Marisa didn't rush her, didn't try and guess what she was saying or smooth things over. She simply leaned her ear in closely.

"La . . . la . . . la."

Marisa stayed stock-still.

"La . . . la mi . . . la . . . la mia casa."

Home. Her nonna wanted to go home.

The doctor had the slightly harried air of doctors everywhere in every language and she adjusted her glasses as she pointed out that their family member was extremely sick and shouldn't be moved anywhere. Lucia pushed her for a prognosis, and the doctor shot a look at nonna on the bed and took her out of the room. When Lucia came back in alone, her face was pale. Nonna, meanwhile, had fallen asleep. Marisa smoothed the dyed black hair. The white roots were coming in. She would absolutely have hated that.

"At any rate, enough now," said the doctor, as Nonna was quite clearly sleeping.

Lucia's jaw was stiff and she was just about to talk to them when suddenly there was a chattering of noise from outside, and, into the room, numbers swollen by the knowledge that the British end of the family was here, Rossis started pouring into the room in a great wave.

Half-remembered distant cousins and aunties descended upon her, demanding hugs and cheek pinches, and before she knew it, they were being borne off to a nearby restaurant, where, somehow, a table for fourteen was commandeered and without ordering or preamble, olives and sparkling water and bread appeared, followed by a rich pot of ragu and a small glass of rough red wine to wash it down with, and many questions about England, and insistence that the awkward teenagers in the ensemble—her cousins once removed, Patrizio and Niccolo—were made to speak English and ask her halting questions about her work while blushing furiously.

It could have been—would have been—daunting, being the focus of so much attention, being surrounded by so many people.

But somehow, today, it wasn't; it was only family, catching her up in a warm, familiar embrace, with all the foibles and daftness and scandal of any normal family, of course, but even so: it was hers, and as the bread was passed around and she grated pepper onto the heavenly ragu with its thick coiled pappardelle, she found, despite the sad circumstances, that she was . . . she was okay. She really was.

Afterward, family members dispersed to have a nap or go back to school, with arrangements to meet up again in the evening, and Marisa finally found a chance to walk with Lucia and find out what was really happening.

It was boiling hot; Marisa hadn't packed anything suitable in Cornwall, so they found a tourist shop that opened over lunchtime, and bought her a huge broad-brimmed hat to protect herself, and a fine white cotton shift that she would never have worn in the UK, but here she could happily float around in.

Then they wandered down to the beach near the port where the huge yachts anchored, and walked past the blue-and-white-striped umbrellas and happy families playing, throwing balls, standing in the water, nattering in bikinis.

The prognosis, as her mother's face had indicated, was not good. Yes, the stroke was awful, but once they'd started doing tests—she had everything, her mother said. She obviously hadn't been to a doctor in years. She was tough as old boots, but basically . . .

Lucia started to sob. It was the strangest thing to be here, in paradise, children eating huge ice creams, couples lingering over the finest seafood and a cool glass of Soave in the shade of the restaurants lining the beaches; teenagers kissing in the water; music playing, and shouts and yells of glee, that there could be so much sadness. Marisa put her arms around her mother.

"Oh, she's old, I know," said Lucia. "And she's had a wonderful life. And this happens to everyone, everyone in the world. Everyone, if they are lucky, loses parents that they love, in the end."

She swallowed hard.

"It doesn't make it any less horrific when it happens to you."

"It doesn't," said Marisa.

Lucia smiled suddenly through her tears.

"It's like when you and Gino were born."

"What do you mean?"

Her mother took her hand as they walked farther up the beach, away from the crowds, splashing through the blissfully cool water, their shoes dangling from their free hands.

"Well, when you were born, I just felt so joyous and happy. Even though, you know, loads and loads of people get to have a baby and feel just exactly the same.

"But it felt such a special private thing to me. And I

suppose this is the same thing in reverse. Just because everyone's been through it doesn't make it any less awful for you; just like knowing billions of people have had babies before you doesn't make yours any less special."

Marisa squeezed her mum's hand.

"But is there no comfort in knowing that you are connected to everyone in the world who's been through this? That so many people have shared this sadness?"

"You sound older and wiser than me," said Lucia, smiling wryly. She turned to look at her only daughter. "You've really been through the wringer, haven't you?"

Marisa couldn't speak, and Lucia held her tight.

"Ah, you were always like that dad of yours," she said, her voice a little thick. "I'm sorry. I just thought . . . I thought I'd get a little girl just like me and we could dress up and have fun together and go to parties and sometimes when you pulled away from me . . . it just hurt so much."

"But I don't need fun," said Marisa, very quietly. "I just need you."

Chapter Sixty-six

It was astonishing how quickly a plan was put together. Everyone knew someone's brother who could help with putting handles in the bathroom or take on shifts, and before the next day's evening meal they were almost organized—by which time Marisa was almost dropping with exhaustion and the unfamiliar sense of interacting constantly, all the time, with other people. Although it gave her energy too, in its own way; everywhere she looked, people were chatting and gesticulating, shouting or laughing out loud.

She had missed this, she thought. All the parties skipped, the weddings postponed, the fun put on hold. How much time she had wasted in that little prison she had built, brick by brick, of sadness and fear, all by herself.

This was entirely different; this was a joint effort. It reminded her of the villagers in Mount Polbearne, all pulling together to repair the causeway and look after people's homes. When one was needed, everyone was there.

And Marisa was all over it: joining in the cooking, helping the cousins with their English homework, debating whether to buy new sheets for Nonna's bed (they decided against it in the end; she wanted familiarity and the ancient embroidered handed down family sheets, in a massive heavy linen nobody made anymore, not new things she wouldn't recognize that might annoy her, they figured). She was also drawn into arguing with the senior clinician, who happened to be German, with excellent English, about the benefits of bringing their grandmother home, something he was adamantly set against, insistent that she would die. Lucia through her sobs pointed out that they'd told her she was going to die anyway and he had made a slightly stiff nod and said, "Well, this will be quicker" and Lucia had said, "Good!" and it had more or less deteriorated from there.

Marisa, used to being around grieving relatives, was able to calmly state their case, and her speaking English seemed to impress him, oddly, even if the old argument—we can free up one of your beds—didn't have anything like the same power here as it would have done in the UK.

Her mother watched, drying her eyes, quietly proud that her unmarried daughter with the mental health issues that she found so hard to brag about was calmly negotiating in two languages in front of everyone, particularly her sister, Ann Angela, and found herself smiling a quiet smile of satisfaction to herself which she hid with her tear-stained handkerchief.

Finally it was arranged. Marisa made a decision. She called Polly and apologized and said that she didn't know when she'd be back, and Polly said lots of people were complaining that the pizzas weren't as good and Marisa said she was very sorry about that and Polly said that was okay, as even not quite as good pizza was still very good and popular pizza, so come back when she was ready.

Marisa was too tired—and her Italian was giving out, it had been a long day—when everyone announced they were going out to dinner at, of course, nine at night. She kissed them all fulsomely but announced she was going to have a quiet night. Tomorrow, with Nonna coming home, was going to be a very big day and she wanted to read her book in the bath and turn in early.

Chapter Sixty-seven

With everyone gone, the house was silent; the cicadas played their little creaky song outside, of course, but she had practically ceased to notice it. She went into the tiny garden and, taking in the warm scent of the lilacs and the herbs, stood under the warm sky.

Perhaps she should stay here always, she thought. Her family was here. The weather was good, it was beautiful, she could find something to do.

But even as she thought it, she realized that she was British; that there was too much about her home country she would always miss, from chocolate digestives to *Fleabag,* that she wouldn't have a hope of explaining here; that she missed her friends so, so much and was going to rectify that as soon as she got home; that she genuinely wanted to go dancing; to go to a party; to eat food that wasn't Italian; to laugh until she was sick. Italy was wonderful, but England was home.

And if she could have the best of both worlds; if she could find her freedom within herself, and only herself— well. That was the most healing thing she could think of, she thought, under the bright starry sky of an Italian summer.

A faint noise pulled at the edges of her consciousness and she frowned. Somebody must be playing the piano near here. How funny. It must follow her everywhere. She frowned and tried to figure out where it was coming from.

That was odd; it sounded like it was coming from inside the house.

Slightly nervously, she turned round again. What on earth was it?

Inside the little kitchen it was louder still; a great crashing epic of a piece, loud and bold, played on a piano . . . Had she left the television on?

Immediately she realized, and felt like a complete idiot. Of course. They'd been out the previous night, but of course—it was coming from the laptop, that was still connected to the flat.

She sat in front of it, even though there was nothing to see in the dark Cornish room. She could hear, though, the great swells of the playing. It sounded absurdly close; close enough to touch. So she simply sat, closed her eyes, opened her mind, and listened. She hadn't really listened before, being too irritated, or sad, or both. But now, here, far away, she let the music take her; music that felt like the rolling of a boat, like a great heavy-masted ship crashing through stormy seas, ploughing up and down through the waves. By the end of it, she felt like clapping, and did so. To her surprise she heard lots of other people too, through the walls, and a resumption of noisy chatter and laughter. Oh my God, he was having a party!

"Alexei," she whispered through the computer. Of course he couldn't hear her. Experimentally she tried a little louder. "ALEXEI?"

But nobody could hear her. She was torn between being insulted at him having a party and not inviting her, admiration for his consideration to wait for her to be gone—and an unexpected desire to be there too.

Chapter Sixty-eight

Marisa had seen lonely deaths in her job. Deaths of people in flats not discovered for months; deaths reported by social workers because there were no family members to love them enough to do it. She had made out death certificates for young drug deaths, and old solitary deaths, and she knew exactly what she was not going to do for her own family.

Nonna was not alone for a second. There was always someone by her side, encouraging her to eat just a little *zuppa del minestrone*, the cure for all ills; or reading to her from the old illustrated Bible on the mantelpiece, or playing her favorite music; changing and washing her, briskly and without sentiment; or simply holding her hand or combing her hair.

For such a voluble woman who had talked and talked and talked, she didn't insist, not anymore, on having something to say, even in the few moments she was lucid and could talk. As if she'd told them all she wanted to say—and they repeated, sometimes in hushed tones, her many pointed lectures on the subjects of their fashion choices, their partner choices, and their life choices, but in every way with affection.

"Oh my goodness, the *trouble* I got when I went to England with Stefano," said Lucia.

"Well, she was right about Stefano," said Ann Angela, earning herself a very Nonna look from her sister.

"Nonna only ever got a telephone so she could ring me internationally and tell me I'd made every single decision wrong in every conceivable way."

Lucia smiled.

"It must have cost her a fortune! All those international calls!"

Everyone laughed.

"No wonder she never bought a new dress."

Nonna slept a lot, nearly all the time, and the doctor came in morning and night to make sure she was never in pain or distressed, but the Rossis were all over it, and not beyond letting her have a sip of her beloved grappa at bedtime, which was quite as it should be.

On the fourth day her breathing started to labor a little and they looked at each other as she became slightly more alert, aware of the breath tight in her body and on her chest, and tugging on the sleeve of everyone who came in and out, and they sat down carefully as she turned to them, one by one, and croaked out.

"*Ti . . . ti voglio bene.*"

And of course everyone said, "I know you do. And we love you too. And everything is well."

And the doctor came for the last time and agreed that it wouldn't be long, but that nothing hurt, and time took on an odd feeling of being extremely elongated—minutes drawing out, punctuated by the sense that every breath was taking longer to come than the previous one, that it might be the last, and they milled, and cooked because they were going to need a lot of food for the funeral, after all, so they might as well put it in the freezer, and neighbors popped in and out quietly in the hush. The priest came and Marisa and Ann Angela got the worst

fit of giggles, in the way you do at the most inappropri-
ate moments, when in the middle of all the solemnity
he turned out to be both radiantly handsome and quite
magnificently camp, and Nonna held on to his robe as
strongly as she'd held on to anyone else's, and intoned,
with a somewhat theatrical flair, the ancient words of
the ritual.

*"Through this holy anointing may the Lord in his love
and mercy help you with the grace of the Holy Spirit.
May the Lord who frees you from sin save you and raise
you up."*

And they gathered around as the day turned to night,
and Marisa texted Alexei for the first time—she didn't
even have his number, she found it on an advert for piano
lessons—and said hello, and that they could hear him
and would he mind terribly playing something?

And he said of course, and she had almost certainly
left her balcony door open again so would she like
him to climb in and grab the laptop so it was closer?
She had told him not to be so daft, he would fall if he
attempted to scale their balconies, but he took this as a
challenge, vanished and reappeared thirty seconds later,
clutching her laptop triumphantly.

It was lovely to see him; she couldn't stop grinning, had
forgotten her crossness.

"Are you comink home?" he said anxiously. "Or have
you gone forever to land of Puccini? Is good land."

"I am coming home," she promised.

"Well, that is good," he said. "That is very good. You
want me to play? Are you sure?"

She had been trying to be subtle but it was impossible

with nonna's old laptop right bang in the middle of the kitchen, the volume turned up to a level an eighty-year-old could communicate in.

"Ooh, is that him?" said Lucia. "Let's have a look then."

"Shut up!" hissed Marisa.

"Is he better-looking than the priest?" wondered Ann Angela aloud. She looked at the screen. "Oh. No."

"Shut up!"

"*Buona sera*, Italian family of Marisa," said Alexei gravely, blinking, which produced much excitement among them, and some giggling among the younger cousins. "What music did your grandmother like?"

Marisa translated, and there was lots of shouting, particularly of popular Italian songs and hymns he simply didn't know, but they finally settled on a gentle program of Verdi and Rossini.

Marisa took the laptop into the bedroom, where the breaths were still faltering and far apart. One of the younger cousins immediately got up and Marisa slipped into their place.

"Hey, Nonna," she said. "Here he is, he's going to play for you."

There it was, almost impossible to feel—the tiniest grasp on her sleeve.

"*Buona sera*, Babushka of Marisa," said Alexei, and beamed cheerfully, then turned to his piano and started with a merry waltz, as other family members crammed into the bedroom to hear.

To Marisa's astonishment, her nonna's eyes opened for the first time in two days. She couldn't quite focus, but Marisa held up the laptop.

"That's him?" she said in a papery whisper. Alexei, oblivious, was concentrating intently on the music, those huge ungainly hands of his now flying as if they were in their natural habitat; a seal in water.

"*Si*, Nonna."

"I like him," she said.

Marisa kissed her nonna as she closed her eyes and settled back to sleep as the music played on and everyone discussed Alexei ad infinitum and Marisa found that she missed him. And much later, at four o'clock in the morning when the world was truly still and all the Rossis were asleep, with her beloved eldest daughter Lucia holding her hand, curled up fast asleep next to her on the bed, Ismarilda Madolina Marisa Rossi woke, bolt awake, eyes wide open, and said, quite distinctly, "Carlo," Marisa's grandfather's name, and then the breathing stopped and Marisa herself in the next room woke with a start and wondered what she could hear.

It took her a little while to realize it was something she could not hear.

Chapter Sixty-nine

The farewells were so teary and heartfelt and emotional, and Marisa couldn't help it; for a buttoned-up, shy person, she would have thought she would hate it but she did not. She loved every second as her cousins spilled out of old cars and surrounded her as she marched through the airport, lamenting as if she was leaving the way Lucia had left: to somewhere cold and distant and expensive with the very real possibility that they might never see each other again.

"I'll be back!"

"Bring your boyfriend."

"Yes, we like the piano player," said several other people.

Marisa rolled her eyes.

"Someone will have to buy a bigger house to fit him," pointed out Gino, who was catching the train in the afternoon which meant the entourage could follow him in the same way.

Marisa frowned at the extra suitcase full of supplies that had been pressed upon her, along with the seeds from her nonna's garden.

"This is going to cost me more in extra luggage than . . . never mind," she said, submitting herself to being hugged and kissed, even by the younger cousins, who had all done very well in their end of term exams and were all vying to come to England to take on shifts at the pizza shop at random, as far as Marisa could figure out.

Her mother was staying. She didn't know how long, and Marisa didn't ask. The house in Exeter was worth a lot now, just through the way things had gone; and she and Ann Angela seemed perfectly happy bickering all day. Who knew, she might stay.

All the way home Marisa felt worn out; tears wrung dry—the funeral service had been crowded and jolly and beautiful, on a sunny day, with wonderful music and happy memories and songs of a life well lived and that, undeniably, lived on in the hordes of cousins and children and family that descended her; the opposite of that gray awful day when her grandfather had gone to a cold grave by himself. Ismarilda was laid next to Carlo, together again, and the grave was laden with sunflowers.

She had mentioned—casually, she thought—to Alexei that she was returning and she told Polly as well (who had replied with a very terse "Thank God") and she hadn't once, absolutely not, well, perhaps just a little, allowed herself to fantasize that he would show up to pick her up from the airport.

He did not, but Huckle did, and she was incredibly grateful to see him, and pleasingly distracted by the twins who had a lot to tell her about what Lowin's party was going to be like and how it was going to be the best party ever and they were having a magician who could disappear and also fly and how there were going to be fireworks and elephants and tigers and also dragons who could fly and you could get on the back of a dragon and it would fly and there was going to be a cotton candy waterfall, and absolutely no snakes (this last from Daisy).

"That sounds . . . sticky," said Marisa.

"Well, you're going to find out," said Huckle. "You're doing the catering."

Marisa scrunched up her face.

"Where am I going to find a waterfall at such short notice?"

"Yay!" hollered the twins.

"I think," said Huckle, with admirable restraint, "we are going to have to work on our expectation management."

It wasn't until he dropped her off at the end of the unpaved road that Marisa started to get truly, properly nervous.

She had missed him.

She had thought she might get over him, that it was a crush born of proximity and desperation. It was not.

But in fact, it had gone quite the other way. She suddenly found she was intensely interested in Alexei; in his passionate moods; his absolute lack of interest in conforming or being normal; his fascinating house and deep interests; the way he threw himself into his work. And the fact that he was, above and beyond anything else, kind. Kind to everyone; to children, to her, to her grandmother. Kind didn't come up on dating apps very often. Funny and kind together even less so—in fact, many of the men Marisa had met in her dating days who announced they had a good sense of humor, were in fact cutting and cruel, or told long jokes and were dull. She couldn't imagine Alexei being either of those things.

He was unconventional . . . but then, she supposed, so was she. So was anyone who ended up in Mount Polbearne, at the end of the world.

She had thought longingly of his large frame, his penetrating eyes, his soft mouth.

She was going to see him as soon as she'd had a shower and got changed; would show off the pretty golden tan her olive skin had picked up; the freckles that had popped out on her nose, the tiny streaks in her dark hair; maybe even—it was a gorgeous day—wear the floaty dress she had bought on impulse; the big silver earrings Ann Angela had convinced her would be just the thing.

Dragging her bag up the road, she suddenly felt distinctly more nervous than she had getting on the plane.

Chapter Seventy

The sun was directly in her eyes as she marched up the hill, which meant at first she couldn't quite figure out what she was seeing.

The door was open to Alexei's house, and there was a lot of noise. The next thing that happened was several large objects were hurled out of the house, including a pair of his boots and his treasured bust of Beethoven (Marisa hadn't known who it was and had once asked "Who is that angry-looking but quite handsome man?" and Alexei had gone into rhapsodies), which smashed straight onto the stony ground in a million white pieces.

Marisa stood stock-still, not knowing what was happening. A loud voice, shouting, came from inside the house. It was obviously Russian and Marisa froze in case they weren't actually shouting, in case this was just what Russian sounded like.

As a teapot hurtled through the door and followed the bust into shattering in pieces, Marisa winced. One, they were definitely angry, and two, that was her teapot that had crossed the balcony one day and somehow never made it home.

The next thing to appear in the doorway was a tiny person.

Marisa blinked in the light, but it was immediately

clear who it was. The girl had an incredibly long neck, but the rest of her was absolutely tiny; a small heart-shaped face, little upturned nose, slender but muscular arms and legs, and a compact and incredibly strong-looking torso.

Her blond hair was pinned ruthlessly tightly on her head, making her neck look even more swan-like than it did already, and her expression was absolutely furious. She didn't stop yelling, kicking things out of her way, walking backward—with utterly perfect posture and poise—down the steps, her feet slightly turned out like a duck.

She turned around at the bottom, hurling a few more insults back up the steps, then saw Marisa, who was conscious she was staring, and possibly had her mouth slightly open, so she closed it, instinctively shrinking back a little.

The tiny woman came up to her, frowning. Her lovely face was spoiled by its malicious, twisted expression. She looked Marisa up and down, several times, then in perfect English sniffed loudly and said, "Well. Obviously it's not *you*."

And without another word to explain herself, she flounced off down the hill, no bit of her fury denting the iron-rod straightness of her back.

All thoughts of getting changed forgotten, Marisa found herself running up the steps. What on earth had gone on?

At the entrance door she stopped. The beautiful sitting room was in utter disarray; tablecloths pulled down, books and papers a whirlwind, the piano lid slammed shut with papers trapped in it.

And there—in that same position and same place she had found herself that very first night, curled up, back to the wall, in the farthest corner of the apartment—was Alexei.

"Alexei?"

He looked up, flinching. When he saw it was her, consternation flashed across his face.

"Marisa . . . I . . ."

He extended a weak hand as if realizing the impossibility of coming up with a reason for why things were how they were.

"Are you all right? Why were you throwing things?"

He blinked his slow blink.

"No. Not me throwink thinks. "

Suddenly, and seemingly to his surprise, a tear rolled down his cheek.

"Oh! Dearest!"

Marisa pulled a tissue from her bag, and in different circumstances he would have smiled, just a little, to see her as organized as ever (no registrar ever goes anywhere without a tissue).

"Was that . . . Lara?"

He nodded.

"What was she doing here?" Marisa found herself asking, even though her heart was shriveling, turning to dust inside her. She didn't need to ask, not really. They'd had a reconciliation, obviously, because he had never been over her, obviously, and now they'd had a fight again, obviously, and now she'd broken his heart all over again, so he was back to square one, which meant that for all her goodwill and willingness to be brave and to live up to her new life—in fact, she couldn't. She couldn't have what she so desperately wanted.

She hid her face to hide how disappointed she was.

Her friend was desperately sad, and it was her job to cheer him up.

"She is dancink nearby. I said, come, see, maybe, what new life I haff."

"So she could share it?" Marisa was incredibly impressed by what a good acting performance she was putting on, even as her heart felt like it was breaking. If she had the slightest doubt about the strength of her feelings for him, it was all gone, now, in an instant, now that everything was lost.

"No. I do not know why. I think I want to say, look, how good I liff without you."

"She didn't agree?"

"No."

"Oh. What did she say?"

"Always. 'Look at you in your little house with nobody to play for and there is people in St. Petersburg and people in Moscow and you are here which is where it is nowhere! And your music is no good!'"

"It's not nowhere," said Marisa. "You love it here!"

"She says I am very, very sad man."

"That's not what it sounds like from my side of the wall," said Marisa.

"She makes me feel so sad."

Marisa sat down next to him against the wall. She barely came up to his shoulder. Her heart felt like it was breaking. But she still had to be a friend for him.

"Well, when you are sad what do you normally do?"

He shrugged.

"Music. But I am too sad for music."

"I cannot believe you are saying that."

He stared at the floor, still distraught.

Marisa sighed. And took a deep breath.

The idea of doing what she was about to do would

have felt utterly preposterous, even before she'd become ill. On the other hand, now she'd found her courage, it felt that she didn't even know how many different ways she could push it if she wanted to. Well. Nothing ventured, nothing gained.

And although the man she had thought about so very much, who had become so dear to her, was sitting next to her, crying about some other stupid girl, she couldn't help it. She was going to try to help him anyway. Because he had helped her, more than he knew.

It had begun to rain, and as they sat listening to the drops against the window panes, she cleared her throat, opened her mouth . . . and started to sing.

In the quietest, most mouse-like voice, barely audible. But it was singing, nonetheless.

> *E cedo a vostri desideri . . .*
> *mi fai la tua amante . . .*

At first he didn't turn, didn't react. Very softly, but tunefully, she carried on with her nonna's favorite song, or at least her favorite song that wasn't a hymn.

> *Lontano di noi sapienza*
> *più tristezza*

Her voice trembled but she thought hard about the words and their meaning:

Wisdom is so far from us . . . there is so much sadness . . . I want a precious instant . . . where we will be happy. I want you.

He turned to her.

"That is beautiful," he said in his low growly voice.

Marisa shook her head.

"It isn't," she said. "I was just trying to reach you."

"Don't stop."

"Do you understand the words?"

"Of course."

"You speak Italian?"

"That song is not Italian. Is everybody's song."

He stood up, finally, and moved toward the piano, beckoning her, then sat down and began to play a simple waltz time.

"Sing with me," he instructed.

"This is so stupid that you know how to play everything."

"Everyone knows this," he said. Then he looked at her. "But your way is my favorite. Sing!"

She was shy now and was speaking more than singing. But somehow the words came to her, even as she realized how intimate they were.

> *Il mio corpo sia tuo*
> – that my body is yours
> *Il mio labbro sia tuo*
> – that my lips are yours
> *Il tuo cuore sia il mio*
> – that your heart will be mine . . .

But her voice remained true, and then Alexei took up the melody again, played it faster and faster till it sounded like an old-fashioned fairground ride, and she leaned against him as he finished with a flourish and turned round, grabbing her and sitting her down on his knee.

"Thank you. You haff cheered me up very much," he said.

"We are two survivors clinging to a life raft," said

Marisa, smiling. "I suppose we have to cheer each other up. That's what friends are for."

But, she thought. But I want to be so very much more than that. I planned so much more than that. Her heart had even leapt when the ballerina had looked to see if she was the person Alexei must have mentioned.

But then she had seen him. In the very depths of despair, completely cast asunder by love for somebody else.

As soon as she said the word "friends" he let her go, as if she was burning him.

"Yes," he muttered "Friends. Of course. That is what we are. Thank you. My friend."

She was standing up.

"I should go," she said. "I'm just off the plane."

"Yes! Oh no! Your nonna! Oh, my *zaichik*!"

He gave her a huge hug and she allowed herself, just for a moment, to feel totally lost once more in his arms, even if she contrasted it sadly with the last time she had stood there: when her nonna was still alive; when she had had so much hope.

"I am so sorry. We shall cling to this life raft together, no?"

"Yes."

Chapter Seventy-one

At least she was busy, throwing herself back into the job. Polly was delighted to see her, and she happily spent several evenings working just with Jayden, who had a seemingly infinite capacity for both eating and discussing pizza.

She had expected the black clouds to descend, had known to expect it, once the reality of a world without her grandmother in it really hit home. And she had, of course, been sad to see the laptop, put back in place by Alexei, showing the interior of the kitchen.

But two odd things had happened. First, the black dog did not descend. She found she mourned her grandmother, of course she did. But it wasn't eating her up from the inside out. She had been there. They had shared her last moments; it had been a good death. She had been present, and her grandmother had not been alone. The absence was sad, the passing was not.

The other thing was, of all things, the ancient laptop. Her mother had still never turned it off. She and Ann Angela were in there every day, cleaning up, bustling around.

They were theoretically getting the place ready to sell, but houses sell slowly in Italy, and from the tone of their bickering they were moving toward a place where the house would perhaps not be sold, and Lucia would stay there and rent out rooms and care for it, so progress was slow—and Marisa knew this because she could hear, all hours of the day and night, when she came in and when she went to bed, comforting Italian chatter and a view of the changing lights of the land far south. It was unimaginably comforting to cook with her mother sometimes, or just say good morning, and Marisa knew that having reestablished their connection, neither of them were in any mood to give it up. So neither of them even mentioned it was there.

And if she was sad about Alexei, well. She had a lot of practice in being sad.

Of course, the day of Lowin's party was beautiful. His birthday was actually at Christmastime—on Christmas Day, in fact—but Reuben had decreed that this was rubbish, and that he must also get a half-birthday which meant that Lowin got a birthday, a Christmas and a half-birthday each year, and his birthday invitations had to be sent out stipulating that he already had all the Playmobil ever made and could they check with the LEGO shop before buying LEGO, thank you.

The twins had been impossible to get to sleep, both insisting on getting a present each for Lowin rather than one between them as there was—they were both firmly of one mind on this issue—nothing worse than giving a shared present, regardless of whether or not people told them that the shared present was worth more than two individual ones, it was still a sorry state of affairs.

Polly and Huckle had exchanged looks—what could they possibly get an eight-year-old whose father regularly took him in a helicopter and had a Rolex?

In the end they had settled for a pizza-making kit from Avery and a set of different-colored baby sparkly nail polishes from Daisy, who had sensibly pointed out that Lowin would have every single thing from the "toys for boys" department and why was nail polish only for girls anyway? Polly was just congratulating herself on having such sensible children and raising them to be so tolerant and open when Avery had shouted, "Because nail polish is SO STUPID and FOR GIRLS," and Daisy had leaned over and whomped him one, which had made Huckle laugh when he should have looked disapproving. As World War Three looked about to break out, Polly announced they were getting changed for the party RIGHT AWAY even though it was three hours away and, as any parent knows, getting a five-year-old to keep an outfit clean for three hours is a feat beyond mortal means.

However, this wasn't Polly's problem, as she was already off in Nan the van with Marisa to get things sorted out onsite, at Reuben's private beach on the other side of Cornwall, its beautiful wild north shore, perfect for surfing.

Reuben's beach was a perfect haven of peace and serenity, or it would be if he didn't have the most ridiculous Tony Stark house on the top of it and a constant stream of comings and goings.

"How are things?" she said as they drove, giving a sideways glance to Marisa. Marisa was looking terribly well, actually. She looked brighter, more alert, more in the world; still quiet, but not the person she'd been when she arrived. "Did I ever tell you," she said, "how I came to live here?"

Marisa shook her head.

"Well. Life had done a number on me," said Polly,

talking about how she'd been practically made bankrupt and lost everything.

"And you met Huckle here?" said Marisa eagerly.

"Yes," said Polly, giving her the side-eye. "Why, have you met someone?"

Marisa squirmed.

"I . . . I thought I had but . . . I think he was only in it for the sandwiches."

Polly stared straight ahead as the van trundled on. They were going slowly so Lowin's ridiculous four-story birthday cake didn't get bashed up.

"Local boy, then?"

"Not exactly."

But Polly was only teasing.

"I know," said Marisa. "It's ridiculous. It was just when I was unwell."

Polly politely said nothing.

"And he was the boy next door . . . but there's nothing there. He's really hung up on his ex."

"Hang on—the literal boy next door? Not the twins' piano teacher?!"

"Oh God, I know," said Marisa. "I feel so stupid."

"Ha! You do know he's really a bear?"

Marisa smiled.

"Well, he's a very sensitive bear." She sighed. "Too sensitive. He's still in love with his ex. Ballerina," she added.

"Oof," said Polly. "*Total* nightmare."

"I know," said Marisa. "Anyway. It doesn't matter. I'm still feeling much better."

"Good," said Polly. "Maybe you can bag one of Reuben's rich mates at the party."

Marisa rolled her eyes. Oh God, Caius would probably be coming too. "How big *is* this thing?" she asked, as Polly smirked.

Chapter Seventy-two

Marisa gasped when she saw the beach, as they lugged huge boxes of ingredients down a sandy path. It was absolutely perfect, like something out of a magazine. Young guys were going up and down, raking the sand. In the middle was an actual real-life circus tent, next to an entire amusement park complete with big wheel, waltzers and, indeed, a cotton candy machine, if not technically a waterfall. The sun shone brightly down on everything.

"Okay," said Polly. "This is going to be just fine."

"'Scuse me," said a cheerful voice, and two young women walked past them on the narrow pathway, carrying between them the longest snake Marisa had ever seen in her life. She jumped and nearly dropped the cake.

"Not scared of a snake, are you?" said the first woman, quite aggressively.

"Yes. A bit," said Marisa, as the first woman sniffed contemptuously. Polly, meanwhile, was looking on with horror.

"Don't listen to her, Janice."

"Aren't they meant to be in a . . . cage or a box or a linen basket or something?" said Polly trying not to look scared but sidling slightly to the side of the path nonetheless. Oh God. Poor Daisy.

"Actually, we believe in freedom for animals? Not caging them?" said the woman at the back end of the snake. "Janice is free-range."

Polly took out her phone and texted Huckle, telling him under no circumstances to let Neil come, however much he liked being in the sidecar. And then she told him not to tell Daisy, and to stay away from the animals' tent. It would be fine. It would be fine. There were a million other things here to distract children, yes?

The girls marched on toward the circus tent, unabashed, even as the snake opened its vast jaws in something Marisa very much hoped was a yawn.

"Daisy is not going to want to see this," said Polly.

"As long as they don't have any free-range tigers," said Marisa, with feeling. "She'll probably be all right. It looks like there's plenty for them to do."

Two men came by with a huge box labeled with several hazard warnings and a lot of exclamation points in Chinese writing.

"What are those?" said Marisa.

"Definitely not fireworks," said the man in a low voice.

"Sssh," said the other guy as they gingerly crept by.

"Why can't they have fireworks?" wondered Marisa. "Is it the beach?"

"Nope, it's normally fine," said Polly. "Unless they're some terribly vast military-grade illegal fireworks."

"Near a loose boa constrictor," said Marisa. "Absolutely nothing is going to go wrong at this party."

Down in the main staging area, all was choreographed mayhem. People were running about with headsets barking serious orders into them like they were organizing a war rather than a party for an unbelievably spoiled eight-year-old. The kitchens were superb—Reuben liked to cook too and used the beach kitchen all year round—and Polly was familiar with it, so she started to unpack the food.

"I have to ask," said Marisa. "I get the pizza element but . . ."

She looked around. There was an entire old-fashioned sweet stand, and an ice cream van giving out free ice cream in every imaginable flavor. Marisa felt a sudden rush of pity for any other kid in Lowin's class at school having a party after this. There was also a fish and chip van parked up, and a fancy-looking plating station.

"Why are we doing smoked salmon canapés? Are kids different these days?"

"Oh no," said Polly. "There'll be a lot of grown-ups at this party."

Marisa raised her eyebrows. Then she thought.

"It has been *so long* since I've been to a party."

"I bet. Well, you can join it when we've finished serving the little brats. They're here from two to four but the party will carry on rather longer than that if my experience of these things is correct."

"I won't know anyone."

"Alexei's coming," said Polly, smiling to herself.

"Is he?"

"Yes. Didn't I say?"

"When I was spilling my guts in the van?"

"Sorry," said Polly. "I didn't think it would help."

"NO! Oh my God."

Marisa looked down at the simple black and white outfit she was wearing.

"Why is he even invited?"

"He's playing Happy Birthday. Only a proper concert pianist will count to play his boy in."

Marisa bit her lip.

"This is money, huh."

"I know," said Polly. "Exhausting, isn't it?"

Kerensa didn't look in the least bit exhausted, however, as she came down from the house, dressed in beautiful beige draped trousers and a top, and hugged Polly. "Hooray! How's it going?"

"Don't you know?" said Polly. Kerensa waved her hands. "Oh, I'm sure Reuben's got it sorted."

They all stopped talking and turned around as a platoon of people dressed as storm troopers marched in formation across the sand.

"Wow. Do you think they're hot?" said Polly.

"Christ, yes," said Kerensa, grinning. "Please come and drink Champagne with me, otherwise it'll be the school mums and if the WhatsApp is anything to go by they are all completely deranged."

"You read the school WhatsApp?" said Polly.

"Ha, not anymore," said Kerensa. "I told them I was coming off it for the sake of 'self care for my own screen-time wellness' and none of those beyatches could do a thing about it. HA!"

Polly laughed too.

"Well, a small one. Huckle can drive home. I'm so tired these days I'd be unsafe whether I have a drink or not."

"I heard," said Kerensa. "You're quite the talk of the region. Reuben wants to talk to you about buying you out for a franchise."

Polly rolled her eyes.

"Unfortunately that only works if you can duplicate the secret ingredient, and there's only one Marisa here."

Marisa smiled and looked embarrassed.

"It's lovely to have you here," said Kerensa. "Welcome."

Marisa thought the woman who lived here would be terrifying, but she wasn't, she was nice.

"It's amazing," said Marisa, honestly. "I've never seen anything like it."

"Welcome to Reuben's world," said Kerensa, rolling her eyes as if you ever got used to it.

Polly turned around at a sound on the water.

"You are kidding," she said.

"Oh," said Kerensa. "He didn't tell me about this either."

"Didn't tell you about what?" came a loud American-accented voice. "Hey. You know they didn't bring the tigers! How are you meant to have a birthday party without tigers?"

"Um, on that?" said Polly, stunned. She went over to Reuben and kissed him. "Happy eighth dad half-birthday."

Round the point was sailing, astoundingly, a proper schooner, flying a Jolly Roger.

"You're having a party with a real PIRATE SHIP?"

"Yuh," said Reuben, as if this was both obvious and reasonable.

The boat tacked around, to be hidden until it was properly needed.

"Are you sure this party is for Lowin?" said Polly, teasing him.

"No," said Reuben, who had no ear for sarcasm whatsoever. "It's for me. Lowin would rather be playing on his Xbox."

"Is that where he is?" said Kerensa. "I should get him into his knickerbockers."

"You're not," said Polly. "Kerensa!"

"What?" said Kerensa. "I am still waiting for my baby

girl and I haven't got her yet, and until then I shall dress up my baby boy how I please."

"Quite right," said Reuben, putting his arm round her. "Look at all this beach."

"It's fabulous," said Kerensa, kissing him.

Polly smiled. "Okay, come on, back to the galley, worker ant," she said to Marisa, who still hadn't quite recovered from the pirates.

"This is . . ."

"It's just his way."

"Why *don't* you sell him the bakery?"

"Because he'd only be doing it as a favor," said Polly. "And we're friends. And I want to keep it that way."

At two p.m. people started to arrive; not in dribs and drabs, like at a normal party, but all at once, in a massive rush, as if everyone had been waiting in the car park on the other side of the dunes until they got the signal to enter, which was in fact exactly what had happened. Lowin's parties had normally been winter affairs but the arrival of the half-birthday was quite a thing.

Kerensa's mother, who worshiped Lowin quite as much as the rest of his relatives and not entirely to the benefit of Lowin, ushered the boy down. He was indeed in velvet pantaloons which made him look, like his doting father, rather more padded in the bottom area than you'd expect from a young boy, and a billowing white shirt.

"He looks like a little prince!" said Kerensa, clasping her hands to her mouth.

"This is a STUPID outfit," said Lowin. "I want an Arsenal kit."

"Darling," said Kerensa. Lowin went up to Polly who gave him a kiss and a cuddle.

"Hello, bruiser. Happy half-birthday."

"Did you get me an Arsenal kit?"

"I didn't. But Daisy and Avery are bringing your presents."

"Is there one between them or two?"

"There's two."

Lowin brightened at this information.

"I *think* they might be snake-related. Well, Avery's is."

"Oh, snakes are super boring, Auntie Polly," said Lowin. "I like pirates now."

"Okay," said Polly, smiling rather tightly.

"And you're going to make me pizza?"

"As much as you like. As long as you keep on the trousers your mum picked out for you."

His face twisted.

"For a bit," Polly whispered. "It's a beautiful day, why don't you lead everyone in swimming?"

She'd already checked: there were about forty lifeguards and a Royal National Lifeboat Institution boat already stationed to look over everyone's special darlings.

His face brightened immediately.

"*And* I have red swimming trunks."

"Those sound like Arsenal swimming trunks."

"They kind of are!"

"Well then."

They exchanged a high five and the boy went off to do his unfortunately dull duty of greeting all his guests, and the slightly better duty of watching the pile of gifts grow exponentially in the afternoon heat, to be borne off by staff to a room in the big house used more or less solely for unwrapping presents.

There were so many people. This was not, Marisa surmised, the kind of party where parents dumped their children and ran, pleased for a couple of hours' freedom. There were huge extended families roaming about, as well as lots and lots of glamorous people who didn't seem to have children at all, strolling around in long silk kaftans or white suits, with glasses of endless Champagne served by waiting staff—even the waiting staff, Marisa noticed, were unbelievably attractive. It was the most ridiculous party ever.

But, she was amazed to notice, she knew almost everyone there. Everyone who came in for pizza; who had waved and said hello up and down the hill. All of the friendly fishing crew. Mrs. Bradley and Mrs. Baillie, complaining about things as usual. Linnet and Denys were there, Denys in his wheelchair down by the water.

"Oh my goodness," said Marisa. "I married those two. I thought Denys was . . ."

"In remission," said Polly. "Some kind of Stevie Wonder miracle, I heard."

Marisa blinked, as more and more people smiled and waved.

But there was only one person she wanted to see.

No. She was here for work. Was already feeling sweaty and the ovens were only just heating up. She put her hand to her cheek and took a long pull of water. Children were coming up to explore, and Polly was patiently explaining that yes they did have lots for everyone, and no there weren't any vegetables on them, and yes they did gluten free and yes they would do one without tomato sauce and yes they would make sure the cheese wasn't too gooey and no there weren't any hidden vegetables in the sauce and, finally satisfied, the children then caught sight of the full-size sweetshop and the ice cream van and the amusement park and were struck more or less dumb.

"I think I'm going to get Daisy and Avery on the waltzers *before* they start eating," said Polly with the hard-earned wisdom of one who has spent an astonishing amount of the last five years cleaning up vomit.

She was actually slightly worried, even beyond Daisy seeing the snake. The twins were of course invited because of the closeness of the two families. But everyone else was eight going on nine; strapping children who were perfectly safe to run in and out of the water, clamber up to the top of the helter-skelter or grab hot fish and chips.

She was also concerned that while the two families spent a lot of time together and Lowin deigned to play with them when there was nobody else around, he was with his own peer group now. She didn't blame him, but he was absolutely the King of the Eight-year-olds today. She hoped Daisy and Avery's cheerful insistence as to how much he was going to love the cards they had specially made for him because he was their very most special friend wasn't going to make them too downcast.

Everyone in the school, from the reception babies up, knew all about Lowin's party and Daisy and Avery were the only chosen few not from year three actually getting to attend, so their status and excitement levels were sky-high. Polly made a mental note to tell Huckle yet again that he couldn't take his eyes off them for a second, however much he himself would be looking forward to seeing his own friends and having a lovely day at the beach. It was a running joke that he was the laid-back parent and she was the fretter, but even on a glorious day like today, she absolutely couldn't relax.

Of course, Kerensa had a horde of spare nannies she'd hired for the day so people could enjoy themselves, but the idea of having to ask—never mind expecting the twins to cheerfully accept a nanny when none of the other children had one—was a completely unlikely scenario. She couldn't deny she was worried.

Chapter Seventy-three

Huckle shook his head, but he was used to Reuben, having known him for a very long time, so wasn't quite as astounded as the other parents.

"Oh God," one was whispering. "I think the party bag is going to be worth more than the entire gift."

Seeing as the party bags contained personalized Nintendo Switches for each child, the parent was not wrong in this assumption, but there was a certain over-the-top quality to everything; the sense that Reuben wasn't actually competing with anyone—because who could—he was doing it for his own pleasure; a sense that money was there to be enjoyed and his generosity was so insane that nobody could possibly hope to be reciprocal. As for vulgar, well, it was fun. So there. Although several of the school mums, on seeing all the beautiful young things who'd also shown up for a party, particularly the bare-chested surfer boys, immediately shared around a lipstick somebody had brought.

"DARLING!" shouted Caius, breezing up to Marisa with two people in tow. Neither of them were Binky or Phillip and both were completely androgynous. One of them had a ring through their nose and the other one had a chain in their hand. Marisa wasn't sure whether they were part of the party entertainment or not. "Please meet my best friends."

He eyed her up.

"You're looking suspiciously healthy and well."

She smiled. "*Really?*"

"Really! I *always* knew I was doing the right thing!"

She couldn't help smiling at him as he leaned in and gave her a big hug.

"Tell, me, *did* we ever sleep together? I remember your food, but I don't remember that."

"We didn't," said Marisa, still smiling at him. He appeared to be wearing a toga, for some reason.

"Well. Aren't *I* the idiot," said Caius, waltzing off, and although he was daft as a brush, it cheered Marisa up tremendously.

As Polly had suspected, the twins were having a difficult time of it. They were used to breaking up at school and hanging out with their own particular friends; here, everyone was taller than them and completely ignoring them.

They had made several attempts to talk to Lowin after he had lazily repeated "nicetoseeyouthanksforcoming" as they had arrived, but he wasn't just not playing with them, he was COMPLETELY IGNORING THEM AS IF THEY WEREN'T THERE.

"Lowin! Lowin!" Avery was saying, jumping up and down in front of the boy's eyeline. "Do you want to open our presents? Open our presents!"

Lowin noticed his friends behind were sniggering at the babies, ignored Avery's entreaties and marched off in the direction of the shooting gallery where somehow miraculously everyone won a gigantic teddy bear on their very first time of trying.

Huckle would have intervened, but he was on snake watch for Daisy and was slightly confused by the long pink ribbon of an aerialist. By the time he turned around, the twins were wandering despondently toward the rides, but they had to go on with each other and Daisy desperately wanted to ride on the carousel, where you could choose whichever pink or white horse you wanted, its name written in gold. Avery sulked and refused to go as only girls were going on them, even though he too desperately wanted a shot, whereupon Daisy started to cry.

Huckle dashed up and tried to distract them with the circus performance, but the children were squirming and the clowns were just weird, until a posse of the boys, led by Lowin, made a strategic intervention just as the magician was on the brink of vanishing a DeLorean, a breed of car completely lost on the eight-year-olds but of huge interest to the parents, and staged a walkout to the sea, shedding clothes at random as they did so.

Daisy and Avery had been extremely frightened by the clowns, and were now clinging to Huckle, even though Avery was desperate to run into the sea where Lowin and his friends were body surfing. Some were even attempting to stand up and do real surfing, none of which Avery was remotely a strong enough swimmer to attempt, and he was gearing up for a tantrum while Daisy sobbed, rather more quietly, at whether or not the tightrope walker was going to fall down.

"Okay," said Huckle. "Uh, do you want to meet . . ."

He consulted a lavishly printed program. There was a huge picture of Janice the snake on page three.

Daisy's sobs turned to howling and Huckle made a

hasty exit to find Polly. By the time they rocked up to the pizza stand, Huckle had two very hot cross children on his hands.

Unfortunately, Polly could do nothing about this as the rush was exceptional and the kids couldn't even get through, being smaller and less shoutier than everyone else there, children and adults alike. Even beautiful models down from London (it had long been a mystery to Polly how Reuben got so many beautiful people to turn up to his parties—she assumed he simply rented them) couldn't, it turned out, resist a slice of the best pizza north of Milan and east of Brooklyn, and they were rushed off their feet.

Huckle thought allowing the twins to choose ice cream might help cheer them up, which it did, temporarily, until they each chose three enormous and clashing flavors—liquorice, bubblegum and popcorn in Avery's case—and, miserably hoofed them into their mouths in a bid to eat them before either the sun melted them or their mother caught them eating a frankly obscene amount of ice cream for a five-year-old. Avery managed about five minutes before being lavishly and noisily sick all over the sand.

There was—of course there was—a chill-out zone, air-conditioned in a marquee, full of soft furniture and changing color lighting. A lot of the mums were in there with younger children and babies and stashes of fizz.

The twins whined about going to the "babies room" when there was so much fun to be had outside, but they were sticky and overexcited and tired and Huckle promised them they didn't even have to go home when the other children went home, so not to worry about it, they weren't missing anything.

In fact, they were missing the wild animal show and, for reasons no child alive could ever have fathomed, a performance by a nineties pop band (which triggered a mass exodus from the mothers, who immediately discovered their aversion to leaving the babies with people they didn't know had suddenly evaporated). But he promised they would get back for the pirate ship Polly had texted Huckle to tell them on no account to miss.

There was a room in the chill-out zone showing the latest Disney movie on a big screen, where several other wan-looking children were sitting, contemplating their early overindulgence ruefully and regathering their strength—and Huckle reflected that if he'd wanted the children to go and watch television somewhere, there were quite a lot of parties that could handle that a little cheaper, but here they were, and it was nice to be cool.

Chapter Seventy-four

"Yeah, I need fifteen pizzas for the Backstreet Boys," said the slightly overweight man with the headset and the black T-shirt in a strong American accent.

"What?" said Marisa.

"WHAT?!" said Polly.

An unmistakable chord started up from the main stage for the soundcheck and Marisa and Polly looked at each other and screamed out loud.

"Um, maybe they could come and pick it up?" said Polly, helpless with laughter when she finally calmed down.

"Could they sign the box?" said Marisa.

"I'M MAKING KEVIN'S," announced Polly.

"Hey, I'm single, I want to make Kevin's!"

The roadie had heard all of this before, a million times, and stared straight ahead, unblinking.

"Gluten-free with no cheese and a rocket topping," he said.

"We don't have any rocket," said Marisa. "Although if you like I will go and personally grow some rocket now and harvest it for you. But only for Kevin's."

The roadie sighed. Everyone backstage was secretly delighted whenever this happened.

"Okay, just give me all pepperoni then."

"I think we should probably give you a hand to deliver

them," said Polly. "You'll never carry fifteen pizzas by yourself."

The roadie was more than 300 pounds and built like a brick shithouse. He gave them a tight smile.

"We tried," said Polly to Marisa, who was spreading basil leaves in the shape of a smiley face.

"This one is *for Kevin*," she said sternly. Then, to Polly, "Can we shut the stand for their set?"

"Absolutely no— JAYDEN!"

Jayden was walking by with his wife, Flora. Like many villagers he wasn't technically invited but had somehow entirely by coincidence found himself down there and even though there were bouncers on the entrance to the beach with walkie-talkies and official lists and ID required, the bouncers were also, when they weren't being billionaire party bouncers—a job which wasn't really full-time in their neck of the woods— mostly Mount Polbearne fisherman, a weakness in Reuben's otherwise flawless organization.

"GET OVER HERE!" said Polly.

"What?"

He looked furtive, as though he'd been discovered.

"Take over the stall and I won't dob you in," said Polly. "Both of you."

They looked at each other.

"Don't you want to see the Backstreet Boys?" Jayden asked his wife.

"Oh God, they're an old person's band," said Florrie, and Polly rolled her eyes and they both took off their aprons and fled.

Kerensa, of course, was up in the wings of the stage, and beckoned them up.

"Do come have a drink with us and the boys afterward," she purred.

"Absolutely not," said Polly. "How could a Backstreet Boy possibly resist the charms of a well-upholstered middle-aged baker with two children? I'd be asking for trouble."

Marisa, meanwhile, had noticed something else, and could barely pay attention as the group took the stage, to a roar of screaming from a group of mums who were having the time of their lives and had forgotten they even had children.

Behind the boys on stage, leaving them plenty of room for dancing, was the most beautiful big shiny black grand piano she had ever seen. It must have been ten feet long, it was ridiculous. Her heart started to beat very quickly. He was going to love it.

"Is that for . . ." She couldn't say his name. "Is that for the piano player?"

Kerensa looked round from where she was dancing away. Then she looked closer at Marisa.

"Ah yes," said Polly. "My business partner loves the piano player."

Kerensa's face beamed with delight.

"There are five Backstreet Boys a foot away from us and you are asking about the gigantic hairy PIANO PLAYER?"

Polly smiled too.

"You have it bad!"

"They're wearing leather skin-tight trousers!"

"I would not like to see the twins' piano teacher in leather skin-tight trousers," said Polly, craning her neck briefly to see if they were out there, then guiltily checking her phone to see that they were safe with Huckle, who was bored out of his mind in the tent, and deciding not to worry about them for five seconds in a day.

Marisa glanced around to see if he was anywhere.

"He'll be in the holding area for performers," said Kerensa. "I can take you there if you like."

"Oh no, I—"

"And now!" shouted out a Backstreet Boy. "Where's the birthday boy?"

There was no response. Lowin was out, doing the purest, most fun thing an eight-year-old could conceivably do on his half-birthday, no matter how much money you spent on it: splashing in some water, surrounded by all his friends.

"We wanna say a special hello to the birthday boy."

Without a word, Kerensa marched onto the stage.

"Well, as I'm afraid he's not here, I guess I'll have to do," she said, proffering her face for a kiss.

Chapter Seventy-five

As soon as the set was over, instead of wafting off to a Backstreet Boy around the place, Kerensa turned to Marisa and Polly with a look on her face Polly knew only too well.

"What?" she said.

"She loves the piano player?" said Kerensa.

"It's not going to work out," said Marisa. "He's hung up on his ex and . . . hang on, I don't *love* him."

"Be quiet," said Kerensa. "He's a man. You're a hot woman. It's a beautiful day."

"And my therapist says you shouldn't look for external validation . . ."

Kerensa rolled her eyes. "Yeah, yeah, yeah." She looked at Polly. "Let me dress her."

"She's not a dolly!"

"Oh, but she is though. Look how pretty! How good will she look in red."

"Better than me," said Polly.

"I'm still here!" said Marisa. "And don't we need to man the stall?"

"I am punishing Jayden for not liking the Backstreet Boys," said Polly, glancing at her watch. "I can spare half an hour."

She smiled.

"You can have the afternoon off. Just bring back a Russian piano teacher. Or a Backstreet Boy. Anything to stop you moping about."

This was so far beyond what anyone had been able to say to Marisa in so long—her demeanor being so truly glum nobody could conceivably have joked about it—that she was completely startled, and then started to laugh. If her friends could take the piss, she must be on the mend.

Marisa looked around Kerensa's dressing room in awe.

"Oh my goodness," she said. Then she looked at Kerensa. "Nothing is going to fit me."

"Hush," said Kerensa. "You're a tiny person. There'll be loads."

She whisked through, professionally, finally returning with a couple of dresses, but discarded the floral prints almost immediately.

"No," she said, as Marisa hopped out of the ludicrously gorgeous rainforest shower to get the pizza off her. "That hair. That skin. You look like Gina Lollabrigida. We need to play up to that."

She dived in again and emerged with a red dress.

"I can't wear a red dress," said Marisa, looking nervous.

"Are you kidding? There's people at that party in *gold* dresses. Of course you can."

The dress had a boat neck and a belted waist that then flared over the hips—it was perfect for little, curvy Marisa.

"And lipstick," said Polly. "Bright!"

"Nooo," implored Marisa.

"Don't be daft," said Kerensa. "Do you want him to notice you or not?"

"I don't want to look trampy."

"Well, how is looking mousy and terrified working out for you?"

"Just let us give it a shot," said Polly. "Is there . . ."

She looked around, just as a waiter turned up with a bottle of Champagne and three glasses.

"Oh God, I like coming to your house," said Polly, grinning. "Do you remember the wedding?"

"Most of it," said Kerensa, grinning broadly, and they smiled at one another.

They fussed around Marisa, making her put the lipstick on but letting her blot it. A bugling noise out of the window alerted them.

"Oh!" said Kerensa, shooting a look at her Cartier watch. "That means birthday cake time. You're on."

"Oh my God," said Marisa, suddenly stricken with nerves.

"We got you," said Polly. "You can't do everything by yourself, you know."

Marisa nodded. If she'd learned anything over the last year, it was this.

Chapter Seventy-six

Alexei had been ordered by Reuben to wear a bow tie and tailcoat which was profoundly uncomfortable in the heat, but he was happy to oblige.

As he took the stage in front of hundreds of people there came a large cheer; he taught many of the children and was a familiar figure at school assemblies and church services, and they all adored him.

He smiled and sat down and played a massive ripple of ornate opening chords, before announcing, "And now . . . for a very special boy . . ."

Lowin had somehow been wrangled back into the embroidered shirt, but the red shorts, dripping wet, were staying stubbornly on. He was sitting on a throne erected at the very front of the crowd, blocking everyone's view.

"I would like everyone to sing with me . . . Happy birthday to you . . ."

Hundreds of people—children, models, gymnasts and Backstreet Boys—happily joined in with Alexei's flamboyant interpretation, as Lowin sat on his chair, fidgeting madly, Mum and Dad on either side and the official photographer, a bullet-headed trendy type, thrusting a camera in his face to do "reportage."

Marisa, shy, had hovered near the back of the crowd,

but Polly wasn't having that, and steadily pushed her forward until she was practically eye level with the stage. Alexei, looking, to Marisa's eyes, extremely dashing, was just reaching the end of the last line, "Happy birthday to . . ."

And at that exact moment he looked up, and caught sight of Marisa, and his voice completely trailed away to absolutely nothing, and the crowd had to finish it for him.

BOOM!

As Alexei crashed some very dramatic chords and arpeggios in an attempt to justify his fee for turning up and playing one song, there was the sound of a cannon going off out at sea.

The crowd's attention turned, and the children's jaws genuinely dropped at the sight of the high-masted pirate schooner coming around the headland, the Jolly Roger flying high.

As one, they charged to the water, screaming and yelling.

At the very front of the gang were Daisy and Avery, Avery having made a speedy recovery as he had heard something in the air about "pirates"

Huckle was desperately chasing them, but it was so bright and so sunny he could barely make out their silhouettes.

Polly caught him on the way. He grinned to see her.

"This is barmy," he said. "That's a British word, isn't it?"

"It is," said Polly grinning. "But it's the right one too."

He smiled and hugged her.

"Goodness. I thought you were working?"

"Taking a short break," said Polly. "I'd better get back to it."

He kissed her. "When the crowd thins out, I have a proposal involving dumping the children in the movie theater, grabbing a bottle of fizz and a picnic blanket and taking a long quiet walk in the dunes," he murmured in her ear.

"I like that idea," said Polly, nuzzling in. "I like it very much."

More cannons went off and they separated, Polly to return to the stall, Huckle to chase the munchkins. He couldn't see a thing in the crowd, the sun was right in his eyes.

"Daisy! Avery!" he called out, although as the "pirates" started throwing ropes over the side and dismounting onto rowing boats, his shouting went unheard.

"Daisy! Avery?"

They weren't down by the water. They weren't splashing around trying to reach the boats.

Neither were they in the now-ignored amusement park, or the cotton candy machine.

Huckle was not a man who lost his cool easily. But his shouting got a little louder.

"Daisy! Avery!"

Alexei was waiting in the wings as Marisa tentatively approached the stage. Everyone else had charged off to watch the pirate ship. He didn't look remotely uncomfortable in his peculiar getup; in fact, it rather suited him, gave a certain distinguished look to his heft.

"You look . . . very nice," he said, shyly. "I thought you workink?"

"I was," said Marisa, stammering. "But, ehm . . ."

She decided it was best just to change the subject.

"That's an incredible piano."

Alexei let out a half-sigh, half-groan. "Oh yes. Come look."

He held out his hand so she could clamber up on stage. His huge paw holding hers was cool and dry; it felt incredibly comforting to have her hand in his.

He opened it up.

"This . . . what a dream," he said.

"Is it worth a lot of money?"

"It is," he said. Very quietly he started to play the theme from *Pirates of the Caribbean*, which was prettier than Marisa remembered, but he kept taking glances at her.

"What?"

"Nothink. You just look . . . Thank you," he said.

"For what?"

"For being kind when Lara came."

"Well. It's hard to get over people."

He frowned.

"What do you mean?"

"I can see why you didn't get over her."

He shook his head.

"But I am over her."

"But you were so sad."

"Because she said I am terrible composer and haff wasted my life!"

"You're kidding."

"Just like you," he said.

"Oh no," said Marisa.

There was a pause.

"But," said Marisa. "I think *you* are terrific."

He looked down at the keys ruefully.

"I will never be famous composer. I will never own piano like this."

"Couldn't you just be a wonderful teacher?" said Marisa. "And a great player? Most people would love to be able to do that."

Alexei looked at her. "Oh, Marisa. You cheer me so."

Marisa couldn't help smiling. "Do I?"

"Oh yes. So beautiful and so kind and the food and . . . well."

She moved closer to him.

Suddenly there was a shout by the stage. It was Huckle, his face a mask of badly concealed panic.

"Have you seen the twins?" he said. "Have you seen them? They're not watching the ship. Are they backstage?"

Alexei leapt off the stool and they both went backstage to have a look, calling their names. They were nowhere to be found, not in the greenroom, or the storage areas.

"Shit," said Huckle. "God."

"We'll go search," said Marisa. "Huckle. There's millions of lifeguards and nannies here, you know that."

"All I know is that we're on the wild Cornish coast and there's millions of people here I don't know and tin mines and surfing waves and rocks and . . . Christ," said Huckle, turning white and grabbing his phone. "Shit, I have to call Polly."

"We'll start looking," said Marisa and Huckle nodded, shortly, grimly.

Before long the entire beach was out searching: the pirates, who had just been readying themselves to do battle with an entire platoon of storm troopers, throwing themselves into it too. The children were half-convinced this was part of the party, and were jealous of the twins for being the ones who got to hide from pirates.

Polly charged up to the road in case they'd got in the way of the cars: Huckle went from food stall to tent, turning things over, shouting until he was hoarse. The terrible paralyzing fear of it; the blind, white panic of missing children.

He reached the wild animal tent, where a large rabbit was being packed away. There were raised voices inside and a short-haired woman came out, looking mutinous.

"Uh, yeah, we have a bit of a situation?" she said. "Only, Janice is missing."

Chapter Seventy-seven

They ran, both of them. Alexei was surprisingly fast for such a big fellow; he pulled off his ridiculous tailcoat and bow tie, shedding a couple of buttons. Marisa ditched her shoes, and grabbed the skirt up round her hips, and they ran like lightning.

"Start at rocks," Alexei said. "Kids lovink rocks."

They clambered around the headland, Marisa cutting her feet and not even noticing, calling and calling.

"Where would they go?" wondered Alexei. "Are there caves?"

They glanced back. There weren't any to be seen.

"The dunes?" said Marisa.

"But there are pirate ships and toys and sweets . . ."

"I know," said Marisa. "Why leave that party? It doesn't make sense."

Alexei looked at her.

"Maybe, for some people, is too noisy," he said.

They looked at one another and dashed on toward the dunes.

She slipped and stumbled behind him. He listened very carefully to the wind, listening for the tiniest change in sounds.

"Come with me," he said, hearing something, the

faintest of sounds; a sound between sounds. A rustle he felt was not right.

"Avery? Daisy?" shouted Marisa, but he hushed her, surprisingly.

She crept along behind him, tiptoeing through the sand—and what she saw made her gasp.

The two children were huddled underneath a large swathe of marram grass, clutching one another, white-faced, Daisy's mouth wide with panic.

And in front of them, rearing and hissing, was the huge snake.

Marisa turned pale. She too was utterly terrified and it took everything in her not to simply bolt. Her throat was dry and she felt absolutely stuck in place.

"Okay," said Alexei very quietly. She looked at him in horror.

"You have a plan?"

He didn't answer. She saw in his face that flash of anger she had seen before.

The snake was waving its huge head, poised to strike. The children were struck dumb with terror.

"Are you ready to take children?" he said. "Be ready."

"You know . . . snakes are really fast!" whispered Marisa, remembering a terrifying documentary.

"Be ready," he said, unsmiling. He took off his shoes and advanced, very quietly, then suddenly, shouted, "NOW!" and, from behind, brought down his heavy shoe on the snake's head while simultaneously grabbing

it round the back of its throat, squeezing it into himself
where it couldn't reach him and shouting a huge stream
of furious invective in Russian at the unsuspecting animal, all the while whacking it.

"Daisy! Avery! Come with me!" screamed Marisa,
and the children, shaken into action, leaped up. She
grabbed their hands and charged back toward the beach,
as all she could hear behind her was furious hissing and
a repeated *whomping* noise, and the crowds on the beach
began to race toward her.

Chapter Seventy-eight

Polly's face worked in slow motion as she saw the twins running toward her. She opened her body like a gate, gathered them in, clung them to her, a warrior queen, fierce in fury and holding them tight, oblivious to their cries or their need to tell her what had happened. Avery looked up, all preferences forgotten.

"Daddy! Daddy! We need you too!"

And Huckle, who had been thundering up behind, completely whey-faced, was hurling himself on top of them, completing the circuit.

Polly looked up to babble at Marisa, but she had already left and was charging back to the dunes.

By the time they got there, the situation had changed considerably. Alexei was standing being shouted at by the girl with the short hair for damaging her snake, which she insisted had been no threat at all, and now he'd given it concussion and Alexei appeared to be apologizing.

Marisa saw red.

"What the hell are you doing letting a snake roam free at a children's party?" she hollered.

"We don't believe in cruelty to wild animals, actually?" said the woman.

"You rent it out for children's parties! If you really

don't believe in it, take it and set the bloody thing loose in South America! And I don't believe you. I've watched documentaries. That thing was ready to go for one of those children."

"Don't talk about Janice like that."

"You are actually going to be sued to South America, and back." said Reuben, who was unable to stop himself clutching his cutlass. "So, I hope that suits you?"

The women sloped off in a hurry after that, carrying the very dazed-looking beast over their shoulders.

"Should have stuck to pirates," said Reuben, half to himself.

He stalked over to Alexei, who was panting slightly.

"You saved my friend's kids," he said. "Tell me what you want. Anything is yours."

Alexei shook his head.

"It was nothink," he said. "It was my pleasure."

Marisa, bold as brass, stepped firmly in front of him.

"But he'd quite like that piano he was playing earlier."

"Oh yeah, sure, whatever, done," said Reuben, wandering off to find Huckle and Polly.

Marisa turned to Alexei, her face bright pink.

"Oh my God! Did you really hit that snake with a . . ."

But before she could finish the sentence, he had grabbed her in his arms and was looking down at her, his whole body trembling.

It had been so long.

She had denied herself human touch for such a long time, hadn't even reached out to a human being. Her loneliness had gone beyond the skin: had been bone deep, soul deep.

And now this. This was something else, something she hadn't felt in a long time, something she hadn't felt in so long she had thought it might be gone forever.

It was the deepest form of desire, a deep low aching, a rush of strong impulse beating in her brain; that it had to be this man, that it had to be now. His lips were full and plump and soft and nothing else could fill her mind than the desire to kiss him, and for him to kiss her back, the way she wanted—needed, absolutely needed to be kissed, firmly, with passion, and confidence and full-hearted conviction. She found herself letting out a small sound, even as the noises of the party faded away completely.

She stretched herself up on her toes, her eyes beginning to close, the scent of him intoxicating, the sunny breeze blowing through the dunes.

His huge hands moved down to circle her tiny waist in the red dress, holding her firmly. But she saw he wasn't moving his head toward her, showed no signs of being about to kiss her.

She panicked. Was he still thinking of Lara? It was the excitement; it had to be. She had been overwhelmed. She looked up at him, terrified, blushing: had she misjudged it? It had been so long since she'd had any male attention—any attention at all, it felt like. Of course she had gone nuts. Of course she had. Oh God. This was awful. And it made things worse somehow that he was a teacher, as if she was a ridiculous student with a crush.

He let her go, gently, sat down in the sand, his arms around his knees looking confused. His brown eyes blinked in that slow way they did.

Marisa looked at him, her embarrassment turning to fury.

"What?"

He shook his head shortly.

"No. Please. I am thinkink," he said. "Sit down, please?"

She refused and instead stood, furiously, a short way away from him, crossing her arms over herself. She wanted to leave, but couldn't bear to.

"I haff to think."

"Oh, do you."

Her tone was sarcastic.

"I haff to think. I think Marisa does not know I am so crazy about her. She does maybe not know what she is doing, maybe she has been unwell, maybe she is just lonely, maybe she does not really care about a bear who lives next door, maybe if I kiss her I will be happy for two minutes and then so sad forever and that will be very bad."

She looked at him steadily.

"Marisa. I cannot be your—"

"Crutch. I get it. You said that."

He looked puzzled.

"But I have to say. Is important. If you want to kiss me . . ."

This was torture. Marisa stood there, torn, uncomfortably aware of her own breathing.

"You have to know. That it is not nothing to me. It will be . . . lot to me."

He looked straight at her, those long lashes fringing those beautiful eyes.

"You are music to me," he said, quietly. "You are a dance, or the whisper of a song. When you are cross, you are Beethoven dreamink of the far seas, and when you are happy you are Saint-Saëns to me, and when you are sad you are Grieg looking on a rainy day, and when you laugh it is Mozart to me. And I would so very much like to make you dance."

This speech took her totally by surprise. She felt the flush rise in her again, but this time it was something else; not humiliation. Something else. The ice that had flooded her veins started to melt.

"So."

He was still seated, his hands now outstretched in a gesture of supplication.

". . . Marisa," he finished, finally.

Very, very slowly and nervously she walked closer toward him, not breaking eye contact.

"I—"

"Enough," she said, finally.

And very carefully she climbed onto his knees, sitting sideways on his lap. He was so solid. He felt like a mountain she could climb. Something immutable; that she could lean on absolutely.

With one hand she pressed a finger to his mouth.

"Be quiet."

And then she traced those wide lips, hard and soft at the same time, so ready to laugh, to shout, to sing.

"Sssh," she said, again, and leaned in and she could feel the beating of his heart, as big as the rest of him, under his shirt, and gently, carefully, traced his lips with her own, tiny brushing kisses, teasing him, light as a butterfly.

"Argh." He made a groaning sound from somewhere deep inside himself. "No," he said. "For me, that will not do."

And with a sudden jerk, his hands pulled her closer to him, much closer; he put one of his huge hands on the side of her head, where it cradled her face, and he bent down and kissed her so fully and deeply and hard and with such intent that every other kiss she had ever had suddenly felt as if they dissolved into nothing in the sea because this—this was full color, full-hearted; this was everything and he was right. He was all or nothing. The heart and the soul and the passion that came out in his playing; that was everything he was, in everything he did. And suddenly he was everything she had ever wanted, more than anything. And he kissed her all better.

Chapter Seventy-nine

The twins just about got to the end of "Twinkle, Twinkle, Little Star" at more or less the same time. Huckle glanced up at Polly, who was going through the post, now Jayden had managed to take over so many shifts at the bakery.

"I'm not sure," he said, "that they're genuinely massive prodigies."

"I LOVE MY PIANO," shouted Avery loudly and they let them play it again.

"Goodness," Polly said, and handed over the letter she'd just opened. Huckle stared at it, then whistled.

"Why is Reuben doing this?"

"He isn't—his lawyers are insisting. If we promise never to sue—which we never would—"

"I would," said Huckle, furiously.

"Well. Anyway," said Polly.

He looked at it again.

"That's a lot of new windows," she said. "And OMG a boiler. OMG. Water pressure in the shower."

"Oh my God," said Huckle.

"I think we each need one piano," said Daisy seriously.

"YES! MORE PIANO!" said Avery, banging his little fists ferociously on the old upright.

"Oh lord," said Polly. "But also, you know . . ."

"What?"

"They haven't finished fixing the causeway yet. It could go toward that . . ."

"You genuinely want to fix the island rather than our windows?"

"Can't we do both?"

Huckle pulled her over to him.

"One of these days," he said, "we are going to have that tropical vacation."

"Eh, you'd be bored," said Polly, kissing him as the twins played a triumphant chorus and Neil moved from one leg to the other on top of the piano, in what was almost certainly not (or, possibly was), a dance.

Chapter Eighty

Marisa sat in the comfortable armchair next to the warm light on the table, fingers poised over the manuscript paper. She was using her old workbook as something to lean on. She had finished filling it in—for now. But she had kept it.

On top was the paper with the five lines, the staves, printed across it.

"I'm really not sure . . ." she was saying.

"No. Is easy. Just listen to me. Every Grumpy Boy Does Fighting. Those are the line notes. Just count, EFGABCDEF. Easy!"

"How is anything that doesn't start on A easy? And I thought you said music started with C."

"Is detail," said Alexei, waving his hand. And he brought his fingers down to play, slowly, and with infinite patience, so she could write it down. She was going back to work part-time, opening a satellite office in Mount Polbearne to deal with the ever-rising birthrate. Nazreen was delighted. So she needed to practice her calligraphy. But she was still part of the bakery, of course.

He played a gentle soft tune that Marisa thought was beautiful. She had a secret theory that he was only a bad composer when he was filled with unhappy and angry thoughts and that when he was happy he might be rather a good one, but it sounded egotistical to say it, so she hadn't mentioned it yet.

"Is for you," he said. And made her write *For Marisa* on the page.

Reuben had been as good as his word, and had immediately sent over the huge piano. It didn't remotely fit in the chalet, of course.

It did, however, fit if you knocked both chalets together.

The day the wall came down, Alexei and Marisa were on separate sides. Brick by brick came out—"This is a right cowboy job," observed the builder. "No wonder there was no noise insulation."—and as soon as the wall was gone, both of them covered in brick dust, she had leapt through the gap and straight into his arms.

She was addicted to him, completely. His calm, quiet control. The absolute mastery of his fingers, of rhythm; his intense connection and extraordinary physicality. She had never known anything like it. He uncovered in her a completely new ability to make the most extraordinary amount of noise.

She was profoundly grateful they had no neighbors.

That night he sat her down with his own laptop.

"There is someone I want you to meet," he said. "She speak no English, I will translate for you."

"Okay," she said, happy as ever on his big lap. She leaned over.

On the screen, a tiny, dark-eyed woman in a headscarf was peering confusedly into a camera.

"Alexei? Alexei?"

There followed a long outpouring of Russian.

"What's she saying?" said Marisa. "What is it?"

"Oh," said Alexei. "She wants to know if you are from good family. What I am eating. But. Mostly. She is very disappointed in my hair."

Outro

I thought I'd write an outro rather than an intro in case I accidentally spoiled anything before we'd even got started, which would be rubbish. But it seems a bit weird, like popping up after the credits. Anyway. Hello! Jenny here. My publishers thought I should talk about this book for a little bit, just because it comes at such a strange time, and why we chose to set it in a non-COVID world. Originally, in the spring of 2020, when I thought everything might be a little quiet for a couple of weeks (ahahahaha), I proposed writing a little book about the lockdown—the first lockdown, in the UK, and promptly did so. Of course, what I, and so many other naive people (my husband says he wants it made clear here that he always said it would last for much much longer so I am putting this in to say yes yes you were right, smartie-pants :)), didn't realize is just how very long and miserably it would drag on, well past the point where it was interesting or fun for me or for anyone else. So, come August, we made the painful decision to scrap the whole thing and start again from scratch, and I hope by the time you have this book in your hands (I'm writing at the beginning of December 2020), things will be looking a lot brighter for everybody, and that it has not been too hard on you and your family.

Writing about long grief is something I have been interested in for some time. There seems to be an idea in our culture that you should be sad and get lots of attention when you lose someone but after a few months you should more or less just get on with things, and of course grief doesn't work like that at all. My mother died five years ago and I still have days when I'm as completely furious about it as if it happened yesterday. So I started to write a story about Marisa, and we took that horrible stupid disease out of the equation altogether because I want to forget it as soon as possible. No trace of it remains, except one tiny bit I really liked and left in: when Alexei and Marisa are throwing kitchen implements at each other over their balconies. Obviously there's no specific reason for them to be doing this in a non-COVID world, but it always made me laugh.

I have made a little playlist of the music Alexei plays, by the way, if you're interested: it's on Spotify and the link is www.tinyurl.com/alexeiplaylist. None of his own compositions feature :).

Jenny
xxx

Acknowledgments

Huge thanks to Jo Unwin, Lucy Malagoni, Rosanna Forte, Milly Reilly, Donna Greaves, Joanna Kramer, Charlie King, David Shelley, Stephanie Melrose, Gemma Shelley, and all at Little, Brown; Deborah Schneider, Rachel Kahan, Rhina Garcia, and all at William Morrow; Felicitas von Lovenburg, Jennifer Lindstrom, Lina Sjogren, Vivian Leandro, Kjersti Herland Johnsen, Nana Vaz de Castro, Ambre Rouvière, Alexander Cochran, Jake Smith-Bosanquet, and Kate Burton. I am very lucky to be surrounded by so much extraordinary professional talent, and I am truly grateful.

It's no surprise really that so many writers play the piano—something solitary and difficult that involves long lonely hours perched in front of a keyboard, you say?—and I found a huge amount of comfort from playing a ferocious amount during lockdown. A variety of teachers and players kept me company (none of whom, I should be clear, are remotely like Alexei, except in how much they encouraged me, a terrible pianist dreaming one day of reaching mediocrity). So, thank you: Liam O'Hare, Martin Cousin, Georgi Boev, Martin Prendergast, Maddy Wickham, Ron Alcorn, Siavash Medhavi, and Fiona Page. Thanks also: Mr. B & bairns, Lit Mix, the Weegies, and family and friends near and far. I cannot express how desperate I am to see the ones who are far, and my fondest hope, dear reader, is that by the time this book comes out, we will all be hugging the ones we love. If by chance this book is accompanying you on a voyage to reunite with someone—I WANT PICTURES. :) Come find me on Instagram @jennycolganbooks or Twitter @jennycolgan.

*Keep reading for a sneak peek
at the delightful first book
in the new four-part
School by the Sea series
by Jenny Colgan*

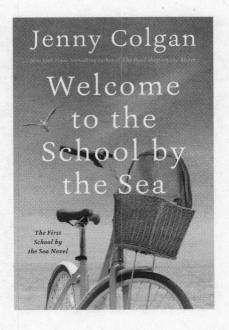

*Available now in paperback
from William Morrow*

Chapter One

Purple skirt *no*. Gray suit *yes* but it was in a crumpled ball from an unfortunate attack of dry cleaner phobia. Black, definitely *not*. Ditto that Gaviscon-pink frilly coat jacket thing she'd panic-bought for a wedding and couldn't throw away because it had cost too much, but every time she came across it in her wardrobe it made her shiver and question the kind of person she was.

Job interviews. Torture from the pits of hell. Especially job interviews four hundred miles away which require clothing that will both look fantastic and stand up to seven hours in Stan's Fiat Panda, with its light coating of crisps. Oh, and that would do the job both for chilly Scotland and the warm English riviera. God, it sucked not being able to take time off sometimes.

Maggie Adair looked at herself critically in the mirror and decided to drive to Cornwall in her pajamas.

Fliss was having a lie-in—among the last, she thought, of her entire life.

I can't believe they're making me do this, she thought. I can't believe they're sending me away. And if they think they're fooling me with their jolly hockey-sticks utter bloody bollocks they can think again. Of course Hattie loves it, she bloody loves anything that requires the brain of a flea, a tennis racket, a boys' school on the hill, and eyelash curlers.

Well, I'm not going to bloody love it. I'll sit it out till they realize how shit it is and they'll let me go to Guildford Academy like everyone else, not some nobs' bloody hole two hundred miles away. Why should I care about being sent so far from London just as everyone else is getting to go to Wembley concerts and on the tube on their own? I'm nearly fourteen, for God's sake. I'm a teenager. And now I'm going to be buried alive in bloody Cornwall. Nobody ever thinks about me.

I'll show them. I'll be home after a month.

Breakfast the next morning was even worse. Fliss pushed her All-Bran round her plate. No way was she eating this muck. She'd pass it on to Ranald (the beagle) but she didn't think he would eat it either. She patted his wet nose, and felt comforted.

"And I don't know for sure," Hattie was saying, "but I think they're going to make me prefect! One of the youngest ever!"

"That's wonderful, sweetie," their mother was saying. "And you can keep an eye out for Fliss."

Fliss rolled her eyes. "Great. Let everyone know the big swotty prefect is my sister. NO thank you."

Hattie bit her lip. Even though she was eighteen months older, Fliss could still hurt her. And she wasn't *that* big.

"Behave yourself," said their father. "I don't want to hear you speaking like that."

"Fine," said Fliss, slipping down from the table. "You don't have to hear me speaking *at all*. That's why you're sending me away, remember?" And she made sure the conservatory doors banged properly behind her as she mounted the stairs.

"Is she really only thirteen?" said her mother. "Do we really have to put up with this for another six years?"

"Hmm?" said her father, buried under the *Financial Times*. Selective hearing, he reckoned. That's all you needed. Though he couldn't help contrasting his sweet placid elder daughter with this little firecracker. Boarding school was going to be just what she needed, sort her out.

Dr. Veronica Deveral couldn't believe they were still interviewing for staff three weeks before the beginning of term. It showed a lack of professionalism she just couldn't bear. She glanced in the mirror, then reached out a finger to smooth the deep furrow between her eyes. Normally she was without a hint of vanity, but the start of the new school year brought anxieties all of its own, even after thirty years, and Mrs. Ferrers waiting for the very last minute to jump ship to Godolphin was one of them.

So now she was short of an English teacher, and with eighty new girls soon turning up—some scared, some weepy, some excited, some defiant, and all of them needing a good confident hand. She put on her reading glasses and turned back to the pile of CVs. She missed the days when she didn't need CVs, with their gussied-up management language, and fancy euphemisms about child-centered learning, instead of simple common sense. A nicely typed letter without spelling mistakes and a quick once-over to see if they were the right stuff—that used to be all she needed.

Still, she mused, gazing out of the high window of her office, over the smooth lawns—quiet and empty, at least for a few more weeks—and up to the rocky promontory above the sea, which started just beyond the bounds of the school, it wasn't all bad. These ghastly "inclusiveness" courses the board had suggested she attend—no one would ever instruct Veronica to do anything—had been quite interesting in terms of expanding the range of people the girls could work with.

They had such hermetic upbringings, so many of them. Country house, London house, nannies, and the best schools. Oh, there was divorce and absent parenting, and all the rest, but they still existed in a world in which everyone had help; no one had to worry about money or even getting a job. Now, wasn't there an application somewhere from a woman teaching in a Glasgow housing estate? Perhaps she should have another glass of mint tea and look at it again.

"La dee dah."

"Shut it," Simone said.

"La dee dah."

"Mum! He's doing it again!"

"Joel!"

"I'm not doing *anyfink*."

Simone tried to ignore him and concentrate on an early spell of packing, which was hard when he wouldn't get out of her tiny bedroom. And, even more irritating, she could kind of see his point. Even she'd winced at the straw boater and the winter gloves on the uniform list, though at first she'd been so excited. Such a change from the ugly burgundy sweatshirt and optional (i.e., everyone wore them if you didn't want to get called a "slut") gray trousers and black shoes at St. Cat's.

She tried to ignore her annoying younger brother, and bask once again in the memory of the day they'd got the

letter. Not the months and months of long study that had
gone on before it. Not the remarks from her classmates,
which had got even more unpleasant the more she'd
stayed behind and begged the teachers for extra work and
more coaching—most of the third years were of the firm
conviction that she'd had sex with every single teacher
in the school, male and female, in return for the highest
predicted GCSE grades the school had ever seen, not that
there'd been much to beat.

She'd tried her best to keep her head high, even when
she was being tripped in the corridor; when she couldn't
open any door without glances and whispers in her direction; when she'd spent every break-time and lunchtime
hiding in a corner of the library (normally forbidden, but
she'd got special permission).

No, she was going back to the day the letter
came. In a heavy, thick white envelope. *"Dear Mr. &
Mrs. Pribetich . . . we are pleased to inform you that
your daughter Simone . . . full scholarship . . . enclosed,
clothing suppliers . . ."*

Her father hadn't said very much; he'd had to go out
of the room for a minute. Half delighted—he'd never
dreamed when he'd arrived in Britain that one day his
daughter would be attending a private school—he was
also annoyed that, even though it was a great opportunity
for Simone, he wasn't paying for it himself. And he worried too for his sensitive daughter. She'd nearly worked
herself ill for the entrance exams. Would she be able to
keep up?

Simone's mum however had no such reservations. She
flung her arms around Simone, screaming in excitement.

"She just wants to tell everyone," said Joel. But
Simone hadn't cared. She'd been too busy taking it all
in. No more St. Cat's. No more burgundy sweatshirts. No

more Joel! No more being paraded in front of Mamma's friends ("No, not pretty, no. But *so* clever! You wouldn't believe how clever!"). Her life started now.

It had to be around here somewhere. Just as she was ferreting with one hand for the last of the Maltesers in the bottom of her bag, Maggie crested the hill in the car. And there it was.

The school most resembled a castle, perched by the sea. It had four towers—four houses, Maggie firmly told herself, trying to remember. Named after English royal houses, that was right. Wessex; Plantagenet; York, and Tudor. No Stuart, she noted ruefully. Maggie mentally contrasted the imposing buildings with the wet, gray single-story seventies build she'd left behind her up in Scotland.

Uh oh, she thought. What was it Stan had said? "The second you get in there you'll get a chip on your shoulder the size of Govan. All those spoiled mimsies running about. You'll hate it."

Mind you, it wasn't like Stan was exactly keen for her to broaden her horizons. He'd been in the same distribution job since he left school. Spreading his wings wasn't really in his vocabulary. But maybe it would be different for her. Let's face it, there had to be more out there than teaching in the same school she grew up in and having Sunday lunch round her mum's. She had to at least see.

Veronica Deveral rubbed her eyes. Only her third candidate, and she felt weary already.

"So," she asked the wide-eyed young woman sitting in front of her. "How would you cope with a difficult child . . . say, for example, one who doesn't think she should be here?"

The woman, who was wearing pale blue eyeliner that matched both her suit and her tights, and didn't blink as often as she should, leaned forward to show enthusiasm.

"Well," she said, in refined tones that didn't quite ring true—junior acting classes, thought Veronica—"I'd try and establish a paradigm matrix of acceptable integral behaviors, and follow that up with universal quality monitoring and touch/face time. I think non-goal-orientated seeking should be minimized wherever appropriate."

There was a silence.

"Well, er, thank you very much for coming in, Miss . . ."

"Oh, I just like the kids to call me Candice. Promotes teacher–pupil sensitivity awareness," said Candice sincerely.

Veronica smiled without using her lips and decided against pouring them both another cup of tea.

Getting changed in a Fiat Panda isn't as much fun as it looks. Maggie tried to imagine doing this in the car park of Holy Cross without getting a penknife in the bahookie, and couldn't manage it. But here, hidden out of sight on the gray gravel drive, it was at least possible, if lacking in the elegance stakes.

She put her makeup on using the car mirror. Pink cheeks, windswept from having the windows open for the last hundred miles, air-con not quite having reached Stan's mighty machine. Her dark, thickly waving hair—which, when properly brushed out by a hairdresser was really rather lovely but the rest of the time required lion taming—was a bit frizzed, but she might be able to get away with it by pulling it into a tight bun. In fact, frizzy hair in tight buns was exactly what she'd expect a boarding school teacher to wear, so she might be right at home. She smoothed down her skirt, took a deep breath, and left the car. Straight ahead of her, the sun glistened off the choppy sea. She could probably swim here in the mornings, lose the half stone caused by huddling in the staffroom ever since she'd left college two years before, mainlining caramel wafers in an attempt to forget the horror that was year three.

Maggie stepped out onto the gravel drive. Up close, the building was even more impressive; an elaborate Victorian confection, built in 1880 as an adjunct to the much older boys' school at the other end of the cove, the imposing building giving off an air of seriousness and calm.

She wondered what it would be like full of pupils. Or perhaps they were serious and calm too. At the very least they were unlikely to have police records. Already she'd been impressed by the amount of graffiti on the old walls of the school: none. Nothing about who was going to get screwed, about who was going to get knifed . . . nothing at all.

No. She wasn't going to think about what it would be like to work here. This was just an experiment, just to see what else was out there before she went back to her mum and dad's, and Stan, in Govan. Where she belonged. She thought of Stan from weeks earlier, when she'd talked about applying.

" 'Teacher required for single-sex boarding school,' " she read out. " 'Beautiful location. On-site living provided. English, with some sports.' "

Stan sniffed.

"Well, that's you out then. What sports are you going to teach? Running to the newsagents, to get an Aero?"

"I'm trained in PT, thank you!" said Maggie sniffily.

"It'll be funny posh sports anyway, like polo, and lacrosse." He snorted to himself.

"What?"

"Just picturing you playing polo."

Maggie breathed heavily through her nose.

"Why?"

"You're frightened of horses, for one. And you'd probably crush one if you keep on eating bacon sandwiches like that."

"Shut up!" said Maggie. "Do you think being Scottish counts as being an ethnic minority? It says they're trying to encourage entries from everywhere. Apply in writing in the first instance to Miss Prenderghast . . ."

"A girls' school with free accommodation?" said Stan. "Where do I sign up?" He thought she was only doing this to annoy him, even when the interview invitation arrived.

"Dear Ms. Adair," he'd read out in an absurdly over-exaggerated accent. "Please do us the most gracious honor of joining us for tea and crumpet with myself, the queen and . . ."

"Give that back," she'd said, swiping the letter, which had come on heavy cream vellum paper, with a little sketch of the Downey school printed on it in raised blue ink. It simply requested her presence for a meeting with the headmistress, but reading it had made her heart pound a bit. It did feel a little like being summoned.

"I don't know why you're wasting your time," Stan had said, as she'd worried over whether or not to take the purple skirt. "A bunch of bloody poncey southern snobs, they're never going to look at you anyway."

"I know," said Maggie, crossly folding up her good bra.

"And even if they did, you're not going to move to Cornwall, are you?"

"I'm sure I'm not. It's good interview experience, that's all."

"There you go then. Stop messing about."

But as they lay in bed in the evening, Stan snoring happilyaway, pizza crumbs still round his mouth, Maggie lay there imagining. Imagining a world of beautiful halls; of brand-new computers for the kids that didn't get broken immediately. Books that didn't have to be shared. Bright, healthy, eager faces, eager to learn, to have their minds opened.

It wasn't that she didn't like her kids. She just found them so wearing. She just wanted a change, that was all. So why, when she mentioned it, did everyone look at her like she'd just gone crazy?

The main entrance to the school was two large wooden doors with huge circular wrought-iron door knockers, set under a carved stone lintel on which faded cut letters read: *multa ex hoc ludo accipies; multa quidem fac ut reddas.* Maggie hoped she wouldn't be asked to translate them as one of the interview questions. The whole entranceway, from the sweep of the gravel drive to the grand view out to sea, seemed designed to impress, and did so. In fact it hardly even smelled of school—that heady scent of formaldehyde, trainers, uneaten vegetables, and cheap deodorant Maggie had gotten to know so well. Maybe it was because of the long holiday, or maybe girls just didn't smell so bad, but at Holy Cross it oozed from the walls.

The doors entered onto a long black-and-white tiled-corridor, lined with portraits and photographs—of distinguished teachers and former pupils, Maggie supposed. Suddenly she felt herself getting very nervous. She thought back to her interview with James Gregor at Holy Cross. "Good at animal taming, are you?" he'd said. "Good. Our staff turnover is twenty percent a year, so you will forgive me if I don't take the trouble to get to know you too well just yet."

And she'd been in. And he'd been right. No wonder Stan was bored with her looking at other options. After all, college had been great fun. Late nights out with the girls, skipping lectures, going to see all the new bands at King Tut's and any other sweaty dive where students got in free. Even her teaching experience had been all right—a little farm school in Sutherland where the kids didn't turn up in autumn (harvest) or winter (snowed in), and had looked at her completely bemused when she'd asked the first year to write an essay about their pets.

"What's a pet, miss?"

"My dad's got three snakes. Are they pets, miss? But he just keeps them for the rats."

Then she'd come back to Glasgow, all geared up and ready for her new career, only to find that, with recruitment in teachers at an all-time high, the only job she could find was at her old school, Holy Cross. Her old school where the boys had pulled her hair, and the girls had pulled the boys' hair, and it was rough as guts, right up till that moment in fifth year when big lanky Stanley Mackintosh had loped over in his huge white baseball boots and shyly asked her if she wanted to go and see some band some mate of his was in.

The band sucked; or they might have been brilliant, Maggie wasn't paying attention and no one heard of them ever again. No, she was too busy snogging a tall, lanky, big-eared bloke called Stan up at the back near the toilet and full of excited happiness.

Of course, that was six years ago. Now, Stan was working down the newspaper distributors—he'd started as a paper boy and had never really gone away, although it did mean he was surprisingly well informed for someone who played as much Championship Manager as he did—and she was back at Holy Cross. They never even went to gigs anymore, since she left college and didn't get cheap entry to things, and she was always knackered when she got home anyway, and there was always marking.

Back in Govan. And it didn't matter that she was still young, just out of college—to the students, she was "miss," she was ancient, and she was to be taken advantage of by any means necessary. She'd ditched the trendy jeans and tops she'd worn to lectures, and replaced them with plain skirts and tops that gave the children as little chance to pick on her as possible—she saw her dull tweedy wardrobe as armor. They still watched out to see if she wore a new lipstick or different earrings, whereupon they would try and turn it into a conversation as prolonged and insulting as possible.

Once she'd dreamed of filling young hearts and minds with wonderful books and poetry; inspiring them, like Robin Williams, to think beyond their small communities and into the big world. Now she just dreamed of crowd control, and keeping them quiet for ten bloody minutes without someone whacking somebody else or answering their hidden mobiles. They'd caught a kid in fourth year with a knife again the other day. It was only a matter of time before one got brandished in class. She just hoped to God it wasn't her class. She needed to learn another way.

The elegant tiled corridor leading off the grand entrance hall at Downey House toward the administrative offices was so quiet Maggie found she was holding her breath. She looked at the portrait right in front of her: a stern-looking woman, who'd been headmistress during the Second World War. Her hair looked like it was made of wrought iron. She wondered how she'd looked after the girls then, girls who were worried about brothers and fathers; about German boats coming ashore, even down here. She shivered and nearly jumped when a little voice piped, "Miss Adair?"

A tiny woman, no taller than Maggie's shoulder, had suddenly materialized in front of her. She had gray hair, was wearing a bright fuchsia turtleneck with her glasses on a chain round her neck, and, though obviously old, had eyes as bright as a little bird's.

"Mrs. Beltan," she said, indicating the portrait. "Wonderful woman. Just wonderful."

"She looks it," said Maggie. "Hello."

"I'm Miss Prenderghast. School proctor. Follow me."

Maggie wasn't sure what a proctor was but it sounded important. She followed carefully, as Miss Prenderghast's tiny heels clicked importantly on the spotless floor.

Veronica glanced up from the CV she was reading. Art, music, English . . . all useful. But, more importantly, Maggie Adair was from an inner-city comprehensive school. One with economic problems, social problems, academic problems—you name it. So many of the girls here were spoiled, only interested in getting into colleges with good social scenes and parties, en route to a good marriage and a house in the country . . . sometimes she wondered how much had changed in fifty years. A little exposure to the more difficult side of life might be just what they needed—provided they could understand the accent . . . she put on her warmest smile as Evelyn Prenderghast knocked on the door.

Oh, but the young people were so *scruffy* nowadays.

That dreadful suit looked as if it had been used for lining a dog's basket. And would it be too much to ask an interviewee to drag a comb through her hair? Veronica was disappointed, and it showed.

Maggie felt the headmistress's gaze on her the second she entered the room. It was like a laser. She felt as if it was taking in everything about her and it made her feel about ten years old. You wouldn't be able to tell a lie to Dr. Deveral, she'd see through you instantly. Why hadn't she bought a new suit for the interview? Why? Was her mascara on straight? Why did she waste time mooning at all those portraits? She knew she should have gone to the loos and fixed herself up.

"Hello," she said, as confidently as she could manage, and suddenly decided to pretend to herself that this *was* her school, that she already worked here, that this was her life. She gazed around at the headmistress's office, which was paneled in dark wood, with more portraits on the wall—including one of the queen—and a variety of different and beautiful objects that looked as if they had been collected from around the world, set on different surfaces, carefully placed to catch the eye and look beautiful. Just imagine. Maggie looked at a lovely sculpture of the hunting goddess Diana with her dogs, and her face broke into a grin.

Veronica was quite taken aback by how much the girl's face changed when she smiled—it was a lovely, open smile that made her look nearly the same age as some of her students. Quite an improvement. But that suit . . .

Veronica was frustrated. This girl was very nice and everything—even the Glaswegian accent wasn't too strong, which was a relief. She hadn't been looking forward to an entire interview of asking the girl to repeat herself. But so far it had all been chat about college and so on—nothing useful at all. Nothing particularly worthwhile, just lots of the usual interview platitudes about bringing out children's strengths and independence of thought and whatever the latest buzzwords were out there. She sighed, then decided to ask one question she'd always wondered about.

"Miss Adair, tell me something . . . this school you work at. It has dreadfully poor exam results, doesn't it?"

"Yes," said Maggie, hoping she wasn't being personally blamed for all of them. She could tell this interview wasn't going well—not at all, in fact—and was resigning herself to the long trip back, along with a fair bit of humble pie dished up by Stan in the Bear & Bees later.

Dr. Deveral hadn't seemed in the least bit interested in her new language initiatives or her dissertation. Probably a bit much to hope for, that someone from a lovely school like this would be interested in someone like her from a rough school. Suddenly the thought made her indignant—just because her kids weren't posh didn't mean they weren't all right, most of them. In fact, the ones that did do well were doing it against incredible odds, much harder than the pony-riding spoon-feeding they probably did here. She suddenly felt herself flush hot with indignation.

"Yes, it does have poor results. But they're improving all the—"

Veronica cut her off with a wave of the hand. "What I wonder is, why do you make these children stay on at school? They don't want to go, they're not going to get any qualifications . . . I mean, really, what's the point?"

If anything was likely to make Maggie really furious it was this. Stan said it all the time. It just showed he had absolutely no idea, and neither did this stupid woman, who'd only ever sat in her posh study, drinking tea and wondering how many swimming pools to build next year. Bugger this stupid job. Stan had been right, it was a waste of her time. Some people would just never understand.

"I'll tell you the point," said Maggie, her accent subconsciously getting stronger. "School is all some of these children have got. School is the only order in their lives. They hate getting expelled, believe it or not. Their homes are chaotic and their families are chaotic, and any steadiness and guidance we can give them, any order and praise, and timekeeping and support, anything the school can give them at all, even just a hot meal once a day, that's what's worth it. So I suppose they don't get *quite* as many pupils into Oxford and Cambridge as you do, Dr. Deveral. But I don't think they're automatically less valuable just because their parents can't pay."

Maggie felt very hot suddenly, realizing she'd been quite rude, and that an outburst hadn't exactly been called for, especially not one that sounded as if it was calling for a socialist revolution. "So . . . erhm. I guess I'm probably best back there," she finished weakly, in a quiet voice.

Veronica sat back and, for the first time that day, let a genuine smile cross her lips.

"Oh, I wouldn't be so sure about that," she said.

Simone held her arms out like a traffic warden's, feeling acutely self-conscious.

"We'll have to send away for these," the three-hundred-year-old woman in the uniform shop had said, as all her fellow crones had nodded in agreement. "Downey House! That's rather famous, isn't it?"

"Yes, it is," said her mother, self-importantly. Her mum was all dressed up, just to come to a uniform shop. She looked totally stupid, like she was on her way to a wedding or something. Why did her mother have to be so embarrassing all the time? "And our Simone's going there!"

Well, obviously she was going there, seeing as she was in getting measured up for the uniform. Simone let out a sigh.

"Now she's quite big around the chest for her age," said the woman loudly.

"Yes, she's going to be just like me," said her mum, who was shaped like a barrel. "Look—big titties."

There was another mother in there—much more subtly dressed—with a girl around Simone's age, who was getting measured for a different school. As soon as they heard "big titties," however, they glanced at each other. Simone wished the floor would open and swallow her up.

As the saleslady put the tape measure around her hips, Simone risked a glance out of the window. At exactly the wrong time: Estelle Grant, the nastiest girl in year seven, was walking past with two of her cronies.

Immediately a look of glee spread over Estelle's face, as she pummeled her friends to look. Simone's mum and the lady were completely oblivious to her discomfort, standing up on a stool in full view of the high street.

"Can I get down?" she said desperately, as Estelle started posing with her chest out, as if struggling to contain her massive bosoms. It wasn't Simone's fault that she was so well developed. Now the other girls had puffed out their cheeks and were staggering around like elephants. Simone felt tears prick the back of her eyes. She wasn't going to cry, she *wasn't*. She was never going back to that school. Nobody would ever make her feel like Estelle Grant did, ever again.

"Now, your school requires a boater, so let's check for hat size," the lady was saying, plonking a straw bonnet on her head. This was too much for the girls outside; they collapsed in half-fake hysterics.

Simone closed her eyes and dug her nails into her hands, as her mother twittered to the saleslady about how fast her daughter was growing up—and out! And she got her periods at ten, can you imagine?! The saleslady shook her head in amazement through a mouthful of pins, till Estelle and her cronies finally tired of the sport and, in an orgy of rude hand signals, went on their way.

Never again. Never again.